THE MISSING PIECE

BOOKS BY KEVIN EGAN

The Missing Piece
Midnight
The Perseus Breed

AS K. J. EGAN

Where It Lies

AS CONOR DALY

Local Knowledge
Buried Lies
Outside Agency

THE
MISSING
PIECE

KEVIN EGAN

A TOM DOHERTY ASSOCIATES BOOK
NEW YORK

THE MISSING PIECE

Copyright © 2015 by Kevin Egan

A Forge Book
Published by Tom Doherty Associates, LLC
175 Fifth Avenue
New York, NY 10010

www.tor-forge.com

Forge® is a registered trademark of Tom Doherty Associates, LLC.

The Library of Congress Cataloging-in-Publication Data is available upon request.

ISBN 978-0-7653-7760-9 (hardcover)
ISBN 978-1-4668-5677-6 (e-book)

Forge books may be purchased for educational, business, or promotional use. For information on bulk purchases, please contact the Macmillan Corporate and Premium Sales Department at 1-800-221-7945, extension 5442, or write to specialmarkets@macmillan.com.

First Edition: April 2015

Printed in the United States of America

0 9 8 7 6 5 4 3 2 1

To MaryLou

ACKNOWLEDGMENTS

Thanks to:

Ben Bova, my agent, and Paul Stevens, my editor, for helping me scale this mountain that was, and now is, *The Missing Piece.*

The Forge staff, including:

Lisa Davis, who managed the production process from Post-it-ridden manuscript to bound book;

Carly Sommerstein (and her Chihuahua), who imposed order on my chaos; and

Diana Pho, for her behind-the-scenes administrative skills.

Three people who shared some of the many secrets of 60 Centre Street:

Major Gerard Fennell, whose knowledge of the building's history is legendary;

Captain Michael Castellano, who led me on a tour that included the presidential bunker; and

Dan Mahoney, the building engineer, who offered to let me climb the dome of the rotunda. (I declined.)

As well as the entire 60 Centre Street community: you all play a part even if you don't contribute a verse.

Loving thanks to the home team, MaryLou, Emily, and Greg. Without their support, none of this means anything.

ACKNOWLEDGMENTS

And finally:

The procedural laws portrayed in the book are not quite accurate. I have done this for dramatic purposes.

This book shares its title with a book written by the late Shel Silverstein. His *Missing Piece* may look like a children's book, but any adult who has ever read it knows that it is much more.

THE MISSING PIECE

CHAPTER 1

The bus churned up the hill, its engine groaning, its tires spewing gravel at each twist in the switchback road. A man pulled himself out of his seat and trudged up the lurching aisle to crouch behind the driver's ear.

"Let me off at Koponya," the man said.

The driver yanked the stick shift out of one gear and jammed it into another. The bus bucked, knocking the man onto his ass. Someone in the second row laughed, and the man glared.

"No one gets off at Koponya," said the driver. The word meant *skull*.

"I do."

The two locked eyes in the large mirror over the windshield. The man's head was shaved, his deep-set eyes were lost in their own cavernous shadows. His slow grin revealed two cracked teeth.

"Yes, maybe you do," said the driver. "Go back to your seat. We have a way to go. I will stop. Koponya." The driver spat.

The man waded back down the aisle. The bus continued upward, the pitch of its engine deepening as the driver shifted into a lower gear. The trees thinned and then disappeared altogether, leaving nothing out the windows but scrub grass, rocks, and sky. The metal fence appeared suddenly, running jaggedly alongside the bus. The swirls of razor wire were gone, the steel poles showed patches of rust.

The driver stopped the bus at the top of the hill and opened the door.

"Koponya, all out for Koponya," he called in a mocking tone.

The man walked down the aisle, intentionally bumping the driver's shoulder with his hip before stepping down the stairwell. The last three years had taught him a simple lesson: avenge every slight.

He jumped off the bottom step and slid several feet on the sloping gravel shoulder before catching himself. The bus pulled away in a black diesel cloud quickly torn apart by the wind. After a few seconds, all was quiet. He cupped his hands over his eyes. The sky was a brilliant blue, the sunlight blinding. Beyond the valley, rows of hills mounted toward the horizon where a curtain of haze hung over Lake Balaton. He backed away from the shoulder, then turned to cross the road. The shirt he had grabbed from the bin that morning was too tight, the pants too loose. The cuffs dragged beneath the heels of patent-leather loafers more suitable for dancing than rock climbing.

Across the road, large boulders blocked the gated entrance to the army base that had been known as The Skull. He climbed between the boulders and settled down out of the wind.

Koponya, his mother had whispered to him during her last visit when his release date had been set. *Hide yourself, and I will find you.*

He took the last plug of beef jerky from his pocket and tore it in half with his teeth. The salty rush filled his mouth with saliva. As he chewed, a deep rumble rose beneath the wind. He swallowed the last of the jerky and raised his head, careful not to expose himself. A battered Yugo idled on the roadside. His mother stood behind it. She wore a long black skirt and a dull gray apron with a matching scarf tied around her head. The scarf and apron rippled in the wind. The neighbor sat behind the wheel of the Yugo, a hat pulled low over his eyes. The man rushed to the car and hugged his mother, but her arms remained at her side. She smelled of potatoes and vinegar.

"We must go quickly," she said.

The man climbed into the backseat, which was littered with bleached chicken bones and crumpled bits of aluminum foil.

The neighbor put the Yugo into gear and headed in the same direction as the bus. At the bottom of the hill, he stopped at a cross-roads with many signposts. The woman pointed left, and the neighbor turned.

"Why not Polgardi?" said the man.

"People have been asking about you."

"What people?"

"The soldiers," said his mother.

The neighbor nodded grimly, and the man sank back amid the bones and the foil.

At Keleti Railway Station in Budapest, they stayed in the car while the neighbor got out to open the Yugo's trunk. The man's mother fished a billfold from beneath her skirt.

"Your passport, tickets, some money," she said. "Not much, but enough."

"Where am I going?"

"To meet your brother."

Cadiz, thought the man. "Why?"

The neighbor slammed the trunk and slowly climbed in behind the wheel.

"Come," said the mother.

A single suitcase stood on the curb. The man recognized it as a battered remnant of his father's fine leather luggage. He gripped the handle.

"In the suitcase is a letter," said his mother. "Don't read it until you get there. You never know who is watching. Speak to no one on the train. You never know who is listening."

She kissed him twice on the cheeks.

"You must never come back," she said. "No matter what happens, no matter what you hear. Promise me."

"But . . ."

"Promise me."

"I promise," he said.

The train pulled out, and the man, sitting alone in the compartment, watched the city pass outside the window. Curiosity about the letter gnawed at him, but he respected his mother's warning and knew he needed to wait.

In Bratislava, a family of three—mother, father, and daughter—joined him in the compartment, heading for Vienna. The man closed his eyes, first pretending and then actually falling asleep.

Some time later, the man opened his eyes. The family was gone, while outside the window a gray smog hung in a forest of blackened trees. He dragged the suitcase down from the rack and opened it on his lap. He pawed through the clothes, but found no letter.

At about the same time the train left Bratislava, the man's mother returned to her home in Polgardi. She filled a pot with water and set it on the stove to boil. A distant rumble shook the house, a blast from the quarry three miles away.

Her eldest had been the talker, she thought, as she sat to peel potatoes. He couldn't keep his mouth shut, and that's how they'd found him. The younger boys were more careful. They would survive.

She peeled the potatoes quickly, the skins falling onto her apron and sticking together in heavy clumps. Another blast from the quarry rolled over the house, rattling glasses in an open cupboard.

She heard something behind her, a creak in the floorboards.

Strange, she thought, believing it connected to the blast, then realizing there could be no connection. She stood silently, listening, until the creak sounded again. Moving quickly, she yanked open a cabinet door. The boy crouched among the big iron pots.

"My little one." She hauled him out and hugged him. "I thought you went home. Why are you still here?"

"I'm hiding," said the boy.

"Hiding from who? From me?"

The boy shook his head. "From the men."

"What men?"

"The men in the dark clothes."

Gravel crunched out front. One car door slammed shut, then another. The woman pushed the boy back into the cabinet.

"Don't move. Don't make a sound."

The boy's eyes widened, frightened by her tone as much as by her words. He sat on a pot as she closed the door.

She stood at the sink, the paring knife in her hand like a dagger. Out the window, the treeless hill stood starkly against the harsh blue sky. The yellow grass trembled in the wind. A boot thumped on the wooden floor, and before she could turn the rope cut across her throat. A hand pried the paring knife from her fingers.

The rope tightened, lifting her off her feet. She kicked, she gagged. The rope lifted her higher. She could feel it dragging across the ceiling rafter. She could see the sink below her, the floor littered with potato skins.

She dangled helplessly, fighting for breath with each jolt of the rope. Finally, as her last breath burned in her lungs, she saw the wine cellar. The forest was green and warm. Her eldest son stood at the door, smiling at her. He stepped back as she floated inside toward a wall of sparkling silver.

In the cabinet, the boy watched through the tiny latticework of the door. He saw dark figures struggling, the paring knife drop to the wooden floor. He heard stifled screams and animal grunts. He watched her feet kick until they slowly gave up the struggle.

The men spoke to each other in a strange language. Then suddenly, one of them crouched. Through the lattice, the boy saw the hard face and the cold blue eyes. He held his breath, terrified that the man would open the cabinet. But the man only grabbed the knife from the floor. In a few moments, the front door closed, the car engines started, and the cars drove away.

The boy pushed out of the cabinet. He crawled beneath the slowly swinging feet, then ran out the back door and over the hill.

CHAPTER 2

"You take the pedestrian knockdowns, the misdiagnosed fatal illnesses, the unpaid promissory notes, the commercial lease pissing contests, and you slog through them all, pretending each is the most important case in the world, when in reality they are all just part of the general din."

Judge Oliver Johnstone poured sherry into two tiny crystal goblets and pushed one across the desk. Waterford, Linda Conover noticed, the same Lismore pattern as the salad bowl that sat in the corner cabinet of her parents' dining room. It had been her mother's "good" bowl, which meant too good ever to use.

Linda nipped at her drink and set the goblet back down. The sherry was the same color as the top of the judge's huge desk, which in the lowering afternoon sunlight took on a reddish cast.

Judge Johnstone knocked his shot back and swiveled his chair to face the window. He had thick white hair, a perpetually ruddy complexion, and craggy features. But those features softened in repose, and as he stared out the window he looked almost wistful.

"But then you get a case like this one, and it's like your first day on the bench again, when you didn't give a hoot about the salary or the pension because you wanted to be a judge. You know it's the case you can wrap your career around. You need to savor it, let it play out, make it last. Because the truth is, no one will remember any of your thousand other cases except the people directly involved. But this one, everyone will remember. This one will be the envy of your colleagues, this one will warm you during the cold nights of your retirement. And believe me, there is no sadder, lonelier person in the world than a retired judge."

He lifted the bottle.

"Another?"

Linda shook her head. She had not touched hers since that first sip.

The judge knocked back his second shot.

"We did it, kiddo. Me and you, you and me. We've shaped this trial exactly the way it should be tried, the way it deserves to be tried."

The judge turned toward the window again with that same wistful stare. The shaping involved several motions the lawyers had presented the previous morning at the final pretrial conference. They were not complicated motions, but they raised serious issues that needed to be addressed carefully. Now here it was, close of business on Friday afternoon, and with an alchemic blend of his gut instinct and her superior research and writing skills, they had crafted what they both considered to be the correct decision. The lawyers would hear it from the bench first thing Monday morning. And then the trial would begin.

"I am concerned about bringing in that exhibit," he said.

"It's part of what makes this trial unique," said Linda.

"I understand. But there are security issues."

"The captain promises a detail of six officers guarding it from the moment it comes out of the armored car till the moment it's loaded back in." She rolled the stem of the goblet between her thumb and forefinger. "It will be here for all of about three hours."

"I'm sure it will seem like much longer," said the judge.

"That's the idea."

The judge poured himself a third shot, then corked the bottle and shoved it into the cabinet behind his desk.

"There could be a book in this," he said.

"Judges can't write books," said Linda.

"Retired judges can."

"Are you trying to tell me something?"

"Like what?"

"That you see this trial as your last hurrah."

The judge grinned tightly, his eyes sliding off Linda and focusing somewhere beyond her. Then he knocked back his drink and held the goblet up to the light.

"Oh no, kiddo. Don't worry. I'm going to stay here till they drag me off the bench."

At eight-thirty on Monday morning, Foxx finished changing into his court officer's uniform and slammed his locker shut. The men's locker room was in the basement of the New York County Courthouse—an old landmark better known by its address of 60 Centre Street—and Foxx needed to get all the way up to the security desk on the fifth floor to begin his day officially by scratching his name on the sign-in sheet. He climbed instead of riding the elevator, choosing a stairwell that turned clockwise as it rose up through the building.

The security desk was in a small lobby where two corridors intersected. Foxx, still huffing, grunted "good morning" to the newbie seated behind the desk. He bent over the sign-in sheet, noting Mike McQueen's name neatly printed on the top line and Gary Martin's name scrawled several lines below. He added his trademark *Foxx* near the bottom.

"Foxx, huh?" said the newbie. "Captain wants to see you."

The captain's office was behind the security desk. Foxx knocked on the frosted glass door, then entered without waiting for a reply.

Captain Kearney sat at a desk as cluttered as a Bosch painting. He wore a wrinkled brown suit jacket and a dingy white shirt with a loosely knotted brown tie. Across from him, Gary Martin, in uniform, sank so deeply in a leather Chesterfield that his knees angled up to his chest. His white-blonde hair was still slick from his shower, his red beard completely covered his shirt collar.

"Please sit down, Officer Foxx," said Kearney.

Foxx weighed the effort of climbing over Gary to reach the other half of the Chesterfield and took the chair opposite Kearney instead.

"I'm switching your assignments," said Kearney. He had cut himself shaving, and a tiny wad of paper clung to his chin as he spoke. "Gary, you're going to Pearl Street, and Foxx, you're taking Judge Johnstone's part."

"Why the hell you doing that?" said Gary.

"Because change keeps us sharp."

"But I've been in Johnstone's part for over a year, and you drop this on a Monday morning?"

"I apologize for the short notice," said Kearney.

"Do you know what's going on in Judge Johnstone's part?"

"I do," said Kearney.

"And so you're going to pull me out and put him in? Don't you think the judge will care? Don't you care?"

"Certainly I care, but I have other considerations."

Gary abruptly stood up. He was a big man who invited comparisons like *bear* and *mountain*. He grumbled under his breath and blew out of the office, slamming the door behind him.

Kearney sighed. He peeled the wad of paper from his chin and flicked it behind his desk, then tore off another shred from a roll of toilet paper and pressed it into place.

"What's this all about?" said Foxx.

"No idea," said Kearney. "When Bev calls, I listen, I obey, I don't ask questions. Find out for yourself if you want to know."

Foxx pressed his hand against his shirt pocket, but his cell phone was still.

"Okay," he said. "Why's Gary so pissed about changing assignments?"

"You heard him. Short notice."

"Doesn't make sense," said Foxx.

"Ask him. He's your friend."

Foxx looked at his watch. Eight forty-five. The usual time that he and Gary and McQueen met to drink coffee and shoot the shit at the start of another day. *Ask him.* He would do just that.

"And what's going on in Johnstone's part?"

"A big trial to determine ownership of an ancient Roman silver treasure," said Kearney. "It should dovetail nicely with your classical sensibilities."

Classical sensibilities, thought Foxx as he punched through the leather-bound doors of the courtroom where McQueen brewed coffee each morning. Four years of high school Latin concluding with an F in Virgil hardly qualified as classical scholarship. In the middle of the courtroom, a custodian worked the levers of a mobile scaffold. The electric motor whined as the platform rose to a darkened light fixture hanging from the ceiling.

The judge's bench resembled an altar. It was made of black walnut and stood on a pedestal above the mottled cork floor. The facade of the bench stretched sideways, encompassing the witness stand on one side and, on the other, the clerk's box where McQueen sat.

"'Bout goddam time you got here," said McQueen.

"Fifty thousand bulbs in building," the custodian called down. "I check them all every day."

"Yeah, yeah. You're a regular Thomas Edison."

McQueen was set up for the day: music played softly from a hidden radio, wax paper remnants of breakfast littered the desk, his thumb held his place in a thick paperback thriller. His judge rarely descended from chambers, so McQueen had the luxury of treating the courtroom as his personal men's club.

"Do you have to be such an asshole?" said Foxx.

"I'm just kidding. Ain't I kidding, Ivan?" said McQueen.

"Maybe," said the custodian. He was a wiry man with closely cropped salt-and-pepper hair and a mustache so thin it might have been a smudge of dirt. The cuffs and sleeves of his blue coveralls were rolled as if several sizes too big.

Foxx poured himself coffee from the pot on the bank of file cabinets, then took his usual spot at the front rail of the clerk's box. The courtroom doors opened, and Gary Martin stormed down the center aisle of the gallery. A leather bag hung from one shoulder and a large backpack dragged along beside him.

"Going somewhere?" said McQueen, peeking around Foxx.

Gary dropped the bag and backpack at Foxx's feet, then fixed himself a cup of coffee and took his spot at the other rail. "Kearney reassigned me."

"So what the fuck do you care?" McQueen had an oily brown beard that somehow sprouted through a moonscape of acne scars. His green eyes swam behind aviator glasses he refused to give up despite being decades out of style.

"Because Kearney's switching me with him." Gary poked a thick forefinger into Foxx's shoulder.

"Same question," said McQueen.

"Because I'm in Johnstone's part for a goddam year, and here it is Monday morning and he's starting a big trial and I'm packing up a year's worth of crap and dragging it to the Pearl Street post."

"Since when do you care about trials?" said McQueen. "You always complain whenever he gets one. 'I gotta handle evidence.' 'I gotta keep track of the jurors.' Pearl Street is the only post easier than this one. After the employees come in, what do you get? A couple of crips in wheelchairs?"

"Maybe I don't want easy," said Gary. "Maybe I want to work, Mike."

"Maybe you want to drool over Johnstone's law clerk," said McQueen. He turned to Foxx. "You ever see her? Nice piece of ass."

Foxx shrugged. He had not had the pleasure. But he wanted McQueen to continue questioning Gary; it saved him the trouble.

"It ain't that, Mike." Gary took a big swig of coffee. "Thing is, I want to be busy because Ursula moved out yesterday."

"Seriously?" said McQueen.

Gary nodded. Big as he was, his head still seemed too big for his body.

"Well, hell, Gary, you knew that was coming," said McQueen.

"Doesn't make it any easier," said Gary. "At least if I was in the courtroom, I'd be busy instead of dwelling on it."

"All right, all right." McQueen arched his eyes at Foxx. "All we need now is him blubbering. Where'd she go?"

"Someone's couch somewhere. She wouldn't tell me, and even if she did I wouldn't tell you. Aw, fuck it." Gary slugged more coffee.

Foxx saw the twinkle in McQueen's eye that usually preceded a wiseass remark. He shook his head, and McQueen swung his attention to the scaffold descending to the floor. The custodian jumped off the platform and flipped the light switch.

"Hey, that was amazing, Edison," said McQueen. " 'What hath God wrought.' "

"Edison didn't say that, you imbecile," said Gary. "It was Bell."

"No, it was Morse," said Foxx.

"What did Edison say?" said Gary.

"Shut up, you feckin' eejit," said Foxx.

"Edison said that?" said McQueen.

"No, I did," said Foxx. "I don't know what Edison said."

The custodian pushed the scaffold through the gallery and out the door.

"See, guys, who the hell needs women when we can entertain ourselves?" said McQueen.

Gary lifted his shoulder bag and backpack and followed the custodian. The sound of his fist pounding the door echoed through the courtroom.

"You're going to piss him off someday," said Foxx.

"Ivan or Gary?"

"Both of them."

"I don't give a shit about Ivan. And I've known Gary a lot longer than you, Foxx. He gets about as angry as Winnie the Pooh."

CHAPTER 3

On the fifth floor of the courthouse, Linda Conover worked alone in the quiet of chambers. It was almost nine fifteen, and Judge Johnstone had not arrived. Odd, she thought—he was always at his desk when she breezed in at nine—but fortunate, as well, because his absence allowed her to key in the edits she had made over the weekend. Linda had never learned how to touch type, but developed her own method in college using two fingers on the keys and her right thumb on the space bar. In straight typing she could reach the amazing speed of thirty-five words per minute. But editing text was a tedious process of moving the cursor within all the hunting and pecking.

Judge Johnstone was not a stickler for details. During his many years on the bench, he had developed a visceral sense of the law that allowed him to judge by instinct rather than by the many books that lined the shelves in chambers. Linda had a different attitude. She loved words, loved to craft decisions that not only could declaim the law but whisper its nuances, as well. Over the weekend, she reread the decision that she and the judge had constructed on Friday and spotted paragraphs where the reasoning could be tighter and sentences that begged for rhetorical flourishes. This was the judge's special case, and a special case called for a special decision. So she had taken out her pen, and in a matter of hours the final draft bled red ink.

Now she was working with one eye on the clock, hitting the wrong keys and missing the space bar. And where was the judge, she wondered.

Finally, she fixed the last typo and printed the decision. As she was tapping the edges together, the phone rang. The robing room number showed on the screen.

"It's me," said the judge. "I was delayed, so I came straight to the robing room."

"No problem. I just finished some final edits on the decision."

"Okay," said the judge, drawing out the two syllables as if thinking.

"Don't worry, there are no substantive changes."

"Well, come down. We still have a few minutes before we begin."

Paul Douglas Leonard White, the fourteenth Earl of Leinster, leaned toward the deeply recessed courtroom window. The title was honorific—the ancient Kingdom of Leinster had not existed as a sovereign realm in hundreds of years—but the family fortune was authentic. One day Leinster would own that fortune outright, but currently the holdings were in trust, an embarrassment for a forty-five-year-old scion but a precaution taken by the late thirteenth earl, who believed, with good reason, that his son was too flighty for the responsibility.

Leinster pulled out from the recess at the sound of the courtroom door squeaking open. His lawyer, Arthur Braman, walked in swinging a large briefcase. A young associate followed, dragging a larger briefcase on a flimsy wheeled contraption that made scuffing sounds on the cork floor. Leinster and Braman locked eyes for a moment, then Leinster leaned back into the recess to look down on Worth Street. One lane was blocked by wooden horses wrapped with bright orange tape, the other was covered by huge metal construction plates that went *clunk-clunk, clunk-clunk* whenever a car or truck drove over them. Leinster winced. That sound was in his head now, and he knew that no matter how hard he tried to shut it out of his mind, the *clunk-clunk, clunk-clunk* would drive him mad.

The time was 9:25 by Leinster's pocket watch. Only five minutes to go before court began, and as Braman and his associate carefully deployed file folders and legal pads on their portion of the large wooden counsels' table, the lawyers for Croatia and Hungary chatted amiably with the lawyer for the auction house. Leinster shook his head, annoyed at how opposing lawyers could be so friendly and cordial before the bell rang. And it was not only American lawyers who behaved like such chameleons. His solicitors back home acted the same way, as well.

"My lord." Braman was at his elbow. He was as diminutive and, in his own style, as dapper as Leinster, with large pleasant features, hair thick enough to mask a comb-over, and a voice that remained smoothly unruffled even in the most heated legal exchanges.

"Mr. Braman."

"How was your flight?"

"Comfortable," said Leinster. Another truck passed over the construction plate, and Leinster tried his best to shut the sound from his mind. "What precisely are we here for this morning?"

"The trial will actually start this afternoon," said Braman. "But last week we all made pretrial motions, which the judge will rule on this morning. These rulings may sound esoteric to you, but they will tell us what evidence the judge will allow us to present and what he will exclude."

"You will explain all this to me, I trust."

"Of course," said Braman. "For now, just keep in mind that the more evidence the judge excludes, the better for us."

"You mean me," said Leinster. "The better for me. I am the one invested in this treasure. You will collect your fee regardless."

With a graceful nod, Braman melted away. Down below, a city bus passed. *Clunk-clunk . . . clunk-clunk.*

If Leinster had known it would have taken this long, if he had known it would have been this difficult and this complicated, he never would have embarked on this quest. Eleven years had passed since James Thatcher-Wood, his solicitor and confidant, came to him with news of a "find" on the Syrian antiquities market: an exquisitely wrought silver urn dating to the fourth century Roman Empire.

"The word is," Thatcher-Wood told him, "it is part of a larger treasure. If you can assemble the entire hoard, the aggregate value would be staggering."

Leinster purchased the urn for one million American dollars. Almost immediately, rumors began circulating about a large silver platter fashioned by the same silversmith. Thatcher-Wood created a trust to act as the strawman in that purchase. Out of available cash, but deliriously interested in pursuing the rest of the treasure, Leinster lined up three investors to bankroll his scheme. The thirteenth earl was still alive at the time and would have approved of neither the deal nor his son's choice of business partners. But, six years, twelve strawmen, and twelve million invested American dollars later, Leinster had assembled a fourteen-piece collection known as the Salvus Treasure.

The entire treasure had an estimated value of seventy million dollars. The plan was to flip it to a museum or a private collection, then divide the profit. But any hope of a sale collapsed when a well-known art historian published an article hinting that the Syrian export licenses, the sole documentation attesting to the treasure's provenance, may have been forged. Prospective purchasers backed off, and the investors turned threatening. Thatcher-Wood offered an alternative plan: a New York auction house was willing to sell the treasure. It was only later, too late in Leinster's opinion, that the contours of this arrangement became evident. First, the auction house would send the treasure on a world tour to drum up interest. Then, as its due diligence, it would notify every government presently existing within the boundaries of the fourth century Roman Empire of the impending auction. Croatia filed a lawsuit to stop the sale, Hungary and Syria joined in, and this interminable litigation followed. The last time Leinster had met with his investors, one jumped across the table and began to choke him. The other two pulled him off, though only reluctantly in Leinster's recollection. Hence Leinster's objection to Braman's use of the royal "we."

Leinster slammed his fist against the window frame. Every time he thought of Thatcher-Wood and this bloody lawsuit he wanted to scream. Arthur Braman was a calm, confident master at the top of his game. If anything else were at stake—a piece of real estate, a bank account, one of his several divorces—Leinster would believe that victory was at hand. But he had encountered so many pitfalls trying to extricate himself from this infernal treasure that he was convinced something else would go wrong.

Each courtroom at 60 Centre Street had a robing room, a small adjunct located directly behind the bench where the judge could relax, confer with lawyers, and, as the name implied, slip into or out of his or her robe. Linda left chambers with the freshened decision in a file folder and took a set of internal stairs down to the third floor. On the 3M level, she passed the jury room, empty now but not this afternoon. Half a floor down, she landed at the robing room door. The stage entrance, she liked to call it.

Judge Johnstone already had donned his robe, and as Linda

opened the door, she caught him pacing with his hands locked behind his back.

"That it?" he said.

Linda nodded and handed over the decision. The judge flipped through the pages with eyes that obviously took in nothing, then lay the decision on the desk. He forced a smile.

"I appreciate all the work you did on this," he said. "But I had an epiphany this morning."

"What kind of epiphany?" said Linda.

"I want to go the other way."

"The other way?"

"With this decision."

"You can't be serious," said Linda.

"I'm perfectly serious," said the judge.

"But after all our . . . why?"

"Think of the jury. Laypeople without any sense of the law, inundated with highly technical expert opinions and extremely confusing factual evidence."

"That's the jury system," said Linda. "The lawyers could have asked for a bench trial. They didn't."

"That doesn't mean I need to go along with them. I'm the judge. I'm responsible for this trial."

"You can't disband the jury," said Linda.

"No, but I can make the trial less complicated."

"You're going to exclude all the evidence that you carefully explained was relevant?" said Linda.

"I didn't explain it yet," said the judge. "Not on the record."

"But you said it to me. All that talk about your special case."

"I've rethought it."

"I don't understand."

"Here." The judge worked his hand through a slit in his robe and handed Linda a coffee shop napkin covered with notes too messy to read.

"But the evidence is what makes this case so interesting," she said. "Excluding all this basically does away with the trial."

"No, it simplifies the trial. And the simpler the trial, the better my chance to settle it."

"How can you settle a trial that involves a unique treasure?" said Linda. "It's not a pedestrian knockdown."

"Because it's not about the treasure," said the judge. "It's not even about national pride. It's about money. Everything is about money, and this is a holdup. If Leinster wants to throw each of the plaintiffs a few million, they'll go away."

"Not if he thinks he's going to win," said Linda.

"He has a smart lawyer. These rulings leave the outcome just enough doubt that he can't take the chance."

"And what about bringing in that treasure piece as a court exhibit?" said Linda. "You and I agreed how important that was."

Judge Johnstone took back the napkin and squinted at his notes. "We did, didn't we?" he said. "Whose motion was that?"

"The auction house," said Linda. "They didn't want the responsibility or the expense."

"I suppose I can stick with that." The judge folded the napkin. "Does that make you happy?"

"Not really," said Linda.

Foxx immediately took in the necessary information as he strolled into the courtroom: six lawyers and a guy dressed like a refugee from Carnaby Street.

"Where's Gary?" asked the court clerk as Foxx drew up. The clerk's desk was perfectly neat, and the bank of file cabinets behind it was totally devoid of any coffee-making paraphernalia.

"Pearl Street," said Foxx. "You got me. Kearney's orders. Who's the dandy?"

"Lord Leinster. You know anything about the trial?"

"Only that it involves a Roman silver treasure and that one piece could be visiting us this afternoon." Foxx eyed Leinster. "When was the last time you saw spats?"

"*My Fair Lady*?" said the clerk.

Foxx laughed.

Behind the robing room door, sharp voices suddenly volleyed and then went silent.

"What's going on in there?" said Foxx.

"Lovers' quarrel." The clerk stood up and told the lawyers to take their places at counsels' table. Then he turned to Foxx. "Tell him we're ready."

Foxx knocked and cracked the door at the same time. Judge Johnstone and his law clerk seemed to be facing off across the desk, the judge with his arms akimbo and the law clerk ripping a thin sheaf of paper in long, slow tears. Foxx had seen Judge Johnstone often, but never the law clerk because he would have remembered the strawberry blond hair, the graceful sway of her back, and her shapely legs. Give McQueen credit, he was right on this one.

"Everyone's ready, Judge," he said.

"Where is Gary?"

"Reassigned. I'm here for now. Name is Foxx."

"I see. Foxx, huh?" The judge glanced at Linda. "Then let's go."

The judge mounted the bench with a swirl of robe while Linda drifted into the clerk's box. Rather than sit, she stood behind the chair, gripping the backrest in a way that told Foxx she had been on the losing end of whatever he had overheard.

The judge pulled the cord on the banker's lamp and adjusted the height of the microphone.

"I have before me four pretrial motions," he said. "I have considered these motions with one principle in mind. The sole issue in this trial is where the treasure was unearthed. That is the lodestar at which I aim my rulings."

The six lawyers all leaned forward, pens poised above legal

pads. In the gallery, Leinster sat in the first row, his arms folded and his legs crossed, one foot bobbing rhythmically.

"First," said the judge, "Croatia will not be allowed to call Anton Fleiss as a witness because his testimony on the unearthing of the treasure would be hearsay. Croatia has until nine thirty tomorrow morning to identify a different eyewitness to the unearthing. If not, the trial will proceed. If so, the court will conduct an immediate hearing on the admissibility of the new evidence."

The lawyers scribbled on their legal pads.

"Next," said the judge, "Hungary will not be allowed to introduce any art historical evidence. Although the evidence may be intellectually interesting and the subject of much discussion among art historians, it does not address the question of where the treasure was last unearthed.

"At this juncture, Hungary may not introduce evidence of the chemical analysis of the soil encrusted on the surface of the cauldron. This is because the chemical composition of the soil, while consistent with the chemical composition of the soil in the area around Polgardi, Hungary, also is consistent with soil in other areas of Eastern Europe. However, I will revisit this issue if Hungary produces an eyewitness to the unearthing. Although there is no potential eyewitness on the witness list submitted by Hungary, I will allow Hungary to identify such a witness by nine thirty tomorrow morning, under the same conditions as previously directed for Croatia.

"Third, because Syria recently discontinued its claim against Lord Leinster, the validity of the export licenses for all fourteen pieces of the treasure is no longer an issue. Therefore, the court will exclude all evidence of the alleged forgeries.

"Finally," said the judge, "the auction house is directed to produce one piece of the treasure to display to the jury during opening arguments this afternoon. Counsel may use the hard-backed, high-definition photographs of the pieces during the trial as exhibits. But this case is too important for the jury to decide without a direct sense of exactly what is at stake."

The lawyer for the auction house stood up.

"We are still concerned about safeguarding the piece."

"I understand your concerns," said the judge. "Your responsibility is to transport the piece here. We will handle the rest. I will see you at two p.m."

As soon as the judge left the bench, Arthur Braman hustled Leinster out to the corridor.

"Raise your right hand," he said.

"What?" said Leinster.

"Your right hand. Raise it."

"What are you talking about?"

Above them, a custodian on a mechanical scaffold unscrewed the cover of a ceiling light fixture. The sound of squeaking metal sent a chill down Leinster's spine, like fingernails on a blackboard.

"This," said Braman. He lifted Leinster's right arm and slapped his hand against the open palm. "It's called a high-five. It's an American form of celebration."

"What are we celebrating?"

"Those rulings. Judge Johnstone practically directed a verdict in your favor."

"All I heard was that Croatia and Hungary had another twenty-four hours to find witnesses," said Leinster.

"If they haven't found credible witnesses yet, I doubt another day will make a difference."

From up above came more metallic squeaking. Leinster shuddered.

"I'll feel better at nine thirty-one tomorrow," he said.

McQueen had been accurate in his prediction about the Pearl Street post. Unlike the front and rear entrances, the Pearl Street door had little traffic and no magnetometers, just a single officer seated at a desk who used experience and perspicacity to determine whether a visitor posed a threat. It didn't take much. After the usual wave of employees rushing to swipe in at the time clock, there had been exactly two wheelchair-bound people buzzing at the bronze door. Gary drummed his pen on the top of the desk. He lifted the cell phone again to check the signal strength. Three bars. He had expected a call or a text, but here he was, halfway to lunch hour, and he had nothing but silence.

He reached into his backpack and fished out the book, still wrapped in the plastic bag from when he bought it on Friday. His twin niece and nephew had an old hardcover edition, the spine broken to show the stitching that held the pages together. They would tuck close on opposite sides of his giant lap and listen while he read the story. The character simply was known as "it," but Gary called him the cheese wheel. The kids liked the book. They liked the simple but evocative drawings and the minimalist but rhythmic text. Gary liked its clever philosophy.

He had used his lunch hour on Friday traipsing from store to store. He wanted to find a hardcover, but at the third store capitulated and bought a trade paper edition. He thumbed the pages gently now so the spine would be pristine. Where do you sign something like this, he wondered, inside cover, dedication page, title page? It wasn't as if he wrote the book and was signing it for a fan. He only wished he wrote the book because it made so much sense.

He closed the book and found a legal pad in the desk drawer. Here was the problem he tried to explain to McQueen. If he was still in Judge Johnstone's part, he'd be as busy as hell, but his mind would be engaged. Here his mind was as silent as the phone.

He scribbled a few words, then crossed them out. He scribbled a few more and crossed them out, too. He dropped the pencil, leaned back in the chair, tried to think.

The sound of the phone startled him. It was the desk phone, not his cell, and he saw the number of the captain's office on the readout.

"Pearl Street," he said.

"Gary." It was Kearney. "I need you to work the lunch hour and the rest of the day. So grab your lunch when you can and report directly to the front steps when your relief arrives."

Gary acknowledged with a grunt and hung up. He leaned back in the chair again and drew the book onto his lap. Maybe something meaningful would come to him if he read it one more time.

CHAPTER 4

At one o'clock on a warm and sunny October Monday, office workers filled Foley Square. People lined up at the sidewalk food vendors, sat beneath the sycamores of Thomas Paine Park, and sunned themselves on the courthouse steps. Halfway down these steps, six court officers watched the midday traffic flow past the courthouse.

"We're getting overtime, aren't we?" said McQueen. "Because there's a lot I could be doing right now."

"Like what?" said Foxx.

"Like reading in the park." McQueen slapped the paperback jammed into his back pocket.

Gary Martin turned around and sneered. Though standing one step below, he still towered several inches over Foxx and McQueen.

Foxx felt the buzz in his chest twice before he realized it was his cell phone and not a burp forcing its way up his gullet. He cupped his hand against the sun and saw "IGGY" crawling across the screen. IGGY stood for IG, which stood for inspector general. Foxx broke away from the pack and climbed up into the shade of the columns to answer.

"Where are you?" said Bev.

"On the front steps, waiting for an armored car."

"He's going through with it, huh? You couldn't talk him out of it?"

"Was I supposed to?" said Foxx.

"No. That was Kearney. He buckled like a cheap table."

"Don't you mean he folded like a cheap suit?"

"I'm not going to debate clichés with you, Foxx."

"Then tell me why the hell I'm here, because we both know it isn't because of my security skills."

"I want you to observe the judge," said Bev.

"Johnstone?" said Foxx. "Why?"

"You don't need to know why," said Bev. "Just keep your eyes and ears open."

Foxx rejoined the security detail, and barely a minute later an armored car nosed against the curb between two orange cones. Two security guards and two workers in overalls got out. The guards stood at the rear of the armored car with their hands on their holsters while the two workers opened the back door and lowered a hand truck and a wooden crate onto the pavement.

Four officers descended the steps to meet the hand truck while Foxx and McQueen hung back, watching.

"You see anything suspicious?" said McQueen.

"No," said Foxx.

"I'm only kidding," said McQueen. "What do you think? Bandits will swoop in and steal this thing? Isn't this over the fucking top?"

"It's a job, Mike. If we weren't doing this, we'd be doing something else."

"I'd be reading in the park, and you'd be . . . what the hell do you do?"

"Try to live the best life I can," said Foxx.

McQueen rolled his eyes.

Down on the sidewalk, the four officers surrounded the workmen as they hauled the hand truck up the steps. Foxx and Mc-

Queen stayed in place, scanning Foley Square until the hand truck rolled safely through the portico and into the lobby.

On the third floor, Foxx unlocked Judge Johnstone's courtroom to let everyone in, then locked the doors behind them. Except for mirror-image reversals, all the courtrooms on the second through fourth floors of 60 Centre Street had the same floor plans. Public entry off the corridor was through double entry doors, each leather-bound and with a small glass window. Inside, there was a shallow gallery made up of nine movable wooden benches arranged in rows of three. A thick wooden rail started at the end of the jury box and continued almost across the entire courtroom before curving to the clerk's desk at the opposite corner. A thick velvet rope hung from hooks at the opening in the rail.

The well was larger than the gallery, and for this trial there were six chairs arranged along the large wooden counsels' table, two for Croatia's counsel, two for Leinster's counsel, and one each for attorneys representing Hungary and the auction house. The bench sat on a riser. There were two doors in the wall behind the bench. The one closest to the clerk's desk opened into the robing room. The other door opened into a small vestibule where stairs led up half a flight to the jury room.

Foxx posted McQueen at the entry doors, Gary at the robing room door, and the other three officers in the well. He took the jury room door for himself and watched the workmen lift the crate onto the table, then pop the lid and pull out fistfuls of straw. When there was no straw left, one workman donned a pair of velvet gloves and slowly lifted the treasure piece out of the crate.

Tucked between courtrooms on the inner edge of the fourth floor was a warren of cubicles where the law department worked. The law department was a pool of court attorneys who drafted decisions for judges because the volume of work at 60 Centre Street was too onerous for any judge and law clerk to handle themselves.

In the one o'clock hour, the cubicles were almost empty, which allowed Linda to drag a chair into Bernadette Symanski's cubicle. The two huddled over their brown-bag lunches.

"I don't know why I'm so mad," said Linda. "I've asked myself that question all morning. He's the judge and I'm not. Simple as that. But he led me to believe that this would be the biggest case of his career and then, just like that and for no reason, he comes in and treats it like any other one."

Bernadette leaned back in her chair. She was Linda's oldest friend and, like her, still saw herself as a Catholic schoolgirl from modest means. Their careers diverged after the bar exam, with Bernadette landing a job in the law department and Linda slaving unhappily through a succession of private firms. It was Bernadette who told her about the opening in Judge Johnstone's chambers, Bernadette who personally delivered Linda's résumé, Bernadette who advocated to both the judge and Linda that they would be a good fit.

"We work for judges," she said. "You work for one and I work for several, but it's still the same deal. Trust builds up, and they begin to rely on us so implicitly that ninety-nine times out of a hundred they do what we tell them. Then that hundredth time comes, and we're surprised?"

"But what he did makes no sense," said Linda.

"To you, maybe. Me, too, if I were in your shoes. But being on the bench is very different from only being near the bench."

"I know, I know. But in this case I don't understand."

"Who really can understand them?" said Bernadette. "The only way would be to become one ourselves. Thank God that isn't in the cards for me."

"Not for me, either," said Linda. "Not now."

In the waning minutes before the afternoon session, the courtroom was quiet. Foxx sat in the jury box, his eyes closed, his breathing slow and deep. McQueen sat on the last gallery bench, reading his paperback. Gary and the other three officers played a hand of hearts at counsels' table. The court reporter, a recent arrival, set up her machine on the apron below the bench.

Foxx opened his eyes, took inventory, and crossed the well to the clerk's desk.

"You got a minute?" he said, nodding toward the robing room door.

The clerk got up, and Foxx followed him inside.

"Something you said this morning stuck in my mind."

"I said lots of things this morning," said the clerk. "I'm surprised any of it stuck anywhere."

"The lovers' quarrel, figurative or literal?"

"Hey, Foxx, you've been assigned to the part for five hours. You think I'm going to tell you something like that, even if I knew?"

Foxx bit the inside of his mouth, summoned his baleful stare.

"Okay, Foxx, this doesn't go beyond us," said the clerk. "What I think? No. What I know? There've been a couple of times I came back from lunch early and found the robing room locked."

"You have a key, right?"

"I do, the judge does, Linda does, so does Gary. Or did. Fact is, I find the door locked at lunchtime, I figure someone doesn't want me in there."

"Who's the someone?"

"I say that, I'd be assuming a fact not in evidence."

"You think Gary knows?"

"Ask him," said the clerk.

Foxx decided to table that suggestion. Today was not the day to ask Gary anything about Judge Johnstone's courtroom. The question could wait till tomorrow. At least.

Foxx returned to his seat in the jury box and closed his eyes. At precisely two o'clock, the entry doors rattled with the sound of someone bumping against them. Foxx took a deep breath and opened his eyes. McQueen got up and peeked out the window.

"It's the lawyers," he said.

"Let them in," said Foxx. "And lock up behind them. Captain's orders."

Linda found Judge Johnstone sitting at his desk in the robing room. His fingers were laced behind his neck, and the chair was swiveled toward the window, which showed the buildings that lined the bottom of Mulberry and the top of the narrow street that climbed into the heart of Chinatown. The judge turned and leaned forward, dropping his elbows onto the desk.

"The piece is out there," he said. "Take a few minutes to look at it."

"I don't think I will," said Linda.

"No, I insist. When I look at it I see something my wife dragged home from Bloomingdale's and stuck in our dining room. At least you can appreciate it, probably more than anyone else in the courtroom will."

His habit of extracting great truths from minute facts irked her. She once had mentioned taking classical art and architecture courses in college. She did well in those courses, well enough that she might have pursued an advanced degree if circumstances had been different. But now, many years and a law degree later, she was just someone who could converse about Praxiteles or the Third Style over cocktails as long as the conversation did not go too deep.

So, because she knew the judge never would let it go, Linda went into the courtroom. There were five lawyers at counsels' table, Lord Leinster seated in the gallery, Foxx in the jury box, and the other officers playing cards on the rail. The piece stood on a small table in front of the jury box. Linda walked closer and had to admit that the urn was quite something.

It was approximately eighteen inches high. The lowest third was spherical with a circular flange that formed a base. The top of the sphere tapered slightly and then flared at the neck. There was a hunting scene depicted on the sphere, Roman soldiers pursuing deer and boar against a mountainous backdrop. The detail was startling, and in the bright light of the courtroom, the silver shined like a full moon on a clear winter night.

"Is there something wrong?" It was Gary Martin, standing at her shoulder.

"Why? Does it look like something's wrong?" said Linda.

"You don't look like yourself."

Linda glanced at Foxx, who sat perfectly still in the foreperson's seat with his eyes closed and his hands palms up on his knees. Could he be meditating, she wondered. He certainly wasn't focused on her.

"Oh, Gary, it's been a horrible day," she whispered. "The judge and I had a terrible argument and I feel sick about it."

"What did you argue about?"

"Legal stuff. It probably would seem like nonsense to you, but it's important to me."

"You're not going to quit, are you?"

"No," she said. "But I feel like it. He told me to come out here and look at the piece before the trial starts. It's like he's trying to make up but doesn't really know how because we never argued like that."

"It's a nice piece," said Gary.

"It's okay, I suppose."

"But you like this kind of stuff."

"You're right, Gary," she said. "Sorry. It's a beautiful piece. Too bad I'm not in a mood to appreciate it."

Gary leaned closer as if to say something else, then melted away.

Linda lifted a hand to the urn, telling herself that she probably never again would be this close to something so old and so valuable. But she felt the eyes of the attorneys on her and hurried back to the robing room.

"Well, then," said the judge. He stood up and lifted his robe off the coat tree.

"You're taking the bench?"

"We're about to start the trial, remember?"

"But isn't this the time to talk settlement?" said Linda. "That was the purpose of those rulings of yours, right?"

"Oh, it was," said the judge, zipping his robe up to his throat. "But I need to hear the openings first. If Croatia and Hungary promise evidence today that they cannot deliver tomorrow, this case will settle easily. Just not today."

Foxx called the courtroom to order as the judge climbed the bench and Linda took her seat in the clerk's box.

"Does anyone have any application before we start?" said the judge. "No? Then bring down the jury."

Foxx went out the jury room door and up a half-flight of stairs to the jury room. There were eight jurors, including two alternates, and as Foxx matched the faces with the jury slips, he recognized the usual collection of waiters, wannabe actors, and stay-at-home housewives who made up the stereotypical Manhattan jury.

After Foxx seated the jury, Judge Johnstone gave a welcoming speech that explained courtroom procedures, apologized for the threadbare courthouse furnishings, and predicted delays when the lawyers needed to argue legal matters out of their presence. As the judge spoke, Foxx stood between the jury box and the witness stand. Twice he nudged the jury door, making sure it was locked. Twice he let his eyes drift toward the nice-looking redhead seated directly opposite the urn.

"In this trial," the judge told the jury, "you will be asked to determine title to a silver treasure that dates back to the Roman Empire. The plaintiffs are the Republic of Croatia and the Republic of Hungary. Each of these countries claims a superior right to the treasure.

"The defendant is Lord Leinster, who you see sitting in the gallery. The auction house that currently holds the treasure is here, as well, though it has no claim. Keep in mind that because Lord Leinster is a defendant he bears no burden of proof.

"I will now turn you over to the lawyers for their opening statements. Be patient, listen carefully, and do not form any conclusions until you have heard all the evidence."

Croatia's lawyer stood up from counsels' table and moved toward the small podium at the far end of the jury box. As he shuffled his papers, the entry doors rattled.

"What's that?" said the judge.

McQueen cupped his hand to the window. "Someone's trying to get in."

"I'm expecting my associate," said Arthur Braman.

The doors rattled again.

"Why are the doors locked?" the judge said, fixing his eyes on Foxx.

"Captain Kearney's orders," said Foxx.

"Captain Kearney does not have the authority to lock my courtroom. We have public trials in America, not Star Chamber proceedings. Unlock that door right now."

McQueen opened the door, and the associate took her seat at counsels' table. Croatia's lawyer cleared his throat and began his opening statement.

"Our story begins during the latter days of the Roman Empire and involves a general named M. Tullius Salvus, whose army operated in what is now Eastern Europe."

Foxx glanced at McQueen, who leaned against the marble doorjamb with his arms folded across his chest. Not exactly standing at attention, thought Foxx, but at least he didn't have his nose buried in his book.

"In those days, Roman generals traveled with their armies like modern-day rock stars, bringing their entire households with them. One of the things that General Salvus carted around as he traveled was a treasure consisting of fourteen silver pieces: five plates, five urns, and four vessels resembling what we might call ice buckets. One piece of the treasure is displayed here to give you an idea of the beauty and exquisite craftsmanship of the treasure whose fate you will determine.

"We will introduce evidence to prove that this treasure, wherever it may have traveled during its sixteen-hundred-year journey to this courtroom in New York City, was last unearthed within the borders of Croatia. We will—"

The entry doors opened, and a man wearing a black ski mask and a loose-fitting maroon warm-up suit shouldered his way into the courtroom. With a boxer's quickness, the man punched McQueen in the gut, then pulled a gun from beneath his jacket and slugged him in the head.

"Freeze," he yelled, sweeping the gun around the courtroom.

A second gunman in a maroon warm-up suit and black ski mask punched in through the doors. He stepped over McQueen, who lay motionless on the floor, then ran through the gallery and vaulted over the rail and into the well. He smacked the microphone off the podium and waved his gun in the face of Croatia's lawyer.

Foxx, frozen at the jury room door, slowly drew his gun. The second gunman grabbed the redheaded juror by the blouse and yanked her over the rail. Then he fixed his eyes on Foxx.

"Drop it," he growled, twisting the muzzle of his gun against the juror's throat.

"Okay, okay," said Foxx. "Just keep calm."

The gunman said nothing else, and Foxx carefully passed his gun, muzzle first, into his left hand as he replayed the gunman's words in his head. The voice sounded husky, as if trying to disguise an accent.

"Here," the gunman growled again. He stamped the floor with his sneaker.

Foxx crouched forward, moving close enough to hear the juror whimpering. He set the gun on the floor, pausing to search for something, anything, that could identify the gunman later. He saw nothing but two black eyes through the slits of the ski mask.

"Move back."

Foxx did. The gunman shoved the juror into her chair, then kicked Foxx's gun into the corner formed by the jury box and the rail.

"Other side."

Foxx crossed to the other side of the well, where the first gunman herded everyone else against the rail. The officers' guns already lay on the floor well out of their reach. Foxx fit himself next to Gary, who was turned sideways as if to shield the judge and Linda.

"What the hell happened?" whispered Gary. "How the hell did these guys get past the mags?"

Foxx shrugged.

"Shit, look at Mike," said Gary.

Blood seeped through McQueen's hair and streamed across his face. One arm bent under his chest, the other twitched at his side. But Foxx concentrated on the gunmen, still hoping to spot one distinguishing characteristic. Both men were athletic and moved with precision and a bare minimum of talk. The word *military* stuck in Foxx's mind.

The second gunman grabbed the silver urn and dropped it into a burlap sack. He whistled two notes, one low and one high, then swung over the rail and into the gallery.

"Everyone face that way," he said, pointing his gun at the bench.

The lawyers, the officers, everyone turned their backs to the gunmen. Gary stood off Foxx's left shoulder, slightly in front. The judge and Linda stood in front of Gary, who lay a protective hand on each of their shoulders.

"Jury, heads down."

Across the courtroom, the jurors doubled over in their seats. Linda, sobbing softly, bent her head toward Gary's hand. Foxx could read her mind. She was scared that the gunmen would shoot them all in the back. But Foxx didn't think so. They were here for the silver urn, and if they wanted to get out of the building they needed to move fast. Sure enough, he heard the creak of a door swinging open, felt the slight change in pressure of the courtroom air. They'll be gone in a second, he thought. Then came the loud, sickening pop of a gunshot.

"Gary?" someone said.

Right in front of Foxx, Gary Martin's hands slipped off the judge's and Linda's shoulders.

"Gary, are you all right?" Foxx cut in front of Gary and lifted his chin. Gary looked confused. His mouth moved, but no sound came out. His eyes focused, then drifted from Foxx.

"You hear me, Gary?"

Gary began to sink. His knee, then his hip, then his shoulder settled on the floor as gently as lying on a bed. A red stain spread on the back of his uniform shirt.

CHAPTER 5

Foxx lit his sixth and last cigarette of the day and lifted his foot onto the low wall at the corner of Duane and Lafayette. The intersection was quiet, just a few cars stopped at the light before heading toward the ramp to the Brooklyn Bridge. There was no foot traffic, either. The last stragglers from the courthouses and office buildings bordering Foley Square were long gone. Foxx blew smoke skyward and pinched his eyes with his thumb and forefinger. In the unearthly quiet, he could almost hear music screeching out of the restaurant around the corner.

Foxx opened his eyes and blinked them dry. The early October sky was a clear, luminous blue, while down at ground level the sidewalks were dark except for the faltering lamplight. Across the square, three huge lanterns hanging from thick iron chains lit the portico of 60 Centre Street.

An arm slipped through his. He tensed until he heard her voice, angling downward from above his left ear.

"Hey, Foxx, whatcha thinking?"

Ursula.

"Ever wonder how birds decide to migrate?" he said.

"I don't know. The weather? The color of the leaves?"

"The weather can be different year to year. Same with the colors of the leaves. But the one constant is the angle of the sunlight. That's their cue. People react the same way."

"Are you about to take wing for Capistrano?" said Ursula.

"I'm talking about memories. The angle of the sun cues intense memories from years past. I remember walking out of the hospital that night. The sky was exactly the same."

"I remember, too. I don't need the sky to tell me." She withdrew her arm and receded enough that the smell of her hair faded. "You have another one of those?"

"I didn't know you smoked."

"I don't," said Ursula.

Foxx shook his pack, and Ursula pinched a cigarette with her fingernails. She was tall and big-boned, the type who looked dynamite in nursing scrubs but somehow raw in a pleated skirt and scoop-necked blouse. Foxx thought she cleaned up nice anyway.

"McQueen sent me to fetch you." Ursula steadied his hand with hers as she drew on the flame from his lighter. "The band is on its last number."

The band, a group of court officers from Kings Supreme, was the reason Foxx had vacated the restaurant.

"What's next on the program?" he said.

"Live auction."

"How is he holding up?"

"Better than last year. You know how he hates to be the center of attention." Ursula took a drag, and a tiny cough clicked in her throat. "But I worry about him. All he does is sit at that computer and search for new information about that damn treasure."

"I don't know what I'd do in his place."

Ursula stubbed out her cigarette, then turned to leave. Foxx grabbed her arm.

"No," she said.

He wanted only to tell her how much he admired her, for coming back, for sticking around, for doing what lots of people always said they would but never did. But those words did not come.

The third annual fund-raiser for Gary Martin offered many ways to separate people from their money, not that any of the many people who packed the restaurant cared. They ate, they drank, they danced, they mingled in ways that violated the stratified caste system of the courthouse because they wanted to support Gary. But even on a night rife with bittersweet bonhomie, Foxx and McQueen, two-thirds of what had been a triumvirate until that day, knew the virtue of variety. And so they had organized 50/50 cash raffles, balloons with gift certificates inside, silent auction items ranging from gift boxes of wine to weekends in the Berkshires. But the big event was the live auction, and McQueen, who could be caustically glib in private, froze up before a crowd, which left Foxx the auctioneer by default.

McQueen sat at an empty table, transposing names and numbers from the silent auction cards onto a master list of donated merchandise. Meanwhile, Foxx paced the dance floor and tapped his finger on the wireless microphone. Each tap thudded in the speakers.

"Give them another few minutes to settle down," said McQueen.

"I thought you wanted me to start right away."

"Who told you that?"

"Ursula."

"Typical woman," said McQueen. "She blames me that he spends too much time on the computer. Then he actually leaves his apartment, and she worries he'll tire himself out. I ask her which is her main concern, the computer or the fatigue, and she walks away."

"The computer was your idea," said Foxx.

"Well, you know the old saying. Teach a man to fish and he'll never starve. Teach a man to surf the web and he'll never stay sane."

* * *

Gary Martin nudged the joystick, and his wheelchair lurched forward. The footrests hit the door, the door swung open, and he was away from the noise, away from the crowd, away from all the people who wished him well but would wake up tomorrow and not give him another thought till next year.

The men's room stank of pungent antiseptic and the floor was dotted with wads of paper towels. Gary rolled into the handicapped stall, where a log of shit turned slowly in the toilet. He pulled the white plastic bottle out of the side pocket of the wheelchair, then unzipped his fly to hang himself out. Well, not exactly hang, because *hang* implied being upright, and being upright was no longer possible. He worked the head of his dick into the mouth of the bottle and let go. The piss hissed as the plastic warmed in his hand.

The door opened twice in quick succession, letting in two distinct blasts of noise from outside.

"Mr. Gavigan," said a man's voice.

"Cut the 'mister' crap. I'm Hugh."

"Of course, Hugh. I sent my résumé to your office last month. I wonder if you've had the chance to look at it."

"I haven't, quite honestly. I'm leaving for a trial in Texas, so if I've seen anything else lately it's only because my secretary stuck it in my face."

"Oh."

Gary emptied his bottle into the toilet and zipped up.

"More than likely," Hugh continued, "she would have passed it on to one of the partners on the hiring committee. They normally respond in a couple of weeks."

"It's been three."

Gary backed out of the stall. One of the men stood at the sink, while the other leaned into a urinal. The man at the sink was short and stocky with a head shaved like a bullet. He wore an olive suit and no tie with the top two buttons of his shirt open. He patted his neck with a paper towel. The other man wore gray pinstriped pants held up by maroon suspenders and a white shirt that had no business looking so starched at the end of a workday. He shook out, zipped up, and turned toward the other man.

"I will talk to the committee tomorrow and see where things stand with your résumé," he said.

"Well, while I have you," said the other, "I just want to reiterate that I've written decisions on virtually every type of civil case. I also have intimate knowledge of the inner workings of the court system. I believe I would be a valuable addition to your firm because . . ."

Gary had a nodding acquaintance with the man named Hugh, and though he never had seen the stocky bullethead before, he gathered he was a law clerk looking for a job. He'd never get it that way, thought Gary, as he kicked through the door and let the sounds of the party drown out the plaintive quaver in Bullethead's voice.

Linda was standing at the bar and waiting for Hugh to return when Gary Martin rolled up into the space beside her.

"Buy you a drink, Judge Conover?" he said.

"I'm afraid I just got a refill." Linda turned and lifted her spritzer. "And it's Linda."

"No, Judge. You earned the title. Using it's the least I can do."

"That's silly. I'm still just Linda. To you, anyway."

"It's a nice sentiment," said Gary. "Not very widespread, but nice."

Linda relaxed against the bar, taking him in. Even in the wheelchair, he still looked like the old Gary. His face huge, his beard full, his hair long and slicked back until it ended in gray-blond curls. His forearms were muscular. His stomach was round, but not as big as she might have expected three years after he took that bullet in the spine.

"You're right. I suppose judges are different." She sighed, but it was not just a physical sigh. She felt as if she exhaled a bit of her soul, reconnecting with her old friend and coworker. "I find it much harder being a judge than a law clerk. I didn't realize what a good thing I had working for Judge Johnstone. Well, I did and then I didn't."

"I always did," said Gary. "Do you ever see him?"

"Not since he . . . you know."

"He visited me a few times when I was in rehab, but he stopped around that same time. Were you surprised?"

"If I was surprised, I don't remember," said Linda. "Things were difficult in chambers. We barely spoke to each other, and I'd already decided, well, I'd already decided a lot of things, but I just hadn't told him yet. Then he dropped the bomb, and I didn't need to tell him."

The bartender reached over the bar and handed Gary a pint of beer.

"Compliments of the lady down at the end of the bar," he said.

Gary and Linda both turned to see Ursula raise a glass.

"You're back with Ursula," said Linda.

Gary sipped, then began to cough as if the beer went down the wrong way.

"Yeah," he finally said, then his voice came fully clear. "And you're married. And a judge. How do those things feel?"

"Individually, fine. Together, not what I expected. This belief that you can have it all, I'm beginning to think it doesn't mean all at once." She shook her head. "Sorry. That sounds self-centered, doesn't it?"

"Not to me," said Gary.

"You don't need to be nice, or even polite."

"I promise I'm not." Gary took a long pull on his beer, then licked the foam from his mustache. "You know, I get flashbacks from that day. Odd things, like random images. It's like every second of that day has come back to me over the last three years."

"Tell me one," said Linda.

"Well, I just today had a flashback of you and me standing in the courtroom and looking at the treasure piece."

"I remember that," said Linda. "Was I ever in a mood."

"Your argument with the judge. It bothered him, too."

"Never said anything to me."

"He told me during one of his visits with me in rehab."

"Really? What exactly did he say?"

Before Gary could answer, Hugh shouldered between them and asked the bartender for a glass of red wine. Then he turned to Gary.

"You made a quick exit," he said.

"Didn't envy you that conversation," said Gary. He backed up. "I'd better circulate. Foxx and Mike keep telling me to work the crowd. Nice seeing you, Judge. You too, Mr. Gavigan."

"It's Hugh," said Hugh, and they both laughed.

"What was that all about?" Linda said after Gary rolled away.

"Your law clerk cornered me," said Hugh. "Did you suggest he send me a résumé?"

"No," said Linda. "I gave him a list of firms I thought were good possibilities, but your firm was not one of them."

"Well, he sent one. And he took the opportunity to ask me about it in the men's room."

"I'm sorry," said Linda. "I'll talk to him."

"No need. I handled it," said Hugh. "Made like I hadn't seen his résumé, though I have. If he thinks he's getting as far as even a courtesy interview, he's sadly mistaken."

"How about this?" Linda snaked her arm around Hugh's and

entwined her fingers in his. "I've had him for two years. You take him for two, turn him into a decent lawyer, and I'll take him back for the duration."

"Why don't we just adopt him?" said Hugh.

He unwound his arm and drained his wine in one long gulp.

"Aren't you going back to the office?" said Linda.

"I am," said Hugh. "That's why I needed that."

CHAPTER 6

Linda sat on the toilet and resumed counting in the old school-yard way of inserting *one thousand* between each number. But the numbers faded again and her mind drifted back to her conversation with Gary Martin. Memory was a strange thing. Everyone could answer the "Where were you when?" questions about the seminal events that happened during their lifetimes. But the tiny events that stuck in people's minds from their own lives were fascinating. Why did we remember what we remembered? She had no answer, but she realized that the shooting in Judge Johnstone's courtroom—"the heist," as it was called in the courthouse—was a dividing line for several lives. Gary's was the most obvious, and it made sense, she supposed, that he would remember standing at the treasure piece with her because it was the last day in his life that he would be able to stand at all. She had no independent memory herself, at least not until he refreshed her recollection.

Her memories of the day took a different track—anger at the judge, fear as the gunmen stalked through the courtroom, desolate loneliness in her apartment that night. And then Hugh called. He had been at a lengthy deposition that day and heard news of the shooting only when he returned to the office in the evening. Quickly piecing the story together, he realized that she must have been in that courtroom. He phoned her immediately, a call that ended six full months of silence following their breakup. They knew that phone call offered them only two choices: stay apart or get married. There was no third way.

The count came back into her consciousness.

Forty-eight one thousand, forty-nine one thousand, Fifty . . .

On the corner of the vanity, the early pregnancy test stick lay on a tissue. The instructions said to pee on the absorbent tip for at least five seconds and then lay the stick flat with the window side up for at least two minutes. Linda, a by-the-book person by nature, followed the instructions to the letter. But unfortunately she had forgotten her watch, and with Hugh up, showered, and dressed, could not risk leaving the bathroom to get it. Her fallback was to count the two minutes in her head.

. . . eight one thousand, fifty-nine one thousand, sixty.

Eyelids tightly shut, chin resting on the V formed by her upturned palms, she could hear the rumble of the elevator rising to the third floor, the rattle of the door as it opened, the squeak of Hugh's shoes in the hardwood hallway before he hit the carpet in the master bedroom.

"Hey, Lindy, you need to come see this," he said.

Good thing she had not tried to grab her watch.

"I'm kind of in the middle of something right now," she said, still keeping count in her head. She had locked the bathroom door, something neither of them ever did, and hoped he did not jiggle the knob.

"Take your time, then. I'm DVRing it."

"Okay."

"Don't you want to know?"

"Surprise me," she said. She could visualize him striding back to the elevator, slick, starched, tie perfectly knotted. He definitely was a morning person. She reached one hundred twenty in her count and, uncertain her timing was correct, decided to count thirty more. Finished, she stood up and, studiously avoiding the test stick, pulled her panties over her hips. She stepped directly in front of the vanity and gripped the edge of the sink basin tightly with both hands. Here goes, she thought.

A blue plus sign filled the round window.

Her hands immediately started to shake, her legs went wobbly. She lowered the toilet lid and sat, trying with little success to breathe deeply.

Keep it together, she told herself. She loosened her fists, unclenched her teeth, and took a deep settling breath until the strength returned to her legs. She splashed water on her face, poked some life into her hair, then dropped the test stick into the pocket of her bathrobe.

Hugh stood at the kitchen counter, staring at the tiny flat-screen TV over the rim of his mug. Linda drew up beside him and insinuated her shoulder under his arm.

"What is it?" she said.

Hugh pressed the remote, running the morning news broadcast back to an image of people, placards, and trees.

"Demonstration at Foley Square," he said. "Started early this morning."

Several people in tattered clothes held signs in front of the wide stone steps that led up to the massive columns of the courthouse facade. She squinted, but the signs were a blur.

"Who are they?" she said.

"Some of your happy customers."

Hugh zapped the TV with the remote, freezing the picture and silencing the reporter's voice-over. Without the dizzying movement, Linda could focus on the signs. One read: INCREASE OUR STIPENDS. Another read: DECENT HOUSING FOR DECENT PEOPLE. A third read: WHERE DO YOU LIVE, "JUSTICE" CONOVER? The screen jumped to a bearded man speaking to a crowd from a park bench.

"Oh dear," said Linda, lowering herself onto a stool.

"What stipends are they talking about?" said Hugh.

Once upon a time, when their marriage was young and Linda's judgeship was new, they talked constantly about the cases that came before her and the cases he took to trial. It was shop talk, Linda believed, but also the cord that bound them. Lately, though, the natural tension between bench and bar had seeped into their relationship. She suspected the motives of every lawyer who came into her courtroom, he doubted the intellectual abilities of the judges assigned to his cases. Shop talk became increasingly rare, but neither of them could ignore a televised protest. So Linda explained how homeless families received monthly rent stipends computed by a formula that was revised every few years. The latest revision went into effect in July, and an advocacy group immediately challenged the new formula in court, arguing that the new stipend was not enough to rent decent housing in a decent neighborhood.

"They want to be able to afford a house like ours?" said Hugh.

"Not exactly," said Linda. "The Department of Social Services calculates the stipends by following a complex system of regulations. The issue is whether the department followed those regulations."

"You don't have Mark working on this decision, do you?"

"Dear God, no," said Linda.

"You?"

"These issues are way too technical for me. I sent it to the law department. Bernadette's got it."

The screen cut to a reporter, who explained that the demonstration began overnight. The police initially cleared the park, but the group obtained an injunction from a judge and they returned just before dawn.

"I wonder who signed that injunction," said Hugh.

"I can give you ten names."

Linda successfully avoided any serious conversation with Hugh for the rest of their morning together. She was in the shower when he shouted to have a good day and not to get caught up in the protest. She counted out a minute in her head to make sure he was truly gone, then she sank to the floor and cried.

At first, Linda saw no protestors in the park, and her immediate thought was that the injunction had been lifted and the demonstration disbanded. But as she crossed Foley Square, she spotted a few people holding signs near a makeshift podium and realized that the hundreds of rabid protestors portrayed on television were two dozen bored unfortunates in real life.

Linda climbed the wide, imposing steps of 60 Centre Street, then rode the judges' elevator to the fifth floor. The old courthouse, originally conceived as circular, ultimately had been built as a hexagon. And nowhere was this hexagonal shape more noticeable than on the fifth and sixth floors, where the judicial chambers lined long narrow corridors that cornered at one hundred-twenty-degree angles. Linda reached her chambers and, having arrived earlier than usual, was not surprised to see the transom dark. She unlocked the door and stepped inside.

The outer office, wedged into an angle of the hexagon, was crammed with two desks, two tall bookcases, and four small tables piled with motion decisions in various stages of completion. Her own office was furnished with a large desk, two sofas, end tables, accent lamps, and the obligatory built-in bookcases filled with dark green case reporters.

Linda plopped herself down into her desk chair and breathed deeply. As disillusioned as she had become with life on the bench, the smell of chambers in the morning still excited her. Today, that mix of wood and paper, of air unmoved since the previous day, precisely recalled her elementary school classrooms. The memory was particularly poignant, harking back to a simpler time when a word like *pregnant* held no meaning for her. Quickly enough, though, both the smell and the memories faded. She took out the box from her purse and lifted the flaps for one more look at the test stick. The plus sign, vague now but still visible, showed in the round window. She dumped the box into the wastepaper basket beneath her desk, shaking the basket so the box settled deep into the plastic liner.

For the next half hour, Linda carefully read and signed several letters she had dictated the previous day. In this quiet atmosphere, performing these mundane tasks, the sight of the blue plus sign in the little window took on an aspect of unreality. She had not dreamed it, of course; she had seen what she had seen. Instead, she doubted the accuracy of the test result, not on any scientific basis but on the simple belief that life would not throw her this curve.

Her staff showed up just before nine o'clock. Karen Pawling blew in like a cyclone and trilled a sprightly "hello" before firing up chambers with her morning ritual of brewing coffee and pulling messages off the voicemail. Mark Garber rolled in like a cloud blotting the sun. His plodding transit across the anteroom door included a grunt that might have been a greeting and a hand flick that might have been a wave.

Karen and Mark were contract hires, which meant that Linda had been obligated to hire them in return for the support of their political club. In New York City, judicial elections usually involved cross-endorsed candidates or Democrats running in solid Democratic districts. The real election occurred at the nominating convention, when the archipelago of neighborhood clubs that controlled the city's politics negotiated the slate of candidates. Often a candidacy came with a quid pro quo: the new judge must hire a law clerk or secretary from the club. Linda was told to hire both.

Karen turned out to be a gem, someone Linda would have hired in a minute if she had been lucky enough to find her on her own. Mark was more of a rough cut—an extremely rough cut. He had a quiet demeanor that came across as intellectual reserve, but that Linda now realized masked a serious ignorance of the law. In conference, he could drop the appropriate legal buzzword at the appropriate moment. But his written work was terrible, and unfortunately civil litigation in New York City required judges to issue hundreds of written decisions each year. Mark's decisions looked presentable to the eye and sounded intelligent to the ear, but whenever Linda parsed the actual language she found that the legal reasoning skipped a beat. Consequently, she needed to perform cardiac resuscitation before signing off on any of Mark's decisions. Though she returned heavily copyedited drafts to demonstrate the smooth style and impeccable reasoning she expected in a decision, Mark simply keyed in the changes on his computer, never taking the obvious hint that Linda's edits were meant to be instructive.

The deal with the West Chelsea Reformed Democrats was that Linda would keep Mark for two years. The two years had less than three months to run, and, problematic as their work relationship had been, Linda still believed that on some mysterious political level Mark had played a role in her becoming a judge. So rather than simply let him go at the end of the year, she had been trying to place him with a private firm.

The phone rang, and "S. Belcher" showed on the tiny screen. Linda picked up immediately.

"Hi, boss," she said, trying for a breeziness she did not feel.

"Morning, Linda. I need to see you. Now, if it's good."

It was good, of course. When the administrative judge called, you made yourself available. Linda pushed up from her desk, steadied herself, then headed out to the anteroom.

"Going up to see the AJ," she said.

* * *

Linda was no sooner out the door than Mark shot her a double bird.

"Now what?" said Karen.

"I went to that goddam fund-raiser last night specifically to talk to Mr. Justice Conover." Mark spat out those last three words, his derisive code name for Hugh Gavigan. "All I got was bullshit."

"Maybe you should have spoken to the judge first," said Karen. "Let her pave the way."

"That's easy for you to say. Your deal is different from mine. You get to stay as long as you like."

"She doesn't need to get rid of you," said Karen. "Two years was the minimum. She can keep you if she wants."

"Right. Like that'll happen. She never gave me a chance and we never really got along. She always nitpicks at what I do."

"She nitpicks at me, too."

"Like hell. She loves you. And me, I have one foot out the door."

"She is helping you," said Karen. "I type the letters."

"And what have they gotten me? Zilch."

"There's still time," said Karen.

"It's October," said Mark. "The year's almost over."

Climbing the stairs to the sixth floor disabused Linda of any idea that the test results were wrong. Halfway up, her stomach went queasy and the edges of her vision darkened. She gripped the handrail until her stomach settled and her vision cleared. The question now was not whether but how far along. She breathed deeply, running the dates through her head. The way life had been lately, the possibilities were not endless.

Sharon Belcher was the administrative judge of the Supreme Court in New York County. Her duties were threefold: carrying her own modest inventory of cases, setting policy for the court as a whole, and administering the court's daily activities. In this third category, the duties ran from the banal, like addressing complaints lodged by a largely uninformed public, to the substantive, like overriding the usual random method of assigning cases to judges.

Judge Belcher's chambers was a modest three-room suite with entry through the secretary's office in the center, the law clerk's office to the right, and the judge's to the left.

"Missed you at the fund-raiser last night," Judge Belcher said, sitting down in a wing chair beside Linda rather than going behind her desk.

"We left early because Hugh needed to go back to the office. He's preparing for a trial in Texas."

"Still the big dog at the firm, eh?"

"He is," said Linda. "I saw the protest on TV this morning."

"Yes. Well. I wouldn't have signed the injunction, but no one asked me. Don't worry, it will blow itself out like they always do."

"I'm not worried," said Linda.

"Good, because that's not why I wanted to see you." Judge Belcher leaned forward. "The Appellate Division is about to hand down a decision in the Roman silver case. I got the call about this last night. In addition to deciding those appeals, the AD wants the new trial to go forward immediately, and the presiding judge suggested that I assign you as the trial judge."

Linda took a deep breath and settled back in her chair. Her stomach felt queasy again, but not for the same reason as when she climbed the stairs.

"The credibility of our court took a big hit three years ago," said Judge Belcher. "Think about it. Gunmen invade a courtroom. A court officer gets shot. It seems like a dream now."

"A very bad dream," said Linda.

"That's why it's important to get this trial done quickly and get it done right. You are the judge in the best position to get it done. You understood the issues in the case then and you'll understand how the AD decision affects those issues now."

"Can I think about it?"

"Sure, just don't take too long," said Judge Belcher, smiling to soften the edge of what Linda clearly understood to be an order.

Linda left Judge Belcher's chambers, but rather than go back to her own she walked a slow circuit of the sixth floor. It was barely nine thirty, and she already had been whipsawed by two surprising developments. She stopped to look through one of the windows that opened over the deep light courts in the interior of the hexagon. Up above, white clouds hurried past the gold roof of the federal court building.

She ran the numbers in her head. She was only a little bit pregnant, as the joke went, and if the Appellate Division ruling was as imminent as Sharon said, she could be done with the trial well before she started to show. And with Hugh leaving for Texas, she would be well into the trial before he returned. But there was another consideration beyond the timing. That day three years ago had been the worst day of her professional life and a pivotal day in her personal life. One rarely had the chance to return to the scene of such a thumping disaster with a clear mission to make amends. And one rarely had a murky future suddenly become so clear.

Linda continued around the rest of the hexagon and poked her head in Judge Belcher's chambers.

"I'll do it," she said.

Judge Belcher looked up from her desk.

"Thank you," she said. "As soon as the decision comes down, I'll cut an administrative order assigning the case to you. As soon as I cut that order, you call the lawyers in for a pretrial conference."

Inside her own chambers, Linda found a cleaning woman emptying the waste paper baskets in the outer office. She never could remember whether the woman's name was Jessica or Jessie Mae, so she merely said "hello," then closed herself in her office.

CHAPTER 7

Gary Martin hadn't expected such a big crowd three years after the shooting. But Foxx scheduled the fund-raiser on nearly the exact anniversary because he believed a phenomenon called cyclic memory would persuade more people to attend. Foxx liked way-out theories. He would read an article in a magazine, then come into the locker room to preach about it because, he would say, it was his duty to edify his benighted brethren.

Gary never bought into Foxx's theories, but this cyclic memory idea stuck because he had noticed it himself in the days leading up to the first two anniversaries. His dreams, which he rarely remembered, suddenly became as vivid as HDTV. They replayed in minute detail the pedestrian aspects of that day—drinking coffee with Foxx and McQueen, sitting alone at the Pearl Street desk, waiting on the front steps to meet the armored car, looking at the treasure piece with Linda. In each dream, he had the conscious sense of being able to avoid the inevitable if he could alter just one of these minor details. It never happened, not even in dreamland, and after a couple of weeks the dreams faded into dull shapes at the edge of his consciousness. In Foxx's terms, the angle of the sun had changed, and the new angle cued not the trauma of that day but the tedium of the many that followed.

This year, the dreams had been different.

Gary awoke on his left side, hard along the edge of the bed. He rocked twice, then rolled onto his back. He could feel the sheets twisted around his waist, but below that, nothing. He used the controller to raise the bed, and the rest of him slowly came into view as the mattress bent itself. Rolling over had left his legs weirdly crossed, like the devil's in a medieval woodcut.

The clock on the night stand showed 10:00 a.m. Damn, he had fallen back to sleep for another three hours after Ursula left. They had returned just before midnight and gone straight to the bedroom. She helped him into bed, peeled down his pants, then dropped her skirt to the floor for the game she called her sexy nurse fantasy.

In rehab, Gary had learned the distinction between psychogenic erections, which began in the brain, and reflexogenic erections, which began closer to home. The nerves that relayed brain signals to the penis traveled through the lower spine, and an injury anywhere higher up interrupted the signal. So while Ursula's sexy nurse act could not get him hard, her direct stimulation certainly did. She straddled him and grinded against him and kneaded him between her thighs. And when the moment was just right, she stuffed him inside.

"I'm very popular on the paraplegic ward," she said, panting, as she spooned alongside him.

"You don't mean that," he said.

"You're right. I don't."

And now, remembering what they had done had no effect on him. He could call it to his mind, but not to his dick.

The phone rang, and Gary dragged himself over to answer.

"They finally turned over the security tapes," said Felix Tyrone. "They're not tapes as such, but computer files. You still up for viewing them?"

"I'm not going anywhere," said Gary.

He used the trapeze suspended from a reinforced beam in the ceiling to lift himself off the bed. He had two wheelchairs. One was the baroque, motorized model that he called his battle chair. It had a height-adjustable seat, a precise steering mechanism, and an engine that reached speeds faster than most people could run. The other wheelchair, the one he dropped himself naked into now, was a light hand-powered model with a mesh seat and backrest designed for the shower. He rolled into the bathroom, waited for the water to heat up, then bumped the wheelchair over the raised tile that prevented the shower from flooding the apartment.

In the months following the shooting, filing a lawsuit had been the furthest thing from his mind. He was so lonely and depressed it took a monumental effort just to open his eyes in the morning, let alone endure hours of physical and occupational therapy. Plus, he knew a thing or two about the law from having stood guard in so many courtrooms. The shooting had occurred on the job, which entitled him to workers' compensation benefits and prohibited any lawsuit against his employer. Unfortunately, with the two gunmen in the wind and none of the litigants responsible for what happened, the court system was the only potential target of a lawsuit.

Just short of three months after the shooting, Felix Tyrone visited Gary at the rehab center. Tyrone had worked as a staff attorney for the legal benefits plan offered by the court officers' union before starting his own firm. He explained that the workers' comp prohibition against suing an employer did not apply to a grave injury, and a partially severed spinal cord that resulted in paraplegia qualified as grave. Like sex in Gary's new world, the revelation piqued his interest but not his desire. Tyrone needed to convince him that suing the court system was neither disloyal nor greedy, then capped his pitch with a commonsense argument: Gary was still young and strong with arms like a weightlifter and hands like a blacksmith. He may not need financial help now, but when the sympathy ran dry and his friends had moved on and he was just a name to the new officers on the job, he might feel differently.

Gary finally agreed to sue, and the court system quickly made a settlement offer that he would have accepted had he been interested in money alone. But Gary was interested in more than money, and Tyrone, who thought the offer chintzy anyway, was happy to press for a trial.

The shower stream turned tepid. Gary shut the water, dried himself off, and rolled back into his bedroom. Then, through a complicated set of maneuvers, he lifted himself onto the bed, dressed, and then plunked himself into his battle chair. He was waiting when Tyrone buzzed from the lobby.

Tyrone was razor-thin, balding, and perpetually rushed. Unzipping his briefcase, he followed Gary to the corner of the living room, where a dual-monitor computer sat on a table high and wide enough for the front end of the battle chair to fit underneath.

"Very confusing stuff," said Tyrone, producing a flash drive. "The feeds are from security cameras inside and outside the courthouse. Putting it together spatially and chronologically is like working a jigsaw puzzle."

Gary stuck the flash drive into the computer's USB port. The screen lit up with file icons.

"Each one a different camera?" he said.

"Forty-three of them," said Tyrone. "You can't fart in the courthouse without someone seeing you."

Gary opened the first file, which showed the front steps of the courthouse from a camera positioned across Centre Street. The steps were bright in the sun, with people ascending and descending at many angles. Halfway down the steps stood a group of six court officers, obvious in their white uniform shirts and dark blue uniform pants, but unidentifiable at this distance. One of them broke away from the others and climbed up into the shade of the portico. Foxx, he recognized from the smooth, swaybacked gait. Less than a minute later, Foxx rejoined the others.

Gary closed that file and opened the next. The view was a high-angle shot of the front steps from a camera at the top of a column. He opened a third file, which was a low-angle view of the magnetometer lines inside the lobby.

"These first several files are the obvious shots of the front entrance, the rear entrance, and the doors on Worth and Pearl," said Tyrone. "The others are from cameras set deep inside the courthouse in places that I've either never seen or don't recognize."

"I'll look at them," said Gary.

"Are you sure you want to?"

"I've gotten past a lot of shit, Felix. I can handle it."

"That's good, because I want to present these feeds as a single narrative of the gunmen exploiting a security breach as they enter the courthouse, move through the courthouse, and exit the courthouse. No one knows the courthouse as well as you."

Tyrone left in his usual rush and promised to phone tomorrow to check on Gary's progress. Gary opened the first camera feed on the left monitor and the second camera feed on the right. He ran the first feed to the point where the hand truck reached the top of the steps, avoiding his own image because seeing himself walk, in the last few hours of his life when he could walk, was too much to bear. Besides, he'd been waiting months to see these feeds, and he needed to focus on the task at hand, not descend into self-pity.

He froze the first feed, then switched to the high-angle shot from the top of the column until the hand truck and its entourage, with Foxx and McQueen trailing behind, passed beneath. He then opened the third and fourth feeds. The third showed the six officers, the two workmen, and the hand truck skirting the mags in the aisle reserved for court employees and attorneys with security credentials. The fourth feed showed two men standing side by side in separate mag lines. Each wore a white T-shirt, while one wore green gym shorts and the other dark jeans. The officers working the mags called them forward. As the two men passed through the mags, Gary knew that these videos would show much more than Felix Tyrone ever could guess.

CHAPTER 8

Ivan and Jessima met at one of their supply closets each day at lunchtime. Ivan's was on the third floor, at the end of one of the six corridors that connected the courthouse's circular core to its outer hexagon like the spokes of a wheel. Though the same size as all the other supply closets, Ivan's was cramped with cartons of CFL bulbs destined to replace the dying incandescents. Jessima's was on the fifth floor, directly across the corridor from the entrance to Judge Conover's chambers. It was well organized with shelves and hooks and easily accommodated her cleaning cart at the end of the day. Ivan's had the virtue of privacy, Jessima's the virtue of space. And so they more often met at Jessima's.

Jessima ate her sandwich quickly, then chewed half a piece of gum as she stripped naked. She hung her jeans on one hook, her bra and panties on another. The floor felt gritty against her bare feet, so she slipped back into her new pair of sneakers that made her the exact right height for Ivan. Sometimes, like today, she put her smock back on, as well. It cut nicely across her thighs and tapered gently at her waist. She left the top three buttons open and spread the collar to expose her breasts.

Ivan knocked. Jessima cracked the door just enough to pull him inside.

Ivan lifted her onto the sink and licked at her nipples as he unzipped his coveralls. Jessima ran her hands up and down his arms. He looked so skinny in clothes, but was surprisingly well-muscled when naked. She tilted herself forward, opening up to accept him. Then she hung, pinned between him and the edge of the sink, her hard nipples scraping against his chest hair. He squeezed her ass, bit her earlobe. Her sneakers kicked.

Yes yes, she panted in his ear. Then, *now now*.

He eased off. She slid to the floor, turned her back to him, and gripped the faucet handles.

Afterwards, folded together over the sink, Ivan rubbed the arch of one foot against the laces of her sneaker. His chin lay in the hollow of her shoulder, his stubble tickling her skin. She reached around to pat his thigh.

"Off with you," she whispered.

He groaned, kissed her shoulder, pushed himself back.

She dressed quickly. He reached down to the coveralls puddled around his ankles and plunged a hand into each sleeve. She unhooked her jacket.

"Going somewhere?" he said.

"I have an errand." She spoke this way, running "errands," meeting "people," scheduling "appointments." At first, he thought these generalities were meant to keep him at a distance. Now he understood them simply to be her way.

She patted her pockets, then pulled back her hair and tied a scarf over her head.

"You don't need to leave," she said.

"Are you coming back soon?"

"Not that soon." She laughed and kissed him on the mouth. "It was nice."

"Only nice?"

"Wonderful. How you say, stupendous." She grabbed him between the legs. "See you later."

Jessima rarely went out of the courthouse during the day, and the brightness of the noontime sun and the noise of the streets assaulted her eyes and ears. Traffic was thick on Centre Street. Skateboarders zoomed around the fountain and launched themselves into the air. A small crowd stood in the park, holding signs and listening to a man speaking from a bench. A loudspeaker amplified his voice, but Jessima could catch only a smattering of words like *justice* and *fairness* and *what's right is right.*

She stayed on the courthouse side of Centre until she crossed over at the intersection with Worth Street. Along the north end of the park, several benches faced the sidewalk. She found an empty one and sat lightly at first, leaning forward on the front slat. The shade felt cool, almost cold. After a minute, she relaxed and settled back on the bench.

Foxx, dressed in jeans and a hooded sweatshirt, lowered the freebie newspaper to his lap and turned the page. Across the park, Ronan Hannigan continued to speak indignantly about "money" and "power" and "the entrenched institutions of the city and state." Foxx remembered Hannigan from Cardinal Hayes High School, a universe they occupied at the same time though in very different orbits. Hannigan had been a champion distance runner, while Foxx only ran from the authorities. Something happened to Hannigan during the summer before senior year. Foxx never knew exactly what, but it was school-wide news when Hannigan quit the cross-country team. Later, well after the college years passed, Foxx began seeing snippets of Hannigan on the local news, a firebrand tackling the many injustices in the city. Foxx had his own idiosyncratic worldview and found himself agreeing with much of what Hannigan said. But the protestors definitely seemed bored, except for a dreadlocked man who circulated among them and unsuccessfully tried to start them chanting.

The speech ended. Foxx took the cell phone from his pocket

and saw he had received a text message from Bev. Texting was her new ploy since he rarely answered his phone and still pretended not to know how to retrieve his voicemail.

I MAY NEED YOU, the text read. Bev loved all caps.

Foxx folded the newspaper and massaged his brow as he counted twenty protestors. He decided on reporting twenty-one, since Kearney would think it more accurate than a round number. Hannigan, down off the bench, crossed Centre Street and headed past the courthouse toward Chinatown. The dreadlocked man walked toward the benches facing Worth Street.

WOMEN EITHER NEED ME OR NOT, Foxx texted back. WHICH IS IT?

The dreadlocked man reached the sidewalk and sat beside a woman on a bench. Foxx trashed his newspaper. He angled out of the park at the corner of Lafayette, then walked back toward Centre on Worth Street. At first he didn't recognize the woman sitting with the dreadlocked man. But after he passed he realized it was the cleaning woman named Jessima.

"I'm protesting today," said Damien. "Not sure what I'm protesting, but neither do any of the protestors." He rolled his paper sign into a long tube and tapped her knee. "What is this great thing you got for me?"

Jessima took the box out of her pocket and the test stick out of the box.

"I found it in her trash," she said. "She must have brought it from home this morning because it wasn't there last night."

Damien gingerly pinched the tester between his fingers and moved it back and forth so that the little window caught the light. Jessima watched silently. Some of the things she found for him were worth something, and he paid her a piece of what some interested party paid him. Some were worthless, and he paid her nothing. She wasn't sure where this one fell.

"Hold this," said Damien.

Jessima held the tester while Damien photographed it with his phone. He checked the picture, then dropped the phone back into his pocket.

"How's the Ruskie?"

"His name is Ivan," said Jessima. "And he's fine."

"Well, when you get tired of him, you can always come back."

"Back to what?"

"I'm hot for you."

"You're hot for every lady you see," said Jessima.

Damien laughed, then shook down his sleeve. His hand lit on her knee. She slapped it away and ran back to the courthouse.

Ivan went out the rear entrance of the courthouse, skirted the basketball courts on the south end of Columbus Park, then turned up a short street into Chinatown. He never expected that he could have someone like Jessima, and now that he had, he craved her, not just the sex, but the idea of her, the comfort of her, the need to keep her all to himself. He had been with her for almost a year now, and he knew there was no going back to life as it existed before her.

The air was cool, but the sun was bright and warmed him through his blue coveralls. He passed several markets in the block leading up to Canal Street. They each featured chicken carcasses hanging from hooks or huge fish lying on ice. As a boy, he had eaten things he would rather forget, but since coming to America he became accustomed to food so far removed from its natural sources that it seemed to have appeared by magic. The Chinatown markets reminded him otherwise, and he passed them quickly until he reached the newsstand where he bought his weekly lottery ticket.

Back at the courthouse, the afternoon mag lines were long. Ivan flashed his ID card at the officer seated at the security desk, then passed the coffee shop and headed up the staircase. Two floors up, he opened the door to his supply closet. On the shelf above the slop sink, a coffee can stood next to a ceramic bud vase with a single silk rose bent crookedly over the rim. The day after he first made love to Jessima, he found the rose wrapped in a paper towel and balanced on the doorknob.

"I never had a woman give me a rose before," he told her.

"I never gave a rose to a man before," she replied.

The rose had stood in the coffee can until a day, some weeks later, when Jessima reached up to straighten the stem and found it embedded in a thick layer of lottery tickets. Dozens of tickets, scores of tickets, hundreds of tickets. Ivan explained that one day he would win and he would use the money to take her away from here. She smiled kindly.

"Men need their dreams," she said.

"It's not a dream if it comes true," he replied.

Still, he sensed her disapproval. She had given him this rose as a symbol of her feelings for him, and he had planted it in a soil of worthless lottery tickets. He brought the bud vase from home the next day, and ever since the rose stood perfectly upright in the long, narrow neck.

Now he stuffed the latest lottery ticket into the coffee can. He knew exactly how much money he had wasted on this stupidity. But one day none of it would matter. As Jessima said, men need their dreams.

CHAPTER 9

Foxx balanced the two pizza boxes on one hand and buzzed two shorts and a long, the not-so-secret code. A moment later, Gary's voice crackled on the speaker.

"Friend or foe?"

"Who is to say what we really are?" said Foxx.

"Oh, it's you," said Gary.

"How'd you guess?"

Foxx stepped off the elevator and into the aroma of something spicy. The people in 4D always seemed to be cooking exotic foods, and tonight's concoction smelled like curry with a hint of coconut. Indian, he guessed, maybe Thai.

The extra-wide door to 4A was ajar.

"Gary," called Foxx as he stepped into the small foyer that had been ornate with engaged columns and arched doorways until McQueen's remodeling crew got done with it. One extra-wide doorway opened into the kitchen, another into the living room, a third into a short corridor that led to the bedroom and bath. In the distance, overheated voices argued about a college football game.

"You here, Gary?"

"Where the hell would I be?" The reply came from doorway number two.

"I got pepperoni and meatball."

"I love you, Foxx."

"Only kidding. Two veggies. Lots of red onion and low-fat cheese."

"Lovely," said Gary, resigned.

"Someday you'll thank me."

"Doubt it."

"I'm inviting myself down the hall for Indian."

"Suit yourself."

Foxx took the pizza into the kitchen. Dried tomato sauce dotted the stove. Rubbery curls of scrambled eggs littered the counter. A pile of dirty plates leaned in the sink. Foxx nudged the faucet lever and held a sponge under the thin stream.

"I hear you, Foxx. Forget the mess. I'm lazy, not helpless."

Foxx shut the faucet and tossed the sponge. He tore the lid off one pizza box, grabbed two beers from the refrigerator, and went into the living room. Gary was parked between the sofa and the recliner. He leaned forward in the battle chair, an elbow balanced on his knee as he wrist-curled a five-pound dumbbell. Foxx set the pizza on the coffee table and popped the beers as Gary finished his set.

"I'll trade you," said Gary.

Foxx lifted the dumbbell from Gary's palm and replaced it with a beer. Gary's face and arms were red, his forehead sweaty.

"Where's Mike?" he said. "Spending my money?"

Foxx laughed. McQueen had his faults, but dishonesty with money was not one of them.

"Might as well give me a slice," said Gary. "They're even worse cold."

McQueen showed up a few minutes later, clipboard in hand.

"How can you stand that stench in the hallway?" he said.

Gary rolled his eyes at Foxx.

McQueen grabbed a beer and wolfed down one slice and then

settled back on the sofa to begin the official post-fund-raiser meeting.

"Our receipts break down like this," he said. "Cover charge minus food netted fifty-one hundred fifty. The auctions, silent and live combined, brought in ten thousand four hundred seventy-five. Both these figures are up from last year. Donations from people who didn't attend came to eighty-five hundred." He unclipped an envelope thick with checks and handed it to Gary. "That figure is down from last year, but that's because more people showed up this year."

Gary balanced the envelope on his lap and thumbed through the checks.

"So we cleared twenty-four thousand one hundred twenty-five," said McQueen. "Now, I propose that we take fifteen thou and ladder another fifteen months of one-thousand-dollar CDs. That gives us a two-year cushion."

"What's the interest rate?" said Foxx.

Gary, still thumbing the checks, did not look up.

"Practically zero," said McQueen. "But that's not the point. The point is Gary can cash in a CD each month if he needs the money. If he doesn't, he can roll it over to the end of the ladder."

"Whatever," said Gary.

"What about the rest?" said Foxx.

"We already made the essential renovations with the doorways and the bathroom," said McQueen. "So I figure, while we still have the people's generosity, we redo the kitchen."

"For nine grand?" said Foxx. "Can you even get a set of plans drawn up for that?"

"C'mon, Foxx. Between you and me, we know every donkey-Irish tradesman in Throggs Neck and City Island. We can dragoon somebody into donating labor and use the money on appliances."

"We should ask Gary what he wants," said Foxx.

Gary closed the envelope and tossed it onto the coffee table.

"New kitchen? Great. Increase the resale value. Plus I can cook all Mike's exotic foods."

"See?" said McQueen. "That's why I don't ask."

Foxx went into the kitchen and came back with the second pie and three more beers. As they ate and drank, Foxx caught Mc-Queen's eye. *Well?* he asked silently. *You start,* McQueen mimed.

"Gary," said Foxx. "We need to talk about something else."

Gary bit into a fresh slice, then extracted a long peel of red onion from between his teeth.

"What's that?" he said.

"The amount of time you spend on the computer."

"How the hell do you know how much time I spend on the computer?"

"Well, Gary," said McQueen, "we think there's reason for concern."

"You're shitting me, right?" Gary looked back and forth from Foxx to McQueen several times before recognition came into his eyes. "Oh, I get it. Ursula put you up to this."

"She didn't," said McQueen.

"Actually, Gary, she did," said Foxx.

"Look, guys," said Gary, "I'm sorry she drew you into this, but what's really going on is she wants to move back in."

"And you're not hopping on that?" said McQueen.

"It didn't work out so great last time, if you remember. Much as I'd like to try again, I'm worried about it not working out because I don't know if I could handle that now. I never had to deal with it then."

They went silent for a while, then Foxx spoke up.

"But you do spend a lot of time on that thing."

"That thing is my salvation," said Gary. "I'm in this chair because of that fucking Roman treasure. What I've tried to do, since I can't do anything else, is learn everything about it. I read art history sites, blog posts, Twitter feeds. I Google 'the Salvus Treasure' twice a day. Yeah, I spend a lot of time on the computer, and Ursula knows exactly why because I've told her. It keeps me from going crazy."

Linda did not know what was going on in the movie, an art film playing on an obscure premium cable channel. But she liked the rhythm of the dialogue, the sudden swells of background music, and, when she looked up from her book, the sepia tones of the cinematography. She did not know what was going on in the book, either, which was a memoir by one of her favorite novelists. But she liked the weight of the book on her lap, the texture of the pages against her thumb, the shape of the print in her eye. The wineglass stood on the coffee table, out of reach now since she had tucked herself back into the corner of the sectional sofa and drawn her legs up under her. The glass had a tiny circle of red at its depth and a faint imprint of her lips on the rim.

She may have dozed. She may have slipped again into deep, transporting thoughts. She could not be sure. What she did know was that when she heard Hugh come in the front door the book was facedown on her lap and the movie credits were rolling up the screen.

She reopened the book and listened to Hugh's progress: the thud of his briefcase, the squeak of his shoes heading into the kitchen, the solid tick of a heavy-bottomed glass on the granite counter, the clatter of ice, the glubbing sound of bourbon and air fighting past each other in the neck of the bottle. Silence then, until he peeked in and said, "There you are," and sat beside her with half a cushion between them. His shoes were off, his tie gone. Wisps of dark chest hair curled over the exposed V of his T-shirt.

"Are you ready for the trial?" said Linda.

"I am now," said Hugh. "The associates flew out today, which left me a big chunk of time to work on my opening statement."

He took a healthy slug of bourbon and settled back to describe his work process, which she had heard many times but did not prevent him from explaining again. He never wrote out his opening statements because a tightly written script sounded stiff in its delivery. He preferred only a general sense of what he needed to say; how he said it was a game-time decision, dependent upon what the plaintiff's attorney had said and what vibe he felt from the jury.

"And you're still leaving tomorrow?" said Linda.

"I need the weekend for final witness prep and to coordinate with local counsel on an in limine motion set for Monday morning." Hugh drained the rest of his drink. "A trial is like a play. You judges don't get to see the rehearsals, the rewrites, the cast changes."

He rattled the ice in his glass. "You want another?"

"No," she said. She had not drank the first glass. She had swirled an ounce of wine in the glass, then kissed the rim before pouring it into the sink.

He took the wineglass into the kitchen, fixed himself another drink, and returned.

"Good book?" he said.

"Some interesting parallels between her life and her fiction, but I prefer the fiction."

He removed the book from her hand, flipped it away, and snuggled against her. He was distracted when consumed with his work, playful when not. And whenever he felt playful, he wondered why she did not feel playful, as well. She tried to relax, stroking the stubble of his cheek as he nuzzled her shoulder. Mountain-time, she had called him during their original dating days, because his five o'clock shadow seemed to arrive by three.

"Hugh," she said, breathier than she wanted to sound.

He mumbled, somehow reached the glass out to the coffee table without his cheek retreating from her neck. And then his hand slipped beneath her and worked between the cushion and her ass.

Their circling before sex had lost its spontaneity, but the hand squeezing her ass was the one unmistakable sign of what Hugh wanted.

Oh great, she thought. He hadn't approached her or shown her any affection since, well, since *that night*, and now, because she needed to have a serious discussion, he turned amorous, which meant he'd get mad if she turned him down and they would spend another night lying side by side, separate psyches in the same bed, each waiting for the other to fall asleep.

Still, as much as she tried to relax so that she could buy time, she stiffened.

"Something up, Lindy?" he whispered.

It was her turn to mumble. But she could not resist a shrug and, despite being two people who earned their living by bending words, they were highly attuned to each other's body language. Hugh felt that tiny shrug. He lifted his head off her shoulder, pulled his hand from her ass.

"Sharon called me in first thing this morning. The Appellate Division is about to issue a decision in the Roman silver trial. She wanted to give me a heads-up."

"Why?"

"Because the AD wants a new trial to go forward immediately. And the presiding judge intimated to Sharon that the panel wants the trial assigned to me."

Hugh backed off onto another cushion.

"Do you really want to try this case?" he said.

"I want to and I need to."

"Because of those pretrial rulings. You were the law clerk, not the judge. You gave him your advice. It was his to accept or reject."

"I still feel I need to make it right."

"And I don't know why this is your responsibility," said Hugh. "I never have."

"Because I was there," said Linda. "Because I should have stood up to him and stuck with my convictions. But I didn't, I couldn't. And the fault was not my reasoning or my research or my powers of persuasion. The fact is, I was cowed. I was cowed by his bluster, by his reputation, by his ability to make me feel like a little girl. I hated being cowed, and that feeling has not gone away one iota."

"I understand all that."

"No. I don't think you do."

With an exasperated sigh that signaled an end to the discussion and to any possibility of sex, Hugh stood up.

"Far be it from me to tell you what to do." He knocked back the rest of the drink. "At least we'll both be occupied."

CHAPTER 10

Foxx left after the pizza was gone. McQueen stayed behind and cleaned the mess in the kitchen, thinking that when they started the renovation he would insist on a heavy-duty dishwasher. He came out to find Gary at the computer.

"I gotta show you something," said Gary. "Get a stool and sit down. This'll take a while."

The left-hand monitor showed a long-range shot of the sun-splashed front steps of 60 Centre Street with a group of six uniformed court officers standing together midway to the top. The right-hand monitor showed a high-angle view of the steps from the top of the column.

"Are these what I think they are?" said McQueen.

"Security camera feeds from that day."

"How'd you get them?"

"Felix demanded them as discovery in my case. You'd be surprised how many cameras there are in the courthouse." Gary minimized the left image to show dozens of file icons on the desktop. "Each of these is a camera. There are forty-three of them."

"Courtrooms, too?" McQueen leaned forward to read the icons.

"Nah," said Gary. "The judges won't permit that, but there are enough cameras in the public areas to chart someone's movements inside the building."

McQueen settled back on his stool.

"Felix wanted the feeds to put together a timeline for the trial. I want them for something else."

"Don't you care about your case?"

"I never cared about my case. If I cared about my case, I'd have taken the settlement offer instead of letting Felix push for a trial. I have something bigger in mind. We are going to find the missing piece."

"The what?" said McQueen.

"The missing piece. You know, that urn those two bastards stole from the courtroom."

"And why do you want to find it?" said McQueen.

"*We*," said Gary. "Why do *we* want to find it? We want to find it because it's worth a shitload of money."

"But it's been in the wind for three years," said McQueen.

"And that's where this comes in." Gary patted the computer tower. "You think I read those blogs and Twitter feeds for my health? You think I read those websites because of my interest in art history? I'm looking for news on the urn, and I haven't seen the slightest hint that it's surfaced anywhere."

"That doesn't mean anything," said McQueen. "It's not like whoever took it is going to broadcast it."

Gary clicked the mouse and brought up a web page on the right-hand screen. A banner along the top showed a head shot of a man with a leonine head of curly gray hair and a thin matching beard. Beside the head shot, the name Dieter van der Weyden appeared in Gothic letters.

"This guy claims to be a descendant of a Renaissance painter. Whether that's true or not, he's one of the foremost art critics in the world and an expert on the Salvus Treasure. He posted this a couple of months ago."

Gary highlighted a section of text.

"'The heist of the urn from a New York City courtroom was the worst thing that could have happened to the Salvus Treasure. In bodily terms, it lopped off a limb. The treasure was greater than the sum of its parts and, conversely, the loss of one of those parts has had a disproportionate effect on the value of what remains. The thugs who stole the urn know this. They can sell it to someone, who might sell it to someone else, who in turn might sell it to someone else again. But they would only be making pennies on the dollar, so to speak. The true payoff can only come from one sale, which will be to the party who prevails at the retrial. If there is a retrial.'"

"Okay, so?" said McQueen.

"So this expert says what I've been thinking for a long time," said Gary. "The piece is impossible to fence and it will command the greatest price once the new trial is held and declares who owns the treasure."

"But there is still an awful big world out there where it could be."

"Could, but isn't," said Gary. "I think the missing piece never left the courthouse."

"That's crazy," said McQueen.

"Except," said Gary. "Now I have proof."

He ran McQueen through the timeline it had taken him hours to piece together: the two gunmen coming into the building, snatches of them moving down several corridors, and then exiting by the rear door just before the courthouse was locked down. The images showed nothing in their hands, not the guns and not the urn.

"So," he said after the last feed ran, "you see anything that looks like the treasure piece leave the courthouse?"

"How do you know these are the guys?"

"They are the guys," said Gary. "You were out cold on the floor, but I was watching those two guys as carefully as I could in case I ever needed to ID them. When I was in the hospital, I replayed those images until I burned them into my brain, because even though I wanted to forget I also wanted to hold on to what I remembered, even if it hurt like hell, because I figured that some day it would matter. I've constructed models of them in my mind. I've only seen them walk, but I know how they would sit, I know how they would lift a fork or drink a beer. I've created them in my head the way a paleontologist can create a dinosaur out of a single bone. Okay? Those are the two guys and they don't have the piece."

"So who's got it?" said McQueen.

"Whoever was their inside guy."

"Who said anything about an inside guy? I never heard anything about this being an inside job."

"That's because no one's ever going to say that out loud," said Gary. "Think about it. Think about how difficult it is to get one gun, let alone two, into the courthouse. Unless . . ."

"Unless you don't need to clear the mags," said McQueen. "A court officer?"

"Anyone who works in the building," said Gary.

"That's five hundred people," said McQueen. "But even if it was an inside job, whoever helped them could have taken it out any time in the last three years."

"You're right," said Gary. "But my theory is the piece is in the courthouse because that's the one place nobody expects it to be. But it's not going to stay here forever. Once the trial is done, it'll be gone. We need to find it now, before the trial comes back."

"How do we do that?" said McQueen.

"My brains, your legs."

"Are you crazy, Gary? We're friggin' court officers. We put our time in, we moonlight for extra cash, then we retire. We don't recover stolen art."

"Doesn't mean we can't."

"This isn't something out of a paperback novel, Gary. This is real life."

Gary lifted himself off the battle chair until his face began to twitch.

"Don't tell me about real life."

"Sorry, Gary. I shouldn't have said that."

Gary dropped himself back onto the seat, panting and red-faced.

"No sweat," he said. "All you do for me, you're entitled to your say. But now I want you to listen to me, not because you're my friend, not because I trust you, but because you and I were the only ones hurt that day. That treasure owes us, Mike."

"I got slugged in the head," said McQueen. "I bled like a pig and I had a headache for a few days. But the bleeding stopped and my headache went away."

"No, it was you and me on the front lines," said Gary. "And if you got permanent brain damage, you'd be getting jerked around the same as me. Look, Mike, we do this and you won't need to run any more fund-raisers. I won't need to guilt-trip guys to come here on Saturdays to run wires and sweat pipes. You can sock something away. Stop worrying about me. Get married."

"Yeah, like who am I marrying?" said McQueen.

"You'll be much more attractive with a wad in your pocket."

McQueen laughed.

"So forget women. You'll have the money to fix up that piece of shit cabin you bought upstate."

"Hey, it ain't a piece of shit. I got big plans for it."

"Big plans you haven't executed," said Gary. "My point is, we can do this, Mike. I've been studying this for three goddam years. We know the courthouse. I know more about the treasure than the so-called experts. We can do this."

"Wouldn't it be better if we had someone else with us?" said McQueen. "Like Foxx."

"No Foxx," said Gary. "I don't want Foxx anywhere near this."

* * *

After a workday, the two beers at Gary's should have been just enough to propel McQueen ten blocks uptown to his own apartment and into a deep, comforting sleep. But seeing the security feeds on Gary's computer scared the living shit out of him. And when that threat faded, Gary ran his insane plan right in behind it. So with sleep a near impossibility, he turned off Broadway and into a pub.

It was a shot-and-a-beer kind of place, empty except for the barmaid and a couple of guys at the far end of the bar. McQueen downed the first pint and pushed the glass forward. The barmaid came back to set up a second, and he slugged that one down, too.

"You want another, or should I hang an IV bag instead?" said the barmaid.

McQueen wanted to respond with one of his patented wisecracks, but the words never made it from his brain to his tongue. The pizza was long gone from his stomach, and the two quick pints hit him hard.

The barmaid took his silence for a yes, drew another pint, and headed back to the two guys. She leaned in close, and each took turns glancing over in a way that McQueen knew they were talking about him. It was stupid to come in here, stupid to down those two pints, stupid not to leave rather than let the barmaid draw him a third. They didn't know how clever he was, how he could summon a wisecrack for any occasion. But the truth was, he never had Gary's knack for small talk or Foxx's ability to challenge the philosophy of a total stranger. He never actually talked one-on-one with another person. He always needed a third ear as an audience for his wit.

He lifted the glass slowly and took a sip. He could feel their eyes slipping off him, sense the cadence in their talk change as their conversation turned elsewhere.

The inquest had begun one month after the heist. The letters summoning them to the IG's office were hand delivered by courier to the captain's office, then distributed by Kearney as the crew signed in the next morning. Twenty-one in all were questioned—ten officers at the front door mags, three officers at the back door security post, one each at the Pearl Street and Worth Street entrances, and the six assigned to the courtroom. The union rep called a meeting, told them all that they were obligated to tell exactly what they knew. A union lawyer would be present outside the hearing room to advise them beforehand, but could not go in for the questioning. *Sounds like a grand jury investigation*, McQueen had quipped. *I suppose it does*, said the union rep.

The inquest lasted five days, two witnesses in the mornings and two in the afternoons. He and Foxx were the last two before the IG and her crew would travel uptown to question Gary in the rehab center. By then, everyone pretty much knew the Q&A routine. *Officer, did you know that a valuable art object was in the courthouse that day? Officer, were you instructed to be especially vigilant that day? Officer, what measures did you personally take to keep the courthouse secure that day?*

He and Foxx walked downtown from the courthouse that afternoon. It was a gray, blustery day, one week before Thanksgiving. The IG's office was on the tenth floor. Foxx went in first. In the waiting room, the union lawyer had leaned in close to McQueen and asked if he had any questions.

I'm good, he'd answered.

Foxx came out after twenty minutes. Walked past, said nothing, met McQueen's eyes only as the elevator doors closed.

Last chance, said the union lawyer.

I'm good, said McQueen.

He expected something he'd seen in many movies about the military—him alone in a chair facing a squad of inquisitors stretched out across a wide table. Instead, the hearing room was cramped with a desk and table in T formation. The IG sat behind the desk, a stenographer on a stool to her right. Six chairs lined the table, three facing three. One was pulled out slightly, and the IG pointed for him to sit there. It still felt warm from Foxx.

The Q&A proceeded like a litany, the general questions he'd heard about in the locker room, then the specific questions tied directly to him. *What did you see when you let that associate into the courtroom? What exactly did Judge Johnstone say about the doors being locked? Do you remember anything about the gunman before he slugged you?*

He answered the questions to the best of his knowledge. He held nothing back. The IG turned the last page in her script. She leaned back and pressed her fingers in front of her face.

I'm sorry to hear that you were injured that day.

McQueen nodded. The IG closed her file folder. The stenographer broke down her machine. McQueen got up and politely pushed his chair back under the table. As his hand gripped the doorknob, the IG called his name. She had one more question.

Did you do anything to provoke the gunman who fired the shot?

No.

He turned and went out the door.

The pint came back into focus, untouched except for that initial sip. He wondered now, as he wondered then, if he had turned away from the IG too quickly.

Gary stayed at the computer, poring over the security feeds, until he was certain that Ursula would not drop by after her evening shift ended. Ursula was spending more time at the apartment these last few months, but she had not crossed the line of actually moving in. Her imprint was more subtle: a corner cleared, a closet rearranged, a dresser reorganized in a way that did not mix plain whites with logoed T-shirts. "At least you can find things," she'd said, though Gary couldn't remember ever having lost anything.

Maybe he lost the occasional thing in the sense of not laying his hands on it right away, but not in the sense of never finding it again. His privacy was shrinking, which wasn't a bad thing if you were in a relationship, provided you wanted to be in the relationship. He needed to think on that a little more.

The wooden box remained in the bottom drawer of the dresser, now covered with neatly folded sweatpants instead of wrinkled shirts and tattered sweaters. Though he often sensed the question form in her head, she never actually asked about the box, which was shaped like a treasure chest with a hasp and a padlock. The key was in his wallet.

The box preserved not only privacy but memories: a pencil dented with teeth marks; two metal badges for admission to the Metropolitan Museum of Art; two ticket stubs for *The Atomic Café*; a matchbook from a Cuban restaurant. He knew from experience that the memories associated with all souvenirs had half-lives that discharged whenever you returned to them. The half-lives of these had spent themselves in the days after he got out of rehab. The book was different. Time and exposure had not changed the minimalist sketches or the simple yet allegorical language. If anything, the book only became more meaningful.

He propped the spine on his dead lap and slowly thumbed through the pages. He closed the book and put it back in the box and covered the box with the sweatpants. He shut the lights, and after his eyes adjusted to the gray tones of his bedroom, began his nightly maneuvers.

The missing piece, his missing piece, was in the courthouse. He knew that for sure.

He lay on his back and adjusted the bed so he would not snore. After a while, he imagined he heard Ursula unlocking the door. But it was only one of those illogical, disconnected thoughts that came on the edge of his dreams.

CHAPTER 11

In the tiny West Clare village of Lisdoonvarna a bed-and-breakfast offered painting lessons to its guests. The owner was an accomplished painter herself who believed that the light of West Clare, reflecting off the Atlantic on one side and the gray stone pavements of the Burren on the other, rivaled the light of Provincetown in Massachusetts. Painters came from places like Dublin, Paris, and Berlin to take formal instruction before breakfast and again after dinner. During the day, when the light was available, they took to the roads and could be seen at easels all over Clare, from the rocky coast near Doolin, to the town square in Ennis, to megaliths standing atop lonely hills.

Lord Leinster discovered the bed and breakfast after the debacle of the Roman silver trial. He had returned to Dublin and, feeling antsy, drove west without a particular destination in mind. Clare called to him, and at nightfall he pulled up in front of the B-and-B. He registered as Paul Douglas, paid for a week in cash, then, after toting his baggage to his room, turned off his cell phone and crawled into bed with the idea of sleeping that week away.

Two days later, he took his first painting class.

Leinster had displayed an affinity for several talents in life. Getting married was one, heeding bad advice was another, losing scads of money (often a combination of affinities one and two) was a third. But his affinity for painting was as real as it was surprising. Within a year of that first accidental visit, watercolor landscapes of the Burren bearing the signature "PD" began to appear in galleries in Dublin and Derry. His first sale went for twenty pounds; he thought he had made a million.

Now he was driving the Burren again. The morning air was cool to the point of cold. But the sky was clear, and as the gray hills filled the distance an idea for a series of paintings came to mind. Dolmen. He would paint dolmen. There was the Brownshill Dolmen down in Carlow, there were fields upon fields of dolmen at Carrowmore up in Sligo. But Poulnabrone, the most famous dolmen of all, stood right here in the Burren.

Historic sites in the west of Ireland appeared without fanfare. There would be no car park, just a few cars nosed into the ditch near a small sign that identified whatever was there to be seen across a field or over a hill.

Poulnabrone was visible from the road, its jagged capstone angling toward the sky. Leinster pulled into the ditch. He opened the boot of the car and pulled out his portfolio and his easel and his backpack. The equipment was bulky but light, and he needed only a single climb over the stile and down onto the limestone.

From a distance, the limestone slabs looked as smooth and seamless as the pavement of a motorway. Up close, they were pocked and fissured from eons of hard, wind-driven rains. Lichens clung to the stones, looking like slapdashes of yellow paint. Soil blew into the fissures, creating a toehold for spindly herbs and delicate flowers. One guidebook called the Burren a "moonscape"; another simply called it "ankle-breaking country."

Leinster dropped his equipment on a flat expanse of rock. The three main stones that made up Poulnabrone were almost perfect table rocks. The two portal stones stood two meters high. The four-meter capstone lay on top. Leinster circled the stones and quickly sketched several different views in his spiral pad. When one of the views spoke to him, he dropped his pad and set up his equipment.

It was not the most convenient of spots. The stone was especially uneven here, the fissures particularly deep. But he eventually leveled the easel and braced it against the breeze. He clamped his board to the easel and started a second, more elaborate sketch.

Leinster was mostly done with his charcoal rendering, the second phase of his creative process, when he heard the car doors slam in the distance. He did not react immediately. In fact, it took several moments for the sounds to register, a few more for his brain to interpret them, and a few more still for him to pull his eyes off the sketch. By then, the couple already had climbed over the stile and were moving unsteadily, hands clasped, toward the dolmen.

Leinster returned to the sketch, hiding behind the easel but sneaking the occasional peek beyond. The couple wore anoraks and floppy hats, fanny packs on their hips, chunky hiking boots on their feet. They veered off as they neared him, perhaps because they respected his privacy, more likely because they wanted to photograph Poulnabrone without him in the frame.

The two stared at the stones for a while, then began to circle toward Leinster. They will bother me soon enough, he thought, but then the two reversed course and returned to their original spot. The man took up beside a portal stone and posed for the woman. Then they exchanged places and the woman posed for the man. Then the man flattened himself at ground level and aimed the camera. He got up, brushed off his clothes, and joined the woman at the portal stone.

The woman fetched the camera and peered at the tiny rear screen. She handed the camera to the man, and then the man turned toward Leinster.

"Hey, buddy, can you help us with something?"

Leinster backed away from the easel, letting his shoulders droop to communicate his displeasure at the interruption.

"It'll take just a second," said the man.

Leinster dropped the nub of charcoal onto the easel tray and pulled a rag from his pocket to wipe his hands. Might as well get this over with, he thought.

"I'm Jay and this here's Dolly." The man held out a hand, but Leinster raised his own to show it was still smeared with charcoal. He did not offer his name.

"We're here from Tampa," continued Jay. "Flying out of Shannon today and we wanted a shot of both of us. But you see, the camera chopped off our heads."

Jay hopped across a pothole to show Leinster the camera screen.

"Not a problem," said Leinster. The faster he took the shot, the faster they would be on the wing back to Tampa.

"You just press this button here," said Jay. He left the camera in Leinster's hands, then took Dolly by the elbow.

The two negotiated the pocks and fissures and potholes to the mouth of the dolmen's chamber. Leinster framed the shot and took the picture.

"How's it look?" Jay called.

"Fine," said Leinster. "Perfect."

"Great," called Jay.

But only Dolly came forward, hopping precariously from stone to stone.

"Go stand with Jay," she said.

"Really, it's all right," said Leinster.

"No, please." She looked at the screen. "You've done us such a big favor. It's such a beautiful shot."

"Fine," said Leinster, not caring if she took his tone.

He walked quickly toward Jay, twice losing his balance but recovering each time. His shoes, soft-soled and without much lateral support, were not suited for traipsing on the limestone.

"That Dolly," said Jay. "She gets an idea in her head, there's no getting it out."

"I suppose that's helpful at times."

"You don't know the half of it," said Jay.

Leinster stood shoulder to shoulder with Jay. Dolly lifted the camera, lowered it, lifted it again.

"You think you're some kind of artist," said Jay.

It took Leinster a moment to realize Jay's challenge was directed at him. Before he could step away, the gun barrel twisted into his spine.

They walked him toward the road. Dolly tucked his right arm against her left side, while Jay prodded him forward.

"We don't want you to trip," said Dolly.

"Ankle-breaking country," said Jay.

"You can't do this," said Leinster. "People will miss me."

"Not for long," said Jay.

Thirty meters short of the stile, Dolly pulled Leinster sideways into a stretch of deeply fissured limestone. Jay dragged the gun barrel up Leinster's spine and pressed it to the back of his head.

"Look down," he said.

Leinster did. A deep and narrow fissure began just beyond his toes.

"Step into it," said Jay.

"What?" said Leinster.

"You heard me. Dolly, help him."

Dolly forced Leinster to point his toes and lower his feet into the fissure, as snug as ski boots.

Dolly stepped away, somewhere behind Leinster. Jay stood in front, aiming the gun.

"I don't understand," said Leinster. "I'm no good to them dead."

"Who said anything about dead?" said Jay.

He pocketed the gun just as Dolly ran at Leinster. She was a big woman, and when she drove her shoulder into his back there was no way he could stay upright.

CHAPTER 12

Damien Wheatley was once an angry man. He had dark skin, a wild Afro, a mouth that pulled his otherwise handsome features into a sneer, and a cheek scar left behind when that sneer provoked a fight with an even angrier man in a homeless shelter. Despite his disposition, Damien had the ability to present himself as polished and educated by imitating manners of speech he remembered hearing on television and radio as a boy. He learned enough about computer keyboarding at a jobs training program to land a job as an intake clerk at the city's Department of Consumer Affairs. He worked two days, borrowed against his first paycheck, and blew the cash on coke.

Three months later, a termination letter caught up with him at a homeless shelter in Brooklyn. Dimly remembering the job at Consumer Affairs, he crossed the river to the courthouse at 60 Centre Street and badgered a clerk in the Office of the Self-Represented to help him draft a complaint. His theory: discriminatory termination; his claim: five million dollars in damages. The lawsuit was baseless, and though Damien lost at every turn, he learned much about the courts and the people in them. He learned that if he acted humble and not angry, asked for advice instead of demanding action, listened quietly instead of shouting over people, there was much that a courthouse could offer an industrious and clever person.

He dropped his lawsuit, bought conservative, second-hand clothes, and braided his hair. He continued to visit the courthouse every day, but carried a legal pad in his hand and a pencil in his pocket. He sat in courtrooms and observed motion calendars. He camped outside the clerks' offices and watched people come and go. He lurked in alcoves and listened to lawyers conferring while their juries deliberated or their trials stood at recess. A courthouse, he came to understand, was organized as a rigid class society. He vowed to befriend everyone from the bottom up, but quickly realized that the bottom was all he needed. The custodians and cleaning ladies, the mechanics assistants and the mail clerks, even the blind man who ran the coffee stand, knew all the information an industrious and clever person like himself needed to scratch out a living.

Damien peeked out from the columns of the Old St. James Church. He wore a gray pinstripe suit from the Salvation Army and a pair of black wingtips from Goodwill. His dreadlocks were tied back. His black carry case held a legal pad, pen, and something he hoped to sell. St. James Place was one of several that cut jagged blocks among the tenements in the neighborhood south of Chinatown and north of the Brooklyn Bridge. At the east end of the block, the sun rose over the river and turned the early morning mist into a buttery light. Damien tucked the carry case under his arm so he could pull back the cuff from his wristwatch. Five minutes to eight. His fingernails were clean.

Ronan Hannigan materialized in the sun-lit mist, arms pumping, legs churning, silky green tank top and shorts rippling in his self-created breeze. He drew even with Damien, threw up his arms, and stuck out his chest as if breaking the tape at the end of a race. Within a few paces he was walking, his thumbs hooked on his flanks, his fingers spanning his narrow stomach. As he traced a desultory arc from the center of the street to the curb, Damien fell into step beside him.

They walked up to the corner and turned back. Hannigan said nothing. His mouth was locked open, stretching the thin beard that defined his jawline. Finally, he forced air out of his lungs, did a deep knee bend, and shook the tension out of his arms.

"You got my call, huh?" said Hannigan.

"I did," said Damien.

"Well, what are you going to do? I'm losing people fast. This keeps up, I'll be making speeches to myself."

"I'll scout around."

"Ten dollars a day. Breakfast at the mission. Lunch provided."

"The others got twenty."

"And half of them are gone. That's the deal. Find me thirty people. You get me thirty people, I'll give you a bonus."

"I have something else." Damien patted his carry case. "Information helpful to your cause."

"What kind of information?" said Hannigan.

"I can't tell you without giving it away. Let's just say it's information you could use in your protest signage, or bring to bear on the judge personally."

"So it's personal information?"

"Of the most sensitive nature," said Damien.

"I don't want it," said Hannigan. "I'm not after Judge Conover personally."

"Sure sounds like you are with the signs and the chants."

"Well, I'm not. I'm trying to help my people, yes. But I'm catching a whiff of something bigger. I want to shine a light on the basic unfairness of the judicial system. It's a club just like Wall Street is a club. The rich and powerful get waved in, while the poor and weak get whatever justice trickles down to them."

They reached an iron gate with a sign for the mission attached by a wire coat hanger. Hannigan opened the gate and closed it behind him.

"I need people," he called back over his shoulder. "Thirty of them by tomorrow. Get them for me."

Linda watched Hugh through the curtain of her hair as he came out of his walk-in closet and laid two golf shirts in an open suitcase.

"You're going to have time for golf?" she said.

"Of course not," said Hugh. "But I can't stay in a suit and tie all day and into the night. I need to be comfortable working late."

"Just kidding, silly," she said.

Her stomach felt queasy. Not barf queasy, but more like burp queasy. She rolled onto her stomach.

"Which of these?" He held two more golf shirts, weighing yellow against red.

Linda took a deep breath and lifted her head.

"I like you in yellow."

Hugh tossed that shirt into the suitcase.

Early in their marriage, they always wrestled with important decisions until they reached a conclusion. Vacation in Italy or France? Buy a brownstone on the Upper West Side or a condo in Battery Park City? Every decision presented binary choices, and they carefully weighed the pros and cons for each. Lately, though, their disagreements sounded like oral arguments in court. She stated her side, he stated his, and then they both went silent as if expecting a judge to decide. But there was no judge, just an inconclusive silence that meant *I'll do what I want.* So it had been last night.

"I'm leaving now," said Hugh.

Linda realized she had dozed off. Her stomach gurgled, and she burped into the pillow before turning over.

"Good luck," she said.

Hugh leaned down, pecked her forehead and her nose, and then kissed her on the mouth.

"Thanks," he said. "Miss you."

"Miss you, too." She dropped her head back onto the pillow and listened to his footsteps recede in the hallway, the squeak and rattle of his luggage, the rumble of the descending elevator. She waited a minute, then pushed up and dropped her legs off the side of the bed. Still naked, she reached for her bathrobe and pulled in onto her shoulders. Was she showing, or did her belly bulge like that because she was sitting?

She went to the window just as Hugh emerged from beneath the stoop and dragged his luggage to the curb. He stabbed a number into his phone and held it to his ear. He paced as he spoke, and he was still speaking when the car service limo arrived to bear him like General Salvus into the hinterlands.

Linda burped and tasted bile. She made it to the toilet just as the heaves gripped her.

CHAPTER 13

Karen put the call on hold but out of habit still covered the mouthpiece before she spoke.

"For the judge," she said. "Sounds important."

"Tell 'em she's late again," said Mark.

Karen sighed, letting her shoulders slump. The judge imposed few rules in chambers, but the one inviolate precept was never, ever admit to the judge's absence from the courthouse during business hours.

"You know I can't do that," she said.

"Who is it?" said Mark.

"A lawyer named Arthur Braman."

"*The* Arthur Braman? Of Carey Hoffenstein?"

"He didn't mention the firm. Is there more than one?"

"Only one that I care about." Mark picked up his phone and connected to the line. "Hello, Mr. Braman, this is Mark Garber, the judge's law clerk. How may I help you?"

"I understand the Appellate Division just issued a decision in *Croatia v. Leinster* and that the case will be remanded to Judge Conover for trial." Braman's voice was smooth and his words carried a slightly wry twist as if he spoke through a smile. "I wanted to confirm that with the judge and schedule a pretrial conference."

"The judge is in conference right now," said Mark.

"Shall I hold?"

"Better that you give me your call-back number," said Mark. "I'll get back to you ASAP."

He hung up and immediately called the courtroom. The phone rang and rang, which could only mean that the clerk was away from his desk.

"What's up?" said Karen.

"The Roman silver case is back," said Mark. "And Braman says it's ours."

He left chambers and ran down the corridor. Forget about the judge and her list of law firms. Forget about Hugh Gavigan and his transparent lack of interest. This could be his lucky day.

In his midtown office, Arthur Braman hung up his phone.

"The law clerk doesn't know a goddam thing about it," he said.

His associate stood across from his desk, holding the decision she had just downloaded from the state law reporter's website.

"Maybe my information is wrong," she said.

"No. No, I'm sure it's right. It makes perfect sense." Braman rifled a thick folder of résumés. Something caught his eye but didn't quite register before he exchanged it for the decision. "Bring those down to Bassano. He'll know what to do with them. I'll buzz you when I hear back from chambers."

The associate turned to leave.

"Wait," called Braman, realizing now what had caught his eye. "Let me see that folder again."

The associate handed it over, then stepped back as Braman paged through the résumés.

"I'll take care of this one," said Braman.

After his brief visit to the courtroom, Mark was even more keyed up than he had been after speaking to *the* Arthur Braman. The clerk had checked the court's computer system and verified that, yes, the Roman silver case was back and had been assigned to Judge Conover for trial by administrative order of Judge Belcher. Seeing those facts on the green-and-black computer screen sent a thrill coursing through Mark's usually stolid body, and he inveigled the clerk to print out the Appellate Division decision. He was chugging up the stairs, the decision rolled like a diploma in his hands, when his cell phone vibrated in his shirt pocket. He stopped, huffing, at the 4M landing, and fumbled the phone out of his pocket. The screen listed the number as "restricted," which was not unusual for large law firms. He gulped a mouthful of air and answered.

"Mark Garber here," he said.

"Hello, Mark. This is Arthur Braman. We spoke just a few minutes ago."

Like I don't remember, thought Mark.

"I just went to the courtroom," he said. "I have—"

"Hold on, Mark, don't say anything else. I want to be completely proper about this."

Mark looked up. Above him, two short flights of stairs zigzagged up to the chambers corridor on the fifth floor. Just a few feet beyond that juncture was the doorway to chambers.

"When you identified yourself earlier," said Braman, "I knew your name sounded familiar. Now I know why. You know what I'm talking about."

"Of course," said Mark.

"Good. Well, now that I have verified the case is assigned to Judge Conover, it would be improper for us to discuss any future employment arrangements until after the trial is concluded."

"I understand," said Mark.

"I know what it's like to send out résumés," said Braman. "Most firms do not give the courtesy of an answer. That will not be the case with us. In the meantime, however, because we will be before your judge and you will, I assume, play a major role in the trial of the case, our communications must be discreet and above-board."

"I understand," said Mark.

"Patience," said Braman, and rang off.

Mark looked at his phone and saw the numbers for the duration of the call blink several times and then disappear. It took a mere one minute and twenty-nine seconds for his entire future to change.

After her third consecutive bout with morning sickness, Linda arrived at the courthouse late enough to consider going directly to the courtroom, where she knew a calendar of pretrial conferences awaited her. But she had bought a box of saltine crackers and a six-pack of seltzer at a deli and wanted to unload the bag in chambers. Karen was at her desk, looking perky in Halloween colors that picked up the reddish highlights in her hair. Mark was absent.

In her own office, Linda dropped the saltines into the big bottom desk drawer and wedged the seltzer into the minifridge. She turned around to find Mark standing in front of her desk.

"Someone named Arthur Braman called for you," he said. "He said that the Appellate Division decided the appeals in the Roman silver case and that you had the trial."

"And?"

"I just checked it out." He unrolled the five-page decision and handed it to Linda. "It's all true."

Linda sat down and skimmed the decision enough to see that the Appellate Division threw out Judge Johnstone's rulings and directed a new trial on all of the evidence.

"Damn," she breathed, then looked back at Mark. "Have you told Braman his information is correct?"

"No," said Mark.

"Call him. Tell him. Then ask him to contact the other lawyers and say that I'm directing them all to come in for a conference tomorrow at ten."

Foxx sat on a bench deep in the park. He wore a houndstooth cap to cover his distinctive silver hair and a brown corduroy jacket to hide his uniform shirt. The protest had hung together over the weekend, but just barely. He counted eleven protestors, including Ronan Hannigan.

His cell phone buzzed. Bev calling. He considered dropping the phone back into his pocket, then decided that if she was calling instead of texting it could be important. Or not.

"The Roman silver case is back," said Bev. "Conover's trying it."

"How did that happen?"

"Appellate Division decided the appeals this morning. Ordered an immediate trial. Didn't directly say who should try it, and with Johnstone gone assigning Conover must have been Belcher's doing, with or without prodding."

"By who?"

"Don't know that. I imagine the public story would be continuity and familiarity with the issues. I want to know why, so you're going into her part tomorrow."

"Kearney already has me observing the park protest," said Foxx.

"He told me. He also told me it looks like it's about to fall apart."

"We did this before. I saw nothing suspicious last time."

"That's because we were too late to the dance," said Bev. "I only found out later."

"The inquest?"

"Later than that. Anyone near you?"

Foxx shifted on the bench, dipping one shoulder and adjusting the phone against his ear.

"No," he said.

"What I am about to tell you is highly confidential."

CHAPTER 14

Halfway through the morning, the maintenance chief told Ivan that he would have butt duty that afternoon because the custodian who usually handled that job needed to rush home to tend to his terminally ill wife. Butt duty meant policing the courthouse portico, the front steps, and the sidewalk down to the curb of Centre Street. Ivan did not mind digging crushed cigarettes off the stone and sweeping them into a dustpan; it was the kind of quiet, mindless, solitary work that he enjoyed. But he did mind that his lunch hour would not coincide with Jessima's. NEED TO WORK, he texted her, adding a frowny face at the end. MISS YOU, came Jessima's reply.

Ivan piled the CFL boxes in his supply closet so that he had room to sit and eat his lunch. Finished, he crossed his arms on the rim of the slop sink and lowered his head for a brief, dreamless nap. Twice he heard footsteps approach in the corridor that dead-ended just past his closet. Twice he thrilled to the thought it might be Jessima coming to see him. But each time, the footsteps receded before reaching his door.

At one o'clock, he began butt duty. The sky was clear, the breeze light, the temperature warm for mid-October. He swept the portico clean and thought he might finish early enough to catch

Jessima at her supply closet. But the good weather had drawn many smokers out from the shelter of the portico, and the steps were a mess with butts wedged in the angles of the risers and stuck in the joints between the slabs. So much for catching Jessima for a quickie.

"Nice protest," Bernadette said to Linda as they reached the bottom of the courthouse steps. "While I write the decision, you take the heat."

They both laughed; the pool of court attorneys was an open secret within the legal community. Still, no one ever would admit that any specific court attorney wrote any specific decision for any specific judge.

Linda had inveigled her friend into a lunch date by promising they would be back inside the courthouse within an hour. Chinatown would have been the closest, fastest choice, but Linda could not face Chinese food after this morning's nausea, so she steered Bernadette to a small Indian joint on a side street west of Broadway.

"I've never seen you order so bland," Bernadette said after the waiter set their food in front of them.

"Just not in a spicy mood today," said Linda. She tore a corner off a piece of naan, dipped it in her saag paneer, and took a bite. The food hit her stomach without incident.

"Now that we're here," said Bernadette, "do you want to tell me the real reason you were so hot to have lunch today?"

"You're my friend. Can't I want to have lunch with a friend?"

"Don't be disingenuous."

"All right, then," said Linda. "True confessions?"

"True confessions," said Bernadette.

They locked pinkies and then pulled them apart.

"The Roman silver case is back," said Linda.

"Really? It's been how long? Three years?"

"Almost exactly. The Appellate Division issued its decision this morning on those rulings that Hungary and Croatia appealed after the mistrial. It also remanded the case for trial."

"Who's getting it?" said Bernadette.

Linda grinned.

"No," said Bernadette.

"Yes," said Linda.

"How did that happen?"

"Sharon called me in last week. Told me the decision was imminent and that I should handle the trial because of my familiarity with the issues, et cetera."

"Like that ever matters," said Bernadette.

"It does this time. Everyone wants this over and done with." Linda speared a piece of cheese and popped it into her mouth. "Plus, I really believe I'm the best judge to handle it."

"And?" said Bernadette, offering her pinkie. Linda reluctantly locked hers and pulled.

"And I confess I do want the chance to make up for the mess Judge Johnstone made of the first trial."

"That mess was not all his fault."

"I'm not talking about the . . . you know."

"I know," said Bernadette. "But I am. Aren't you worried about handling this case after what happened? Even a little?"

"There's always a little worry somewhere in your head after something like that," said Linda. "But I tell myself that whatever was going to happen already happened. What does worry me is taking the bench with my idiot law clerk to guide me."

Bernadette leaned back in her chair and leveled her gaze at Linda.

"I get the feeling there's something you're not telling me," said Bernadette.

Linda lifted her pinkie. Bernadette hooked hers and then tried to pull away, but Linda would not let go.

"This is the truest of true confessions," she said.

"I can see that," said Bernadette.

"I mean it. I'm going to tell you something that no one else knows," said Linda. "It needs to stay that way."

"I get you," said Bernadette.

Linda held fast. "Do you?"

"Unless you're going to hold my pinkie forever. Then I'll reconsider."

Linda let go.

"I'm going to leave the bench," she said.

"What?" said Bernadette. "Why?"

"'With what I most enjoy contented least.'"

"What the hell's that?"

"Shakespeare. A line from one of his sonnets. I just don't feel I'm in the right place, and if you're not in the right place you can't enjoy what should make you happy."

"So what's so bad?"

"Nothing I can put my finger on," said Linda. "I guess being a judge isn't what I thought it would be."

"Another complaint about judicial pay?" said Bernadette.

"The pay isn't the issue. With what Hugh brings home, my salary is pocket change. The respect is there, too, though I don't feel I command the same respect as Judge Johnstone."

"You need to stick around longer than two years for that."

"You're right. Maybe it's just impatience. Maybe it's the suspicion I'm missing out on something."

"Like what?"

"I don't know," said Linda. "But having this means that I can't have that. Whatever that is."

"Kids?" said Bernadette.

"No," said Linda. "Maybe."

"Are you pregnant?"

"No. Definitely not." Linda lifted her pinkie, but Bernadette didn't take it. "Look, this has been something on my mind for a while. Like background noise that I hear only when it's quiet. At night, you know. But it's crystallized now that I have the case. It can be my exit music. My last hurrah."

"Sure was for Judge Johnstone."

"Not in the same way," said Linda.

Bernadette leaned back, tossed in her napkin.

"But I was not kidding when I said I can't rely on Mark," said Linda. "I want you to work the trial with me."

"I'm not your personal court attorney. I work for other judges, too."

"It won't be wire to wire and it won't be every day. You know how trials go. There will be dead time when the lawyers have other commitments."

"I'll think about it," said Bernadette. "That's all I can say for now."

"Thanks," said Linda. "That's all I can ask."

"Tell me, are you planning this exit to avoid firing Mark?"

"Not at all," said Linda. "I've actually been helping him connect with some firms."

"Any prospects?"

"Not yet."

"Don't you think he'd want to be in the courtroom for this trial so he could make a connection with one of those lawyers?" said Bernadette.

A laugh burst from Linda's mouth.

"He wouldn't have a snowball's chance with any of them," she said.

Back in chambers after lunch, Linda settled into her chair and opened a can of seltzer. Mark had piled several motion folders on her desk, and she looked forward to a quiet afternoon of reading, editing, and more likely rewriting his decision drafts.

Jessima appeared in the doorway with a dustrag in her hand

and a can of furniture polish in the pocket of her smock. She came in every other afternoon to dust the shelves and furniture, and Linda, pleasantly surprised by the quality of Mark's first decision draft, waved her inside and promptly forgot about her.

Linda read a second decision draft and found that one surprisingly good, too. Had Mark been dogging it these last two years? Had he come to understand the message behind all her painstaking edits? Or had he, with time running out, suddenly decided to apply himself in a campaign to convince her to keep him beyond the end of his contract?

After reading the third decision draft, she pressed the intercom button. Mark appeared in the doorway.

"Come get these, please," said Linda.

He walked slowly to her desk and picked up the three files. He didn't even glance at the decisions, which were clipped to the outside of the motion folders. He never did.

"Good work," said Linda.

"Uh, thanks, Judge."

"Very good work, in fact."

He shifted the folders from one hand to the other and tucked them under his arm. In the corner, Jessima sprayed furniture polish and wiped the top of an end table.

"Could you get something for me?" said Linda. "Middle file cabinet, bottom drawer. There's a Redweld way in the back."

Mark slowly left the office. He disappeared momentarily to drop the folders on his desk, then crouched at the file cabinet, which was visible through the doorway. He dug out the Redweld, then carried it back.

"This is about the Roman silver trial?" he said. "I never saw this before."

"No reason you would," said Linda. "No reason for me to think about it before today."

"Copies of old court papers?"

"Mostly. Some other stuff, too. Time to get myself reacquainted with this."

"If you need me to do anything, just let me know," said Mark.

"Sure. Thanks," said Linda, trying not to sound dismissive.

Ivan finished with butt duty just before two o'clock. He dropped off the broom and dustpan at the head custodian's office, then rushed up the stairs to the fifth floor. As he reached the last angle of the hexagon, he heard the distinctive sound of Jessima's door closing. The idea that she had just returned to her supply closet excited him. He reached the door and knocked, but a moment passed and he knew that the sound must have been her leaving. He shoved off in pursuit with the sudden brainstorm of inviting Jessima to dinner at his apartment tonight. The quickies in the supply closet were great; just thinking about them, sometimes just passing Jessima's door, could make him hard. But he wanted to make love to her in his own bed, wanted to wake up next to her in the morning and do it all over again.

The idea propelled him down the elevator, through the rotunda, and up along the mag lines until he finally caught a glimpse of Jessima pushing through the revolving door and onto the portico. She must be looking for me, he thought, and felt a stir.

Ivan reached the top of the steps just as Jessima reached the sidewalk. She had angled sharply to the right, passing close to the corner of the stone pier that jutted out from the portico. Below the pier, the steps extended to their greatest width before reaching the sidewalk. Out on the sidewalk, standing in a tree well that now lacked a tree, was a man with long dreadlocks and a gray suit. His hand closed on her elbow.

Ivan stopped dead on the steps, then drifted toward the edge of the pier for cover as Jessima and the man settled on a bench in the small park beside the courthouse. The man touched her knee.

Jessima slapped Damien's hand away from her leg, then twisted her entire body to look up at the steps. She had felt someone watching, but she saw only the usual faceless crowd rushing up as lunch hour died and the many courtrooms within the huge courthouse opened for their afternoon sessions. She saw no one she recognized, no one she knew, no one who would care that she was talking to Damien. She was his most dependable contact in the upper reaches of the courthouse, picking up scraps of information as she moved unobtrusively from chambers to chambers, dusting, wiping, sweeping, peeling out the plastic liners from the trash cans. There was much to be learned from the garbage of the ruling class, and at 60 Centre Street the judges were the ruling class.

"The Roman silver case is back," she said.

Damien cocked his head toward her in a way that sharpened the scar on his cheek. "Who has it?"

"Conover," said Jessima.

Damien stroked his chin. Despite the grime on his knuckles, his fingernails were perfectly manicured.

"Goddam," he said.

CHAPTER 15

They lived in a fifth-floor walk-up, and on his treatment days Matyas could make it only to the fourth floor before his head began to pound and his legs began to tremble. Andreas carried him the rest of the way. He would crouch, and Matyas would lie on his back and hug him tight around the neck. Andreas would straighten up and lock his forearms under Matyas's thighs. Only when they were inside the apartment did Andreas deposit Matyas into the chair where he would spend the rest of the day alternately slugging bottles of water and bottles of Gatorade to replenish the fluids the chemo squeezed out of his body in long, exhausting runs.

The call came while Matyas lolled weakly in the chair. Andreas took the phone into the hallway. He was back five minutes later.

"That was Luis," he said.

Matyas stirred, then settled back and closed his eyes. If he recognized the name, he gave no sign, which was disconcerting since Matyas had been the one to contact Luis, cultivate him, and ultimately pump him for information.

"Luis," Andreas repeated.

"I know." Matyas groaned. His eyes popped open and he pitched forward as if seized by pain. But the spasm passed, and he settled back again.

"What did he want?" he said.

"It's back."

"The trial?"

"Yes," said Andreas.

"Did he say anything else? Give you any details?"

"Only that there will be a conference tomorrow. The lawyers and the judge. He will tell us more afterward."

Matyas struggled to sit up, then let gravity drag him down again. He reached toward the small table, his hand groping blindly. Andreas steadied his wrist and guided the water bottle into his hand. Matyas lifted it to his lips. Always slight, always sharp, Matyas was now a husk of what he had been, his mind slowly darkening. He sucked the water like a baby, then let Andreas take the bottle from his hand.

"I will," he said, "be ready."

He turned sideways and closed his eyes.

McQueen found Gary's apartment quiet except for the rattle of dice. In a corner of the living room, a fan swept back and forth, its white noise dampening the street racket from down below. Ursula sat on the couch, Gary in his battle chair with the coffee table between them. They were playing backgammon.

"Hey," said Gary.

Ursula said nothing.

McQueen had let himself in as he always did, and he could sense Ursula's disapproval that he had a set of keys to the apartment. In his mind, this was a sure sign that she planned to move in. Soon.

He went into the kitchen and grabbed a beer from the fridge. He could feel Ursula's eyes follow him as he crossed behind Gary and settled onto the recliner. He could sense more disapproval about that, too.

"Hey, anybody mind if I watch TV?" he said.

"Only if you keep the sound down," said Ursula.

McQueen thought he saw Gary wink, telling him to play along. He zapped the TV with the remote and quickly lowered the volume to zero. The baseball playoffs were on. McQueen had been a better-than-average high school player, gave up the game in college, then returned as a star shortstop on a short-lived courthouse softball team. Baseball meant nothing to him now, and these two west coast teams meant even less. He ran through the channels, found nothing to hold his interest, and turned off the TV. Ursula seemed to relax. She was dressed in nursing scrubs and sneakers, her hair pulled back and her face fresh. McQueen agreed with Foxx that Ursula looked great in scrubs and probably even better out of them. He actually had dated her once long ago, a double fix-up along with Gary and another nurse. Ursula took an immediate liking to Gary, and the two talked over and around McQueen until he switched seats to get out of their way. He didn't mind. Fix-ups never worked out for him, so what was one more wasted night? But then Gary and Ursula started seeing each other seriously, and McQueen felt a twinge of envy because Ursula now carried his best friend's imprimatur.

"Hey," he said, "remember those cheap old cardboard checkerboards that folded in half? Remember how the other side always had backgammon? Well, I used to think that 'backgammon' was German for 'game on the back.' "

Gary laughed. Ursula rolled the dice.

"Get it, Ursula?" said McQueen.

"Yeah," she said. "Funny."

McQueen leveled the recliner and closed his eyes. He didn't really know all that much about women, certainly not as much as Foxx. But he did know that a shared sense of humor was an important part of any relationship. He hoped Gary and Ursula laughed at the same things because she sure never laughed at anything he said.

McQueen concentrated on the fan. The white noise was sooth-ing, the breeze just strong enough to send a pleasant chill up his spine. He listened to the dice and the quiet, comfortable chatter that passed between Gary and Ursula. He gathered that she was working the midnight shift, but would leave soon to meet some of her friends for a bite at their local near the hospital.

"Damn, how'd you do that?" said Gary.

"A mix of luck and skill," said Ursula.

McQueen heard the shuffle and click of the game being put away. He opened his eyes enough to see Ursula standing and stretching, her arms raised and fingers laced over her head. He closed his eyes again, not because he didn't want to look, but be-cause each time Ursula caught him staring he sensed another up-tick in her animosity.

"See you, Mike."

McQueen kicked forward and blinked his eyes as if he had been dozing.

"Yeah, Urse," he said. "See ya."

"Don't keep him up too late," she said, and leaned down to kiss Gary.

"I won't," said McQueen. "I'm half asleep already myself."

Gary trailed Ursula out into the foyer, said a second good-bye, then closed the door behind her and threw the deadbolt. McQueen got out of the recliner.

"What's this?" he said as Gary rolled back in. "You being pun-ished? I mean, no TV, no radio. The computer ain't even on."

"Ursula wanted me to spend the entire day with her without any distraction. We went to the park, had lunch, tooled along Fifth Avenue, had dinner. Then, well, you saw backgammon."

"And you played along?"

"It's called compromise," said Gary. "Sometimes you need to compromise. Not that you'd know anything about that."

"I never needed to, and now I don't want to," said McQueen.

"You'll see when you get a girl."

"Right, the girl I'll get when I have a wad in my pocket. But when I have a wad in my pocket, I won't need to compromise. Foxx would call that circular reasoning."

"Foxx," said Gary, shaking his head. He pushed the throttle on the battle chair and rolled to the computer table.

McQueen watched as the computer booted up.

"First time all day?" he said. "Truly?"

"Yep," said Gary.

"Then I guess you don't know."

"Don't know what?"

"The trial is back."

"When did that happen?"

"Today," said McQueen.

"And you don't call me?"

"Well, first of all," said McQueen, "I didn't find out till late this afternoon because I'm not exactly on the memo distribution list. And when I did find out, I didn't call because I thought you already would have seen something about it on the web. I didn't know that you'd actually spent a whole day offline."

Gary took a breath as if he could erupt, but then the courthouse web page splashed onto the left-hand monitor. He clicked the mouse and tapped the keys. More web pages popped, shuffled, and scrolled until he found what he wanted.

"Holy shit," he said.

He spun the battle chair to face McQueen.

"You have any idea who's assigned the retrial?"

McQueen shook his head.

"Linda."

"Really?" said McQueen. "Ain't that a kick."

"A kick?" said Gary. "You think this is a coincidence? You think they put this case in the wheel and her name popped up?"

"Didn't think about it. Not in the five seconds since you told me."

"Well, think about it. Judge Johnstone's retired. Linda was his law clerk when he had the case. No other judge in the building knows squat about it. What do you think?"

"Someone wanted her to get it," said McQueen.

"Exactly."

"But who?"

"Belcher, maybe. The AD probably. That doesn't matter. What matters is how it affects us."

"How it affects us? You're here. I'm there. I doubt that treasure piece will come in as an exhibit."

"Linda knows the case," said Gary, "which will affect how fast the trial will start and finish, which affects how much time we have to do what we gotta do."

"You know how long trials take," said McQueen. "We'll have a year, maybe more."

"Uh-uh. Look at this. Pretrial conference tomorrow at ten o'clock."

"Geez," said McQueen.

"Geez is right. This trial is on a fast track. You need to get into that courtroom tomorrow and find out exactly how fast."

"Just walk in?"

"You got a problem walking into a courtroom?"

"Not if I have a reason."

"You don't need a reason. You're a court officer. You can go anywhere you damn well please."

"I suppose I can go in and talk to the officer," said McQueen.

"Whatever makes you feel better," sighed Gary. "But you need to get into the courtroom and find out everything you can. When the trial will start, how long it will last. Because this is it, Mike. The clock is running and we need to find that missing piece before it runs out."

"Gary, do you really think—"

"No!" Gary slammed his fist onto the armrest. "Don't you dare start fading on me now."

"I'm not, Gary, it's just—"

"Just what, Mike? Your fear? Your laziness? I need you to put your paperback novels away and get off your ass and act like you're with me. Because I'm right, Mike. I know I'm right. That piece is in the courthouse, and we're going to find it. And you know why we're going to find it? Because we deserve it. We put our lives on the line that day. We deserve every goddam penny we can make off that piece. So are you with me or not?"

McQueen took a deep breath. "I'm with you, Gary."

"Good. Get us a couple of beers. We gotta get to work."

The cell phone buzzed next to Ivan's ear. He lifted his head off the cradle of his arms and blinked his eyes. The small table was dappled with wet circles. He tipped the bottle, splashing vodka over the rim of a shot glass with "I ♥ NY" stamped in red and black. The cell phone went silent. He had not looked at the screen, another small victory on a night when small victories were the best he could hope for.

Across the table, the curtains sucked against the open window, then billowed back inside. The building was breathing, he told himself. From outside came the rumble of a truck passing on the street, random voices, snatches of music. The sounds had stitched themselves together when he first sat down to his bottle, but now they flew apart in his head.

He knocked back the shot, slammed the glass onto the table. He looked at the phone, which showed another missed called from Jessima.

"Ha," he muttered as if stage-whispering for an invisible audience. "Nice try."

He had avoided her for the rest of the day, swiping out fifteen minutes early so they would not meet at the time clock, taking a different subway line so they would not cross paths on the platform, turning off his phone so he would not receive her calls. When he got home and turned on the phone, the messages rained down on him. Voicemails, texts. He heated two Jamaican patties in his toaster oven, ate them only to have solid food in his stomach before he turned to the bottle. Darkness fell, along with the level of vodka in the bottle, along with his ability to think coherent thoughts.

The cell phone buzzed again. This time, a text message came through: CALL ME. I NEED TO TALK. J

"Fat chance." His stage-whisper seemed to come from somewhere outside of himself. He shut off the phone, crossed the small room, flung himself on the wrinkled sheets of his narrow bed. He felt a visceral need to deny himself to her and he tried to summon his defiant, I'll-show-you attitude that had helped him through so many lonely nights. But those thoughts would not come. Instead, he heard her say that he was a good and decent man, that she never had met anyone quite like him, that she reserved a special place for him in her heart. He always had feared that his own disbelief or lack of confidence would undo him. Now he wondered if his constant need for reassurance was just too tiring for her.

He drifted off to sleep and found himself in that dream once again. This time it started in the courthouse. He was walking the fifth-floor corridor, approaching Jessima's supply closet with a sense of trepidation. He wanted to turn around, but his feet kept moving. The door loomed closer, and behind it he could hear grunting and panting. He tried to run, but the feet that had brought him where he did not want to tread now refused to carry him away. The closet door unlatched and slowly swung open. The noises inside grew louder and more guttural. He pushed the door closed, but it would not latch and swung open again, as if the closet were too small to contain what was happening inside.

Finally, he unstuck his feet. He began to run as the corridor changed to that same familiar field from long ago. He ran up the hill, batting aside the tall grass. He could feel the man behind him, the one with the cold blue eyes and thin hawk nose. At the top of the hill, a gust of wind stopped him dead. Behind him, the man moved easily through the tall grass. Ivan started to run again, but another man rose up in front of him and smacked him to the ground.

Ivan woke with a start. He swung his feet off the bed, bent double with his head in his hands. His heart fluttered like a dying bird.

CHAPTER 16

Linda waited till well into the evening before she called Hugh. He was an hour behind in Texas, and she imagined him being in court till five, fighting rush-hour traffic back to his hotel, showering the day off his body, and then having dinner. This last item was the shaky one, given Hugh's habit of ignoring basic bodily functions like eating and sleeping when he was on trial. The call kicked directly into voicemail. She left a message, then unpacked the light dinner she had picked up at the deli: grilled chicken breast, brown rice, and an iceberg wedge salad with only the barest hint of balsamic vinaigrette. She would have loved a glass of wine, but she stuck with her seltzer.

Hugh called back an hour later.

"The Appellate Division issued its decision at nine thirty this morning," said Linda. "By ten o'clock, the case was assigned to me for trial, and by ten fifteen the lawyers were calling. I'm holding a conference tomorrow."

"Fast work," said Hugh. "What did the AD do?"

"Reversed all of Judge Johnstone's rulings."

"You expected that."

"Yes, but it's different to see it in writing. And some of what the AD said could have come right out of my decision."

"Except no one ever saw that."

"True."

"Do you feel vindicated?" said Hugh.

"It's more satisfaction. No, maybe you're right. I do feel vindicated."

"I still don't understand what happened between you."

"It's a chambers thing. If you haven't worked in one, you never would understand."

"Then I never will."

The conversation descended into banalities. Linda interrogated him on the flight, the hotel, the associates, the trial. Everything was fine, Hugh said, except for the jet lag. Linda laughed at that one, equating a flight from New York to Houston with setting the clocks back in the fall. But Hugh explained that his circadian rhythms were finely tuned, and without the precise amount of sleep at precisely the right time, he fell seriously out of rhythm.

The line beeped.

"That you?" said Linda.

"Local counsel," said Hugh. "I need to take this."

"Love you," said Linda.

"Me, too," said Hugh, and cut the connection to pick up the call.

Linda went into the kitchen and stared into the refrigerator. An open bottle of pinot grigio stood on the shelf. She took it out, pulled the cork, and breathed in the rather subtle bouquet.

What the hell, she thought, and mixed an ounce with a full glass of seltzer. She barely tasted the wine, and when she crawled into bed the thought that the Roman silver case would waltz into her courtroom tomorrow hit her like a sudden slip on ice.

They were through their third beers, and McQueen had fallen silent. Gary sat sideways at the computer, his thumb worrying a loose ply on the tabletop. One computer monitor displayed a history of 60 Centre Street compiled by the New York State Courts Historical Society. The other showed an architectural plan of the mezzanine level between the third and fourth floors of the courthouse.

"What's up, Mike?" he said.

McQueen grunted.

"C'mon, Mike. Talk to me."

McQueen sighed. "You know, Gary, when I don't think about this too closely it all makes sense to me. But when I walk out the door and you're not in my ear, I think there are too many leaps of logic."

"These aren't leaps of logic," said Gary. "Leaps of faith, maybe, but not logic."

"Yeah, well, maybe that's the problem. Faith is something you either have or you don't."

"I have enough for both of us."

"Maybe," said McQueen. "But what if I find it? What if it really is in one of those places you showed me? Then what?"

"Good question, Mike." Gary turned completely away from the computer to face McQueen. He punched a fist into his other palm, then let both hands drop onto his lap.

"In the courtroom before the trial that day, Linda told me she had an argument with Judge Johnstone. She said it was about legal things." Gary tapped the right monitor. "According to the Appellate Division, Johnstone ruled that a lot of Croatia's evidence and a lot of Hungary's evidence couldn't come in.

"Croatia's story was that the treasure was dug up on one of Marshal Tito's vacation compounds near the city of Pula. A soldier would testify to the unearthing. Hungary's story was that is was dug up in a forest near the town of Polgardi by a quarry worker self-educated in Roman antiquities. Problem was, the quarry worker was long dead, so Hungary needed to rely on chemical analysis of soil crusted on the pieces and the artistic similarity to a Roman-era silver tripod in a Hungarian museum and definitely dug up in Polgardi. So there was lots of evidence for the jury to chew on, but the way Johnstone ruled basically gave the trial to Leinster.

"Now the trial will be the way Linda thought it should be. If I had to bet on a winner, my money would be on Hungary because it gets to put in all that evidence. And Hungary winning is the best scenario for us."

"Why is that?" said McQueen.

"Well, first, we'd be dealing with a government, not a flake like Leinster."

"But we don't know anyone in the Hungarian government."

"Yes, we do," said Gary. He clicked the mouse, typed furiously in a dialogue box, and pulled up a web page with a much retouched photo of Robert Pinter, the lawyer who represented Hungary. "He's Hungarian. Born near Polgardi. Lived there till he was fourteen."

"The same Polgardi where the treasure was found?"

Gary smiled at McQueen's slow enlightenment.

"He's tied into the Hungarian community. The embassy in Washington. The consulate here at the UN. How do you think he landed a big case like this?"

"I thought he just got lucky," said McQueen.

"Luck has nothing to do with it. Connections do. So after we find the piece, after the trial ends, after we know the rest of the treasure is on its way to some Hungarian museum, we hire Pinter to negotiate with the Hungarians."

"They'll deal with us?"

"They'll deal with Pinter," said Gary. "And he'll deal with us because we aren't thieves. We didn't steal the thing. We found it fair and square, just like the guy who dug it up. He'll know that. He'll be a national hero, and we'll be rich."

"What if Leinster wins?" said McQueen.

"Leinster ain't gonna win," said Gary.

"What if Croatia—"

"Hey, Mike, anyone ever tell you you're a negative person?"

CHAPTER 17

Linda felt better than she had in days. She had awakened without nausea, chomped a full sleeve of saltines before leaving home, and, by the time she arrived at the courthouse, felt hungry enough to buy a buttered roll at the coffee shop. She sat at her desk, tearing off chunks of the roll with her teeth, reveling in the sensation of a full mouth, wondering again whether her morning sickness had been illusory, her test results an error.

"Uh, Judge?" said Mark.

"Sorry," Linda said, and quickly wiped the butter from her lips with a napkin. She was so enthralled with the solid feel of her stomach that she had not seen him walk into her office.

"Court officer called. All of the lawyers are in the courtroom."

"Thanks. Tell him I'll be right down."

"Do you want me down there with you today?" he said.

"What about your motions?" She brushed the crumbs from her lap, then stood up from her chair.

"Well, I thought with this being an important trial, I should come down to meet the lawyers and get a feel for the issues in case you need me to research any rulings you might need to make."

Linda came out from behind her desk and shooed Mark ahead of her into the anteroom.

"I doubt anything substantive will come up today," she said. "This is more of a scheduling conference. Let me feel them out. I'll call if I need you."

Linda took the nearest set of internal stairs down to the second floor, then followed a catwalk corridor halfway around the hexagon to her robing room. She found Bernadette waiting inside.

"Fancy meeting you here," said Linda.

"Don't get too excited," said Bernadette. "I can't rearrange my schedule like this every day."

On floors three through six, the center circle of the courthouse floor plan was an enclosed corridor. On the second floor, it was an open gallery with alternating brass rails and marble pilasters. Down below was the black and white marble of the rotunda floor inlaid with brass symbols of the zodiac. Up above was the rotunda dome, with its dazzling WPA mural depicting in six lunettes the History of the Law from Hammurabi to Lincoln.

Ivan steered a wide dust mop along the gallery. He already had worked the corridors on the third and fourth floors, using the dust mop as an excuse to peek into each courtroom. Only the second floor remained.

Ivan turned down the last of the corridors that shot off the gallery like the spokes of a wheel. The doors to the two courtrooms were near the outer end of each spoke. In between, steam radiators and hardwood benches lined the walls. Dust collected under the radiators and the benches, but dust no longer was on Ivan's mind because Robert Pinter sat on one of the benches with an old man. Pinter, looking more heavy-set and gray than the last time Ivan saw him, leaned an elbow on a thick briefcase while he pored over an open file on his lap. The old man wore a brown suit and black orthopedic shoes. He had a long thin neck that matched his long thin legs, which were crossed, and his long thin arms, which were folded in such a way that his sleeves rode up almost to his elbows. A red feather poked out of the band of his brown fedora.

Ivan pushed the mop along the opposite wall. At the end, he lifted on his toes to look through the square window in the door of Judge Conover's courtroom. Two lawyers sat at counsels' table. Pinter could have been in court on any case, the old man sitting beside him could have been any client or any witness. But the other two lawyers were proof. Ivan glanced back at Pinter. For a moment, the lawyer lifted his eyes off the file as if picking up on a smell or a sound or perhaps even a memory. He never looked Ivan's way, and then the old man snorted and diverted his attention. Ivan carefully leaned the mop handle against the wall, then took a dust rag from his pocket and went inside the courtroom.

Foxx had expected curiosity seekers: reporters, an art critic or two, court employees interested in the return of the trial. He was wrong. The only extraneous person in the courtroom was Ivan, who seemed more interested in dusting the deep window recesses than in the courtroom proceedings. Which hadn't started yet, though he heard the judge speaking to someone in the robing room.

He stood beside the bench and watched the third lawyer pull up a chair at counsels' table. He remembered each of them from the first trial and noticed the subtle changes brought on by three years of time. Arthur Braman had a tad more gut and a bit less of a comb-over, but still moved with the regal bearing of a partner in a white-shoe firm. William Cokeley, the lawyer representing Croatia, now seemed more calm and seasoned than the youthful brat of three years ago. He still dressed in the slightly crass manner of a suburban attorney who might walk in any day mixing stripes and plaids. Robert Pinter looked grayer and more bristly. A sole practitioner in a legal landscape dominated by huge firms, he litigated with a chip on his shoulder, and that chip, Foxx guessed, had only grown larger. Foxx wandered over and leaned down with his fists on the table.

"Where's the other guy?" he said.

"The auction house?" said Braman. "I called him yesterday. Says he can't be here today, but he'll appear for the trial."

"Then I'll tell the judge you're ready," said Foxx.

"As we'll ever be," said Braman.

Foxx pushed off the table. He had one speed in the courtroom: slow; one demeanor: calm; one message he wanted to convey: don't bother me.

He opened the robing room door to find Judge Conover and Bernadette Symanski chatting across the desk. He had an affinity for these Catholic school girls who grew up as the standard-bearers for their working-class Italian or Irish or Polish families. Hell, he'd knocked knees with enough of them.

"We are ready," he said.

"Thank you, Officer," said Judge Conover.

Bernadette mouthed *hello, Foxx,* and he winked in return.

"Do you want the lawyers in here?" he said. Judges usually held pretrial conferences in the robing room.

"This case is all in the courtroom." Linda stood up and lifted her robe off the coat tree. "And all on the record."

Foxx went back outside and held the door slightly ajar. Except for Ivan, the only other new person to appear was McQueen. The judge signaled she was ready. Foxx pounded his fist on the rail of the clerk's box and called the courtroom to order. The lawyers stood, Judge Conover climbed the bench, and Bernadette settled into the clerk's box.

Foxx strolled through the well and into the gallery, where Mc-Queen sat in the last row.

"Just like old times," he whispered.

"Not quite," said McQueen.

* * *

"Mr. Cokeley, I am going to start with you," Linda said from the bench. "Judge Johnstone excluded the testimony of Anton Fleiss. The Appellate Division reversal means that Fleiss may testify. Do you still intend to call him?"

"Unfortunately not," Cokeley said, standing up. "Mr. Fleiss died in May. However, I understand that a new witness has been located and will arrive in time to testify."

"Do you have the name of this witness?"

"I don't," said Cokeley.

Both Pinter and Braman began to rise, but Linda waved them down.

"You don't know the name of your own witness?" she said.

"It's complicated," said Cokeley. "As you might expect, most of the soldiers who participated in the unearthing of the treasure are either dead or retired. Yugoslavia broke up, and it took the Croatian military authorities some time to locate this witness and obtain his consent. I understand he only agreed to testify yesterday."

Linda glanced down at Bernadette, who sat in the clerk's box taking notes, then back to counsels' table.

"Mr. Pinter, you had something to say?"

"This is a new witness," said Pinter. "I believe we have the right to depose him."

"Mr. Braman?"

"I agree, Your Honor. Especially since Mr. Cokeley knew five months ago that Anton Fleiss would be unavailable to testify."

"I did not know five months ago," said Cokeley. "I found out only two weeks ago when I reached out to advise him that the trial would be imminent.

"Now about the deposition, Your Honor, the Appellate Division did not disturb Judge Johnstone's ruling that allowed both Croatia and Hungary twenty-four hours to identify and produce witnesses to the unearthing. Croatia's position is that the twenty-four-hour period never expired because the courtroom invasion occurred and then the judge declared a mistrial. It is as if the clock stopped and will not start running again until we reconvene to start the trial anew."

"But, Your Honor," said Pinter, "the deposing of a newly discovered witness on the eve of trial, even during a trial, is basic trial procedure."

"We all know that," said Cokeley. "But the discovery phase of this case ended long ago. Judge Johnstone did not reopen it with his decision. He simply gave Croatia and Hungary an additional twenty-four hours to produce witnesses. He said nothing at the time about adjourning the trial for depositions if either party found such a witness. The Appellate Division did not disturb that part of the ruling."

"There are some principles so basic and so obvious," said Braman, "that there is no need to state them."

"Is that why you didn't bother to appeal this issue?" said Cokeley. "It was too obvious?" He turned his attention to the bench. "The fact is that this witness was in the same military detail as Anton Fleiss at the unearthing. He saw everything that Fleiss saw and, from what I understand, will testify just as Fleiss would have testified. If counsel need to prepare to cross-examine him, they can review Fleiss's deposition."

"Mr. Cokeley, when will this witness arrive?" said Linda.

"End of the week."

Linda glanced down at Bernadette, who made a subtle slicing motion across her neck.

"I am going to reserve on this issue," she said. "Now, the decision allows the admission of Hungary's art historical evidence. Mr. Pinter, are you prepared to present this evidence?"

"I was prepared then and I am prepared now," said Pinter.

"I have a problem," said Braman. "I plan to call Dieter van der Weyden as a witness to dispute Hungary's art historical evidence.

However, Mr. Van der Weyden has proven, let's say, difficult to corral."

"Then I suggest you get some cowboys out to rope him right away," said Linda. The lawyers all laughed politely. "We will have some time before we reach your case."

"I understand," said Braman.

"The decision also directs that Hungary be allowed to present its soil sample evidence without the need to connect it to eyewitness testimony," said Linda. "Mr. Pinter, you are prepared to offer that evidence, I take it."

"I am, Your Honor," said Pinter. "And I have additional evidence to prove that the treasure was unearthed in Hungary."

"What kind of evidence?" said Linda.

"A witness and documentary evidence," said Pinter. "I have a witness in possession of a letter written by the mother of the man we believe found the treasure in a forest near Polgardi."

"The quarry worker?" said Linda.

"Yes."

"Who is the letter addressed to?"

"The woman's two younger sons."

"And who is the witness?" said Linda. "One of the sons?"

"A neighbor," said Pinter. "He saw the woman write the letter, which she intended to give to one of her sons, but later found the letter in his car. He has had it ever since."

"Why didn't he return it to the woman?" said Linda "You said they were neighbors."

"He tried, but she was dead."

Linda leaned back in her chair. She knew about the murder of the mother, but this letter was something completely new.

"What is the content of the letter?" said Linda. "Briefly."

"Briefly, Your Honor, the woman explains to her two younger sons how her eldest son found the treasure, tried to sell the treasure, and later was murdered for his troubles."

"That does not sound like eyewitness testimony to me," said Linda.

"But it is," said Pinter. "She describes seeing the cauldron in the ground. She also describes helping her son lift it out of the ground using tools borrowed from the same neighbor. She also goes on to postulate who murdered her son and why. And let me stress that the letter was written just before she herself was murdered."

Linda allowed Pinter's statement to settle.

"Anyone?" she said.

"This is the first time any of us have heard about the letter or the witness," said Arthur Braman. "But just off the top of my head, I can think of numerous reasons to exclude this evidence. First, Judge Johnstone did give Hungary time to produce a witness to the unearthing. Now, assuming but not suggesting that you adopt Croatia's argument that the clock never ran on that portion of the rulings, this neighbor was not an eyewitness to the alleged unearthing."

"This is a two-step process," said Pinter. "The witness introduces the letter. The letter was written by someone who was present and describes the unearthing. Documentary evidence is the equivalent of testimonial evidence."

"Let's assume that I adopt Croatia's argument," said Linda. "What is your next basis for exclusion?"

"Authentication," said Braman. "Who knows whether this woman even wrote it?"

"The letter is self-authenticating because the witness saw her writing it," said Pinter.

"It's self-serving," said Braman.

"That's not true," said Pinter. "The letter would be self-serving only if it was written by the party in interest. This woman is not the party in interest. Hungary is. Therefore, the letter is not self-serving."

"Then it's hearsay," said Braman, "if he is offering it for the truth of its contents."

"But the letter clearly falls under an exception to the hearsay rule," said Pinter. "The letter admits to finding the treasure. The treasure is covered by Hungary's laws on antiquities, and these laws require that anyone who finds antiquities must turn them over to the government. They didn't, so this letter is an admission against interest because it basically admits that they violated Hungarian law.

"Further, the letter supports Hungary's claim that the quarry worker was murdered by soldiers from the Yugoslav army who also stole the treasure and staged its discovery at Pula."

"This is absurd," said Cokeley. "We thrashed this issue out last time. The Hungarian authorities ruled the quarry worker's death to be a suicide. Mr. Pinter did not even challenge that ruling on appeal."

"That's all changed now," said Pinter. "The Hungarian authorities have reopened their investigation and have classified the deaths of both the worker and his mother as suspicious. The letter bears this out."

"Even more ridiculous," said Cokeley. "How can a letter written by the mother be proof of her murder?"

"If the letter comes into evidence, it comes in for all purposes," said Pinter. "In the letter, the mother explains to her two younger sons how and why their older brother died. She explicitly fears for her own life, as well as the lives of her sons. And, as I said, the witness will testify that the mother died in the same manner as her eldest son on the same day that she wrote the letter."

Linda leaned forward, resting her chin on one hand and drumming the fingers of the other on the bench.

"Are you going to show us the letter?" she said.

"Of course, Your Honor." Pinter pulled a file folder from his briefcase and fanned several copies of the letter with his thumb. He gave one copy to Foxx, who handed it up to Linda, and one each to Cokeley and Braman.

Linda rolled her chair to the side of the bench, and she and Bernadette read the letter together over the rail.

"This is a close one," Bernadette whispered. "Reserve decision and ask for memos. We may need a couple of days on this."

Face time, Mark Garber thought as he went down the back stairs. He needed face time in the courtroom. No smiles, no winks, no knowing nods. Just simple face time to show Arthur Braman that he was someone who Judge Conover relied on. He didn't need to do anything or say anything. He just needed to stand in the courtroom for a few minutes, listen to the proceedings with a somber look on his face, maybe whisper something innocuous to the judge.

Mark had walked through robing rooms thousands of times and often could sense if something important was happening in the courtroom. This was one of those times. He twisted the courtroom doorknob so the latch would not hit the striker, then pushed the door open a crack. He could see the judge sitting on the right side of the bench and reading a sheet of paper that lay on the rail. The courtroom was silent. He cracked the door another inch and saw Bernadette Symanski standing in the clerk's box and reading that same sheet of paper.

He let the door fall shut, ran through the robing room, chugged up the stairs, and burst into chambers.

"Gotta go," Karen Pawling said into her phone and hung up.

Mark punched the back of his chair and kicked his trash basket.

"What's going on?" said Karen.

Mark gripped the windowsill behind his desk, bent over, and took very deep breaths.

"I asked her if she wanted me in the courtroom," he said. "I thought, hey, this is a big trial with serious issues. I could help her with her bench rulings. Not that I care about that. I really wanted to be in the courtroom to put myself in a good light with the lawyers. You know, so I could find a goddam new job after she lets me go. But she tells me that she wouldn't be discussing anything substantive today, just scheduling, and that she wanted me working on motions up here. So I go down to the robing room, crack the robing room door, and you know what I see? I see that goddam Bernadette Symanski on the bench with her, whispering in her ear."

"Mark . . ."

Karen took him by the hands and rubbed her thumbs against his palms. He liked that feeling, and for a moment he seemed to calm down. But then he shook free, squeezed past her, and rushed out of chambers.

CHAPTER 18

"How do you know what I think?" said Ivan.

They sat on the bench where Pinter and the old man had sat earlier. Ivan's mop still leaned against the wall near the courtroom door. He twisted the dust rag in his hands.

"I work for him," said Jessima.

"You work for the courts, like I do."

"Yes. We both work for the courts." Jessima looped her arm around his and laced her fingers together. Ivan did not flinch, did not move, did not react in any way. "He sells information. I help him find it."

"What kind of information?" said Ivan.

"About cases, about judges. Mostly judges. I spend a lot of time in chambers, sometimes alone, sometimes not, but always without anyone caring what I see or hear. It's like I'm invisible."

Ivan knew how that felt.

"He pays you for what you find?" he said.

"Only if someone pays him," said Jessima. "Last week, he told me to find something about Judge Conover."

"What kind of thing?"

"Anything she would not want anyone to know," said Jessima. Ivan removed his arm from hers and slid ever so slightly away.

"I like Judge Conover," said Jessima. "She is a good lady. I wouldn't want to hurt her. But I found something and handed it over to Damien."

"So, that's his name?"

"Yes. Damien Wheatley. I thought you knew."

"Why? Because you think I would sell him information?"

Jessima sighed. She did not want to fight; she wanted only to explain.

"Damien told me that the person he thought was interested did not buy it."

"Who did he try to sell it to?" said Ivan.

"The protestors in the park."

"Them? They're just a bunch of homeless people."

"But they have organizers," said Jessima. "And Judge Conover has their case."

Ivan leaned forward and pressed his fists into his eye sockets. When he finally lifted his head, his eyes were red from rubbing.

"How could you do such a thing?" he said.

"I do it for us," said Jessima. "I save the money he pays me."

Ivan stared at her and then right through her. He realized that he should be touched. He realized that with all his doubts about her, this explanation for what he saw should be exactly what he wanted to hear. She loved him, she planned for a future with him.

"You don't need to steal for him anymore," he said. "I will take care of everything for us."

She took back his arm, hugged it to her side, and slid close to him. He could read her mind just as surely as he could hear her breathe and feel the cushion of her hair on his square, bony shoulder. She thought he meant the lottery, and the fact that she didn't say anything to ridicule him meant something, too.

Jessima pecked his cheek. Then she got up and ran past Mike McQueen toward the rotunda gallery.

Ivan thought that McQueen would walk right over him. But

the officer stopped just short and lifted one foot onto the bench to corner Ivan against the armrest. Ivan resisted the urge to rub the wet spot left by Jessima's lips.

"I need to get into the plenum," said McQueen.

"The what?" said Ivan.

McQueen hooked a hand under Ivan's armpit and pulled him to his feet.

"Don't play dumb with me, Romeo."

But McQueen could not tell whether Ivan was playing dumb or just plain dumb. He repeated the word several times, then explained that *plenum* meant a space filled with matter, but in the context of an old building it meant a storage area, and in the specific context of this courthouse it meant a hidden storage area. No hint of recognition or understanding lit Ivan's dull gray eyes. He allowed McQueen to drag him out to the circular gallery and beyond the elevator bank to the metal door labeled with a capital A. He said nothing as they climbed the stairs behind that door, up past the 2M level and then past the third floor. The A stairwell, though public, was rarely used. It ran from the basement up to the sixth floor, and on each of the landings had grimy windows that opened onto the interior light courts, an ancient architectural technique for illuminating large buildings.

"So what do you think of the trial?" said McQueen.

"What trial?"

"I don't believe this." McQueen shook his head. " 'What trial?' Do you have any clue what goes on around you? The Roman silver case. In front of Judge Conover. You were just in the courtroom."

"I was cleaning windows," said Ivan.

"Cleaning windows, replacing lightbulbs. I've never seen someone so devoted to the sense of sight."

"What do you want from me?" said Ivan.

They had reached the landing on the 3M level, and McQueen stopped at a door painted the same metallic green as all the window frames and sills in the stairwell. It was four feet tall by three feet wide and raised a foot above the landing. He jiggled the knob.

"Open it," he said.

"No one is allowed without permission."

"I have permission from Captain Kearney."

"I don't have a key," said Ivan.

"Don't lie to me, Romeo. All you custodians have keys to this door."

Ivan seemed to weigh his choices, then fished a key ring from the pocket of his coveralls. Shaking, he tried one key after another.

"Hey, cut the crap," McQueen said after the third key jammed halfway into the keyhole. He grabbed the ring and flipped through the keys until he found a manufacturer's stamp that matched the stamp on the lock. The key slipped easily inside.

"Fuckin' genius," said McQueen. The key turned easily, and the door swung open.

"What are you looking for?" said Ivan.

"Let's just say I'm conducting a general search for a specific thing," said McQueen. "In other words, none of your goddam business."

"Maybe I have seen this thing."

"Yeah." McQueen snorted. "If I need your help, I'll ask."

He pushed the door fully open and stuck his head inside. The plenum was dark and dry, the air smelling of cement and dust.

"There any light here?"

Ivan reached past McQueen's shoulder and flicked a switch on the inside wall. A line of bare bulbs lit up. Dim and yellow with grime, they curved into the distance, their light diminishing until they went dark. McQueen pulled a flashlight from his belt and switched it on. The beam flickered until he pounded the flashlight with the heel of his hand. He played the beam inside. The plenum was narrow, criss-crossed by metallic ductwork installed during the early 1990s. Tucked close to the wall were piles of old furniture.

"Don't these lights get any brighter?"

"No," said Ivan.

McQueen let go of the door, and it slowly began to swing shut.

"You stand here," he said.

Ivan did not move immediately, so McQueen pulled him into place.

"You hold this door all the way open."

Ivan straddled the raised threshold, his back against the door. McQueen crouched through the doorway and carefully straightened up inside.

"You sure these lights don't get any brighter?"

"They don't."

"Goddam black hole," he said. "Don't move. I need all the light I can get."

Slowly, his eyes adjusted to the dim light, reaching a point where the plenum looked gray and shadowy instead of dark. He took one step forward and felt something crunch beneath his shoes. Glass, maybe, or tiny bits of cement. He took another step and felt the edge of a duct brush the top of his hair.

"Damn," he said, flinching. He looked back. Ivan stood against the door, staring at him. *You think this is fun?* he wanted to say. But he decided the less he said, the quicker he'd get in and out of here. He took a deep breath, crouched under that duct, scissored over another one, then shuffled between an old wooden desk and a wooden chair missing three legs. He accidentally kicked the chair, and thought he saw something dark scurry out from underneath and disappear into the shadows.

"Hey, Ivan, are there any rats in here?"

"Yes."

"Shit," said McQueen. "Why didn't you tell me?"

"You didn't ask," said Ivan. "Find what you're looking for yet?"

"Don't get funny. You ain't funny."

McQueen scissored over another duct and reached the last of the lightbulbs. He played the flashlight into the darkness, hoping he wouldn't see something he'd rather not see.

"Hey, are there any more lights here?"

"There is another switch."

McQueen ran the flashlight beam along the wall. He saw a patch of bubbled plaster and rust stains running down to a puddle on the floor. He thought he saw something furry dart away, but told himself it was just the power of suggestion. Finally, he found the switch, and another set of yellow lights came on, curving away from him until again going dark. More metal ducts caked with dust, more broken pieces of furniture, more rust stains on the walls.

"Hey, how far does the plenum go?" he called back.

"Halfway around."

Great, thought McQueen. By *around*, Ivan meant the building's circular inner core. McQueen was barely into this semicircle, and he already felt the slow creep of fear, the hair bristling on the back of his neck, the involuntary shudder, the uncomfortable sense that many tiny eyes were watching him.

He swept the beam from wall to wall. There was one duct to climb over, another to crouch under, and then a few feet of clear floor space where several broken chair legs gathered together in a campfire heap. He would take it that far, he decided, because nothing was here. Nothing obvious, anyway. Searching half the plenum was good enough for him. He could tell Gary he'd scoured the place top to bottom and end to end. How would Gary know the difference?

He reached the first duct and carefully swung one leg over so he would not brush against the dust. He shined the flashlight up ahead. That campfire pile looked like the last bits of furniture between him and the patch of darkness. That was good; that definitely meant halfway was all he needed to go. He played the beam on the pile. He thought he saw something glint within, and rather than feel the creep of fear, he felt a surge of something more optimistic. The thrill of discovery.

He crouched under the next duct. The campfire was five feet away. Something definitely was inside, something smooth and metallic. Not very shiny, more like something tarnished. He tried to recall what the urn looked like that day in the courtroom, but he hadn't paid it much mind. He remembered it was silver, though, and silver tarnished. He knew that much.

He stood up, took one step, and then another. Then he kicked the campfire. The pieces fell like bowling pins. But the darkly shining object inside was no ancient Roman urn. It was a rat.

"Oh, shit!" said McQueen.

The rat reared on its hind legs, and McQueen swung the flashlight like a baseball bat. He felt the flashlight catch the rat below the neck, lift it into the air, and hurl it into the darkness. The flashlight beam died. Claws scrabbled on the floor, but McQueen couldn't tell if the rat was running at him or away from him. He threw the flashlight at the sound, then scraped over the duct and began to run, ducking and vaulting until he reached the door.

"Outta my way," he shouted, elbowing Ivan aside. He dove out onto the landing.

"What happened?" said Ivan, pulling the door shut.

"Biggest fuckin' rat I ever saw. Musta been two feet long. Red eyes, red mouth, claws like razors."

Ivan twisted the doorknob.

"Don't," said McQueen. "He could be right there."

But Ivan only smirked, opened the door just enough to reach inside, and switched off the lights.

"Was the rat really two feet?" he said.

"If it was an inch," said McQueen.

CHAPTER 19

Back at his office in midtown, Arthur Braman unhappily reviewed what had transpired in Judge Conover's courtroom. Judges had a way of being unpredictable, but the book on Judge Conover was remarkably consistent. She had a generous idea of what constituted relevant evidence.

The phone buzzed, and Braman picked up.

"I have Lord Leinster on the line," his secretary said.

"Put him through," said Braman. The line scratched, then connected. "Hello, my lord. I've been trying to reach you since yesterday morning, our time. I hope everything is all right with you."

"Everything is most definitely not all right," said Leinster, his words clipped and his voice weak. "I am in hospital. In bloody Galway City."

Before Braman could ask even a simple *why*, Leinster dove right into a story that was extremely hard to follow. Words stuck out as if typed in bold and all caps, words like *BURREN* and *PAINT-ING* and *TOURISTS* and *BROKEN ANKLES*. The story had a beginning, a middle, and an end, but to Braman it made no sense.

"So you were painting," he said, as if trying to summarize a witness's confusing testimony, "in this place called the Burren and two tourists attacked you."

"They weren't tourists. They were posing as tourists. They came to deliver a message. From, you know . . ."

Braman slumped in his chair. *You know* was code for the investors, which itself was code for the people Leinster never mentioned by name and whose existence Leinster never actually admitted, though Braman had sensed them. They were Leinster's dark companions.

"And so?" he said.

"Where are we with the trial?" said Leinster.

Braman sketched it quickly, the Appellate Division ruling, this morning's conference, the evidence that the judge would likely admit. Lots of news, none of it good.

"That can't happen," said Leinster. "I can't afford it. I won't survive it. I'm going to be hobbled for life, and that life will be a short one if I don't pay them off."

"Are you suggesting I try to settle this case?"

"I'm suggesting I need twelve to fifteen million dollars to get them off my back."

"How do I arrange that?" said Braman. "You're the defendant. Defendants usually offer to pay the plaintiffs."

"You're the lawyer," said Leinster. "You tell me."

"Ivan let you in?"

McQueen was on the courthouse portico, close enough to where a pair of clerks stood smoking cigarettes that he thought they might have heard Gary's scream go through his head and out his other ear. He quickly strode off and squeezed through the metal stanchions set up to block off the far south side of the portico.

"Gary, Gary," he said, less to mollify than to buy time until he reached the wrought-iron railing that overlooked Pearl Street.

Still, Gary seethed.

"I told you not to involve anyone else."

"He's a fuckin' janitor, Gary."

"I don't care. You need a key, you get it from the captain's office."

"So you don't want me to involve Ivan, but you want me to involve Kearney."

"You don't involve Kearney, you eejit." Gary paused to take a deep breath, obviously trying to calm himself, maybe also recognizing that McQueen wasn't only his legs but his eyes, his ears, his hands. His man on the ground. "What did you tell Ivan?"

"Nothing."

"Nothing? He just let you in because you're a nice guy?"

"I can be very persuasive," said McQueen.

"Did he ask why you, a court officer, wanted to get into the plenum?"

"Oh yeah. I told him I was conducting a general search for a specific thing."

Gary went silent for a long moment.

"So what did you find?" he finally said.

"Dust, lots of broken furniture, a rat."

"Did you get through the whole place?"

"Yeah," said McQueen. "What do you think?"

"I think if you saw a rat you'd run like hell."

"I didn't see the rat until I reached the far end. And, yeah, I did run like hell. Practically knocked Ivan on his ass."

"He was in the plenum with you?"

"Nah. I had him hold the door open. For extra light."

"Okay, listen," said Gary. "From now on you work alone. You don't tell Kearney, you don't tell anyone. If you meet anyone while you're searching, you don't give them this bullshit about a general search for a specific thing. You tell them you're looking for a laptop, or an engagement ring, or a necklace. Got that?"

"Yeah," said McQueen.

"And did Foxx tell you why he's been reassigned to Linda's part?"

"I didn't ask him."

"Good. Don't. And stay out of the courtroom," said Gary. "Here is where I want you to look next."

Mark needed two laps around the outside of the courthouse to calm himself, and now that he was calm he tried to fashion a credible explanation for why Bernadette Symanski sat beside the judge during the pretrial conference. He could tell Braman there were lots of motions in chambers. He could tell Braman he needed to work on the big motion involving the homeless shelter stipends. Braman certainly would have seen the protestors outside and Braman certainly would believe that Judge Conover would want her own law clerk, not a court attorney in the pool, to draft such a politically and socially important decision. It wasn't true, of course. The motion had gone directly to the law department and was assigned to Bernadette.

But whether Braman bought these bogus explanations was beside the point. What worried Mark was the possibility, actually the probability, that Braman intended to observe him during the trial and read the judge's rulings and decisions as evidence of his legal skills. But now, with Bernadette riding shotgun in the courtroom, there would be nothing for Braman to read.

Mark took another lap. At the start of his fourth, his cell phone vibrated. "Restricted" showed on the screen. Mark quickly answered.

"Mark?"

"Hi, Mr. Braman, let me explain that the woman you saw on the bench with the judge, she—"

"Never mind that," said Braman. "I need your help with something else. Are you with me?"

"Yes," said Mark.

"The judge told us to come back Friday," said Braman, "when she will rule on several evidentiary issues."

"I know," Mark lied. He didn't know a goddam thing of what happened in the courtroom this morning.

"I have a problem that can't wait till then. Now, I understand that you have the authority to schedule a conference if the situation dictates."

"I do," said Mark. He cleared his throat and deepened his voice. "What is your exact problem?"

"It's a client relations problem," said Braman, "directly connected to the trial."

Mark stayed silent for a few seconds, pretending to mull this over.

"Well," he said, "a client relations problem on the eve of trial is one of those situations."

"So I take it I have permission to phone opposing counsel and say that chambers has scheduled a conference for, say, ten o'clock tomorrow?"

"You do," said Mark.

CHAPTER 20

Grotzky sat in a chair while Pinter paced behind him, holding a legal pad with pages of questions and answers. Pinter had located the old man back in June, shortly after his contact in the Hungarian mission informed him of the untimely death of Anton Fleiss. He had flown to Budapest and rented a car to drive to Polgardi. Grotzky showed him the letter, the remains of the draft cart decaying in the tall grass behind the toolshed, the roof of the old Szabo house just visible over the brow of the hill. Pinter read the letter carefully, then constructed a series of questions on that same legal pad and wrote down Grotzky's answers.

Grotzky seemed to have slipped since June. Maybe it was the flight from Budapest, maybe it was the imminence of the trial, maybe it was the sight of the courthouse earlier today. Grotzky's command of English had totally evaporated.

"Tell me about that day," Pinter said in Hungarian.

"Karolina asked me to drive her to meet her son," said Grotzky. "He was being released from prison. Three years for burglarizing a jewelry shop. I found her in her kitchen writing a letter. She took the letter and a book and an old suitcase, and we went out to the car. I put the suitcase in the trunk, and she used the book as a lap desk to finish the letter as we drove."

"To the prison?" said Pinter.

"No. She had arranged to meet her son at Koponya. I told her no one goes to Koponya, but she said that she did."

"Koponya? The abandoned military base?" said Pinter.

Grotzky nodded.

"So you drove to Koponya. Did she say anything about the letter?"

"She told me it was addressed to her two sons. The younger one was getting out of prison. The older one had been gone for a while."

"Where?"

"Somewhere west," said Grotzky. "Spain, maybe, or France."

"Then what?"

"We reached Koponya. I stopped the car and saw someone step out from the big boulders at the front gates. Karolina and her son embraced and spoke and got back into the car. I drove to Keleti Station in Budapest. I opened the trunk and got back into the car while they said their good-byes. Then he went off to the train.

"I drove Karolina back to her home. Then I went to mine. Sometime later, I needed to look in the backseat and saw the letter lying on the floor. I drove to Karolina's house. It was quiet. I knocked. There was no answer, so I opened the door and went inside. I found Karolina hanging from a rope in her kitchen. She was dead."

"Why did you hold on to the letter for all these years?" said Pinter.

"There was no one to give it to," said Grotzky. "I had no address for her sons."

"Didn't they return for their mother's funeral?"

"No. As far as I know, no one in Polgardi ever saw or heard from them again."

McQueen was easy to tail, Ivan thought, as he peeked around a corner and saw the officer heading for the door to the C stairwell.

McQueen had a stupid certainty that left no room for imagining that an underling, especially an immigrant custodian, would have the brains or the balls to observe him. Ivan waited for the stairwell door to close behind McQueen, then hurried to the B stairwell. Both the B and C stairwells descended to the county clerk's file room in the basement, and Ivan, lighter and quicker on his feet, was waiting in the file stacks when McQueen finally landed. McQueen hitched his belt, made a lousy attempt at joking with one of the file room workers, then clomped down a set of circular stairs to the subbasement. Ivan approached slowly, waiting until he heard the last of McQueen's footsteps ringing on the metal stairs before heading down himself.

The subbasement occupied the same hexagonal footprint as the courthouse above. But instead of a central rotunda, there was a physical plant where the engineering crew worked the steam and water and electricity behind locked metal doors. Instead of a lobby, there was a courtyard of sorts with orange painted walls. Instead of courtrooms and back offices, there were oddly shaped rooms painted a flat white that had faded to dingy gray. Many were empty except for broken brooms and damp wads of paper and had the word *clear* scratched into the paint. Others were filled with painting supplies, custodial supplies, huge sacks of rock salt, metal shelves sagging under the weight of file boxes stuffed with stenographer notes or old court papers.

One room, the largest and darkest, was marked with grimy civil defense signs. Inside stood wooden desks with disassembled radios, cots without mattresses, and rolling chalkboards with detailed survey maps. This had been a fifties-style fallout shelter, then the city's first emergency command center, then the bunker where Ike or JFK or LBJ would ride out a nuclear attack if they were in the city when the Reds pushed the button. Now it was a relic, perpetually musty from the underground pond that regularly rose through the cracks in the concrete floor. Few people who worked in the courthouse knew this piece of history existed.

Ivan did. He watched from behind a corner as McQueen came out of the bunker and unfolded a sheet of paper to orient himself. After McQueen fixed his position, he struck out with a purpose. He moved quickly from room to room, switching on the lights and, it seemed to Ivan, noting which rooms were empty and which were not. It took him almost half an hour to cover every accessible room before he returned to a room with many shelves of steno notes. Water covered the floor. McQueen tiptoed on a crude path made from wood scraps, plastic tiles, and soggy newspapers. He reached the first shelf, peeled the lid off a file box, and poked his hand inside.

Ivan backed away from the door. If he had any doubts, they were gone now. The plenum and the subbasement were places a court officer rarely tread, especially a court officer as lazy and unadventurous as McQueen. He took one more look at McQueen elbow deep in a file box. But the futility of McQueen's search wasn't the point. The point was that he was snooping in all the right places.

Ivan backed away from the door, climbed the circular stairs to the basement, then took the C stairway to the third floor. He closed himself into his supply closet and turned the deadbolt. He sat on the sink and allowed himself only shallow breaths so as not to make any sound, so he could dissipate, disappear, merge his molecules with the air. Just as he had done the day the men came.

The subbasement wasn't as skeevy as the plenum. It was big and it was bright and, even though he couldn't see them, McQueen knew there were other people around. Somewhere. But the water gave him the creeps because he knew it wasn't water that leaked from old rusted pipes, but ground water that welled up from the old Collect Pond that once occupied this area of New York and, even with all the pavements and buildings, never quite went away.

He heard footsteps from outside, then saw two guys from the engineering crew in the doorway.

"Need any help?" said one.

"I'm good," said McQueen.

But he wasn't. His feet suddenly felt cold, and he looked down to see the water was over his soles. He stepped onto a plastic tile.

"Shit," he said.

He didn't like rooting around in all these boxes. He couldn't drop them onto the floor because of the water, so he had to search them in place. Many were over his head, so he couldn't see inside and his arms quickly tired. After the first dozen boxes, he just lifted the lid and ran his hand across the top. If he didn't feel anything metal—and he didn't feel anything metal—he lowered the lid and moved on to the next one. After a dozen of those, he didn't bother with the lid. The boxes were all the same size, all stuffed to the gills with blocks of steno notes. They all weighed the same, give or take an ounce or two, so he began to lift them off the shelf. If the urn was inside, the box would feel lighter. Or maybe it would feel heavier. He didn't know and he didn't care. He just wanted to get done with this room and get the hell out of here.

Gary never would know the difference.

The sun sank lower, and the evening shadows filled the light court outside the supply closet window. Time crawled past. At five minutes to five came a gentle rap on the door, a tiny jiggle of the knob, a soft whisper of his name. Ivan held his breath, feeling Jessima linger and then walk away slowly. He waited another half hour before slipping off the sink and shouldering his backpack.

Ivan knew where all the security cameras were and also where they weren't. They weren't in the courtrooms or in chambers because the judges refused to have anyone spying on their business. But they also weren't in the catwalks, they weren't in many of the stairwells, and they weren't in the airspace over the rotunda.

He checked the entire third floor. All the courtrooms were locked up and dark. No one walked the corridors, no one waited for the elevators. On the third floor, the inner circular corridor was eye level with the rotunda dome. The windows were large and set almost five feet above the corridor floor, so Ivan dragged a bench into place. The window wasn't locked because its weight was enough to insure no one would open it. After some pounding and shaking and prying with a screwdriver, Ivan loosened the window enough to fit his palms under the sash. Then, imagining himself a weight lifter, he pressed upward. The window resisted, then squeaked, then steadily rose one foot, then two feet, then three. That was enough. Ivan took a deep breath and swung his leg over the sill.

"Hey!" someone yelled. It was a court officer. "What the hell are you doing?"

Ivan pulled himself back down onto the bench.

"Oh, it's you," said the officer.

"I need to check the purge fan," said Ivan.

"Now?" said the officer.

"Forgot to do it earlier," said Ivan.

The officer slid beside the bench and peered out the window, down at the dome and up at the sky.

"Better you than me," he said.

The officer moved on, and Ivan swung back over the sill. Going out the window seemed dangerous, but the dome filled the entire space so there was nowhere to fall. A set of metal stairs began at the sill and followed the curve of the dome to a narrow ladder that ran straight up the cupola. At the top of the cupola was a cylinder that housed a purge fan that would kick on and suck air out of the rotunda in case of a fire. Attached to the cylinder was a square box with a pull-down handle. The fan was cleaned and tested once a year.

Ivan locked an elbow around the top rung of the ladder. The sky had turned a dusky gray, and the lights inside the third-floor corridor burned brighter. The court officer was long gone; no one was watching. With his free hand, Ivan grabbed the box handle and pulled.

The urn stood inside the box.

Ivan stuffed the urn into his backpack. He climbed down the ladder, descended the stairs, and went in through the window. A camera blinked in the ceiling, but he knew it caught nothing but him going out the window with his backpack and returning with his backpack. Nothing in between.

He closed the window and replaced the bench. He saw no one in the corridor, no one in the A stairwell. On the 3M landing, he unlocked the door to the plenum. The hinges squeaked like a scream in the silence.

He closed the door behind him and, turning on his penlight, swiftly negotiated the ducts and broken furniture until he reached the scattered pieces of wood that marked the limit of McQueen's search. He lowered the backpack to the dusty floor, crouched beside it, and swept the thin beam of light back and forth. For an instant, pinpricks of light flashed back at him. He made hissing sounds with his lips. From the darkness came tiny scratchings.

Ivan opened the backpack and pulled out the urn. He knocked aside the pieces of wood, stood the urn against the wall, and used the wood to build a campfire around it. Not the greatest of hiding places, but McQueen already had looked here once and Ivan knew he never would look here again.

He heard more scratchings and turned the penlight beam toward the sound. Three feet away, the rat he had named Bors reared on its hind legs. Ivan reached into the pocket of the backpack. The cellophane crackled as he loosened a peanut butter cracker.

"Here," he said, holding out the cracker.

The rat lowered itself and crept up to Ivan's fingers.

"You be a good boy, Bors," Ivan whispered. "You protect my treasure."

Out in the street, Andreas shivered. He had rushed here after getting a call from Luis, and on the shaded street his thin jeans and light windbreaker were no match for the rapidly cooling air. A police cruiser tooled past, and Andreas feigned a sudden interest in the faded menu curling in the glass case beside the door to a bar. He had been waiting damn near forty-five minutes and worried that everyone on the street had noticed.

It was much later when Grotzky came out of the building with the lawyer named Pinter. The breeze had calmed as dusk settled. The traffic on nearby Church Street passed uptown with a whisper. Andreas watched from beneath the scaffolding as the two men shook hands and then parted ways. Pinter headed east and Grotzky west. For a big man, Pinter was light on his feet, while Grotzky, thin as a stick, walked with excruciating deliberation, his right foot dragging. Andreas, who walked only at one speed, gave him a long head start.

Eventually Grotzky crossed the busy West Side Highway into the relative quiet of Battery Park City. He limped past a line of new but quaintly designed brick town houses, then out to the promenade that ran along the Hudson River. He stopped there and gripped the metal railing with both hands. The sky over the river was fuzzy with gray early evening clouds. The sun, descending toward New Jersey, was red.

Andreas watched Grotzky for a while, then joined him at the rail. Grotzky did not turn, did not react to Andreas's proximity in any way. But Andreas knew the old man sensed him.

"*Jó estét,*" he said. Good evening.

Grotzky lifted one hand off the rail and shifted his entire body to take in Andreas. His eyes searched for a moment before stiffening into recognition and then ultimately softening into a glaze of profound sadness.

"How did you find me?" he said in raspy Hungarian.

"We are all like moths to a flame," said Andreas.

Grotzky replaced his hand on the railing and focused on the red sun.

"I have something for you," he said.

"I know," said Andreas.

"It is in the apartment where I am staying," said Grotzky.

They walked back past the town houses and turned down a street lined with high-rise condominiums. As Grotzky limped, Andreas struggled against his urge to drag the old man along with him. In front of the building, the doorman crouched in front of a toddler's stroller and twisted a long white balloon into the shape of a dog. Inside the lobby, the concierge shouted into a phone. The elevator opened immediately. Grotzky pressed 16, and the doors closed. As far as Andreas could tell, no one had noticed them, though of course there would be cameras. There always were cameras.

"How much is Pinter paying you?" he said.

"Enough to come here and not go back," said Grotzky.

"A fair trade for your lies."

"I turned over what I found."

"You held on to what you stole."

They reached the sixteenth floor. The corridor was clean, bright, and quiet, completely devoid of any discernible smell. The apartment itself was as sleek and as well-appointed as the lobby and the corridor.

"Here," said Grotzky, "look."

The windows of the living room faced the river. The sky had

turned a darker gray since they'd left the promenade, the sun had flattened as it touched the horizon. Andreas took in the view, the flat-screen television hanging on the wall, the granite coffee table, the plush, chocolate brown upholstery of the sofa and chairs, the wine goblets sparkling in a glass cabinet. He thought of Matyas in their own apartment, slouched in a chair propped up by a brick, slugging tap water from a plastic bottle.

Grotzky sat on the couch and opened a briefcase on the coffee table. Inside were many papers—envelopes with Hungarian stamps, yellow sheets with blue writing, snippets of news articles. From this, Grotzky removed a photocopy of a four-page letter.

"I found it in my car. You remember, my old Yugo."

Andreas remembered the backseat with its scraps of aluminum foil and dried chicken bones. He held the letter in his hands. His mother's handwriting, beautiful and evocative.

"You were already gone," said Grotzky.

"She could have mailed it to me."

"It was already too late."

We know that now, thought Andreas, don't we.

"What did they pay you, those soldiers?" he said.

"It's not what they paid. It's what they promised." Grotzky lifted a hand to his neck and squeezed. "You were too young. You don't remember. But in those days, Luca spent every night in the tavern near the forest. He was frustrated to be sitting on a fortune but unable to sell it because he trusted no one. I told him to turn it over to the government. They would reward him, I said, for this contribution to the rich history of our people. But he didn't trust the government, either. And so he drank every night, and when he drank he talked. They would have found him anyway."

"He would not have gone with them," said Andreas. "He was too smart."

"Too smart, but also too dumb," said Grotzky. "When he was a boy, sitting in the flea market in Budapest, he would watch the soldiers pass the tables. They called him Roman Boy and made fun of the coins and chariot nails he tried to sell. He wanted them to see what the Roman Boy found, and he paid for it."

Grotzky excused himself and disappeared down the hallway. A few moments later, Andreas could hear the halting stream of an old man peeing. He went into the kitchen and slid open the drawers until he found the neatly folded dish towels. He held one beneath the faucet, carefully letting it soak up every molecule of water it could hold.

Later, before leaving the apartment, he inverted his reversible jacket, changing it from blue to red. He unfolded the ballcap from his pocket and pulled the brim low on his face.

In the lobby, the concierge still shouted into the phone. On the sidewalk, the doorman twisted a red balloon into the shape of a monkey while the toddler slept in the stroller. The sky was dark now, and on the subway ride back to Queens and the apartment he shared with his brother, he read the letter more than twenty years too late.

CHAPTER 21

Ursula's plans had changed, so instead of being alone in his apartment Gary had a living room full of nurses. They were easy on the eyes, but right now Gary didn't want easy. He wanted to hear that McQueen found the missing piece. But McQueen hadn't called, and so Gary sat in the living room and tried to smile as the nurses laughed and talked over each other and told stories about people he didn't know.

He wasn't in a good mood and hadn't been all day. Even before the bullet clipped his spine, he'd been prone to the occasional darkness. It afflicted him without warning, the way other people suffered from migraine headaches or asthma attacks. He would wake up and his life—the same life that satisfied him the night before—was somehow wrong. He'd feel generally irritated, as though the least little thing could set him off emotionally. Low-energy days, he called them, and he would consciously try to avoid the people he cared about because he needed to preserve his reputation as the sunny Gary Martin, everyone's friend, everyone's Teddy bear.

The phone in his pocket buzzed. McQueen, he saw when he scooped it out. Finally. He weaved the battle chair through the crowded living room, waving the phone at Ursula to signal he had a call rather than a surge of antisociability. In the bedroom, he spun a quick one-eighty so that he faced the door in case anyone followed him in.

"Yeah, Mike," he said. He hated answering the phone in a hopeful or desperate way, though on a low-energy day he couldn't summon much beyond deadpan.

"Where the hell are you?" said McQueen. "A goddam chicken coop?"

The noise from the living room seemed even louder in the bedroom. Gary closed the door.

"Ursula has some friends over. Better?"

"Yeah," said McQueen. "That subbasement is big as the goddam Roman catacombs. Lots of the rooms are empty, but there's still a shitload of places to look. I started with a room full of steno notes."

"And?"

"Nothing there, Gary."

"Okay," said Gary. He forced himself to cough because he suddenly felt he might cry, as he did on other low-energy days.

"You all right, Gary?"

"Fine," he said, coughing again.

"Getting a cold?"

"Nah. Seltzer. Went down wrong. Tickling my throat."

"I'm going to keep looking," said McQueen. "The subbasement will take me a while, but you let me know if you have any other ideas."

He senses something, thought Gary.

"I will when I get a chance," he said. "You know when these nurses get together."

"You're a better man than I am," said McQueen.

"Maybe," said Gary. He ended the call and bent his neck back hard against the headrest. Those fake coughs hadn't fooled McQueen. He knew he was talking to someone on the verge of tears, and the amazing thing was that Mike didn't toss one of his stupid-ass wisecracks. He may not earn the Nobel Prize for compassion, but he still sounded like he cared. He sounded like a friend.

And so a sob now ripped itself free in Gary's gut like a bubble of air belched from the muck at the bottom of a pond. Gary let it come. He felt he could sit here all night and blubber like a teenage girl, but there was just that single sob and it was over. He pulled his heavy head forward and wiped a tear from beneath his eye. He blinked, looked around the bedroom. Outside, the nurses howled over a story about an ER doctor. Gary wished he could pull himself onto the bed and let himself drift in and out of sleep till the morning. But the bed was covered with jackets and shoulder bags, so he rolled to the dresser and opened the bottom drawer.

He never unlocked the chest with Ursula in the apartment, but if he couldn't drift himself out of his low-energy state he needed something. He pulled out the book, locked the chest, closed the drawer, and then spun the chair so that his back faced the door. This is good, he thought. He would read the book from cover to cover, then go back into the living room and endure the rest of Ursula's party.

"Hi."

One of the nurses stood on the other side of the bed and pawed through the jackets. Gary closed the book over his thumb.

"Hi." He needed a moment to remember her name. "Jen."

"Just looking for something. Sorry. What are you reading?"

Gary lifted the book to show the cover.

"Great book," said Jen. "I read it to my kids practically every night. They didn't get the half of it, but they liked it."

"Same here. I used to read it to my niece and nephew. I still do, when I see them. But it's not like it was before. They always sat on my lap."

"I'm sorry," said Jen.

"Yeah, well, it's not all that. They're three years bigger, too."

"Time does march on," said Jen. "You know, the amazing thing about that book, about all his books, is how deep he gets with just a few words and simple sketches. He's so philosophical."

"I know," said Gary.

"And, like, I never read it the same way twice. Sometimes, it's just a stupid cheese wheel looking for the hunk that was cut out of it. And sometimes, it's a real person with real dreams and desires."

"I hear you," said Gary. "Sometimes I watch *Casablanca* and I believe Ilsa truly loves Rick. Other times, I think she's lying her face off just to use him."

"Well, I don't know about *Casablanca*, but I know this book. And if you ask me, it's all about you and Urse."

"Yeah," Gary riffled the pages front to back. "I think so, too."

At first Andreas thought Matyas was dead. His brother was crumpled in his chair, his head pressed on the armrest, an arm dangling to the floor. His foot had kicked the water bottle, which lay on its side with its contents now a dark circle in the brown carpet. For a moment, Andreas felt a sense of relief, then pity at the sight of his brother's composed features resembling the face he'd had as a boy, then sorrow at the realization that the boy was gone forever.

But then Matyas twitched, and Andreas saw he wasn't dead but sleeping painfully, his body curved around the exact spot where the first tumor grew inside him. There were many tumors now, not just the primary as the doctor explained. It was like a jailbreak.

Andreas lifted the bottle off the floor and placed it on the table beside the chair. He cared nothing about the carpet, nothing about the landlord or the security deposit. Soon enough, none of those trifles would matter.

He gently patted his brother's cheek.

"Matyas," he said. "Matyas, I'm back."

Matyas opened his eyes, which darted around as if taking stock of his awkward position. Then he pushed himself up and blinked. The lamplight in the room was bright, the window dark.

"Andreas," he rasped.

"Yes."

"What time is it?"

"Late," said Andreas. "Are you thirsty?"

Matyas nodded, and Andreas took the bottle into the kitchen to refill it from the faucet. When he returned, Matyas was sitting fully upright, feet on the floor, face no longer boyish.

"Did you talk to Pinter?" he said. He accepted the bottle and took a slug.

"I went to his office, but could not see him," said Andreas.

"Luis?"

"I will call him later," said Andreas. "Are you hungry?"

"Very."

Andreas went into the small, cluttered kitchen. He set oil to heat in a frying pan, sliced three potatoes, then dropped the slices into the sizzling oil. He beat four eggs, then poured them in. Fifteen minutes later, he set up a snack table in front of Matyas and served him a wedge of potato and egg. Matyas ate silently, and Andreas remembered how much they had talked together as boys and how unfortunate it was that they spoke so little to each other now. In normal circumstances, Andreas expected he would regret these silences. But these were not normal circumstances.

Matyas finished eating, and Andreas cleared away the plate and the snack table. When he returned, Matyas's head already had lolled sideways, his body already beginning to twist around the spot in his side.

"Come," he said, lifting Matyas under his arms. "Up with you."

He walked Matyas into the bedroom, tucked him into bed, and turned off the light. He was washing the frying pan when his cell phone rang. Though it no longer mattered, he took the call out into the hallway.

"That Croatian witness," said Luis. "I have his name."

After the call ended, Andreas went back into the apartment. He stood in the hallway outside the bedroom door and read the letter again as he watched his brother sleep.

CHAPTER 22

Ivan remembered being on butt duty the morning Luis tapped him on the shoulder. Luis, a paralegal for attorney Robert Pinter, had walked him through the tedious process of filing his immigration papers, had phoned when his permanent residence status had been approved, and had delivered the letter of recommendation from Pinter that got him his job in the courthouse. Ivan often saw Luis filing papers in the county clerk's office or answering calendar calls in the motion courtroom. They might nod, exchange banal pleasantries, or, as they had on one occasion, chat over coffee in the lobby. A tap on the shoulder was something different.

There were a couple of guys in the park, Luis explained. They needed to talk to him about something important. He called them *paisanos*, which Ivan understood to mean anything from relatives to neighbors to countrymen.

Ivan wanted to finish butt duty, but Luis said the *paisanos* would not wait and led Ivan across Centre Street. The sky was bright, the air crisp, and the shadows sharp. The two men looked like brothers, one slight and the other brawny. Luis performed the introductions, added that they all three hailed from Polgardi, then lifted his hands as if to say *I'm done*.

The talk was small at first. This person, that shop, the quarry that dominated the town. Ivan ran their names through his head. Matyas and Andreas. Surname Szabo, which was common enough in Hungary. Their faces slowly began to look familiar, but he couldn't have known them. They were so much older, and he had been gone from Polgardi for so many years. What would they have cared about a young boy like him? And then he remembered.

"Was Karolina Szabo your mother?" he said.

The younger brother, Andreas, began to speak, but Matyas punched him in the arm.

"It doesn't matter," Andreas told his brother, then turned to Ivan. "Yes, she was our mother."

"I played in your kitchen," said Ivan. "I remember your pictures on the refrigerator. I . . ." He went no further.

Matyas invited Ivan to sit beside him on a bench and told Andreas to stand behind them and keep watch.

"For who?" said Ivan.

Matyas pointed two fingers at his own eyes, tapped one against his ear.

"We need your help," he said.

He explained that their older brother, Luca, had been obsessed with finding Roman artifacts in the countryside around Polgardi. As a boy, Luca filled glass jars with coins, chariot nails, shards of painted pottery. On Saturdays, he would ride with their neighbor Grotzky to a flea market in Budapest and sell these trinkets for forint coins. Later, around the time he took a job at the quarry, Luca convinced himself that a large Roman settlement once stood in the forest at the edge of town. Studying the land, he identified the footprints of ancient buildings and dug test holes inside the largest of these until his spade struck the lid of a bronze cauldron. It took days for him to dig around it, a full day to lift it out, another day to haul it on a draft cart borrowed from Grotzky to a shack that had been a wine cellar. There he pried off the lid and found fourteen pieces of beautifully wrought urns, bowls, and trays, all solid silver. Later, much later, after the Yugoslav soldiers came, pieces of what was called the Salvus Treasure began to appear on the Middle Eastern antiquities market.

"A trial over the ownership of the treasure starts next week," said Matyas. He handed Ivan a piece of paper showing a judge's name, a room number, and a date. "One piece of the treasure will be on display. We are going to steal it."

"Why?" said Ivan.

"Because it is ours," said Matyas. "Because our brother was murdered over it. Our mother, too."

"Bastards," Andreas snarled above them.

"What is your plan?" said Ivan.

Matyas explained it, stressing the need for an inside connection. Someone just like Ivan.

"And you steal the piece. Then what?"

"We sell it to whoever wins the trial. Get back some of what is rightfully ours," said Matyas. "It is worth millions."

Andreas snorted. Ivan looked back and forth between the two brothers, saw the tension there.

"I need to think about this," said Ivan.

"See?" Andreas told his brother.

Matyas raised a hand. "There is no time to think," he told Ivan.

"Five o'clock," said Ivan. "We meet right here."

Ivan went back into the courthouse and shut himself in his supply closet. He lifted the coffee can off the shelf and sifted through his many losing lottery tickets. He already knew he would help them. He owed them that much after what he had seen as a helpless boy in the kitchen where he played. But their plan was too stupid and too obvious to succeed. And he wanted it to succeed because he would demand a cut of whatever they made selling the treasure piece. It would be his lottery.

He spent the afternoon dry mopping the corridors on the courtroom floors. But in his mind he was calculating sight lines and escape routes. At five o'clock he met the brothers in the park and redrew their plan, erasing the weak parts and inserting his own ideas. The brothers agreed. Willingly, thought Ivan, though he supposed they had no choice.

On Friday, Ivan stuffed his duffel bag with the warm-up suits the brothers would put on after they entered the courthouse. On Monday, he lugged in the two guns, waving pleasantly to the officer at the first-floor security desk before veering off to swipe his ID card at the time clock in the corner of the lobby.

They met at one thirty that afternoon in a little-used men's room half a flight up from Ivan's supply closet. The brothers pulled the warm-up suits over their gym shorts and T-shirts. Ivan, wearing gloves, handed over the guns. At two o'clock, Ivan climbed the A stairway to the 3M level, unlocked the door to the plenum, then returned to the third-floor landing. At five past two, he heard a gunshot. A few seconds later, Matyas and Andreas burst into the stairwell. Matyas handed over the burlap sack that held the treasure piece. Ivan ran up to the plenum. The brothers stripped off their warm-up suits, flew down the stairs, and exited by the back door before the courthouse locked down.

Ivan spent the entire afternoon in the plenum. He sat on the floor, cradling the treasure piece in his arms. It was an urn with a round bottom and a long neck that ended in a thin spout. He rubbed the urn with his thumb, feeling the low-relief detail through the scratchy burlap.

He heard shouts in the stairwell, footsteps climbing, descending, pounding on the landings. Once he heard the door handle jiggle and he expected next to hear a key sliding into the keyhole. But that was it. No one returned to the plenum door for the rest of that long afternoon.

When it was time, Ivan crept carefully toward the dim outline of an old wooden desk. He eased open a drawer, angled the urn crossways inside, then eased the drawer shut. He let himself out of the plenum and locked the door behind him. He returned to his supply closet, quietly but not stealthily, in case he was spotted. He stayed in the closet long enough to compose himself and change out of his coveralls and into his street clothes. He pulled on his jacket and shouldered his empty duffel bag. He took the elevator down to the rotunda. There were court officers everywhere and police and men who looked like detectives.

Several employees gathered at the revolving door. A police officer frisked each one as a court officer searched whatever they carried. Ivan waited his turn. He wanted to ask what happened, what the gunshot meant, whether the brothers had gotten away. But he dared not ask; he simply let himself be frisked and searched and then he pushed through the revolving door.

CHAPTER 23

Ronan Hannigan jumped out into traffic and waved the truck to the curb along the west side of Thomas Paine Park. The driver rolled down the window, then tore an invoice from a clipboard. Inside the park, Damien Wheatley lifted a foot onto a bench and leaned backward to stretch his spine. The protestors had dwindled to six people, all of whom stood on the other side of the park, directly in front of the courthouse. Their banners drooped, the lettering of their signs ran with the moisture of a heavy morning dew.

Hannigan folded the invoice into the waistband of his running shorts. The driver and a helper got out of the truck and lifted the rear gate. Hannigan took a quick look inside before wandering over to Damien.

"This is the masterstroke," he said. "I got this idea during yesterday's run. I get all my good ideas when I run. It's like ideas get shaken out of deep corners of my brain."

"You have six people," said Damien. "I can't find you any more."

"You will," said Hannigan. "I'm changing the context."

The driver swung into the back of the truck and pushed a long cardboard box into the hands of his helper.

"A tent?" said Damien, reading the print on the box.

"Not a tent," said Hannigan. "A tent city."

Damien closed his eyes and shook his head. Hannigan grabbed his arm.

"I thought, hey, I have the injunction allowing me the use of the park," he said. "Why not use it to the max? So I'm running, and the ideas are tumbling like glassware in an earthquake, and suddenly it comes to me. This is all about housing, so I'll give my people a place to live while they protest. At first, I thought one big tent, like a revival meeting. But there are too many trees for one big tent, so I thought a few smaller ones. Then a few more, then a few more after that, and it became a tent city in my head. I talked to my lawyers . . ."

"You have lawyers?" said Damien.

"Of course I have lawyers. You think I'm doing this on my own? I talked to my lawyers, and they reviewed the language of the injunction and said it was broad enough to include the use of nonpermanent structures; in other words, tents."

"How many?"

"Six for now. They each accommodate twelve people." Hannigan turned to look at the six sorry protestors across the park. Then he handed Damien a thick stack of single-ride MetroCards. "You got a lot more to offer now, so work your magic."

Across the park, Ivan walked slowly toward Andreas with his hands deep in his coverall pockets. Andreas sat leaning forward on a bench, a thick fist propping his chin. He looked like that statue, Ivan thought, which was kind of funny because Andreas was the brother who always seemed to react without thinking.

"Where is Matyas?" said Ivan.

Andreas looked up. He took in Ivan for a moment, then leaned back and sighed.

"Matyas is not well," he said.

"But wasn't he doing better?"

"He was until the last chemo. He always feels bad for a day. But this is the third, and he is still . . ." Andreas held a hand flat out. "So, what is this about?"

Ivan sat down beside Andreas, his hands still in his pockets.

"Someone is on to us," he said.

"Who?"

"A court officer."

"Why do you think he is on to us?" said Andreas.

"Because he is not just any court officer. He was one of the officers in that courtroom. He was the one you slugged, the one guarding the front door."

"He was not much of a guard," said Andreas. "So, did he come to you and say, 'I know you have the urn'?"

"It was not so clear," said Ivan. "He told me to let him into the plenum."

"The what?"

"The plenum. It is a storage area. Most people in the courthouse don't know about it, even people who have worked here for many years. All the custodians have keys. It was where I hid while you and Matyas escaped."

"Why did he want you to let him in?"

"He said he was looking for something."

"Did he say it was the urn?"

"No."

"Then he could have been looking for something else."

"That is true," said Ivan. "But earlier that day, the lawyers on the case were in the courtroom with the new judge. He was in the courtroom, too, not working but watching. He found me after the conference ended. I asked him why he needed to get into the plenum, but he wouldn't give me a straight answer. I tried to follow him inside, but he told me to hold the door. I could see from his flashlight that he went as far as the place where I once hid the urn. Then a rat chased him out."

"Some brave guard," said Andreas.

"Later, I followed him down to the subbasement," said Ivan. "There are many storage rooms there. He looked in each one."

"So?"

"I kept the urn down there for a time, too," said Ivan. "It was like he was reading my mind."

"Where is it now?"

"Back in the plenum. He won't go back there again. He's afraid of Bors."

"Bors?" said Andreas.

"My name for the rat."

Andreas shook his head.

"Don't worry about the guard," he said. "It won't be much longer that you'll need to keep him fooled. What about the other guard?"

"Still in a wheelchair," said Ivan. "Paralyzed from the waist down."

Andreas clapped a hand on Ivan's shoulder.

"I will be in touch," he said.

The courtroom was deathly quiet. Foxx sat in the front row of the gallery, his posture perfectly straight, his hands cupped on his lap and his eyes closed. The court reporter straddled her steno machine, thumbing through a fashion magazine. Arthur Braman had ducked out a few minutes earlier to take a phone call, which left only Billy Cokeley at the counsels' table. The clock built into the back wall of the courtroom clicked, and the big hand lurched forward another minute. Robert Pinter was now half an hour late.

Inertia, coupled with an unpleasant fatigue and an upset stomach, kept Linda on the bench. She surreptitiously broke a saltine cracker and slipped half past her lips, the gesture reminiscent of a priest snapping a large, newly consecrated host into three pieces to fit into his mouth. Similarities between the church and the courts, between the ecclesiastical and the legal, had dogged her all morning. They went beyond equating altar with bench, pulpit with witness stand, choir with jury box, and sacristy with robing room. Instead, they settled on how the courts, like the church, had no standing army, no physical manifestation to enforce their rulings, but relied on a shared understanding with their respective flocks.

She glanced at Mark, who sat in the clerk's box, reading a motion file he had brought down from chambers. He had offered, again, to sit in on the conference, and she, for two intertwined reasons, had agreed. For one, Bernadette needed a solid day in her cubicle to draft the pretrial decision and, once that was done, work on the homeless stipend case. For another, Arthur Braman had requested the conference for reasons that were still unclear, and with a case like this prudence dictated that another set of eyes and ears be present, even if those eyes and ears belonged to Mark. Smart he wasn't, but honest she felt he always would be.

Braman returned to the courtroom and noisily took his seat at counsels' table. In the gallery, Foxx opened one eye.

"Mr. Braman," said Linda. "You did notify Mr. Pinter of the conference, correct?"

"I spoke to him directly," said Braman. "I told him ten o'clock sharp."

The clock on the back wall clicked off another minute: 10:32.

"And can you give us a hint about why you needed this conference?"

"With all due respect, Your Honor, I prefer to wait until all counsel are present."

Linda considered that for a moment, then whispered to Mark.

"Call Pinter's office and find out what's keeping him."

Mark went into the robing room and came out a minute later to crouch beside Linda.

"His paralegal says he was called away on an emergency. He'll be here as soon as possible."

Linda scowled, then, after Mark sank back into the clerk's box, plucked another saltine from the sleeve. She was still nibbling when the courtroom doors opened and Robert Pinter slumped in dragging his litigation bag behind him.

In the gallery, Foxx stirred into action. He slid smoothly toward the doors, checked the corridor, then took up a position just inside the well. Pinter, meanwhile, parked his cart and yanked back his chair. Rather than sit, he planted his hands on the table and leaned heavily forward. He looked haggard and slack, his suit jacket wrinkled, his belly straining against his belt buckle.

"I apologize to the court and to fellow counsel," he said. "Something came up."

"An emergency, we understand," said Linda. "Did you attend to it?"

"Not quite," said Pinter. "I don't know how to say it, so I'll just say it." He pushed up off the table. "My witness, Grotzky, is dead."

The words sank through the silent courtroom, and Linda felt herself sinking with them. She started to speak, then realized she would not be able to form a coherent sentence. Finally, as Pinter lowered his hands back onto the table, she pulled up over the front rail and told the court reporter she wanted everything taken down on the record.

"All right, Mr. Pinter," she said. "Tell us what happened."

"I was to have breakfast with him this morning," said Pinter, "but he did not answer the door. I became concerned, so I asked the concierge to let me in. Grotzky was on the kitchen floor, still dressed in the same clothes as when I saw him last evening. The police came. They are treating it as suspicious."

"Suspicious as in murder?" said Linda.

"That's the only type of suspicion I know," said Pinter. "And it wouldn't be the first time someone with direct knowledge of the treasure's discovery was murdered."

"What is that supposed to mean?" said Billy Cokeley, jumping to his feet.

"You know exactly what that's supposed to mean," said Pinter. He did not move or raise his voice, as if too weary to exert himself.

"Counselors," said Linda. "Whether the death was a murder, or an accident, or from natural causes has no bearing on the trial right now, other than what effect the unavailability of the witness has on the admission of the letter Hungary seeks to present as evidence."

"I will brief you on that," said Pinter.

"Do," said Linda. "I expect additional briefs from all of you addressing this new issue. Nothing fancy. They can be letter briefs, but they need to be delivered to chambers by nine thirty tomorrow."

The lawyers all nodded.

"Fine," said Linda. "Give me five minutes, and we'll start."

Alone in the robing room, Linda phoned Bernadette.

"Big doings," she said. "Hungary's new witness. Grotzky. The guy who had that letter all these years. He's dead."

"Seriously?" said Bernadette. "You think it's related?"

"The cops think it's suspicious. If it is, I'd lay money it's related."

"That simplifies my research. No Grotzky, no way the letter gets into evidence."

"Not so fast," said Linda. "I want that letter in evidence."

"But how?"

"I don't know right now. I just asked for additional briefs."

"You have a conference? I didn't know you had a conference today."

"Arthur Braman asked for it. I don't know why, and he won't say just yet. You're busy with more important things right now, so I asked Mark to act as a second set of eyes and ears. He can handle that."

"When are the new briefs due?"

"First thing tomorrow."

"But you promised your ruling tomorrow."

"I'll move it to Friday," said Linda. "If we get jammed, there's always Monday."

She hung up. A moment later, Foxx opened the door. He had the most striking blue eyes, and right now those eyes stared so intently that Linda looked away. When she glanced back, the stare was gone, and she wondered whether the effect had been the light, or her indigestion, or her nerves.

"Mr. Braman wants to see you alone," he said.

"Very well," said Linda. "Send him in. Mark, too."

Foxx held the door open as Braman and then Mark filed in.

"Please have a chair, Mr. Braman," said Linda.

Braman sat directly across the desk from Linda, while Mark dragged a chair to the right and slightly behind the lawyer. Different angle, different view, different take, thought Linda. Maybe Mark wasn't so dumb.

With everyone settled, Foxx gave Linda an ironically courtly bow and receded into the courtroom. As soon as the door closed, Braman exhaled wearily.

"I have a serious problem," he said. "My client wants out. He does not want a trial. He wants to recoup his investment and go home."

"That certainly is a major change in your client's position," said Linda.

"Well, just among us." Braman turned slightly to include Mark. "My client's personal funds went only to purchase the first two of the fourteen pieces. The other twelve purchases were bankrolled by a consortium of investors."

"I sense air quotes, Mr. Braman."

"You sense correctly, Your Honor." A smile flickered on Braman's face. "These investors are not the type of people Lord Leinster's father would have approved of. They have been problematic right from the start, but my client has been able to, if not control them, at least mollify them. The theft of the urn changed the landscape. Basically, my client has been in hiding ever since."

"From his investors?"

"They are not happy that their investment has been tied up in court. They even think that my client may have arranged for the theft as a means of diminishing their return and increasing his."

"I don't follow," said Linda. "Maybe I'm dense."

"You're not dense, Your Honor. The idea makes no sense to me, but I can't control what people think." Braman took a deep breath as if shifting gears. "Anyway, Leinster was attacked last weekend."

"Physically?" said Linda.

Braman nodded. "In the middle of nowhere. The back of beyond, as the Irish call it. He's taken up painting. Believe it or not, he's actually quite good. He was painting when two people posing as tourists approached him. They broke his ankles."

"Ankles?" Linda said, emphasizing the plural. "How?"

"It is too horrific for me to repeat," said Braman.

Linda glanced at Mark. This was not the type of talk anyone expected to hear in the robing room, or coming from the genteel Arthur Braman.

"So, what do you propose?" said Linda.

"As I said, my client wants out. He wants to recoup his investors' stakes, pay me, and go off somewhere by himself and continue painting without constantly looking over his shoulder."

"This would cost, what?"

"Fifteen million," said Braman. "He relinquishes all title and claim to the treasure, and Hungary and Croatia can continue to litigate."

"So, we are not talking a global settlement."

"No. This is a divestment."

Linda ran the ramifications of the offer through her head.

"All right," she said. "Let me talk to them."

Braman left the robing room.

"What do you think?" Linda asked Mark.

"Interesting," he said.

"I think it's crazy, but," she said, "sometimes crazy works."

The door opened, and Cokeley and Pinter entered and sat down.

"As it turns out, Mr. Braman wants to talk settlement," said Linda. "Lord Leinster offers to divest himself of all title and claims to the treasure for a price that your two clients would share and the trial would continue between the two of you."

Cokeley looked at Pinter, who stared down at his own lap.

"Anybody?" said Linda.

"What price is Lord Leinster asking?" said Cokeley.

"In the fifteen- to twenty-million-dollar range," said Linda.

Cokeley guffawed. Pinter kept staring down.

"Split between us?" said Cokeley.

"Precisely," said Linda. "The treasure as an aggregate was worth, what? Seventy?"

"That was before the heist," said Cokeley.

"So, what's the value now? Sixty? Fifty-five?"

"Depends on who you speak to," said Cokeley.

"But no matter who you speak to, the value of the treasure is significantly higher than the cost to each of you of letting Leinster out of the case."

Cokeley grunted. Pinter shrugged. Linda looked at Mark, who arched his eyebrows.

"Either of you want to speak to me privately?"

"I do," Pinter said quietly.

Cokeley slapped his knees, then stood up and left the robing room.

"Look, Judge," said Pinter, "this might be a creative way to handle this case, but it's just not going to fly. I have my evidence, Cokeley has his. If my evidence is good enough to prevail over his, it's good enough to prevail over Leinster's. Same if Cokeley prevails over me. So why would either of us pay to get Leinster out of the case?"

CHAPTER 24

McQueen covered two rooms in the subbasement before the damp air started to clog his lungs. One room had three shelves with more boxes of steno notes and the other was the old presidential bunker. He approached the steno notes as he had the previous day, starting out by diligently removing enough paper bricks to feel for the urn and then gradually devolving into lifting and dropping the file boxes to gauge their weight. The bunker was an easier and more interesting search. There were no shelves, no boxes, just the old wooden desks, the broken radios, and the skeletal remains of the cots. It would have taken him all of about five minutes to open and close all the drawers. But then he began finding stuff. First came the old bottles of Anacin and Alka-Seltzer and Tums. Real bottles made of glass, not crappy plastic. Then came the old issues of the *Daily News*, faded and moldy but still readable. He spread one from December 1964 on the top of the desk. He had forgotten how bad the Giants were in the mid-sixties. But there it was in black and white, the final NFL standings with the Giants in the cellar of the Eastern Conference at 2-10-2.

He found a few issues of *Life* magazine, and would have pored over the pictures if he hadn't started to wheeze. He went back to the courtyard, then up the circular stairs to the basement level, then out to a stairwell. As he opened the door, he heard a voice speaking in the harsh, guttural sounds of a foreign language. He had studied two years of Spanish, now long dormant in his brain. He could recognize French and knew a smattering of German from a summer of hanging out in some bars in Yorkville. This was nothing he'd ever heard before.

A man stood on the landing. He leaned heavily into the corner, his left arm extended to brace himself against the wall. For a moment, McQueen thought the man was sick and he instinctively thumbed the intercom attached to his shoulder. Then he recognized the man was Pinter. He wasn't sick; he had someone—a much smaller person—pinned to the wall.

Pinter went silent until McQueen started up the stairs. He resumed talking, lower now, but in that same guttural language. As McQueen turned onto the next flight, he could see down into the corner. The man Pinter had pinned to the wall was Ivan.

Ivan was at the bottom of the stairwell, lining a trash can with a fresh plastic bag, when he heard a voice speak the name he hadn't heard in years.

"Istvan."

He turned to see Pinter descending the stairs, his cart clopping behind him, each footfall jolting his entire body. At bottom, Pinter hip-checked the trash can out of the way and plowed toward Ivan, who avoided a collision by ducking into the corner.

"You must help me," Pinter said in Hungarian. His hand shot over Ivan's head and thudded against the wall.

"I cannot help you."

"You owe me."

"I owe you nothing." Ivan tried to worm his way out of the corner, but Pinter slammed his other hand against the wall and bent his elbows to pin Ivan's head between them.

"Grotzky is dead."

"Who is Grotzky?"

"He was sitting with me outside the courtroom yesterday morning. I saw from the way you stared that you recognized him. Your neighbor from the old country. Your neighbor, and Karolina Szabo's neighbor."

Ivan went still, and Pinter relaxed his elbows.

"I brought Grotzky in to testify at the trial. He had a letter that Karolina Szabo wrote the day she was murdered. It is an important letter. Now that he is gone, I need another witness to swear to seeing her write it. You were her neighbor, too."

"I was only a boy," said Ivan.

"But old enough to remember."

"I saw no letter. I will not lie."

"You will not lie, huh?" said Pinter. "All of a sudden, you are an honest man? Let's see how you feel when Teresita crawls out of the woodwork, looking for cash. I'm sure she won't lie, either."

"I haven't seen her in years."

"Doesn't mean she's not waiting for the right moment to come back into your life."

Ivan went perfectly still.

"I thought so," said Pinter. "Luis will be in touch. He'll prep you and show you a copy of the letter to refresh your recollection. I don't expect you to testify till next week at the earliest. You work in the building, so it's not like you'll need a whole lot of time off. What could be more convenient than that?"

Pinter slapped Ivan lightly on each cheek. Then he grabbed his cart and trudged up the stairs, leaving Ivan slumped against the wall.

Arthur Braman was barely back at his office before the world, or at least the world as defined by the Roman silver trial, crashed around him. Leinster had phoned again in his absence, a call that his secretary described as "demanding and abusive." The settlement conference had been a disaster. Sure, Pinter and Cokeley each dutifully promised to convey Leinster's offer to their respective clients and recommend that they consider it carefully. But Braman knew bullshit when he heard it; if he were in their shoes, he wouldn't recommend that offer, either. Next up were the pretrial rulings, which were certain to go against him. The single bright spot was the untimely death of Pinter's witness, but even that was negligible because weakening Hungary's case only strengthened Croatia's.

He buzzed his secretary and asked her to summon his two litigation associates. They arrived at his desk quickly. He explained the new development, and they furiously took notes. He nodded in the direction of one, and she headed off to begin work. The other associate remained.

Braman closed his office door. For years, generations actually, the associates his firm hired had rolled off a single assembly line with the same intellectual and cultural pedigree—white, male, Northeast Corridor, double Ivies. That had changed, slowly and imperceptibly at first, before accelerating in recent years, and the associate who sat before him—Darius was his name—was the apotheosis of this new, multicultural template.

"I need Judge Conover off the case," said Braman.

Damien Wheatley had to concede that Hannigan was right. Many of the same lowlifes who had dissed him only yesterday now jumped at the chance to occupy the tent city in Foley Square.

"Hey, you're doing great," Hannigan told him over his cell phone. "Thirty-two showed up so far."

Thirty-two, thought Damien, translated to three hundred and twenty dollars. Not bad, but nothing like he could make on the Roman silver case if he could come up with an angle.

"The tent city needs a catchy name," said Hannigan. "Something like Stipend City or Conover Square. You have any ideas?"

Damien, way uptown near Riverside Park, tried to catch the attention of an old man with a flowing white mustache and leathery, sunburned skin. The man's head, weighed down with a scuffed Mets batting helmet, bent forward so that his chin rested on his chest, his wrist flicking a cup in a rhythmic jangle of nickel on tin.

"Conover Square," said Damien. "It's in the middle of Foley Square and it sounds like Hanover Square."

"Yeah, with all its Financial District associations," said Hannigan. "I like that."

Hannigan rang off, and Damien tried again with the old man. He waved his hand, then crouched into his line of sight. The man's eyes were closed.

"Hey, wanna make twenty bucks?" said Damien.

The old man only flicked the cup harder. A nickel popped out and rolled a slow arc on the sidewalk until Damien stomped it with his foot. He picked up the nickel and plunked it into the cup.

"God bless," said the man.

One block farther on, a man sat on a bench with a blanket spread on the sidewalk in front of him. Pictures lay on the sheet, and as Damien drew closer he saw they were charcoal sketches of buildings.

"Five bucks each," said the man. "Three for twelve."

The sketches weren't worth five bucks, or four bucks, or anything at all. They weren't even on drawing paper but on lined sheets ripped from a spiral notebook.

"How about I give you twenty bucks and you keep your pictures," said Damien.

The man cocked his head, waiting for the catch.

"You just need to spend some time down at Foley Square."

"Where's that?"

"Downtown. Got a tent city growing there. Shelter. Three squares."

The man stroked his chin. He had a salt-and-pepper beard. Dandruff powdered his shirt where his gut protruded.

"Don't like downtown," he said.

"Then screw you," Damien said and walked away.

This was a waste of time, begging the crazy homeless to join Hannigan's protest when the Roman silver trial was back. He opened his phone and scrolled through his contacts. He still had the numbers: Arthur Braman's, Robert Pinter's, the small hotel where the woman named Natalija stayed last time. He clearly recalled the black Town Car stopping alongside him on Broome Street, the back door opening on a dark interior that made the pair of legs all the more obvious. They were long legs, crossed at the ankles and shaped elegantly by open-toed heels. Natalija had blonde hair, sharp features, sinewy arms. She took a long drag on a cigarette and blew the smoke to the ceiling. When she spoke his name, she sounded like a spy.

"Thank you for meeting like this," Darius said as he guided Mark into a small park filled with office workers eating take-out lunches.

Mark had been surprised by the phone call. Surprised, intrigued, and ultimately worried enough about its impropriety to pay cash for a two-trip MetroCard for the subway rather than use his regular unlimited monthly pass that could track his movements if this meeting ever came to light. Still, he had come, and when he told the judge he might take an extra hour for lunch, her reaction had been a distracted if pleasant *whatever*, as if he needed more proof of his low standing in the pecking order of her esteem.

"Mr. Braman has a concern," said Darius. He held a file folder on his lap.

"I know. I tried to explain the division of labor in chambers and that I might not always have the judge's ear."

"It's not that."

"Oh," said Mark.

"Mr. Braman believes that Judge Conover should be disqualified from trying this case."

"Disqualified?" Mark performed a quick mental calculus. Disqualified equaled not trying the case. Not trying the case equaled him being cut off from all contact with Arthur Braman. Arthur Braman equaled his last best hope for future employment.

"Mr. Braman believes that she formed a definite conclusion about the case when she worked as Judge Johnstone's law clerk," said Darius. "He believes this indicates bias, which is a ground for disqualification.

"He also thinks that she could be aware of, perhaps even in possession of, inadmissible evidence that may influence her handling of this trial. The bell that can't be unrung, if you will.

"But, as you understand, a disqualification motion is a difficult one to bring and an even more difficult one to win. High risk, high reward. It can't be based on a lawyer's thoughts or feelings or impressions. That's where you come in. We hope. We want you to give us an affidavit."

They were sitting on the edge of a large concrete planter filed with mums and ornamental bushes. The lunch crowd was beginning to disperse. No one was within earshot.

"I don't know," said Mark. He plucked a few bark chips from the planter and crushed them in his hand.

"I understand," said Darius. "It is no small thing to give an affidavit to disqualify your judge from trying a case. But you are our only window into chambers. If we decide to use your affidavit, and we won't know that until we actually have it in hand, you will lose your job. But then, we know you're out at the end of the year anyway, right?"

Mark nodded.

"And your political club, the West Chelsea Reformed Democrats, will not help you get a new job, right?"

Mark nodded again. Darius opened the file folder just enough to reveal it held Mark's résumé.

"You fucked up a few clerking gigs."

"Hey, those judges weren't rocket scientists," said Mark.

"We understand," said Darius. "These are political jobs and sometimes they end for political reasons. Judge Conover is several cuts above your prior bosses. But you're in a funny little box."

"It's not so funny," said Mark.

"You're right," said Darius. "And maybe you're not cut out for the court system. Maybe your future lies elsewhere. So think of this as a head start on the next phase of your legal career."

"With your firm?" said Mark.

"That's not for me to say because I'm not privy to those decisions," said Darius. "What I can say is that this gambit is Mr. Braman's idea. He has a plan. He always has a plan, and his plans always account for every vagary and every ramification."

They did not go to the firm. Once Mark agreed, Darius steered him two blocks downtown to a building that housed several physical therapy practices. They rode the elevator to the fifth floor, then followed the corridor to a nameless office suite. Darius unlocked the door to a white, windowless office with a gray industrial carpet, a desk, and three chairs. A stenographer sat in one of the chairs.

"You'll talk," Darius told Mark. "I'll refine what you say, and Rosemary will take it all down. She'll print it, we'll shape it, and we'll have your affidavit. It will take an hour at most."

And so, Mark began to talk. He recounted his first meeting with Judge Conover on the first day of her term. He had been sent by his political club with a letter of introduction that spelled out the conditions of his employment, and the judge, after reading the letter and folding it back into its envelope, spoke at length about what she expected from her law clerk and what she hoped to achieve on the bench. The Roman silver trial—and the heist and the shooting of the court officer—had occurred only fifteen months earlier and was still raw in the judge's memory. She explained how that trial, both factually and symbolically, had been the springboard to her judgeship.

Darius shaped the trial and the prospect of the retrial into a continuing theme. Mark allowed that the judge "might have" mentioned how she would handle the retrial if given the opportunity, "routinely scanned the *Law Journal*" for news on the status of the appeals, and "occasionally spoke in low tones about the case" to someone on the phone.

"Do you think she was plotting to have the retrial steered to her?" said Darius.

"I never thought of that, but yeah," said Mark. "Her husband has a lot of clout at Sixty Centre."

"We know all about him," said Darius.

The stenographer gathered the scattered bits together into a series of numbered paragraphs and printed what they had composed so far. Mark read it, seeing how deftly Darius's embellishments strengthened the affidavit.

"Is there anything else you could offer?" said Darius.

"Oh yes," said Mark. "There's this file."

CHAPTER 25

The administrative office on the seventh floor consisted of one large room with six large desks and many file cabinets. A door at one end connected to the private office of the chief clerk, while double doors on the opposite side opened into a well-appointed conference room. By four forty-five on most weekday afternoons, the occupants of the six desks were gone for the day. A closed door indicated that the chief clerk was not in attendance, and the open double doors showed no conference was in session.

Despite Gary's passionate certainty, McQueen hadn't bought the idea of the missing treasure piece being hidden in the courthouse. But he'd definitely gotten a weird vibe from that meeting between Robert Pinter and Ivan and now felt more engaged.

The file cabinets had employee personnel files arranged according to job titles. There were security titles, legal titles, clerk titles, and support titles. McQueen didn't know Ivan's last name. He didn't, for that matter, even know if Ivan's name even was Ivan. He had used the name derisively for so long he couldn't remember whether Ivan had volunteered it or whether he had made it up himself. So he started at A in the support titles and worked forward. Since each file contained a photocopy of the employee's photo ID card, there would be no missing Ivan, whatever his name was.

Of course, Ivan's given name was not exactly Ivan, and, of course, his surname began with a Z.

McQueen spread the file on the nearest desk and photographed each document with his cell phone. Then he closed the file and wedged it back in the drawer at the very end of the alphabet.

Just before five, Linda wandered into the anteroom. With nowhere special to go and nothing special to do, she planned on staying in chambers until six, when she could phone Hugh and not interrupt his day in court. Karen had gone, and Mark sat at his desk, his fingers poised over his keyboard and his eyes staring through his monitor.

"Mark?" she said.

He jerked as if startled, blinked his eyes, then focused on her.

"I wanted to thank you," she continued, "for sitting in on that conference today."

"It's my job," he said. "Besides, all I did was sit there."

"It may seem so, but it's important to have someone else in the room."

"Glad to help," he said.

"So, what do you think?"

Mark tilted back in his chair and gripped the armrests.

"I thought Mr. Braman proposed an interesting idea. But even if Hungary and Croatia take it, the trial isn't any simpler."

"You're right about that. Do you think they'll take it?"

"I doubt it," said Mark.

"Why?"

"No reason. Just a feeling. Maybe if he asked for less, but it sounds like he's tied in to that number."

Linda tapped her watch. "Almost five. You don't get overtime, you know."

Mark forced a smile.

Linda wandered slowly back into her office and took a can of seltzer from the minifridge. At a distance, she could hear Mark shutting down his computer and grabbing his things. He called "good night" and then the outer door shut and when the squeaking sound of his shoes faded in the corridor it was quiet enough that she could hear the seashell hissing of the bubbles in her seltzer can.

Her desk was empty. She had signed everything she needed to sign, read everything she needed to read, and still had an hour to kill. She sipped the seltzer, then considered whether it was time for her to look in that file. She had been thinking about it ever since returning from the courtroom this morning. Luckily, work kept her occupied.

She was about to get up when she heard the outer door open and shut. She heard nothing else, but definitely sensed a presence in the anteroom. On the underside of her desk was a button that tripped an alarm in the captain's office. Every judge's desk in every chambers had that button, but to her knowledge no one ever had pressed it.

"Hello," she called.

A moment passed, and then Foxx stepped into the doorway.

"Sorry, Judge," he said. He had a pile of motion folders tucked under his arm. "Didn't know you were still here."

"I am," she said. "My husband is on trial in Texas, and with the time difference I was waiting to call him."

"I'd keep the door locked if I were you."

"Really? Why?"

"Those protestors outside. They have a few more than this morning."

"I don't think of them."

"No?" said Foxx. "What do you think about?"

Linda straightened herself in her chair.

"Are those today's motions? I'll take them here." She patted her desk blotter.

Foxx came through the doorway and set the folders down. "Anything else you need?" he said.

Linda stared at his eyes, trying to see what she thought she had seen this morning. Nothing was there.

"No thanks," she said, "but you can lock the door on your way out."

Foxx left chambers, and Linda worked through the pile of motions. They all were relatively thin and relatively straightforward, the kinds of motions with such clearly indicated results that she wondered why the lawyers needed to file them. But that was big-city litigation; no one ever gave in.

She dashed off several notes to Mark, telling him how each motion should be decided, and lugged the pile out to his desk. She looked at her watch. Still half an hour to go. She checked the door—Foxx indeed had locked it—then opened the Redweld that lay on her desk since Mark had dropped it there a few days ago.

Linda began putting this file together before there was a first trial, before there ever was a case pitting Croatia and Hungary against Lord Leinster. It began with a magazine article that combined her two great academic loves, fine art and classical civilization. Had she come from money, she might have pursued an advanced degree in art history, traveled to Rome or Florence, and found a job in one of the great museums. Practical and working-class, she got her law degree instead, but occasionally delved back into what might have been. The article focused on a Roman silver treasure with a murky provenance that was sitting in a New York City auction house.

Metal work, even precious metal work, did not usually interest Linda. She preferred sculpture (especially Greek marble), painting (the Third Style was her favorite), and architecture (as much as she loved 60 Centre, seeing Corinthian capitals atop fluted columns irked her). But the full-color catalogue showing the fourteen treasure pieces, stunningly bright and amazingly detailed, was quite something.

She read an article about the owner, Lord Leinster, and wondered why he was so hot to sell the treasure. She heard, vaguely, about a lawsuit, an injunction, countries claiming rights of patrimony. For a brief spell, the Salvus Treasure, as the collection was called, was all over the media. Articles appeared in such disparate magazines as *Playboy*, *Harper's*, and *Natural History*. Each brought their own particular slant to the ancient treasure, with *Playboy* running a gauzily sexy photo spread of Croatia's minister of culture and *Natural History* describing the top ten archeological excavations of Roman settlements in post-Soviet Eastern Europe.

But the article that made the most sense appeared in an obscure Hungarian magazine called *Az Igazsag*, The Truth. The article carefully considered the claims of all three plaintiff countries: Syria, which issued the export licences, Croatia, which claimed that the treasure was unearthed by soldiers at one of Marshal Tito's vacation compounds, and Hungary, which claimed a young quarry worker found the treasure in a forest near what had been the border with Yugoslavia. *Az Igazsag* clearly believed Hungary's story was the truth.

Linda had visited the county clerk's office and pulled the case file. Despite the intriguing backstory, the file was boring as hell, full of motions and legal briefs but devoid of any sense of what truly was at stake. The lawsuit faded from her consciousness. The collection of articles, now in a Redweld folder, fell farther back in a chambers file cabinet. And then, one day, a group of lawyers walked into Judge Johnstone's courtroom. The Roman silver case was assigned to him for trial.

Linda thumbed past the *Playboy* spread, the *Harper's* article, the *Natural History* list. Behind them was what she really wanted to see, the translation of the *Az Igazsag* article and behind that the tear sheets from the magazine itself.

There always was a gap between absolute truth and what passed for truth in a court of law. Judge Johnstone's rulings had jammed a crowbar into that gap and jimmied it wider. The Appellate Division closed that gap, but it was not enough for her. She wanted to fill it in, smooth it out, and paper it over into a seamless surface of absolute truth. This file, this totally improper collection of inadmissible evidence, was the urtext of her intentions.

She read the translation, then glanced at the photos in the original article, all except the police photo of the Hungarian quarry worker dangling from a noose. The photo had given her nightmares back then; she didn't want any now.

For Mark, an unsettled day deteriorated even further the moment he left the courthouse. Darius had skillfully pitted Mark's frighteningly real prospects of unemployment against his wobbly loyalty to Judge Conover. Self-preservation won out. Mark had read thousands of affidavits related to hundreds of motions in his checkered court career, but never had given his own. The power of the words that Darius extracted and the stenographer typed, coupled with the act of signing his name, had been intoxicating. Judge Conover *had* prejudged the case; Judge Conover *did* maintain that file of inadmissible evidence.

But now, walking in the cool, bracing air of an autumn evening, the hangover set in. The story he spun in his affidavit seemed as shaky as his future and as wobbly as his loyalty. Man, had he fucked up.

His wife sounded totally bonkers when she answered the phone. Mark could visualize Baby Phyllis clamped onto her shoulder like a leech, hear the rhythmic shrieks that bored straight to the part of the brain that caused his stomach to turn.

"I'm going to be late tonight," he said.

"Again? What is it now?"

"A meeting at the club."

"The club?" his wife said. "I thought you were done with the club."

"Technically not."

"I don't understand why you need to go there, with the way those people treated you."

"I need to be bigger than those people," said Mark.

"You need to be home," she said.

By then he was outside a Tribeca local frequented by the after-hours courthouse crowd. The bar was packed—familiar faces out of uniform, in wrinkled shirts, with loosened ties. He shouldered in close enough to catch the bartender's eye, ordered two pints, then retreated into a corner. He slugged down one pint, then stared at the other. The beer looked bright gold, the bubbles endlessly ascended to join the perfectly white head. He was having one of those moments when the world stopped zipping by in a blur but froze into a hi-def image of some pedestrian object.

He had made his choice. Despite all her promises, the judge could not help him and so he needed to help himself. Sure, giving that affidavit was stupid. As soon as the judge paged through Arthur Braman's order to show cause tomorrow, he was finished. Word would flash around the courthouse. *Garber sold out his judge.* But he couldn't think about that now. There was a much wider world beyond the courthouse. And if he made it with Arthur Braman's firm, that wider world would be his. He lifted his second pint, but his heightened perceptions were gone, and the beer just looked like a beer.

"What kept you?" said Hugh.

"Working," said Linda.

"This late?" It was five forty-five by his watch, which meant it was six forty-five her time.

"Waded through three of Mark's decisions, then previewed today's pile of motions. Where are you? It sounds so quiet."

"Local counsel's office," said Hugh. "Everyone else is in the conference room. I can see them through the glass partition. What's going on with your trial?"

He carefully poured himself a bourbon from the minibar, neat, because he did not want Linda to hear the tinkling of ice. For ten straight minutes, she recounted every turn in this morning's conference. Hugh listened closely enough to get the gist and, when he felt it was expected of him, opined that Arthur Braman's offer was inventive.

"Of course," he concluded, "a lawyer needs to be inventive when his client fears for his life."

"You don't have that particular problem with your clientele," said Linda.

"Proof that corporations are not people."

"I wish you were here."

"Me, too," said Hugh. "But I'm not. What's going on with that protest?"

He heard a knock at the door. Soft, tentative, barely a brush of knuckle on wood. He set the glass down quietly, rushed to the door with his thumb muffling the mouthpiece, and peered through the peephole. Local counsel waited in the corridor. He opened the door and stepped back, a finger touching his lips as local counsel followed him inside. The door closed with a whisper.

"They set up several tents in the park today," said Linda. "And my court officer told me the number of protestors has grown."

"Give it a wide berth on your way home." Hugh crouched at the minibar and snaked his hand past the bourbon to the vodka. "And get Bernadette to knock off that decision. Win or lose, they'll go away."

"She's already helping me with the trial," said Linda.

"That must sit well with Mark," said Hugh.

"Actually, his work has improved lately. I got him involved in the trial today, and we even had a pleasant conversation tonight. I keep thinking he has a wife and a baby."

"He's a big boy. He knows the deal. Everything ends at some point," said Hugh.

"I know, but . . ."

"Then keep him. The West Chelsea people won't mind. He stays with you, that's one less problem on their plate." Hugh carefully set the two bottles on the counter beside the olives and the martini glass, the bowl of ice and the silver shaker. "Look, it's late here and it's even later there. Get out of chambers, avoid the protestors, and have a good night. Tomorrow you'll find out that Hungary and Croatia will buy out Lord Leinster and that Mark's found a new job."

"Thanks for your confidence," said Linda. "Love you."

"Ditto here," said Hugh. He cut the connection with a jab of his thumb, placed the phone on the minibar, and turned around just as local counsel stepped out of her skirt.

CHAPTER 26

Linda needed to disengage for the evening and, as she stepped out of the Worth Street entrance, she felt this was the perfect evening to disengage. The weather was poised between warm and cool. The sun was setting earlier, but after a clear day the twilight held on beautifully with rose-colored clouds creating a faint haze that forgave the city its many faults. She crossed Worth and stood at the corner of Centre to look back at the courthouse. The huge columns, bathed in that same reflected light, took on a pink cast.

I still work here, she told herself, and felt something she hadn't felt in a long while: a swell of pride.

In the park across the street, six large tents stood among the sycamore trees. They looked festive, as if a carnival would begin once night fell. But Linda remembered Hugh's warning, and rather than continue past the park on Worth, she gave the tents a wide berth by heading up Centre.

She took three trains instead of one and got off at Columbus Circle. She had well more than ten blocks to home, but the night was beautiful and the sidewalks and cafés were filled with an upscale Lincoln Center crowd.

She noodled along, nosing in and out of random shops, browsing for the perfect take-out dinner. Her tender stomach made her decision for her—stuffed shrimp from one store, sweet pepper hummus and sesame flatbreads from another. Time passed, and she found herself standing outside a maternity shop.

In the display window, crib mobiles gently revolved: biplanes, winged unicorns, bears on balls. The door opened, and a couple carrying pink bags came out. Behind them, a nursery rhyme played to music. The air, for one breath, smelled of talcum powder. Just as her stomach had decided her dinner, her heart drove her inside.

At first, she felt like an intruder. Was she even pregnant? she thought. Of course she was. Those tests don't lie; neither had her roiling stomach and her morning retches. Still, the store was a totally alien world to her, the tiny clothes, the pastel colors, the soothing music. Was there, somewhere in the back room, a bunch of babies napping?

She noodled here as she had noodled on the street, sampling the feel of the different fabrics.

"How far along?"

Linda looked up. On the other side of the display table, a young woman folded stacks of onesies.

"Not very," said Linda. She paused for a moment, then added, "My husband doesn't even know yet. You probably never get that."

"It's New York. We get lots of things," said the woman, who gradually did not seem so young to Linda. "Some women want to keep it to themselves for a while, almost like a jealousy thing. Some want to get used to the idea, especially if it's their first. Is this your first?"

"Not the first time," said Linda. "The other ended quickly. My husband never knew. We lead very busy lives."

"Don't we all."

"So there's the jinx factor, too."

"I get it," said the woman. "How long have you known?"

"I took a home test last week."

The woman finished refolding and slid to another display table.

"Not to tell you what to do, but you'd better see your doctor soon."

"I plan to," said Linda.

"Don't plan. Do."

Linda smiled as if to agree. She circled off to another table, inspected the tiny sweaters without messing their perfect folds, then noticed it was closing time and left the store. She loved the privacy of a big city. Here she was, knowingly pregnant for several days and not telling her husband or her best friend or her immediate staff, yet blathering it to a total stranger at a store ten blocks from her house. As duplicitous as it seemed, getting the news out of her head and into the world relieved her.

"Tell me again," said Gary. "What put you on to Ivan?"

McQueen took a deep, exasperated breath. He had explained all this when he first got to the apartment, but Gary was at his computer, one hand on the mouse and one eye on the monitor as he connected McQueen's cell phone to his computer with a very short cable. He clicked the mouse, and a program opened.

"I was coming up from the subbasement and found Pinter in a stairwell, leaning hard into the corner like he was sick. Then I saw he was talking to Ivan. The conversation didn't sound pleasant. It wasn't even a conversation. It was all Pinter."

"You heard what he said?" Square icons appeared on the monitor, like playing cards dealt facedown on a table.

"Heard it, but couldn't get a handle on it. It wasn't English, but the tone was clear. He sounded pissed as hell. I figured I should check out Ivan's background, so I went to the admin office and pulled his personnel file."

Gary clicked the first icon, which opened to an image of a gray and white cat.

"You took a picture of a cat?" he said.

"It was cute," said McQueen. "What? I can't like cats?"

Gary shook his head. He clicked the next icon, and a document in a foreign language replaced the cat.

"It's a Hungarian birth certificate," said McQueen. "The next page is the translation."

There was the birth certificate, immigration papers, an application for a green card, the green card itself, a marriage certificate, and a letter of recommendation.

"Pinter handled the green card application," said McQueen.

"Yeah, and he wrote the letter of recommendation for Ivan's job at the courthouse," said Gary. "So?"

"So, of all the lawyers in New York, Ivan goes to Pinter?"

"All the Hungarian immigrants do," said Gary.

"But they're both from Polgardi," said McQueen.

"Hungary is like fuckin' Rhode Island," said Gary, "so two people from the same region isn't that big a coincidence."

He closed the program, disconnected the cable, and handed the phone back to McQueen.

"I know you have a history with Ivan," he said. "You bust his balls, he reacts, you bust his balls some more. You think that's fun, fine. But I don't want that dragging you in the wrong direction. We don't have much time."

Linda wandered along slowly, her hunger overcome by the reality of sharing her secret with the woman in the maternity shop. Near the intersection of Broadway and Amsterdam, she stopped in front of a Halloween shop. The costumes in the window were amazingly detailed and amazingly expensive, mixing the current vogue of horror and sci-fi movie characters with old standbys like vampires and werewolves. On the sidewalk, several store employees staggered in the latest zombie gear. Lurid body parts littered the pavement.

Linda bent down to look at a corner of the window where tiny costumes were displayed. Next year, she would be shopping here for her baby's first Halloween costume. She already knew what she would choose—a princess for a girl, a pirate for a boy.

She moved on, thinking on whether the Upper West Side was a good place to raise a child. It certainly seemed good enough when they'd bought their brownstone here, but children weren't specifically in their game plan then. She wondered if they were now, at least in Hugh's mind. The real action for families with young children was now in Tribeca. You couldn't walk a block without passing old textile buildings converted into preschools or dance schools or birthday-party venues. Maybe, if they moved down to Tribeca, she would reconsider her plan to leave the bench.

Up a few more blocks and across the last street, Linda turned toward home and found herself alone. It always amazed her how this could happen in New York City. You could turn a corner and go from being a face in the crowd to perfect solitude. There must be some kind of theory that explained this phenomenon, something connected with particle flow or liquid dynamics or Brownian motion. Right now, there were just sensations: the quickly fading traffic noise from the avenue, the deep pools of shadow cast by trees that still held their copper-colored leaves, the lonely scuff of her shoes on the sidewalk.

But she saw she was not quite alone. Across the street, an odd face floated above the roof of a parked car. The face was bright white, artificially white, and very long and thin. For a moment, Linda almost stopped walking as Foxx's warning about the protestors wound back into her head. But this was her neighborhood, she told herself. It was a safe neighborhood, literally miles from the protestors in Foley Square.

Linda cocked her head and focused well enough to see that the bright white face actually was a mask. The mask creeped her out, but at the same time she realized it was the falsest of false alarms, probably a customer from the Halloween shop. Still, she glanced over several times until she passed him. She was three doors away from home, three pools of tree shade ribbed with bands of streetlight. One band lit someone standing at the curb and wearing a black cape and a black conical hat. This person seemed to be talking on a cell phone, though Linda, only one door away from her own, heard no conversation.

The attack came swiftly and from behind. He yanked at her purse, spilled the packages from her hands. Linda immediately went into survival mode. *It's a mugging. Give it up. Nothing is worth getting hurt.*

But he pushed her forward and tripped her up. She crashed painfully to the sidewalk, wrists and knees instantly burning. She started to crawl toward her stoop.

The kick came from the side, to her stomach, so hard that it lifted her into the air and dropped her to the ground. The pain was so intense that she could not scream, could not cry, could do nothing other than breathe, *Oh my God, no. Oh my God, no.*

He kicked her twice more in the gut before she tightened herself into a ball. After that, she went numb. Hazily, through her tears, she saw the one who had been across the street drag her attacker away. Then she rolled over and groaned.

No one came because no one saw and no one heard. Linda lay in a fetal position until she was certain they were gone and would not return. She pushed herself up, forced some deep breaths, then lifted herself onto the first step of her stoop. She hung her head between her knees and checked herself. Her wrists ached, her knees burned, her stomach roiled. But when she probed with her hand, she felt nothing wet, nothing bleeding, just the pain and shock and horror of the attack.

She took a few more deep breaths before sitting fully upright. The sidewalk was deserted on both sides in both directions, something that was inconceivable for most of New York, but not on her quiet street. She pulled herself up by the bannister rail, held it until she was sure she could toddle on her own without falling or fainting. Her purse and grocery bags lay on the pavement, scattered but untouched. Two steps and she reached her purse, two more and she snagged her grocery bags. She turned back and reached the stairs as her vision blackened around the edges. She slumped against the bannister until she breathed the light back into her eyes.

She climbed slowly, unlocked the door, and stumbled inside. She lay on the hardwood parquet, panting with exertion and gasping with pain. The front door was still open, the night air rolling in. She kicked it shut, then reached into her purse for her cell phone and hit the speed dial.

"It's me," she said.

CHAPTER 27

Linda answered the door wearing a bathrobe and slippers. She was not visibly bruised, but her face was ashen and she was hunched over as if tortured by a terrible stomach ache.

"Thanks for coming," she whispered.

Bernadette took one arm, Foxx the other, and they walked her into the nearest room, a den with leather furniture and floor-to-ceiling bookcases. Bernadette sat beside Linda on the sofa. Foxx took a chair. Linda's knees, exposed now, were skinned red.

"What happened?" said Bernadette.

Linda started to speak, then fixed her eyes on Foxx.

"I thought he should be here," said Bernadette. "So?"

"I got mugged. Right outside. Two of them. They wore Halloween costumes."

"What kind of costumes?" said Foxx. He got up and circled behind the chair to part the curtains. The sidewalk directly in front was empty. Across the street, a portly man held a leash while a white poodle nosed around a tree well.

"Thin white masks with a black mustache and pointy beard."

"Hats and capes?" said Foxx.

"How did you know?" said Linda.

"A Guy Fawkes costume." Foxx turned away from the window. "Go on."

Linda haltingly recounted the attack.

"Did they take anything?" asked Bernadette.

"No."

"Did they say anything?"

"No," said Linda. "The one who actually attacked me kept kicking at me until the other one dragged him away."

"You didn't call the police?" said Bernadette.

"No."

"You need to report this."

"No. No police."

"Then you need to go to the ER."

"No. No hospital."

Bernadette reached her hand toward Linda's stomach, and Linda cringed.

"I think you should step outside," Bernadette told Foxx.

Foxx went into the hallway, then down onto the stoop, then onto the sidewalk. The portly man with the poodle had gone, and except for the avenue traffic passing at opposite ends of the block, nothing else moved. Foxx circled the tree where Linda said her attacker had waited. No footprints, no cigarette butts, no candy wrappers. He walked partway up the block, crossed the street, and walked back on the other side. He didn't know what he was looking for and did a good job of not finding it.

Back at Linda's stoop, he took out his cell phone to call Bev. Then he thought better. Linda hadn't reported the mugging to the police, hadn't gone to the ER, hadn't done anything to create a blip on Bev's radar screen. Technically the mugging hadn't happened. Yet.

The front door opened, and Bernadette came down the steps.

"She finally agreed to see a doctor," she said, hugging herself. "Not any doctor. Her doctor."

"At this hour?" Foxx put a hand on Bernadette's shoulder and rubbed it with his thumb.

"When you're a judge and the wife of Hugh Gavigan, doors open for you."

They all three took a cab through Central Park and then crosstown to a building in the block between Park Avenue and Lexington Avenue. Bernadette pressed numbers into an intercom, and a voice came over the speaker.

"It's Judge Conover," said Bernadette.

The door buzzed, and they went into the lobby and rode the elevator until it opened directly into a waiting room with the name of the medical group spelled out in stainless-steel letters on the wall behind the reception desk. This was Foxx's first clue.

The waiting room was deserted until a door opened on one end and a man pushed a wheelchair toward them. He was fiftyish and stocky, dressed in khaki pants and a dark blue polo shirt, his arms roundly muscled and hairy, a gold watch heavy on his wrist. He held the wheelchair steady as Bernadette lowered Linda onto the seat.

While Foxx waited in the reception area, Bernadette wheeled Linda into an exam room. Linda slowly removed her clothes and put on a gown. Then Bernadette helped her climb onto the examination table. The doctor, whose name was Lander, returned wearing a white smock, a white cap, and white latex gloves.

"When did you find out?" he said.

"Last week," said Linda. "Assuming it's true."

"I'll double-check, but how far along, assuming?"

"Eight weeks," said Linda.

"Fine," said the doctor. "I'm going to examine you, then we'll have the visit you should have arranged the minute you found out."

Dr. Lander listened to Linda's heart, drew two vials of blood, took her blood pressure, then placed her finger in a plastic clip attached to a machine that monitored the oxygen in her blood. He told her to lie back, placed her legs in the stirrups, and palpated her abdomen before lifting her gown to probe gently inside. Muttering to himself, he rolled another machine next to the table and performed a transvaginal ultrasound to make sure there were no injuries the gross exam missed.

"You are either very strong or very lucky," Dr. Lander told Linda as he rolled the machine away. Then he turned to Bernadette. "Help her dress. I'll meet you in my office."

Back at the brownstone, Linda gazed up at the front steps.

"The doctor told her to avoid stairs," said Bernadette.

Foxx held out his arms, offering to carry Linda up the steps.

"No need," said Linda. She led them to an iron gate and an incline that sloped down to a door beneath the stoop. Inside, Linda pressed a button, and a machine rumbled.

"An elevator?" said Bernadette.

"I never told you?" said Linda. "It came out of Hugh's first big trial. Horrible wrongful birth case, well-to-do parents, a little girl profoundly retarded because of cerebral palsy. Hugh led the defense team. The jury returned a verdict of sixty million. The defendants appealed, but Hugh convinced both sides to settle for twenty. The parents bought this brownstone and renovated it for complete handicap access. Anyway, they weren't here very long before they suddenly didn't need all this anymore. They offered Hugh the right of first refusal at a discounted price. They were grateful he worked the settlement because it gave them more time with their little girl rather than fighting an appeal."

The elevator stopped rumbling, and Linda opened the door, which looked just like any other door except there was a small elevator car on the other side. Bernadette and Linda stepped in. As Foxx followed, the inside doors began to slide shut. Linda pulled Foxx out of the way.

"No electric eye," she said.

Foxx got off at the first floor and went into the den while Linda and Bernadette continued up to the third floor. He was paging through an old *New Yorker* when the elevator rumbled again.

"She still refuses to call the police and still hasn't called Hugh," said Bernadette. "At least she agreed to stay home tomorrow."

Foxx turned two more pages and then put the magazine aside.

"Why an OB/GYN?" he said.

"That's something I'm not comfortable sharing," said Bernadette.

Foxx got up from the chair and parted the curtains. A single leaf shook free from a tree and glided to the sidewalk.

"I'll stay the night, too," he said.

"I thought you might. There are two guest rooms upstairs."

"That's one more than we need," said Foxx.

Bernadette laughed and headed to the elevator, shutting lights as she went. Soon it was dark and quiet, well short of midnight, but with a much later feel. Foxx pried off his shoes and stretched out on the sofa. He listened to Bernadette's laugh in his head. He could read many types of laughs—the sardonic, the ironic, the wry—but not that one.

He woke up some time later to the sound of the elevator. He opened his eyes as someone came into the den. He expected Bernadette, but then the curtains parted and street light sliced the darkness. Linda. Silently, Foxx sat up.

"So, which is it?" he said.

Linda shook at his sudden words, then turned toward him.

"Which is what?" she said.

"The gynecologist," said Foxx.

Linda dropped the curtain and plunged the den back into darkness.

"The way I figure it," Foxx could see her gray figure settle into the chair, "there are two possible reasons you go to a gynecologist. One is that the attack was a sexual assault. The other is you're pregnant and you needed to make sure nothing happened."

"It's the second." Linda curled up in the chair. "I found out only last week. Didn't tell anyone, including my husband, until I told Bernadette tonight. So now you know, too, and I didn't want anyone else to know just yet."

Foxx waited.

"Don't you want a guest room?"

"I'm not a guest," said Foxx. "Are you worried?"

"I haven't sorted it out yet. But I do feel better with you here. At least for tonight." Linda stood up, her grayness hovering in the dark. "You'll keep my secret?"

"Is that a court order?"

"Yes," she said with a hint of a laugh. "It is."

"You got it," said Foxx. "But could someone know you are pregnant?"

"No. Wait. You think the mugging was planned?"

"I think if someone wanted to send you a message, this might be the way."

"Earlier tonight, I went to a maternity store and struck up a conversation with a sales clerk," said Linda. "I didn't exactly tell her, but she assumed it."

"How long before the attack?"

"Fifteen minutes."

"Then the answer is just you, me, and Bernadette," said Foxx. "Let's keep it like that."

"I'll need to tell Hugh."

"Sure you will. Let me know when you do."

"You don't think Hugh . . ."

"I just want to keep things clean."

"Why? You're only a court officer. Sorry, that didn't come out right."

"It came out exactly right," said Foxx. "I am only a court officer. But I'm your court officer."

He could sense something in the dark. A smile, maybe, or just a nod of understanding. She said a soft "good night," then moved through the shadows to the elevator.

CHAPTER 28

The phone jarred Linda awake at exactly eight o'clock. It was the landline, which she and Hugh nicknamed the telemarketer/ robo-call line. But the caller ID readout showed Hugh's cell phone, and so Linda answered.

"What's going on?" said Hugh.

"Nothing." Her mind spinning, Linda quickly sat up and dropped her feet over the side of the bed. "Is something wrong?"

"Just that I haven't been able to get in touch with you. Left two messages last night. Called this morning and your cell phone kicked into voicemail."

"It's off, charging," said Linda, relieved that Hugh's mild fit at being thwarted meant she could get through this call without affirmatively lying. "What's up?"

"The judge has a conflict this afternoon," said Hugh. "We'll work only the morning, so I'm coming home for the weekend."

"Didn't you know this last night?"

"Not until well after we spoke," said Hugh. "The judge's law clerk called and said the judge wanted us to know."

"Why not tell you when you got to court today?"

"The other side had a witness flying in. The judge knew that. Didn't want to inconvenience anyone."

"I suppose that makes sense," said Linda.

"Don't you want me to come home?"

"Of course I do. I'd love it."

"You won't be too busy?"

"You know me, party city since you've been gone. I can still cancel the Saturday-night orgy."

"I meant the trial."

"It starts Monday," said Linda. "I have some rulings to issue, some witness problems to resolve. Normal stuff."

"Are you all right?" said Hugh.

"Do I not sound all right?"

"Actually, you sound like you could break into a coughing fit."

Linda cleared her throat. "How's that?" she said, injecting some steel into her voice.

"Better," said Hugh. "My flight gets in some time after seven. It was the only direct flight that worked."

"Great," said Linda. "I'll send the cabana boy home at six."

She never was so playful over the phone, she thought after she hung up. Must have been a form of post-traumatic stress disorder.

She went into the bathroom and studied herself in the mirror. Her face was pale, but unmarked. Her wrist felt tender, but it was not swollen or bruised, so it likely was just a sprain. But the scrapes on her knees were still bright red, and she wondered how much they would heal before tonight.

She threw on a bathrobe and went down to the kitchen, where Foxx stood barefoot at the counter. A skillet sizzled. The coffee-maker dripped. Three mugs stood in a row nearby.

"I hope you don't mind," said Foxx. He produced an egg in his hand, almost but not quite like a magician. "I like breakfast so much I usually eat two a day."

"Eggs or breakfasts?"

"Both."

"Like a hobbit."

"I wouldn't know about that," said Foxx.

"How do you like them?"

"Scrambled."

"Dry?"

"Very."

"Throw in two for me."

She watched him crack the eggs into a steel mixing bowl and whip them with a whisk. His hair was rakishly mussed, his bare arms well-muscled. She might have taken more notice if she was of a mind. She wasn't, but she had to admit that he cut a much different figure out of uniform than in one.

Foxx divided the eggs onto two plates, poured two cups of coffee, and joined Linda in the booth that served as a breakfast nook.

"Hugh is coming home tomorrow night," she said. "That was him on the phone."

"Because of what happened?"

"I didn't tell him."

Foxx squinted over the rim of his mug.

"Phone calls with Hugh are very to the point. He told me he was coming, the reason, and the time. No diversion, so it was easy not to tell him. Anyway, I'd rather it be face-to-face." She forked a clump of egg into her mouth. "And I'm going to the courthouse today. I can just as easily rest in chambers as I can here. But more importantly, in the clear light of day, I think the attack may have been a message. I don't want to give them what they want."

"Any idea who they are?" said Foxx.

"Well, there's the trial," said Linda. "Lord Leinster was attacked a few days ago in Ireland. Two people sent by investors with a stake in the treasure broke his ankles. It's why we're having the settlement discussions now. He wants out."

Foxx scraped together the last bits of egg with his fork.

"That's good to know," he said.

"Then there are the protestors," she said. "Increasing their number increases the chances one of them might do something violent. But really, I have six hundred cases in my active inventory and I've probably disposed of double that since I became a judge. That's a big pool of unhappy people, and you can't ever be sure how other people perceive you."

"How do you want people to perceive you?" said Foxx.

"As a judge who goes where the evidence and the law takes her, rather than a judge who tries to fit the evidence and the law into some preconceived result. Basically, as a good judge."

"Not as a good person?"

"Is it possible to be both?"

"Theoretically," said Foxx. "But I rarely see it."

They finished breakfast in silence. As Foxx cleared the plates and loaded them into the dishwasher, Bernadette came into the kitchen.

"I thought we were both sleeping in today," she said.

"Hugh woke me up," said Linda. "He's coming home tonight. And now that I'm up . . ."

Foxx turned away from the dishwasher, and Linda briefly but obviously locked eyes with him.

"You're going to the courthouse," said Bernadette. "Even though the doctor told you to stay home."

"He didn't say that exactly," said Linda. "He said to rest and avoid stairs."

"I was there, remember? It wasn't a suggestion. It was a prescription."

She looked back and forth between Linda and Foxx, then poured herself a cup of coffee and headed back to the elevator.

"I just thought of something," said Linda. "I took the early pregnancy test here last week, and since I didn't want Hugh to find it, I brought it to the courthouse and tossed it out in chambers."

"So, your staff knows?" said Foxx.

"No," said Linda. "Someone else."

Ivan's plan was to hide out till the weekend, and right now he was almost halfway there. He knew Pinter would send Luis after him and that Luis probably would come looking for him at the courthouse and then, when he didn't find him, stake out his apartment from the bodega across the street.

Ivan twisted slowly to ease the pressure of the support rod that dug into his kidneys. Even this slight movement shook the fold-out bed, and Jessima's breathing changed as she rose toward wakefulness and then sank back to sleep. Ivan drifted off himself. It had been a long, eventful night, the events playing out across the flimsy mattress at angles and in positions much different from those in the supply closet.

Eventually, Ivan got up to pee and when he returned Jessima was sitting up with the sheet wrapped tightly around her, from her breasts to her knees, and with her dark hair pulled back from her face. Ivan could see immediately that the sex play was over, that it was time to pay up with the explanation he had deferred from last night.

"Pinter wants me to testify at the trial," he said, answering the question that had hung in the air between them since he had followed her home from the courthouse. "He wants me to testify about things that I didn't quite see, things that I saw but was too young to understand, and things I saw and never will forget."

"What things?" said Jessima.

"About a letter and a woman and a murder."

Jessima said nothing, but moved her head in a way that demanded he continue.

"She was a neighbor with two grown sons and a third long dead. I would visit her to get away from my own house, and she treated me like her little boy. Gave me treats to eat and trinkets to play with. Let me help her cook.

"I never saw her write any letter, but I remember the day Pinter says she wrote it. I was at her house, and she was getting ready to meet her youngest son, who was being released from prison. She had an old suitcase on her kitchen table and was waiting for a neighbor to pick her up with his car. I sat with her. She looked sad, I remember thinking. And then came the sound of the car horn. She lifted the suitcase off the table and told me to go home. I always came and went by the back door. So as she left the kitchen, I only pretended to leave. Instead, I hid in a cabinet below the counter.

"The cabinet had big iron pots. The doors had thin slats that I could see through. I sat on a pot and waited for her to come back. Even then, I was a patient boy. I could sit and wait for hours, so I sat on the pot and waited for her to come home, and when she opened the cabinet door I would jump out and surprise her.

"I heard the front door open, but instead of her footsteps I heard thick boots and sharp whispers. I held my breath and slid back deeper among the pots and pans, but I could still see through the lattice. There were four men in dark clothes. They were looking for her.

"They left. Slammed the door. Drove away. I stayed in the cabinet, too scared to come out even when she returned. But she found me, and I told her about the men. We heard a car pull up outside. She pushed me back into the cabinet and told me not to make a move or a sound.

"They made quick work. One muffled her screams, another held her wrists, a third fit the noose around her neck and then threw the rope over the rafter. I could see her feet through the slats in the cabinet door. They kicked, then they swung, then they were still. One of the men crouched to pick up the knife she had dropped. He looked through the lattice, right into my eyes, but he did not see me.

"Pinter needs me to testify because his other witness is dead. If I refuse, he will bring my wife to the authorities."

"Your wife?"

"Ex-wife. Pinter arranged the marriage so I could stay in America."

Jessima laughed. "The government has more important things to do than deport someone like you. You work, pay taxes. You add value to society, not look for handouts."

"Good of you to say," said Ivan. "But it's not the government I fear. Those men from that day, they will be at the trial, too."

CHAPTER 29

Foxx shoved the ottoman under Linda's desk so she could keep her feet elevated while she worked. The outer door opened, and Karen called "hello" from the anteroom before crossing the doorway to hang up her jacket in the closet.

"I'll check back periodically," said Foxx.

"Thanks," said Linda. She pushed back from the desk, testing how far she could roll before her feet slipped off the ottoman.

"You have nothing scheduled in the courtroom, right?"

"Once I postpone the settlement conference, I won't. I'll wait for Mark to handle that."

"Good. You stay here. Lunch, too."

"I'll order in."

"And I'll tell Karen to keep the door locked at all times." Foxx read the look on Linda's face. "Don't worry. I won't tell her why."

Karen balked when Foxx told her about locking the door. They never locked the door, so she would need to remember her key when she used the ladies' room, or filed papers in the clerk's office, or collected hand deliveries at the security desk. Foxx leveled his baleful stare, and she agreed that keeping the door locked was a good idea.

Jessima's supply closet was a few paces away from Linda's chambers. Foxx glided close. He listened, then knocked. No answer. He listened again and, detecting no presence inside, headed down the corridor. Foxx knew Jessima's schedule because he observed and then cobbled his observations into a comprehensive picture of the courthouse. Jessima cycled through every chambers on the fifth and sixth floors twice each day. In the mornings, she emptied the trash. In the afternoons, she dusted and polished. Her cleaning cart always marked her location.

Foxx covered the fifth floor, then climbed up to six and covered that floor, too. Jessima's cleaning cart was nowhere in sight. Interesting? Yes. Coincidental? Maybe. Sinister? Well, someone involved in an attack on a pregnant judge might stay home from work the next day.

"That officer was here," said Karen. "The one with the eyes. Foxx. He said the captain wanted the door locked."

"Why?" said Mark.

For the second time since Mark sat down, Linda called for him from her desk.

"Her again," whispered Karen.

"I heard her the first time," Mark snapped, then shouted that he'd be a second before lowering his voice to Karen. "Does the captain think something could happen to her?"

"He didn't say," said Karen.

"Whatever," said Mark. He got up and went into Linda's office.

"I want to postpone today's conference till Monday," said Linda. "Give them all a good long time to think about settling."

"Okay," said Mark. Something about her looked different, and it took him a moment to realize that she was slouched in her chair, which made her appear smaller. "You want me to call the lawyers?"

"I want you to organize a conference call, and when you have all three on the line, send it in to me."

"I usually ask one of the lawyers to organize the call."

"I want this one organized from here."

"But . . ."

"I have my reasons," said Linda.

Mark went back to the anteroom.

"She sounds like she's in a good mood," said Karen.

"So am I," said Mark.

"No kidding," said Karen.

"What's that supposed to mean?"

Karen opened a steno pad. "Give me the numbers," she said. "I'll organize the call."

Mark read off the phone numbers, then said, "Look, Karen, I'm sorry. I'm just worried about something today."

"What?"

"I'll tell you later," he said.

It took Karen some time to organize the conference call. Billy Cokeley was en route from White Plains and needed his cell phone patched in. Arthur Braman was in the men's room. Robert Pinter's call went into voicemail, which referred to an alternate number that, luckily, he answered.

"Hold for Judge Conover," said Karen when she had all three. And then she said to Mark, "Tell her it's ready."

Mark went into Linda's office. She told him to sit and hit the speaker button.

"Thank you all and sorry for the short notice," she said. "But I'm postponing today's conference till Monday morning. Frankly, I'm not ready to rule on the pretrial motions and I believe you could use more time to consider Lord Leinster's offer."

The lawyers were silent.

"Has there been any movement on that?" said Linda.

"Robert Pinter, Your Honor. Not on my end."

"This is Bill Cokeley, Judge. The ministry of culture has settlement authority, and I have not been able to speak to the minister. But she will arrive at JFK later today."

"And you will speak to her?"

"I will," said Cokeley, "and to be candid, for whatever it's worth."

"Do your best. Mr. Braman, anything from you?"

"No, Your Honor."

"All right. Monday morning. Nine thirty. Let me know if you resolve any part of this."

Jessima eyed Foxx over the door chain, one hand clutching her bathrobe collar tight to her throat. Foxx could feel a lick of dry heat from the steam radiator, smell a mix of onions and human sleep.

"Yes?" she said.

He knew that she didn't recognize him out of context and out of uniform, so he held up his shield for her to see, then let it dangle from the lanyard around his neck. She closed the door, slipped the chain, opened up again, and turned sideways to admit him. She still held her bathrobe collar closed. Beyond her, standing beside an open sofa bed with rumpled sheets, Ivan pulled a T-shirt over a surprisingly well-muscled torso.

"Do court officers spy on absent workers?" he said. "We called in sick."

"I'm not spying," said Foxx. "I have a few questions."

"We don't want your questions," said Ivan.

"The questions are not for you." Foxx turned to Jessima. "A few minutes, and I'll be gone."

In two quick strides, Ivan inserted himself between them.

"Don't," said Foxx.

"It's all right," Jessima told Ivan.

Ivan backed off, but not very far.

"Last week," said Foxx, "Judge Conover threw away a pregnancy test stick in her chambers. Did you see it?"

Jessima looked at Ivan, then back at Foxx and nodded carefully.

"I found it in her trash basket," she said.

"What did you do with it?"

"I took it to someone."

"Who?"

"Damien Wheatley," said Jessima. "He collects information around the courthouse."

"What does he do with the information?"

"Uses it. Sells it."

"And you find him this information?"

Jessima moved to the edge of the sofa bed and slowly sat down. Ivan sat down beside her.

"Does he give you money?"

"Sometimes. But not this time. He told me he tried to sell the information, but couldn't."

"To who?" said Foxx.

"He didn't tell me."

"What does he look like?"

"He has dreadlocks," said Jessima. "Usually dresses in suits like he's a lawyer. Lately worked on the protest in the park. He found homeless people to hold signs."

Foxx climbed out of the subway station at the bottom of Foley Square to find many more protestors and much more activity than earlier that morning. Scores of protestors marched in a circle with their signs raised over their heads. Satellite trucks lined Lafayette Street for the entire length of the park. TV correspondents took up positions on the sidewalk, doing stand-ups in front of cameras.

Foxx spotted a tent with a hand-lettered sign above the entrance flap that read ADMIN. The protestors started to chant something about "good homes for good souls." Foxx couldn't make out every word, but he definitely did not hear the name *Conover.* Maybe it was too tough to rhyme.

As Foxx reached the admin tent, the flap parted and Hannigan emerged. He walked quickly, flanked by two men with the stereotypical look of storefront lawyers. Beards, ponytails, spectacles, corduroy suits. One shouted directly into Hannigan's ear as they brushed past.

"You've been discovered. This is your chance."

They headed toward a makeshift podium balanced on a bench. Hannigan climbed up, grabbed the legal pad, and tapped the microphone until the chanting stopped.

"There are two courthouses inside that building across the street," Hannigan said. "One courthouse is for the wealthy and the powerful. They send finely dressed lawyers to plead their cases in front of welcoming judges. These lawyers and judges have a silent understanding. They are all part of the same team dedicated to one goal—to preserve, protect, and defend those who hold the financial, political, and social power in this city. The other courthouse is for the poor and oppressed. In other words, for the people just like us. For us, the judges are not so welcoming. The justice they dispense is neither swift nor just.

"Sure, some crumbs may fall from the table when it means nothing to them or they want to appear compassionate or concerned in front of their liberal friends. But if you go against the system, as we are going against the system, if you try to right a wrong, as we are trying to right a wrong, or if you are trying to obtain a decent human living environment, as we are trying to obtain a decent human living environment, we see how slow and unfair justice can be.

"We are in a unique position to shine a light that exposes the two courthouses in that building. Our judge, Judge Conover, has had our case for seventeen days. That is seventeen days that we have been on the streets. I'm sure that doesn't sound like a long time to her. I'm sure she'll get to it when she gets to it. But now we have another complication. A big case has stolen her attention. It is a squabble over the ownership of an ancient Roman treasure. Do any of you own an ancient Roman treasure?"

Hannigan cupped a hand to his ear, and the crowd shouted, "No!"

"Neither do I. Do any of you care about an ancient Roman treasure?"

Again, he cupped a hand and again the crowd shouted, "No!"

"Neither do I. But we should care because on Monday, Judge Conover is starting a trial in that case. And unless she finds the time to decide our case before then, our case will be delayed even longer."

Hannigan kept speaking, but Foxx stopped listening. In his mind, it was the same orchestrated prattle spoken in public forums since the days of the Romans. Eventually, Hannigan piped down. There were some songs, some chants. And then Hannigan jumped off the bench and walked with his lawyers back to the admin tent. Foxx followed at a distance. When the lawyers departed without Hannigan, Foxx lifted the flap and ducked inside.

Hannigan looked up from a folding table where he scribbled on a legal pad. He still had the leprechaunish aspect of a prominent forehead and a red beard that Foxx remembered from high school.

"That was something else," he said. "Damn, that felt good. Are you here to help?"

"No," said Foxx. "I'm looking for Damien Wheatley."

"Don't know him," said Hannigan. He started scribbling again, his eyes narrowing in concentration and forcing Foxx from his consciousness.

Foxx slammed the table hard enough that the plastic top cracked.

"Hey, what the . . . Who the hell are you?"

Foxx whipped out his court officer shield, then stuck it back in his shirt.

"You want to try that again?"

"All right, all right," said Hannigan. "Damien helped me with the protest. He recruited people, set up the tents. But he left here two days ago, and I haven't seen him since."

"What about last week?" said Foxx. "Did he try to sell you information?"

"What kind?"

"About Judge Conover?"

"He said he had something," said Hannigan.

"Did he tell you what it was?"

"That would have been giving it to me, not selling it to me. Anyway, I refused."

"Because you're so upstanding?" said Foxx.

"No, because this isn't about Judge Conover."

Foxx grabbed Hannigan's shirt and pulled him over the table.

"This is most definitely about Judge Conover because the information he wanted to sell you was very personal."

"I told you, he didn't tell me what it was."

Foxx pushed him back onto his chair.

"The info was that she is pregnant."

"Why would I be interested in that?" said Hannigan.

"Because no one else knows she is pregnant," said Foxx. "Not even her husband. And the reason I'm interested is because she was mugged last night by someone who knew she was pregnant. Beat her down, kicked her repeatedly in the stomach."

"I wouldn't get involved in something like that," said Hannigan.

"Why? Because you're such a nice fuckin' guy?"

"No, because like I told you, I'm not after Judge Conover personally," said Hannigan. "Look, I know her track record. She clerked for one of the most conservative judges on the Manhattan bench. She'll likely dismiss my case the way her old boss would have. I expect to lose, but I'm playing a long game here. Get a decision. Appeal it to the AD, where the judges are more remote and more liberal."

"Does Wheatley understand this?" said Foxx.

"You mean, did I tell him what I just told you? No. Why should I? I paid him to find people to carry signs and chant slogans and live in tents. I didn't share my legal strategies with him. Did he attack the judge? I don't know. But if he did, it wasn't because of me. And I never would have wanted, never even hinted that something should happen to her. Scaring her off the case would just delay the whole process."

CHAPTER 30

In chambers, time moved slowly for Mark. Darius had promised to bring the motion to disqualify by order to show cause. He implied that Mr. Braman himself would present it at the conference. But then the conference was cancelled, and here it was, past two o'clock, and there was no sign of the motion to disqualify. Mark's thoughts on what this meant flipped back and forth. Arthur Braman thought the affidavit was too weak, which was good, or maybe it was bad. Arthur Braman had decided not to disqualify the judge, which was bad, or maybe it was good.

Mark read a motion while Karen wheeled a cart with two dozen signed decisions down to the clerk's office for filing. The door to the judge's office was closed, but the light on Mark's phone console showed she was on the phone and occasionally her voice rose high enough for Mark to hear. He could not make out the actual words, but he recognized the machine-gun cadence. She was peppering someone with questions, Bernadette most likely. Well, that was one thing he wouldn't miss.

Karen returned from the clerk's office and parked the cart alongside her desk. The phone rang.

"Sure," Karen said. "Someone will be right out." She hung up and turned to Mark. "Two orders to show cause at the security desk. Wasn't there something you wanted to tell me?"

Too late to confide in her now, Mark thought. His heart began to race, but he managed to fake a weary sigh.

"I'll get the orders," he said.

An order to show cause was a procedural method for bringing a motion before a judge. A lawyer drafted the order, which usually scheduled a quick court date and could grant immediate relief like the stay of a trial or the postponement of a deposition. The order was supported by affidavits, affirmations, and exhibits and then was submitted to the judge for signature. Judge Conover signed several orders to show cause each week, and Mark's role was to screen each one. The judge trusted Mark enough to sign the routine orders without reading a word of the supporting papers. But an order to show cause that asked for immediate relief needed to be handled with care. Mark usually read through the papers first and either jotted notes or attached yellow stickies to the important points. Then he discussed the issues with the judge. Sometimes she might quickly stroke her name on the signature line. Other times she might muse on her options aloud before deciding aye or nay. And occasionally, less now than at the start of her term, she would ask Mark to leave her office and then call her husband for advice.

The officer at the security desk handed Mark two folders. The folders were thin, which meant the orders were likely routine. Mark wandered slowly away from the desk and looked into the first folder. A lawyer wanted to be relieved from representing a client who had stopped paying his fee. It was a relatively common order to show cause, as routine as routine got. The other one, despite its slim feel, was anything but routine, and Mark settled on a nearby bench to read.

It was from Arthur Braman's firm and asked that the judge stay all proceedings in the Roman silver case until she determined Lord

Leinster's motion that she disqualify herself from the trial. The papers had all the production values typical of a large midtown firm. Impeccable typing, a crisp format, perfectly aligned papers that stayed open when you flipped them. Darius supplied the affirmation, which gave the legal rationale for disqualification. Beneath that was Mark's affidavit, which gave the factual basis. Mark read through it quickly; it was word for word what he remembered.

He got up from the bench and took the long way around the hexagon. There was no way he could fake this. As soon as the judge saw an order to show cause in the Roman silver case, there would be no discussion, no stickies, no verbal musing. She would take it onto her lap and read every word. And when she saw his name at the top of the affidavit . . .

Mark looked at his watch, fixing in his mind the date and time of his anticipated demise.

The long route took him past the library and, without thinking, he ducked inside. The library usually was unoccupied now that each chambers had several computers with subscriptions to legal research sites. But even devoid of the law clerks and their buzzing intellectual undertone, it maintained a tired grandeur. Heavy wooden tables with built-in bankers' lamps butted up against large, drafty windows that looked out over Foley Square. Light fixtures made of brass and marbled glass hung on thick chains from the high ceiling. Hard-bound books, rarely disturbed anymore, crammed the bookcases and exuded the comforting smell of old paper.

Mark sat at one of the tables. He pushed the two folders against the divider, planted his elbows, and covered his face with his hands. He needed just one more day. One more day would get him to the weekend. He would handle the order to show cause on Monday, when the judge would be distracted by the onset of the trial. Hopefully too distracted to focus, or too invested to give the long shot of an order to show cause a minute of her time. He could be flip about it. *Hey, Judge, get this. Lord Leinster wants you to disqualify yourself.* And the judge would summarily scratch a big X across the order to show cause and scribble "Rejected, LC" at the top.

Yes, he could see that scene clearly on the backs of his eyelids. But that would be Monday, not today.

He opened his eyes and focused on the mezzanine above the bookcases. In the old days before computers, law clerks staked out work spaces at the tiny desks on the mezzanine. Now, after carefully climbing the metal stairs that would ring with too heavy a footfall, he found the desks abandoned. He walked the length of the mezzanine, then retraced his steps to a four-shelf bookcase jammed with heavy volumes of a dusty *Decennial Digest*. The space between the bookcase and the wall was just wide enough for the order to show cause to fit.

Back in chambers, the judge's door was open and the judge herself sat working at her desk.

"There was only one," Mark told Karen, then went into the judge's office.

The judge sensed his presence and seemed to notch a thought in her head before looking up. The Redweld lay near a corner of the desk, wrapped up tight with two thick rubber bands.

"Routine order to show cause," said Mark. He flipped back the front page, and Linda scratched her initials on the signature line. She absently muttered "Thank you," then returned to her work.

"All right if I leave early?" he said.

"Fine with me," said Linda. "Big weekend plans?"

"Maybe," he said, then added, "actually, yes."

CHAPTER 31

Mark's early departure allowed Linda to work one on one with Bernadette in chambers and not bruise his fragile ego. They accomplished much in the space of two concentrated hours, not only arriving at the rulings Linda would issue on Monday, but also talking out the problems Bernadette encountered in drafting the decision on the homeless stipend case.

"Drink?" Linda said after they packed up.

"What do you have?" said Bernadette.

Linda opened the minifridge and looked inside.

"Seltzer," she said.

"Anything else?" said Bernadette.

"Flavored seltzer."

"I'll go with the straight stuff."

Linda popped open a can and divided it between two plastic cups.

"You know," she said, "Judge Johnstone and I sat together just like this on the Friday before the trial. He kept a bottle of sherry in his desk. Sorry to be such a Puritan." She lifted her plastic cup. Bernadette lifted her, and they both mumbled *salud*.

"That was the afternoon he blathered about what the trial meant to him."

"I'm not as invested as you were," said Bernadette.

"I don't plan to change my mind, if that's what you mean. Anyway, Hugh will be home, and we have a lot of ground to cover. Some good, some bad. Luckily, more good than bad."

Mark pulled to the curb and leaned on the horn of the rental car. His apartment was a fourth-floor walk-up, and it took some time for his wife to realize that the horn was meant for her and was not part of the general Lower East Side din. Finally, the curtains of the front window parted. Mark popped out and waved his arms.

"What are you doing home?" Rita yelled down after lifting the window.

"Pack your bags," he yelled back.

There wasn't much discussion. There never was much discussion when Mark came up with a plan. They just set about executing the plan, which here meant packing for a weekend away with a six-month-old.

"Mystic?" Rita asked. "What's there to do?"

"There's a seaport with old whaling ships, a great aquarium, neat places to eat."

"But why are we doing this? I mean, now."

"Because it's a nice thing to do and the kind of thing we should do."

Soon they were on the FDR Drive, fighting their way uptown in the madhouse of a weekend exodus.

"And how are we doing this?" said Rita.

They talked about money often. Money, and the lack thereof, hovered like an unwelcome guest over every discussion. They made a practice of never mentioning the guest by name. Mark couldn't say he had it covered because that would imply he had money stashed away, and the implication would lead to an argument because Rita would ask why he always seemed to have money when he wanted to spend but cried poverty whenever she complained about the things that she needed. Anyway, it wasn't true. He had no more money in his pocket than he had yesterday or last week or last month. Instead, he had quietly activated a credit card that had been buried in the back of his sock drawer for weeks, still gummed to the welcome letter announcing its promotional APR.

"I'm trading on the future," he said.

Rita slumped in her seat. She knew the code.

"No, no," said Mark. "This is a good thing. A different future."

"A new job?"

"Let's say serious headway toward a new job. I'll know soon."

They peeled off the FDR and tracked New England signs through the Bronx. Traffic was stop and go.

"Still leaf season," said Mark.

Rita stared silently out the window. Silence was a sign that she didn't believe him. He needed her to believe him, at least long enough to get through the weekend.

They were clear of the city, cruising toward the Connecticut line, when Mark's cell phone sliced off another thick slab of silence. He plucked the phone from his pocket. Darius. The sixth call since he departed chambers.

"That about the job?" said Rita.

"Nah." Mark silenced the phone and dropped it into his pocket. "Someone else."

Foxx steered Linda across Worth Street to hail a cab out of sight from the protestors. As soon as they climbed inside, Linda got on her cell phone. She ordered a nonalcoholic bottle of Champagne, a bottle each of Bordeaux and Sauvignon blanc, and an assortment of French cheeses for delivery.

At the brownstone, Foxx followed Linda under the stoop.

"You don't need to come in," she said.

"Yes, I do," he replied.

There was no further discussion. Foxx swept the entire house and then, after Linda closed herself in the bath, he took up his position at the front window. The delivery arrived, and he answered the door. By the time he stuck the Champagne and the Sauvignon blanc and the cheese in the refrigerator, he could hear the whoosh of water filling the bathtub.

Linda sank to her neck in the bathwater and watched the soap bar bob among the wavelets. She was glad now that Foxx had insisted on coming inside and glad that he planned to stay. She had not been fearful at all during the day. She worked without last night's demons barking on the periphery of her consciousness. But now that night was here, the demons slipped their leashes. At least with Foxx downstairs she could bathe without every creak sounding like a footstep and every car horn sounding like a scream.

And she needed to bathe. She needed to soothe herself, but more importantly she needed to transition from work life to home life, from judge to wife, from wife to expectant mother. Things happen for a reason, and she understood now that the identity and motive of the muggers were not that important. She had promised herself ever since her professional debacle with Judge Johnstone that she never would back down. The mugging would not scare her off the trial or stop her from defying the protestors. The court system could not function on fear or intimidation, and if the court system could not function—if society could not rely on a civilized way of resolving disputes—then society was one more step down the road to hell.

She got out of the tub and wrapped herself in a thick towel. Steam clouded the mirror, and as she stared at her blurry reflection she thought of her father. He was an even-tempered man who sought to achieve a measured joy in his life. He believed that a well-lived life was a combination of effort and luck and that, unfortunately, luck usually trumped effort. She would get mad at him, especially during her high school and college years, for the way he always seemed to focus on the dark side of a good thing. The "yes, but" she had called it. Now she realized the dark side wasn't dark. It was reality.

She wanted to be happy tonight. She wanted to welcome Hugh home and celebrate the news she now needed to share with him. The mugging had accelerated the timeline of her plans, and they needed to start rearranging the furniture of their lives. Yes, eventually, she would be able to look back and realize that she had the good marriage, the happy family, the satisfying career. Just not all at once.

McQueen dragged himself up the stairs and out through the door into the basement corridor. His hands were grimy from rooting through dozens and dozens of transfiles crammed with strips of stenographic notes. His feet were cold from splashing through puddles of water that welled up from the ancient pond under the courthouse. His tongue tasted like he had licked the chalk off a blackboard. Yet he felt good. In the schematic floor plan that he kept folded in his pocket, he'd been able to cross off several more rooms where the treasure piece definitely was not hidden. He would come back on Monday, recharged, and start all over again.

Day was done, and all but a few people were gone from the courthouse. He climbed the ramp up to the locker room, washed the grime from his hands, exchanged his uniform shirt for a pullover sweater, then took advantage of his solitude by lighting up a cigarette. He still had a long way to go. Many rooms still remained in the subbasement, and he still didn't know where Gary's whimsical notions would send him next. The roof, maybe, or the ductwork, or crawl spaces in the masonry. But for reasons he could not articulate, he felt confident. Unbelievable as it seemed, he had taken on Gary's faith as his own.

He smoked one more cigarette to replace the chalk on his tongue with the more pleasing taste of tobacco. Then he took the elevator to the main floor and allowed the night guard to unlock the front door. Across Centre Street, garlands of tiny white lights glowed festively in the tent city. He angled down the courthouse steps, aiming toward the subway entrance. On the way, he called Gary's apartment. Ursula answered.

"Hey, Urse," he said.

"Oh. Mike."

"Don't sound so happy to hear from me. Gary around?"

"Well, not exactly."

"What the hell does that mean?"

"He's around," said Ursula. "He's just kinda, I don't know, low."

"Sick?"

"Not physically."

McQueen heard a voice in the background.

"It's Mike," Ursula told Gary. Then she told McQueen to hold on.

"Hey," said Gary.

That one syllable sounded exactly the way Ursula described Gary. Low.

"You okay, Gary?"

"Been better. Just one of those days, you know? They happen."

I know, McQueen almost said. He needed to tread lightly when Gary was low. He couldn't even hint that he understood any of what Gary felt because in Gary's mind no one could.

"Just wanted to tell you," he said. "I went through four rooms in the catacombs today. Didn't find anything."

"That's supposed to be good?" said Gary.

"Not really," said McQueen. "But for some reason I came out of there feeling good. I don't know why."

"Maybe because it's Friday?"

"I don't think so. It's more of a feeling that I'm getting warmer. Like I could find this thing."

"The conservation of stupid beliefs," said Gary.

"What?"

"Einstein's theory. Matter converts to energy, energy converts back to matter. Nothing is lost, everything balances. Same with you and me. I believe the piece is there, you disbelieve it. You start to believe, I begin to doubt."

McQueen tried to summon a wise remark to bring Gary back, then thought better. He had convinced himself of some fanciful things in the past—college, a professional baseball career, the interest any number of unreachable women had in him. But there always was a saner, more rational voice in his head, and eventually that voice would break through the delusions and ask, *Am I crazy?* So it might have been with Gary.

"Sorry," he said.

"Yeah. Me, too," said Gary. "Maybe I'll feel better tomorrow."

Out of the bath, Linda dressed in denim jeans, a square-necked top, and thin slippers. She would have liked to welcome Hugh in a negligee, but since Dr. Lander told her to stay away from sex for a few days she did not want to start something she could not finish. Her physical changes seemed obvious now, as if the mugging and doctor's exam had given her body permission to let go. Her breasts felt bigger and her hips looked wider.

The second guest room, the one Foxx refused to use the night before, doubled as a computer room. After some trial and error, she created a greeting card with "Something Nice Is Happening" on the outside and the image of a bassinet and the word "Surprise!" on the inside. She slipped the card into an envelope and wrapped it with a purple ribbon, a deliberate mix of pink and powder blue.

Down in the kitchen, she set the cheese on a crystal serving plate and plunged the fake Champagne and the Sauvignon blanc into a silver bucket of ice.

Foxx watched from the doorway.

"Is this corny?" she asked.

Foxx shook his head.

"Good. Hugh and I have much to discuss, none of which he knows yet, so I want the discussion to follow a particular sequence."

"Good news first, I take it," said Foxx.

"Is that a question or an observation?"

"You tell me."

"We discussed children once a long time ago," said Linda. "Unfortunately, our discussions don't resolve into conclusions. They just lie there, like old magazines on a coffee table. Sometimes we pick them up again, sometimes we don't."

"And this?"

"We haven't. But it's not my first pregnancy, either. So I've had this discussion before. At least in my head."

"What happened?"

"A miscarriage," said Linda. "It was so early on, Hugh never knew. I never told him. Never told anyone else, not even Bernadette. That was part of the reason I haven't told him about this, even though I'm much further along already."

"Part of the reason?" said Foxx.

"The rest is superstition. It didn't work last time, obviously, but this time I can't keep it from him without keeping the mugging from him, too. That's just not possible."

Linda's cell phone rang. She held it to one ear and pressed her finger in the other.

"Yes . . . oh, you are . . . didn't expect you so early. . . . Okay . . . fine. See you in a few."

She pocketed the phone and looked at Foxx.

"That was Hugh. He's landed. Already in a limo. Just entering the tunnel. So I think you can go now."

"You don't want me to wait till he gets here?" said Foxx.

"Better not. You being here begs questions I don't want to deal with till later."

Linda followed Foxx to the front door. There was a bittersweet feel to this departure, as if once Foxx was gone she would be separated from something forever. She had no idea what that something might be, but as she watched him go down the steps, she had the odd sense that it would not have been inappropriate to kiss him good-bye.

Linda waited in the den until she heard the limo trunk slam. She yanked open the front door just as Hugh reached the stoop. She hugged him before he dropped his bags and searched out his mouth for a long kiss.

"Geez," he said, dropping his bag so he could peel her off his face, "you'd think I was away for a year."

"Don't you like a warm welcome?" she said.

"Of course I do." He hugged her lightly and kissed the top of her forehead through her hair.

"Come this way," she said, pulling him toward the kitchen.

But he closed the door, made sure the latch caught, and moved his bag against the wall.

"Let's sit a sec," he said.

They went into the front room and sat on the couch.

"Don't you want to take your coat off?" she said.

He was wearing a thin black raincoat. He stood up, slipped it off, and lay it carefully over the arm of the couch. Linda sensed something strange in him, a distance that she could not put off to fatigue, distraction, or his famously ridiculous jet lag. He sat back down, slightly farther away from her. He looked at the floor and rubbed his knees.

They both spoke at the same time.

"I . . ." they said, and then stopped as if startled.

"You start," Linda said after a moment.

"No, you start," said Hugh.

She was completely off her game. Like a rookie lawyer flustered by the first question from a hot bench, everything she planned to say went right out of her head.

"How is the trial?" she asked instead.

"Actually," said Hugh, "there is no trial."

"You mean it settled?"

"No," said Hugh. "There is no trial. Was no trial. Never has been a trial."

"Well, were you in Texas to drum up business? You were in Texas, right?"

"Oh, I was in Texas, but not to drum up business."

"Hugh, you are scaring me a little."

"Well, I'm afraid I'm going to scare you some more. I want a divorce."

"Come again?" said Linda.

"I want a divorce."

"I don't understand," said Linda.

"Do I need to draw you a picture? I went to Texas to see someone I met when I actually was on trial there last year."

"Who is she?"

"Her name is Carla Sue Cole. She was local counsel for the trial. She was—"

Linda got up. Hugh grabbed her arm, but she shook him off and rushed into the kitchen. She stood over the counter, looked at the cheese platter, the ice bucket, the wineglass and Champagne flute, the cocktail plates and the cocktail napkins, and with one swipe of her forearm, knocked it all onto the floor. The platter exploded, the plates shattered, the bucket bounced and rolled, spilling its melted ice.

Hugh ran in. He stared silently at the mess, then focused on the last remaining thing on the counter—the envelope with the purple ribbon.

"What's this?" he said.

"Nothing," said Linda, grabbing it. "Never was."

She ran down the hallway and out into the street.

CHAPTER 32

They were on a daybed on what had been a front porch of a cottage on the back end of City Island, but which was now enclosed with jalousie windows. The jalousie slats were open to let in the briny air off the Sound. Beyond the marina, lights danced on the dark water—buoys, boats, a half-waxen moon. In a month or so, Foxx would drag the daybed inside and tape plastic sheeting over the jalousies. But for now, the porch was warm. He had half-induced, half-worked Bernadette's top over her head, and at that point, Bernadette digressed. She wanted to talk about history, their history, as in their previous encounters, while Foxx tried deflection by saying that their history was removed enough in time to be irrelevant. Bernadette disagreed. She stopped him from toying with her bra strap, and there stood the state of play when a taxi screeched to a stop on the broken pavement that was Foxx's street. The taxi idled for a minute, then a door opened and slammed shut. A figure stepped gingerly through the potholes to the tilted concrete slabs that led to the front steps. The taxi accelerated backward, then swung into a turn, its headlights sweeping across its former passenger.

"Holy shit," said Bernadette.

She snatched her top and ran inside as footsteps clopped on

the wooden steps. Foxx sat up on the daybed. A hand cupped it-self to the jalousie door. A pair of eyes peered through a glass panel.

"Hello?" called a woman's voice.

Foxx got up. The woman backed away, allowing room for the door to swing open. She wore jeans and a white top too thin even for the warmish late October air.

"Hi, Judge," said Foxx.

"I didn't know where else to go."

She stepped around the door, tripping on the threshold and fall-ing forward. Foxx caught her under the arms. An envelope skit-tered across the porch floor.

Foxx lifted Linda onto the daybed. Bernadette came out onto the porch, her top tucked in, her hair smoothed back behind her ears.

"What's going on?" she said.

"Hugh." Linda belched. She leaned forward over the floor, gripped the edge of the daybed mattress, and opened her mouth as if to vomit. But she only belched again, then gulped air before she leaned back and hugged her stomach.

"He wants a divorce," she said.

She started to cry. Bernadette sat beside her, and Linda buried her face in her shoulder. Foxx backed away. He shifted his weight from leg to leg, listening to Linda sob, watching Bernadette pa-tiently stroke her hair. He noticed the envelope near the doorway into cottage. He picked it up. The flap was unsealed, the front had "Hugh" surrounded by a heart drawn with a pink marker.

"Tell me," said Bernadette.

Linda could not tell very much. She had run directly from her house to a diner on Broadway and only after withstanding a bar-rage of text messages and voicemails, none of which she read or listened to, did she sort through her narrow range of options and decide that returning home was not one of them. A call to Berna-dette's cell phone went right into voicemail, so she searched the web and found an address for someone simply listed as "Foxx" on City Island.

She finished her skimpy account and looked at Bernadette and then at Foxx. Foxx handed her the envelope.

"Clever, huh?" She forced a laugh. "My way of telling Hugh that we, I mean that I am pregnant. I don't know why I took it. Or maybe I do. There is no other way he would know."

"We think," said Foxx.

"No," said Linda. "I hate him now more than I've ever hated anyone. But he wouldn't do that."

Foxx said nothing else. There was no point in arguing the pointless. He didn't think that Hugh had been involved in the mugging, but he raised the possibility just in case. He went into the kitchen, opened a can of ginger ale, and brought it out to Linda. By then, the two ladies were sitting face-to-face, heads bowed, conversing as if they were conferring on the bench. Foxx went back inside and sat at his old aluminum table.

Bernadette came in twenty minutes later.

"She wants to spend the night here," she said.

"What about you?"

"My plan all along."

The cottage had two bedrooms, and the wall between them was paper thin. Bernadette made a grilled cheese sandwich—about all Linda said she could stomach—while Foxx found a pair of sweatpants and a T-shirt for Linda to sleep in.

Linda ate the sandwich and drank another ginger ale, then retired to the spare bedroom. Foxx imagined she might look cute in the sweatpants and T-shirt, but never saw her. Bernadette went in to visit, and the two started talking. Foxx returned to the daybed. He drank one beer, then fetched another, and then a third. He smoked a cigarette and thought about how shitty people could be to each other. Then Bernadette finally came out and supplied more evidence to substantiate his theory.

"I never liked him," she said. "But I always thought Linda was a smart lady and knew what she was doing. He was there almost a week, saying he was on trial when he actually was shacking up."

"I hate people," said Foxx. He slouched low, his head resting on the bolster pillow that lined the wall, a beer on his stomach.

"Not everyone, I hope," said Bernadette.

She lifted the beer from his hand and straddled his legs to sit on his knees.

"Persuade me," said Foxx.

She grabbed the hem of her top and reversed it over her head. Somehow, the bra that had bedeviled him earlier went along with it.

Later, naked, they shut off all the lights and got into bed. Sounds bled through the wall, though neither could tell if they heard Linda tossing on a cheap mattress or sobbing at the demise of her marriage.

"We'll need to be quiet if we have a second act," whispered Bernadette.

"Fitzgerald said there are no second acts in American life," said Foxx.

"That was a hundred years ago." Bernadette massaged his thigh with her knee. "There are nothing but second acts in American life now. Thirds and fourths, too."

"It's like I woke up blind and now I need to relearn the world around me," said Linda.

She and Bernadette sat at the flimsy kitchen table and drank coffee.

"Sure, I still have my other senses, but without my sight I don't really believe what I smell, taste, touch, and hear."

"Did you have any inkling at all?" said Bernadette.

"Consciously, no. He's a lawyer with a national practice. He has a trial in Texas. He prepares for it, or gives a damn good show of preparing for it. So no, I had no conscious inkling. But subconscious? Maybe I've known it all along, but it surfaced as my personal dissatisfaction."

"With being a judge?" said Bernadette.

"Among other things." Linda sipped coffee, then pushed the mug away. "I was thinking last night, before Hugh got home, that there were three aspects of my life I needed to prioritize. Now it's only two."

"Have you thought about who you'll retain?" said Bernadette.

"I don't know any lawyers in the matrimonial bar. What I want to do is put this all off until after the trial."

"You can't sweep this under the rug. A trial is a trial. Your divorce will have long-range implications for your life."

"If it comes to that," said Linda. "Until I get served with papers, there is nothing to do. I'll have twenty days to hire an attorney and serve an answer. The trial could be finished before that."

"This is not the time to start cutting things too fine," said Bernadette. "You need to establish interim living arrangements. You ran out in a panic last night, but maybe he should be the one to move out and leave you in possession of the house. Maybe he wants that."

"I'm sorry I imposed on your night with Foxx."

"You didn't impose."

"I had no idea. Well, maybe a little. When did this start?"

"It didn't start," said Bernadette. "It's an old story that restarted. And this is not what I want to be talking about."

"Then what is?" said Linda.

The jalousie door creaked, and Foxx stood in the kitchen doorway, dark against the bright morning sun. He dropped a bag of bagels on the counter, poured himself a cup of coffee, and took it onto the porch. Perfect silence settled in the kitchen. Foxx looked out over the water. It took a moment, as always, for the shell of the old prison to spin into focus. But once it did, that was all his eyes could see.

A chair scraped in the kitchen, and a moment later an arm slid around him. Bernadette. Foxx blinked, and the prison receded into the background.

CHAPTER 33

Across the street was code for the firm apartment, which actually was two blocks away in a high-rise condominium. Occupancy was short-term, a courtesy and convenience for out-of-town clients or trial witnesses. This time it was both.

The firm driver had picked up the present occupants late the previous afternoon at JFK, where they arrived on a flight from Zagreb. According to the driver, neither the flinty old man nor the elegantly beautiful woman had said a word on the long slow drive from the airport. Not to him, not to each other. Nor did the old man want to see anyone, particularly his lawyer. He was too tired from the flight.

Billy Cokeley left his office with a file, a legal pad, and the transcript of Anton Fleiss's deposition from almost four years ago. He also carried a bag of hot chestnuts, which Natalija Radic, the minister of culture, had whispered over the phone last night would be a nice gesture.

Natalija opened the apartment door. She kissed Cokeley on each cheek, then led him into the living room. Orkan Stjepanovic sat at the table in the dining area and stared out the window. He wore a bathrobe, pajamas, slippers. He said nothing when Natalija introduced Cokeley as "our lawyer," just slowly turned his head to meet Cokeley's eyes and then just as slowly turned away again. He had a thin face, a hooked nose, wiry white hair tight to his skull, and tiny blue eyes. *Flinty* was an accurate description. He never knew his driver had such a way with words.

Natalija opened the brown paper bag and placed the chestnuts in front of Stjepanovic. Stjepanovic took one in his mouth, chewed, and then swallowed. His stern expression did not change. Cokeley caught Natalija's eye, and she lifted her brow as if to say *go ahead.*

Cokeley cleared his throat.

"Mr. Stjepanovic," he said.

Stjepanovic did not react. It was as if he had not heard, so Cokeley repeated himself louder. Still, no reaction.

"He prefers to be called *Pukovnik,*" said Natalija. "Colonel."

"I'm sorry," said Cokeley. He leaned toward Stjepanovic, his hands folded on the thick deposition transcript. "*Pukovnik* Stjepanovic, I appreciate you traveling such a distance to give your testimony. Let me explain what will happen."

Natalija translated. Stjepanovic waved his hand, annoyed.

"Stop," Natalija told Cokeley.

She traded words with Stjepanovic, and then Stjepanovic rose unsteadily and shuffled around the corner and down the hallway.

"He gets cranky when his bladder fills," said the Natalija. "I told him to pee. And now I'm going to tell you what you need to know. Colonel Stjepanovic is not Anton Fleiss. He was stationed along the Hungarian border. He and his men often crossed into Hungary. They socialized in Hungary, they had friends in Hungary, and they had financial interests in Hungary that they sometimes needed to protect. You will go into none of that."

"I won't be the only lawyer to question him," said Cokeley.

"The colonel can handle himself quite well," said Natalija. "His bladder is the problem, not his brain or his tongue or his forbidding personality."

Stjepanovic shuffled back into the dining area and sat down. He seemed to Cokeley to be in a marginally better mood, at least until his bladder filled again.

Cokeley patted the transcript.

"This is what Anton Fleiss said," he explained. "Right now, we need to go over your testimony. I will ask you the questions asked of Anton Fleiss. I expect your answers will be the same."

They covered all the same ground: Marshal Tito's summer retreat at Pula, the excavation for a swimming pool, the spades hitting the lid of a large bronze cauldron, the fourteen pieces of silver inside. Cokeley did not probe, did not try to shake any of the colonel's unswerving answers. That was a job for Pinter and Braman. And from the harsh glare in the colonel's eyes and the haughty turn to the colonel's mouth, good luck with that.

The call started while Linda was in the bedroom, and now she was pacing the kitchen. Bernadette had gone to a family function that started in the afternoon and would last long into the night and did not include Foxx. Foxx himself sat on the porch.

"I don't want to fight," said Hugh. "We're sensible people. We're lawyers. We should be able to work things out and get all this behind us so we can move on."

All this? thought Linda. What was all this? What part of all this was her fault?

"What are your plans?" he said.

"My plans? You think I went to bed last night and woke up with a plan?"

"You could start by telling me where you are."

"None of your business," she said. "A friend's house."

"Bernadette's, right?"

"Wrong."

"We need to talk. You rushed out last night before I could explain."

"You explained everything clearly enough."

"We still need to meet," said Hugh. "While we have the time."

"Right. We'll meet and talk. Because we're sensible lawyers. Because we can work things out and get it all behind us and move on. I hear you, Hugh. I hear the code behind your words. You want to talk so you can get what you want and how you want it."

"That's not true."

"Isn't it? I don't see the rush, and you're not going to stampede me."

"The rush is that I'm not going to be here," said Hugh. "I took a leave of absence from the firm. I have a flight back to Texas at noon tomorrow."

"Oh," said Linda. The swiftness of this change in the landscape dumbfounded her.

"And in the meantime, you can stay in the house while I'm gone, of course without prejudice to a later determination of possession and ownership."

"You know what, Hugh? You're an asshole." She cut the connection and tossed the phone onto the kitchen table and stormed out to the porch. Foxx shoved over to one side of the daybed and patted the bolster pillow. Linda sat down, but did not sit back.

"You can tell me to shut up," said Foxx, "but I'll say it anyway. He is an asshole."

"You expect an argument from me?" Linda sat back now and tried to pick out whatever Foxx found so engrossing on the water. "What's out there?"

"See that island with the brick building?"

Linda squinted. "I do now."

"That's Hart Island and the brick building was the Reformatory Prison. My father ran the mess hall there. A launch would come to that dock to pick him up in the morning, then bring him back at night. Every day, all weather."

"That was a different sort of commute," said Linda.

"Yeah, it was." Foxx looked at her. "So?"

"He said he's leaving tomorrow. Going back to Texas. I don't know for how long, but I know I don't want to see him. Can I stay the night? I understand without Bernadette here you might feel uncomfortable."

"Why would I?"

"Right," said Linda. "Why would you."

McQueen found Larkin in a bar on Columbus Avenue a few blocks south of a renovation project Larkin managed as a general contractor. Larkin had big shoulders and a big gut that expanded into a surface where he could rest his big arms when he sat on a barstool. His red hair, pulled back into a ponytail, was white with dust. It was late afternoon. The sunlight was on the wane, and so was Larkin's sobriety. McQueen tapped his shoulder, reminded him of the appointment they had arranged to eyeball Gary Martin's kitchen.

"Right, lad," Larkin said, addressing McQueen's reflection in the mirror behind the bar before pushing his pint glass toward the bartender.

The bartender refilled the glass, and Larkin knocked it off in two pulls. The scene repeated itself three more times before Larkin pushed himself off the stool.

Outside, McQueen turned in the direction of Gary's apartment.

"For fook's sake," said Larkin. "Where's the fire?"

"We're an hour late," said McQueen.

"You are, I'm not," said Larkin. "Your friend's misfortune is not my occasion for charity."

McQueen walked on, keeping two paces ahead of Larkin as if to drag him along by gravitational pull. Larkin grunted and complained, then grunted some more. Twice he veered off into alleys, once to pee, the other to take a snort from a little brown bottle in his pocket. He came out jangled after that stop, but complained less. They arrived in front of Gary's building. Larkin looked it up and down, then wandered off while McQueen rang up. Ursula answered.

"I'm here with Larkin to look at the kitchen," said McQueen.

"This isn't a good time," said Ursula.

"It's never a good time to renovate. But it's worth it."

"I'm talking about right now. This minute. It's not a good time."

"Let me talk to Gary," said McQueen.

"Mike . . ."

"Jesus, Urse, I got this guy here. Let me talk to him."

"Fine," said Ursula. "Gary, Mike's outside with a contractor. They want to look at the kitchen."

"Not now," Gary said in the background.

"Hear that?" said Ursula. "Now is not a good time, just like I said."

"Yeah, thanks a lot." McQueen turned to explain to Larkin, but Larkin was gone.

Foxx gave Linda a fresh pair of sweatpants and a fresh T-shirt, then ran a load of wash that included the clothes Linda wore when she fled her house. With the clothes in the dryer, Foxx walked to the boulevard and then down to Artie's. He smoked a cigarette on the way. Somehow he'd gotten in four so far.

Foxx ordered take-out shrimp fra diavolo over linguine and fillet of sole with potato croquettes. A couple of the old-timers were at the bar, clerks who had retired from 60 Centre and moved out of Manhattan to City Island because New England was too far away.

"Got a hot one back at your place?" said one of them.

"Just hungry," said Foxx.

They jawed while he waited, offered him a shot of Jameson, which he took, then accepted a second round, which Foxx stood. Foxx walked the boulevard with the take-out swinging in a white plastic bag. He made sure no one was following him, then turned up toward the back end of the island and home.

Linda sat at the kitchen table. She had commandeered his bathrobe and made herself a cup of tea.

"You have an interesting library," she said, holding up a Dover edition of Yeats's poetry.

Foxx dealt out two plates and assorted silverware. They ate in lengths of silence punctuated by short bursts of small talk until the wall phone rang and Foxx reached up to take it down.

It was Bernadette with music playing in the background. They exchanged pleasantries, then Foxx handed the phone over to Linda, who reported on her conversation with Hugh, listened to some advice, then handed the phone back to Foxx.

"He's a self-absorbed ass," said Bernadette.

"I'm trying to eat," said Foxx. "Artie's take-out."

"Enjoy. I'm going to be stuck here pretty late."

"I'm turning in early."

Foxx cleaned up while Linda browsed his bookcase. He closed the jalousies and locked both the outer door and the inner door, something he never did but thought was prudent under the circumstances. He told Linda what lights to leave on and what lights to turn off, then went to bed.

He fell asleep until a creaking sound woke him from a vague dream. The shades of the back window were up, showing that clouds had rolled in and turned the sky a fuzzy orange. A latch clicked, and his door opened wide enough to show a dark shadow against gray light. The door closed and the latch clicked. Gradually, the image reversed, the shadow now gray against the darker wall.

"You awake?" she whispered.

"I am now."

"Can't sleep."

"Bad night or bad food?"

"Night," she said. "Mind if I stay in here?"

He slid over to make room. She sat with her back to him. Then she lifted her legs and stretched out on top of the covers. Foxx said nothing. He thought back to McQueen's remarks on the morning of that day, and later, his first sight of her when he interrupted her argument with Judge Johnstone. The curly hair, the straight back, the nice legs. He could feel the damp air seeping into the cottage as it always did at night. She'd get cold soon. She would resist at first, hug herself, draw up her legs, pull her hands back into her sleeves. But eventually she would lift the covers and crawl underneath with him.

CHAPTER 34

Foxx returned Linda to the brownstone late Sunday afternoon. Though Linda had fled in a panic on Friday night, she remembered to grab a set of keys from the hook inside the front door. Such presence of mind told Foxx that she was more grounded than she was letting on. Inside, they swept the house together, Foxx to make sure the doors were locked and no one was lurking, Linda to see what Hugh might have taken. Not much, she concluded, except for two large suitcases and a lot of warm-weather clothes.

Hugh had not touched the mess in the kitchen. Linda could imagine him stepping around the shattered crystal, the puddle of water, and the runny cheese while sipping coffee and talking to his new girlfriend on the phone. He might even have snapped a picture and sent it with a cover email, saying, "See? See what she did?"

But now the puddles had evaporated and the cheese stank. Bernadette arrived, and the three began to clean up. As they unstuck the last remnants of cheese and swept up the last shards of crystal, the phone rang. Linda answered, and a grim expression immediately crossed her face. Foxx and Bernadette locked eyes briefly, each reading the other's mind that the caller was Hugh.

"Yes . . ." Linda said, then ". . . yes . . . yes . . ."

She went silent, looking down and rubbing her thumbnail.

"That's ridiculous," she eventually said. "You're the administrative judge. You run the courthouse. This is your decision."

Bernadette exhaled, relieved that the caller was not Hugh, but Foxx listened hard. He could hear Judge Belcher's tiny voice leaking around Linda's ear. No words, just cadence. She was selling something.

"Fine," said Linda. "No, I'm not okay with this, but what do you want me to say? Okay. Tomorrow. Good night."

She killed the connection and slammed the phone onto its cradle.

"Judge Belcher," she said. "Called to inform me that those protestors plan to march into my courtroom tomorrow."

"You're kidding," said Bernadette. "Why?"

"Well, apparently this rabble rouser Hannigan who put the whole thing together has been making speeches about there being two court systems, one for the rich and one for the poor. The press picked up on this, not the tabloid press, but the *New York Times* and the *Wall Street Journal*, and now this Hannigan wants to bring these two court systems together in my courtroom because I'm going forward with the Roman silver trial while I delay my decision in the homeless stipend case."

"I'm sorry," said Bernadette. "I should have gotten it done."

"It's not you," said Linda. "They still would be outside protesting even if I issued a decision last week."

"Is there a plan?" said Foxx.

"Oh yeah. Sure. Extra court officers. You'll have a lot of company tomorrow."

Andreas sat at Matyas's bedside and waited another eternity for his brother to draw his next breath. His cell phone rang. He took it out of his pocket, saw that it was Luis calling, and answered. There was no reason to remove himself from Matyas anymore.

"Tomorrow," said Luis. "Most of the morning and into the afternoon."

"Thank you. I will talk to Ivan."

"Good luck. I've been trying to serve him with a subpoena. He must be hiding."

"I will talk to him," said Andreas.

He ended the call and turned back to his brother. Matyas's breathing caught, then resumed as someone knocked on the apartment door.

The nurse did not look like a nurse, at least not to Andreas's expectations. She wore a leather jacket, jeans, and boots. Her hair was long and teased, thick as a handful of straw.

"Sorry," she said, shedding her jacket. "One of my other patients . . . I needed to wait around. Where is he?"

Andreas pointed down the hallway to the wedge of light spilling out from the bedroom. He watched from the doorway as she examined Matyas.

"His breaths," he said. "They stop for long time."

The nurse nodded, slid the bell of her stethoscope to another part of Matyas's chest. His ribs were visible beneath his skin. The nurse read his blood pressure and took his pulse. Andreas noticed that she did not smile or frown but just went about her business. When she was done, she took Andreas into the hallway.

"He is now actively dying," she said. "His blood pressure is low. His pulse is slow. His breathing is shallow. Sometimes it stops, like it hits a snag."

"What means 'a snag'?" said Andreas.

"It gets caught. Stuck." She hooked one hand around the other. "But then it starts again."

"How long?"

"Could be days, a week. I can't predict." She rooted around in her backpack and pulled out a plastic bag holding thin syringes filled with yellow liquid. "This is morphine. Keep it in the refrigerator. It helps with the pain."

"He has no pain," said Andreas.

"It also helps him to breathe. His breaths won't snag. But"—she paused—"this is the final descent. Once you start with this, he is not coming back. Has he been talking to you?"

"Some yesterday. A little today."

"That usually ends when you start with this. Not always, but usually. He may be able to hear you. But if you want to have a back and forth, better have it before you start with this."

She showed Andreas how to administer the morphine, told him to keep the empty syringes, warned that when it was over all twenty-four needed to be accounted for. She wished him luck and she wished him well, told him she understood, though he doubted that she did. She gave him a magnetized card with the hospice phone number. She told him to call if anything changed, otherwise she would return in two days.

Andreas let her out the door, then returned to the bedside chair. Matyas's eyelids fluttered, his breathing sounded smooth.

"My brother," said Andreas. "Can you hear me?"

"Yes," said Matyas. His eyelids opened fully for a moment, then closed. His breath hit another snag.

Andreas could not waste any more time. He told his brother exactly what he planned to do. He told him that it was all they were left with. Matyas's breath snagged again, and this time Andreas shook him.

"You understand?" he said.

Matyas made a tiny sound.

"I have your blessing?"

Again, a tiny sound.

Andreas felt his face tighten. He blinked against the tears that filled his eyes. He pushed the first syringe between his brother's lips. He waited a full minute, listening as Matyas breathed smoothly. Then he pushed a second syringe.

Andreas pushed eight in all, deciding without any reason that eight would be enough. He dropped the empties back into the plastic bag and wedged the bag in the crook of Matyas's elbow.

After his brother's last breath, Andreas picked up his duffel bag and left the apartment. He did not lock the door behind him.

CHAPTER 35

The nebulous confidence McQueen had felt exiting the subbasement on Friday afternoon suddenly coalesced into words as he shaved his neck on Monday morning. Ivan had possession of the urn, which meant that Ivan had been involved in the heist. And if Ivan was involved in the heist, why shouldn't he go to the police, the IG, even the captain with his suspicions? Because he really didn't know; he only felt. And though sometimes what you felt was more true than what you knew, he wasn't one hundred percent convinced what he felt was true. Besides, Ivan having the piece didn't mean he was directly involved in the heist. The security tapes showed that the two gunmen, neither of whom resembled Ivan, had fled the courthouse and left the piece behind. Maybe Ivan was holding it for them, or maybe they were gone forever and Ivan had stumbled upon it. The police had investigated, the IG had investigated, everyone in the building had been treated like suspects. If the police and the IG both had passed over Ivan, why shouldn't he?

Because he felt it.

And though McQueen's feelings were not proof beyond a reasonable doubt, they were strong enough that the razor blade slipped and a line of blood oozed pink beneath a thin layer of shave cream.

McQueen never cut himself shaving. The cut only proved his theory to be correct. He knew exactly where he would find the missing piece.

Ivan was in his supply closet when the call came.

"I'm in the park," said Andreas.

Ivan immediately took the A stairwell all the way down to the basement and headed toward the back door. Unlike the front entrance, which was well known from TV and movies, the back entrance was used mainly by deliverymen, the handicapped, and employees returning from lunch in Chinatown. The security post was a backwater, consisting of a single magnetometer and three court officers. Going out the back was a longer route to the park, but Ivan worried that Luis might be waiting out front with a subpoena in his pocket. As he passed the magnetometer, a poster board showing the head shots of two men caught his eye. The shots had the grainy look of security camera images, but the resolution was clear enough that Ivan recognized Andreas and Matyas. Hand-lettered at the top was a single word: WANTED.

Outside, Ivan turned up his collar and crossed Worth Street to give the courthouse the widest possible berth. He reached the corner of Centre Street and spotted Andreas pacing behind a bench with a duffel bag hanging from his shoulder.

"What took you so long?" said Andreas. He dropped the duffel bag at Ivan's feet.

"What's this?"

"My tools. I have a small piece of business to attend to," said Andreas. "It's none of yours."

"You won't be able to get into the courthouse," said Ivan.

"Why not?"

"There are pictures of you at every entrance."

"What pictures?"

"You and Matyas. They are from security cameras three years ago."

"I am much more handsome now," said Andreas.

Three years ago, Andreas had long, unruly black hair shot through with strands of gray. Now it was cut so short that the scars above his hairline showed like craters on the moon. Ivan had heard of boxers who led with their chins. Andreas led with his forehead.

"You take this inside and don't worry about me."

"What about the urn?" said Ivan.

"The man you need to talk to is Robert Pinter."

"Why do I need to talk to him? I thought Matyas would handle everything."

"Matyas is dead," said Andreas. "The piece is yours."

"What about you?"

"You, me. What does it matter in the end?"

"But he's a lawyer."

"He's not just a lawyer. He has the connections to broker a deal with anyone, no matter who wins the trial. For a fee."

"But he wants me to testify about the letter your mother wrote."

"Oh." Andreas looked into the distance, thinking. "So testify. Maybe then Hungary will win. That will make your conversation with Pinter more pleasant."

McQueen usually rushed down to his courtroom after signing in at the fifth-floor security desk. Out of sight, out of mind was his theory. If the captain didn't see him, he wouldn't reassign him to a post where he actually would need to work. But this morning, McQueen lingered. He could see the banker's lamp burning like a bright oblong through the frosted glass of the captain's door. Diagonally to the right, the door to the operations office was fastened back. The office was empty, so McQueen slipped in and grabbed the key to the plenum.

McQueen quickly walked past the security desk to the inner circular corridor. An elevator dinged, and he held his breath as the door opened on a messenger with a hand delivery destined for one of the chambers. McQueen ducked into the A stairwell. He took the stairs silently, landing on the balls of his feet and pressing his hand against his belt to prevent his equipment from jingling. He stopped at the fourth floor and listened carefully. Not a footstep above or below. Then he eased down to the 3M level, unlocked the door to the plenum, and closed himself inside. He flipped the light switch and saw the dim bulbs curve into the darkness. The air smelled less musty, the layers of dust didn't look as thick. But the difference was only in his perception. Last time, he was here on Gary's orders; now, he was here on his own conviction.

He swept the flashlight from side to side as he swung over and bent under the ducts. Occasionally, he opened the drawer of an old desk or lifted the seat of an old chair. But that was just habit. Because he knew where he would find the piece. He felt exactly where it would be.

The plenum turned, and he hit another light switch. Halfway along the next arc was the empty wall where he had kicked aside the pile of broken chair legs and found the rat. He could see that the legs had been gathered together and leaned upright against the wall in a neat conical pattern. A tingle crawled down his spine, then broke into an involuntary shiver. But this wasn't a shiver of fear. It was a shiver of anticipation. He played the flashlight beam and could see something round and dull gray through the gaps in the chair legs. He measured the length of the legs against his memory of the urn. They were long enough to hide the urn inside.

He stepped close and toed at one of the legs. It moved easily, so he worked his toe behind it and flicked his foot. The chair legs tumbled like bowling pins.

The urn stood against the wall. It was the size and shape he remembered, the long narrow neck, the tonguelike spout, the spherical bottom. But it was dull gray rather than a shiny silver. The figures were blurry rather than cut in sharp relief. And it stood not on the flanged base that he remembered but on a bed of fur.

McQueen lifted the urn. The base peeled away from the fur, which slowly wriggled, then stretched, then rose. It was the rat.

The rat reared on its hind legs. It hissed. It scratched the air. McQueen reacted with a swift kick. His toe caught the rat squarely under the front legs, lifting it off the floor and dashing it against the wall.

CHAPTER 36

McQueen spun the padlock and pressed his forehead against the cold metal of his locker door. Holy fuckin' shit, he said to himself, I just locked a five-million-dollar piece of silver in my locker. He needed to call Gary ASAP.

The locker room door opened, and footsteps and a gust of voices swept in. McQueen pushed himself off his locker. Four, five, eight court officers filed in and formed a semicircle in the area behind him. Captain Kearney followed, dragging two plump green garbage bags.

"Join us, Michael," he said, "this involves you, as well."

McQueen inserted himself into the semicircle, peeking between a couple of taller heads. Kearney rarely descended to the locker room, where his brown suit and priestly manner were at odds with the blue uniforms and crass language. He shoved his hands into his pockets and rocked on the balls of his feet. On either side of him, the garbage bags slowly settled with the pull of gravity.

"Today, this morning," he said, "the protestors from the park will march into the courthouse and into Judge Conover's courtroom. They have the permission of the administrative judge and they are to behave in accordance with an agreement worked out with their lawyers. They will enter the courtroom and sit in the gallery. They will not speak or disrupt the proceedings in any way.

"Though we expect a peaceful and silent demonstration, it is still incumbent upon us to provide security in a way that we can quickly react should the need arise. These bags contain clothes from the St. James Mission. You are to dress in these clothes. After you dress in these clothes, you are to infiltrate the protest in the park. Leave by the rear entrance and walk to the park via Worth Street. Walk singly, not even in pairs. Do not acknowledge each other, but be aware of where you all are. The march will begin in an organized fashion on the other side of Centre. Fold yourselves in among the protestors. Keep your spacing. All the protestors, as well as yourselves, will go through the mags. In the courtroom, there will be a crew of three officers. They will know who you are and that you will be randomly dispersed among the crowd. They might seek you out with their eyes, but don't acknowledge them in any way. Any questions?"

No one said a word.

"One more thing," continued Kearney. "The trial in front of Judge Conover is the same trial where our own Gary Martin was shot. Keep that in mind."

Foxx called the courtroom to order, then drifted to a spot in the well where he could face the judge and still eyeball the lawyers in quarter view.

Linda switched on her banker's lamp.

"Is there anything before I rule on the pretrial motions?" she said.

"There is, Your Honor." Arthur Braman stood. "My firm submitted an order to show cause on Friday. We have not heard whether it's been signed."

"An order to show cause in this case?" said Linda. "On Friday?"

"That's correct," said Braman.

"I signed one order to show cause on Friday afternoon. But not in this case. I would have noticed that. What time did you submit it?"

"Early afternoon, I'm told," said Braman.

"Where?"

"Through the proper channels," said Braman. Proper channels meant that the order would be screened by a back office clerk, then sent to chambers for the judge to sign.

Linda leaned back and caught the eye of her court clerk. The clerk immediately tapped his computer keyboard, then climbed the bench.

"Computer shows the order to show cause was submitted Friday at two thirty-five," he said.

"Excuse me," Linda told the lawyers.

She went into the robing room and called chambers. Mark answered.

"Do you know anything about an order to show cause in the Roman silver case? Computer shows it came in at two thirty-five Friday."

"I'll look around," Mark.

"Do," said Linda.

She went back to the bench.

"The order never reached chambers," she said. "We are looking for it, and when we find it I'll consider it. Meanwhile, I will issue the rulings."

"But, Your Honor," said Braman, "you must consider the order to show cause before you issue your rulings. Otherwise the order is moot."

Linda gazed down severely at Braman.

"Explain," she said.

"The order asks that you disqualify yourself."

"On what ground?" said Linda.

"I prefer to have the papers speak for themselves."

"Do you have copies?"

"My associate handled the matter. He's been waiting on a call from chambers since Friday. He's en route now."

"Mr. Braman, you are here, I am here, opposing counsel are here. What are your grounds for my disqualification?"

"That you have prejudged the case," said Braman. "And that you are in possession of inadmissible evidence."

"I have prejudged the case?" said Linda. "Because I was the law clerk to the judge who had it the first time? And what if he were still on the bench? Would you have made the same motion to disqualify him?"

"I would need to examine the circumstances," said Braman.

"Right," said Linda. "And what is the nature of my inadmissible evidence?"

"This is why you need to see the order itself. The supporting papers amply justify disqualification."

"Mr. Braman, you didn't bring copies, so you are unprepared. Your associate is on the way, but he is not here. We will continue to look for the original. In the meantime, the trial will start."

"But, Your Honor, the order asks for a stay of the trial pending your decision on disqualification."

Both Pinter and Cokeley shot to their feet.

"Easy, counsel." Linda waved her hand, telling them to sit down. "Mr. Braman, I can't imagine your papers setting forth any valid reason for disqualification, let alone a stay of the trial. Nice try, but we are moving on."

"I object," said Braman.

"No kidding," said Linda.

Braman sat down.

"Now for my rulings on the pretrial issues," said Linda. "First, Croatia is permitted to present the evidence of the new witness, Colonel Orkan Stjepanovic, in place of the testimony of Anton

Fleiss without the need for a pretrial deposition. Since Colonel Stjepanovic was with Anton Fleiss during the alleged unearthing of the treasure, his testimony will be substantially the same.

"Second, Hungary may present art historical evidence and chemical soil analyses without any eyewitness testimony. However, the letter Hungary intends to present requires qualifying testimony from an eyewitness, and for that I don't see how it can be admitted now that Grotzky is dead."

"I have a subpoena out for another witness," said Pinter. "A custodian who works in this building. I met him many years ago and filed his resident alien application, but have seen little of him since."

"Can I say I am somewhat suspicious of this witness," said Braman. "We should at least get a chance to examine him before he takes the stand."

"He's not under my control," said Pinter, "and my process server has not been able to serve him."

"Can't he serve him here?" said Linda.

"He seems to be in the wind," said Pinter.

"What will he testify to?" said Cokeley.

"He was a neighbor of the Szabo family," said Pinter. "He was much younger than the two younger sons, but would spend time with the mother. I believe he was in the house the day she died. I believe he saw her writing the letter. I also believe he witnessed her murder by a group of former Yugoslav soldiers led by Colonel Stjepanovic."

"That's absurd," said Cokeley.

"And how do you know this?" said Linda.

"A story he told me many years ago," said Pinter. "The story made no sense to me at the time. Now, with what I've learned since, it does."

"He must have been very young," said Linda.

"He was," said Pinter. "But sometimes the most accurate memories are the ones from childhood."

"And sometimes they are completely false," said Cokeley.

"The weight of the evidence would be for the jury to decide," said Pinter.

The door of the courtroom opened, and Ivan walked in holding a piece of paper. He stopped at the rail. Linda caught Foxx's eye and lifted her chin. Foxx took the paper from Ivan and brought it to the bench.

"The subpoena has been served," said Linda. She looked at Ivan. "Mr. Zoltar, you know this means you are to testify in this trial. The subpoena cannot be ignored."

"I know," said Ivan.

"In addition to that, I am going to direct that all the lawyers question you before you come to court," said Linda. "This way, they will hear your testimony beforehand. Do you understand?"

"I do," said Ivan.

"Good." Linda handed the subpoena to Foxx, who walked Ivan out of the courtroom.

"Anything else?" said Linda.

"I want to say on the record that I take exception to all of your rulings," said Braman.

"Of course, Mr. Braman," said Linda. "I would expect no less."

CHAPTER 37

McQueen, being McQueen, took his damn time walking from the locker room to the park. He was the last of the eight officers to head out, and by the time he crossed Worth Street the seventh officer was fifty yards ahead of him, shambling along in striped pirate pants and a knockoff Brooklyn Nets jersey. The getup McQueen had grabbed from the plastic bag included oversized jeans held up by a rope, a stiff wool poncho that reeked of mildew, and a mismatched pair of high-top sneakers. He worked his hand under the poncho and pulled out his cell phone. There was no guarantee Gary would answer, not the way he sounded when last they'd spoken. But four rings in, Gary picked up. His "hello" didn't exactly sound sprightly, but it was a definite improvement.

"Hey, it's Mike. Guess what I'm doing? Heading to Thomas Paine Park dressed like a bum."

"Really?" said Gary. "And why am I interested?"

"Because I'm going undercover with a bunch of protestors marching into Judge Conover's courtroom."

"During the trial?" said Gary.

"You got that right."

"Who's protesting what?"

"Bunch of homeless. They have a case before her. They think

she should have decided their case before starting this one. Obviously, they don't know how the courthouse works."

"And what the hell are you going to do?"

"Keep the peace. Make sure nothing happens. There are eight of us, plus three in the courtroom."

"Have fun," said Gary.

"There is something else," said McQueen. "I found it."

"Say again."

"I found it."

"Found what?"

"What are you? On drugs? I found the urn, the missing piece, whatever the hell you call it."

"Mike, don't start playing games with me."

"I'm not. I found the fucker."

"Where?"

"In the plenum," said McQueen. "Remember when I told you I thought Ivan was involved? I took a gamble on that. I figured if he's hiding the piece and he knows I'm looking for it, he might move it somewhere he knows I already looked. Turned out I was right."

"Jesus, Mike, you really have it?" Gary sounded fully alive now.

"I do, Gary. We're gonna be rich. We're gonna be fuckin' rich."

"Not so fast, Mike. Get a hold of yourself. Where is it now?"

"In my locker."

"Mike . . ."

"Nobody saw me. I wrapped it in a plastic bag and got it into my locker without anyone seeing me. And it doesn't look like it looked in the courtroom or on the internet. Ivan must have covered it with wax. But I chipped some away, and it's silver underneath."

"This is good. This is great." Gary spoke slowly, as if mulling many thoughts at once. "You need to bring it to me tonight. Not too early. Wait till after dark. I gotta be sure it's just you and me."

KEVIN EGAN

"You just name the time, Gary, and I'm there."

"Eight. I'll call if I want you earlier. And make sure you carry your gun. I don't want anything happening to you on the way up."

"You got it, Gary. We're gonna be fuckin' rich."

"We're at first base, Mike. We still need a hit or two to get us home."

"We'll get those hits, Gary. I know we will."

"Eight o'clock," said Gary. "Not a minute earlier unless I call."

After a brief recess, Linda went back on the bench as the courtroom clock jumped to 10:45. The lawyers sat at counsels' table with Billy Cokeley closest to the jury box and the attorney for the auction house the farthest away. Pinter, Braman, and Darius took up the middle. There were no spectators in the gallery, no Lord Leinster minding Braman's every word and every move, and no treasure piece on display.

An officer slipped in through the jury entrance, holding the door so that it closed without a sound. He nodded to the judge, meaning that the last of the jurors had arrived. At the back of the courtroom, Foxx pushed open one of the double doors and spoke to the officer in the corridor. He came back in and shook his head, meaning that there was no sign of the protestors.

"I'm told the jury is here and the protestors aren't," Linda announced. "Therefore, unless there are any preliminary matters, we will begin."

Arthur Braman rose to his feet.

"Your Honor, my associate arrived during the recess, and I now have copies of the order to show cause. I request that you sign it now and I can serve all counsel."

"The original hasn't turned up," said Linda. "Do you represent that the copies are true copies of the original submitted on Friday?"

"I do, Your Honor."

"Give it here," said Linda.

Braman gave the order to Foxx, who handed it up to Linda.

"Don't go away," she whispered. She took a pen and, without giving the order a look, scratched a big X across the top page and signed her name in the corner.

Foxx handed the order back to Braman.

"You didn't even look at it," said Braman.

"Didn't need to," said Linda.

"Then I request permission to go to the Appellate Division and apply for a stay of this trial pending an appeal of your denial of my order to show cause."

"You have my permission to go up whenever you please," said Linda. "But I will not stop the trial in the meantime. You get a stay from the Appellate Division, and of course I will abide by it. But I'm not going to deny your order to show cause, then adjourn the trial so you can rush uptown and appeal it. That would be granting your relief by other means."

Braman leaned down to whisper to Darius, then finally sat.

"In that case," said Linda, "bring down the jury."

The officer disappeared through the jury entrance and climbed half a flight to the jury room. He returned a few minutes later, announcing, "Jury entering," and holding the door as the eight jurors filed in and took their seats in the jury box. He then handed the ballot cards to the judge, who quickly scanned the cards and attached names to faces. These were all routine steps at the start of any trial, but today freighted with drama because each was a step closer to the point in the first trial when everything went wrong.

Linda began her welcoming speech to the jury. Her early versions were verbatim knockoffs of Judge Johnstone's canned speech, but her more recent endeavors contained enough personal flourishes to make them her own. The question today was whether to make any reference to the first trial. She opted against that, and as she finished she felt confident in her decision.

Billy Cokeley moved to the podium. As Cokeley gave his opening statement, Linda scanned the courtroom: the court officer standing with arms folded at the jury room door, the head and shoulders of the other officer in the corridor outside, Foxx at the corner of the well. She listened as Cokeley reached that exact point in his opening, the words that had haunted her for three years, ". . . evidence to prove that this treasure, wherever it may have traveled during its sixteen-hundred-year journey to this courtroom in New York City, was last unearthed within the borders of Croatia. We will . . ."

The skies did not darken, the courtroom did not explode, no gunmen burst in through the doors. As Cokeley promised credible eyewitness testimony from a man who had been a distinguished officer in the Yugoslav army, Linda found herself breathing normally again. She already had gone further in this trial than Judge Johnstone in the last.

McQueen was not good at estimating numbers of people. There could have been fifty, there could have been one hundred. But whatever the number, it was large enough that McQueen and the seven other officers fit themselves into the group without being noticed.

A man in charge of the protestors shouted some commands, and the protestors ambled toward a set of metal stanchions. The stanchions were positioned to funnel them to a point at the curb where they would cross the street two-by-two to another set of stanchions that would shunt them to the brass rails running up the center of the steps. Eight officers wearing bulky flak jackets waited on the other side.

McQueen fell in behind a man with a thick neck, broad shoulders, and a pronounced limp. The protestors moved slowly, across the street, onto the sidewalk, up the many steps. The revolving doors were pinned back to create a free-flowing entrance. Officers in the lobby waved the protestors through, then distributed them in the three mag lines. McQueen moved past the man with the limp and settled in behind a pair of protestors who appeared to be husband and wife.

Beyond the mags, the three lines joined and curved into the rotunda. An officer separated the protestors into groups of ten, each group standing in front of one of the three elevators programmed to stop only at the second floor and then return to the lobby.

McQueen cleared the mags. An officer swept him with an electric wand, so poker-faced that McQueen wondered if he recognized him. McQueen shuffled onto an elevator and rode up. From the elevator, he and nine homeless protestors followed signs halfway around the inner circle to the corridor that led to Judge Conover's courtroom. A court officer stood outside the doors. Inside, Foxx directed the protestors to the gallery benches. McQueen ended up seated on the center aisle. He looked around: Linda Conover on the bench, the lawyers at counsels' table, the jury in the box. Arthur Braman stood at the podium, waiting for the commotion to subside before continuing his opening statement.

Is this ever weird, thought McQueen.

The man with the limp was in the third car to open on the second floor after McQueen's. He lagged behind the other protestors, then peeled off into the A stairwell. He climbed quietly to the third floor, limped into the circular corridor, then down one of the spokes. There was a doorway at the end of the corridor. Beyond that was a set of stairs leading up to a men's room, and beyond the stairs was the door to Ivan's supply closet.

KEVIN EGAN

"Hey, you," called a man dressed in striped pirate pants and a basketball jersey.

The man with the limp broke into a run, reached the stairs, and took them two at a time. The stairs went up half a flight to a small landing, then reversed up to the men's room. He stopped midway up the second flight and crouched alongside the wall to wait for the man in the pirate pants, who he knew was a guard dressed to blend in with the protestors. Footsteps approached, paused, then padded on the stairs. As the guard turned up the second flight, Andreas's uppercut caught him under the ribs and lifted him into the air. The guard hit the wall and melted to the landing.

Andreas hurried up into the men's room. According to Ivan, it was rarely used by anyone except the few employees who knew it existed. Andreas opened the door to the third stall. The gun, wrapped in a nylon warm-up suit, was lodged behind the base of the toilet. Andreas tossed the warm-up suit aside and shoved the gun into his belt.

Down on the landing, the guard began to stir. Andreas stepped over him, then turned back. He pulled the guard up by the shirt, waited for his eyes to open, then grinned before slugging him in the jaw.

After he rang off with McQueen, Gary rolled the battle chair to the computer table. At first, he considered rolling right under the tabletop and activating the lift control. But somehow the vision of components toppling like buildings in the wake of Godzilla did not match his euphoria. Instead, he cupped his right hand around the base of the left monitor and swept it off the table. Then he cupped his left hand around the base of the right monitor and swept that off the table, too. Both monitors shattered on impact, sending thousands of glittering black shards across the hardwood floor. He dropped the keyboard beneath his feet and rolled the battle chair over it, back and forth, back and forth. The frame cracked and the keys flew off like kernels of popcorn. He pummeled the mouse with his fist.

He drove into the bedroom, opened the drawer, and lifted the treasure chest onto the bed. He sifted through the souvenirs, no longer concerned about dissipating the half-lives of these memories. He took the book onto his lap and read it cover to cover.

Later, he heard Ursula let herself into the apartment. Quickly and quietly, he returned the book to the chest and the chest to the drawer.

"Oh my God!" Ursula cried. "Gary! Gary!"

"In here," he called.

He heard a rush of footsteps. She burst into the bedroom, a look of horror on her face that dialed back into confusion when she saw him calmly parked beside the bed.

"Gary, I . . . the computer . . ."

"I know, Urse, I know. Don't worry."

She leaned against the battle chair and hugged him hard at the shoulders. He inclined his head against her and wrapped an arm around her waist.

"I'm turning over a completely new leaf," he said.

CHAPTER 38

The protestors kept straggling in. The officer who had been in the corridor was now in the courtroom, acting like a church usher squeezing parishioners into crowded pews. Foxx marked each of the undercover officers in his head—he counted seven of the eight, but except for McQueen they were easy to miss.

"Call your first witness, Mr. Cokeley," said Linda.

Cokeley stood. "Croatia calls Colonel Orkan Stjepanovic."

The officer at the door leaned out into the corridor. A few moments later, Stjepanovic stepped through. He was very tall with an erect bearing and a slow, stately gait. He wore a full uniform, which was too big for what remained of his bony frame. He crossed the well, mounted the witness stand, and took the oath with the help of a Croatian interpreter.

"Good morning, Colonel Stjepanovic," said Cokeley. "I want to ask you about an incident that occurred near the city of Pula in 1980."

Stjepanovic listened to the interpreter's translation, then leaned back in the witness chair as if to divorce himself from a scene he plainly felt was beneath him. A big man with a bad limp came through the courtroom door. Stjepanovic watched as the officer jammed the man beside McQueen.

"First," said Cokeley. "Where is Pula?"

"It is on the Istria peninsula in the Adriatic Sea."

"At that time, it was part of Yugoslavia, correct?"

"Yes."

"And now?"

"Objection," said Arthur Braman.

"Overruled," said Linda. "The witness is a colonel in the army. He can read a map."

"And now?" continued Cokeley. "In what country is Pula now?"

"Croatia," said Stjepanovic.

"And what were you doing in Pula in 1980?"

"I was assigned to a detachment that acted as personal bodyguards for the Marshal."

"That would be Marshal Tito?" said Cokeley.

"Correct."

"Now, I direct you to a day in March of that year. Do you remember what happened?"

"The Marshal wanted to build a small swimming pool," said Stjepanovic. "His estate already had a large one, but he wanted one that would be filled with saltwater for health reasons. Our detachment was to dig out the area for the pool. We worked in two-man shifts. The shift before ours defined the perimeter of the pool. We were digging down within that perimeter."

"You said we," said Cokeley. "Who else was on your shift?"

"Anton Fleiss," said Stjepanovic. "We were down over one meter when his shovel struck something hard. We had struck rocks through the entire shift, but this was much bigger. We dug around it and realized that it was not a rock but some sort of metal. It was smooth and round like a lid."

"A lid to what?"

"A cauldron."

Cokeley lifted a remote control from the podium. An image of a cauldron appeared on a flat-screen monitor on the wall behind

Stjepanovic. The cauldron was large and pockmarked, bronze in color except for black charring on its bottom and lower sides.

"Is that the cauldron?" said Cokeley.

"Yes."

"And you dug it out of the ground within Marshal Tito's compound near Pula, in what is now Croatia."

"Yes," said Stjepanovic. "It took all day to dig around it and four men to lift it out of the hole."

"And then?" said Cokeley.

"Liar! Murderer!"

McQueen froze, eyes wide open, as Andreas stood up and pulled a gun from his pants. The officer at the door rushed toward him. Foxx instinctively opened his holster guard.

Time slowed. Andreas raised his gun and aimed it at Stjepanovic. Stjepanovic tilted his head, a haughty smirk on his face. Andreas squeezed the trigger. A red dot appeared on Stjepanovic's forehead. Then his head snapped back and his entire body twisted out of the chair.

Foxx got his gun out of his holster.

"Drop it," he said.

Andreas looked at Foxx, then he looked down at McQueen.

"Finally," he said. "It is finished."

Andreas moved as if to drop his gun, then quickly raised it to his mouth and blew his own head off.

The rest of the day passed in a blur for Foxx, Linda, Bernadette, and even McQueen. There were the NYPD detectives, of course. And there were the IG investigators Bev had dispatched the moment word of the shooting reached central administration. After that, there were the reporters.

By close of business, the identity of the shooter and his motives were well known. His name was Andreas Szabo, and he was the brother of Luca Szabo and the son of Karolina Szabo. Luca

Szabo was the quarry worker who found the Salvus Treasure in a forest near Polgardi, Hungary. He had been murdered in 1980 by a detachment of Yugoslav soldiers, who then staged the unearthing of the treasure on Marshal Tito's vacation compound. The leader of that detachment was Orkan Stjepanovic. Years later, when the Hungarian magazine *Az Igazsag* ran a feature story documenting the Hungarian provenance of the treasure, Stjepanovic returned to eradicate the rest of the Szabo family. He found only Karolina.

All this information was found neatly printed on sheets of a legal pad in a large zippered plastic bag inside Andreas Szabo's flannel shirt. There also were Andreas's identification papers, the letter written by his mother on the day he left Hungary, a photocopy of the *Az Igazsag* article, and a tattered photo showing Luca Szabo holding a plate from the treasure.

There was no mention of the missing piece.

Foxx insisted on escorting Linda home, and Linda insisted on traveling by taxi, and so they rode uptown together.

"I have something to tell you," said Foxx. The taxi had just crossed Canal Street, and they were clear of Foley Square and the gravitational pull of the courthouse. "I was not assigned to your part by coincidence."

"Captain Kearney moves in mysterious ways," said Linda.

"Not Kearney," said Foxx. He pointed upward.

"Sharon?"

Foxx pointed upwards again.

"I give up, Foxx."

"The inspector general."

"I see." Linda looked out the window for a block, then back at Foxx. "Why you?"

"That's a long story."

"Tell me."

"Some other time. There's something else you need to know first." Foxx pulled the cell phone out of his pocket, frowned, then dropped it back in. "That was the IG."

"Why didn't you answer?"

"Because I didn't want her to tell me not to tell you."

"Her timing is that good?" said Linda.

"Not always. Actually, hardly ever," said Foxx. He pressed his hand to his chest, feeling the phone vibrate. Bev again, no doubt. Maybe her timing was that good. "You ever study astronomy?"

"Me? God, no," said Linda.

"Neither have I," said Foxx. "But I've read about it, and what surprised me is how many interstellar objects aren't directly visible. Like black holes. You can't see them, but you can find them by observing the behavior of objects around them."

"What's your point, Foxx?"

"You and Judge Johnstone had a serious disagreement that day, right?"

Linda nodded.

"To you, it was a philosophical disagreement. You thought he should have a full-blown trial. Let in all the evidence. Let the jury decide on all the facts. He wanted to restrict the evidence as a way of forcing the parties to settle. Am I right?"

"Close enough," said Linda.

"But it was odd behavior, especially after all the work you had put in preparing for the trial, especially those pretrial rulings."

"That's right," said Linda. Her voice sounded small, as if she knew she was about to hear something she did not want to hear.

"What you didn't see was the black hole." Foxx waited a moment for Linda to react. She didn't, not visibly, and he went on. "After the heist, all the officers connected with security that day were interviewed by the IG. Judge Johnstone was interviewed, too.

Not about the trial or his rulings, but about insisting the court-room doors remain unlocked when Captain Kearney ordered otherwise."

"That was within his rights," said Linda.

"But it wasn't common sense," said Foxx. "Anyway, the IG investigation wrapped up just before Thanksgiving. In mid-December, the IG got an anonymous phone call that Judge Johnstone had been bribed to rule in Lord Leinster's favor."

Linda said nothing. She turned away from Foxx, who could still see her reflection in the window. She swallowed hard.

"The IG recalled Johnstone under the pretense of reopening the investigation of the heist. Instead, she confronted him with what the caller had said. He admitted everything."

"Which was?"

"Afraid I'm not privy to that," said Foxx. "But I do know that he never collected on the bribe. That allowed the IG to offer her deal: retire and it all goes away."

"Who bribed him?"

"The obvious answer is Lord Leinster since he benefited from the rulings. But the IG suspects it could have been Croatia since, as matters stood had the rulings gone as originally planned, Hungary likely would have won."

"How did that help Croatia for Lord Leinster to hold on to the treasure?" said Linda.

"Live to fight another day? Cultural antipathy? We saw how easily that urn disappeared. Maybe Croatia thought the treasure would be less secure in Leinster's hands."

"What do you think?"

"Generally, things are what they seem until proven otherwise," said Foxx.

"And then?"

"Well, the IG thought whoever tried to bribe Johnstone might try to influence you. And not necessarily by offering money. That's what got me assigned."

"So, the mugging was related to the trial."

"That's what the IG thinks," said Foxx.

"And now?"

"Another opening, another mistrial," said Foxx.

"Sounds like a song."

"Yeah, an old one."

They reached Linda's brownstone. Foxx went in with her and made sure nothing was amiss. Doors secure, windows locked, closets devoid of bogeymen. After he finished, they stood in the foyer. A definite sense of the bittersweet hung in the air.

"Bernadette will come by to fetch me tomorrow morning," said Linda. "She suggested it, and I thought why not. She's the only person I feel really has my best interests at heart. Present company excluded."

Foxx reached for the doorknob.

"I guess this is it," said Linda. She smiled and lifted her hand. Her palm felt warm against his.

"See you tomorrow at court," said Foxx.

"That you will."

"We'll always have City Island."

"That we will," said Linda.

Outside, Foxx headed toward the park instead of toward Broadway. He stopped where the shadows were darkest and stared at Linda's stoop. His phone buzzed; Bev again.

"Yeah."

"Well, well, well. Fancy catching you on the phone."

"I don't want to be reassigned just yet."

"It's over, Foxx. You stay with her until she formally grants a mistrial tomorrow. Why? You think it was the protestors?"

"I don't know what to think. But right now she needs some stability."

"You? A stabilizing force? You know, Foxx, you have some sense of humor."

"No," said Foxx. "I have a sense of the absurd."

McQueen waited for the call that never came, then arrived at Gary's apartment building at precisely eight o'clock. They'd made it to first base, he thought, but with today's shooting they might be stranded there without scoring. The case was headed for a certain mistrial, which would delay the determination of who owned the treasure. So they'd be sitting on the piece for a while, unless Gary had some other brilliant idea. Which he might. After all, he figured out that the piece was still in the courthouse.

McQueen had wrapped the piece in several plastic grocery bags, then laid it sideways in a paper shopping bag. He took the elevator to the fourth floor and did not smell any cooking coming out of 4D. That was a good sign. The door to Gary's apartment was locked, so he let himself in with the key Gary had given him. He wondered what would happen when Ursula finally moved in. She'd probably demand that he hand it over. He doubted he would give a shit, being that he'd be rich as all hell someday.

Gary sat in the battle chair just inside the living room.

"Did you hear what happened at the courthouse?" said McQueen. "Another goddam shooting during the trial."

"What?" said Gary. "Who?"

"A witness. Tell me you didn't hear."

"I didn't. Is everyone else okay?"

"An officer got slugged in a stairway on three. Probably followed the shooter there when he picked up the gun."

"Another inside job, huh? Ivan?"

"I'd bet on it, but no one's figured that out except me, and I'll keep that quiet till we do something about this. He ain't going anywhere."

Gary spun his chair and rolled toward the computer table. The plywood top was clear—no monitors, no keyboard, no mouse.

"What happened to your computer?" said McQueen.

"Stupid me," said Gary. "I got so excited when I hung up with you that I hit the lift button instead of the joystick. *Kaboom!*"

"That's not like you, Gary," said McQueen, assuming it was a joke until he saw the shattered monitors facedown on the floor.

"Yeah, but it's not like me to find out we're rich," said Gary. "So, what happened? Who was the witness?"

"An old Yugoslav soldier named Stjepanovic," said McQueen. He recounted what little he had heard of Stjepanovic's testimony, then added, "The guy who shot him was sitting right next to me."

"Jesus, Mike, do they know who he is?"

"They know everything," said McQueen. "It was all neatly wrapped up in a plastic bag."

He explained what the police found and the rumors circulating the courthouse.

"Pure revenge. I suppose that's understandable. It's stronger than a lot of emotions," said Gary. "So, what are we waiting for?"

McQueen set the shopping bag on the coffee table and lifted the piece out by the neck. He stood it upright and peeled down the plastic bags one at a time.

"Like an artichoke," said Gary.

McQueen lifted the urn and swept the bunch of bags onto the floor.

"It's smaller than I remember," said Gary.

"The wax takes off the shine," said McQueen.

Gary rolled up to the coffee table. He stared at the urn for a long time, moving his head slightly to change the angle, as if to prove to himself that it was a real, three-dimensional object and not a mirage, a will o' the wisp, fata morgana. Then he stood it on his belly.

"Solid," he said. "Heavy."

"Must have taken Ivan forever to drip all that wax," said Mc-Queen.

Gary set the piece back on the coffee table. He took out a pocket-knife and carefully scraped off a section of wax to expose the silver beneath.

"Pretty good shine," he said. "I suppose this'll melt right off."

"So, what we do next?" said McQueen.

"What we do next is have a drink."

"I'm talking about selling the thing."

"And I'm talking about celebrating," said Gary. "What do you want?"

"Beer, I guess." McQueen started for the kitchen. "What about you?"

"Sit, Mike. I'll get them."

"No, it's—"

"Mike, sit. You've been my eyes, my hands, my legs for all this. The least I can do is get us a couple of beers from the fridge."

McQueen sat. He heard the refrigerator door open, bottles rattle, silverware tinkle.

"Hey," he called in. "We can go bigger on the kitchen now."

"That we can," Gary called out.

"We even can pay people to do the work instead of sucking up to guys like Larkin."

"Yeah. Who needs Larkin?"

"Maybe whoever we get to work on your kitchen can work on my cabin."

"A two-fer," said Gary. He rolled back out, one huge hand holding the two mugs of dark beer by the handles while the other worked the joystick.

"That one," he said.

McQueen took it.

"Cheers," he said.

"Cheers," said Gary.

They clinked mugs, then took long slugs. Gary rested his beer on his lap while McQueen settled back onto the couch.

"Who woulda thought Ivan was involved in this," he said. "Not me, that's for sure. But in a way, it makes sense. Inside guy. Comes from the same town where the treasure was found."

"I wonder if he realizes he doesn't have it anymore," said Gary.

"Who the hell knows?" said McQueen. "What's he going to do about it, anyway? What are we going to do about it? A mistrial means more delay before we can find a buyer."

"Are you in a rush?" said Gary.

"Not really." McQueen took another long slug. "But retirement is beginning to look good after being involved in two courthouse shootings."

"You were involved?"

"You know what I mean. I was there both times, inches from the shooters." McQueen slugged again, shorter this time, then held up the mug to the light.

"Something wrong, Mike?"

"Nah, just . . . ah, nothing." He set the mug down and rubbed his eyes.

"Geez, Mike. Don't go falling asleep on me. This is the biggest night of our lives."

"Yeah, sure is," said McQueen.

"Here." Gary raised his mug. "Another toast. To Ivan. May we remember him forever."

McQueen leaned forward. They clinked mugs and they both drank to Ivan. McQueen went to set his mug down, but missed the table. It lay on the floor, froth spilling onto the rug.

"Sorry, Gary," he said, groping for the mug. "Shit, when Urse sees this mess."

"Don't worry about Ursula," said Gary. "This is my place, remember."

"Yeah, Gary, right. Your place." McQueen's head dipped, then lifted. His eyelids fluttered. "Tired."

"Been a long day, Mike. A long haul. But you know, Mike, there's something that's been bothering me for a while. See, when the IG came to the rehab, she asked me a bunch of questions about that day. She asked me whether anything provoked the gunman to shoot. I told her no, but I was lying."

Gary hooked a hand under the coffee table and reversed the battle chair to drag it out of the way. Then he nudged the chair against the couch so he could lift McQueen's chin and slap his cheeks. McQueen's eyes fluttered, then rolled, then opened halfway.

"I lied to the IG because I knew you lied to the IG. Because it did me no good to tell the truth. You understand?"

McQueen moaned.

Gary dropped McQueen's head, rolled into the kitchen for a handful of paper towels, then rolled back to sop up the beer. By the time he finished, McQueen was dead out.

First thing Gary did was search for McQueen's service piece. It looked clean and felt heavy, like an old friend. He popped the magazine, saw it held all fifteen rounds, then slammed it closed.

"Thank you for listening," he said. He lay the piece on the coffee table, then began to yank off McQueen's sneakers, strip off his pants, pull off his sweater. McQueen barely groaned. Gary tossed the sweater one way, the pants another in a depiction of wild abandon. Then he dragged McQueen onto his lap and drove into the bedroom.

Ursula lay on one side of the bed, facedown and naked. Gary raised the battle chair and dumped McQueen onto the other side. He pushed McQueen close, then sandwiched one of Ursula's legs between McQueen's. As a final touch, he removed McQueen's glasses and folded them onto the night stand. No matter how crazy things got, McQueen was always careful with his glasses.

CHAPTER 39

Long after Foxx departed, long after she ate a light dinner of grilled chicken, rice pilaf, and sautéed asparagus, long after she had changed into sweats, Linda nestled in the corner of the sectional in her living room. The television was off, the radio was off. She had lived through the day's news and did not want to hear it again. Instead, a mix of classical music played softly from the speakers above her head. Linda had never had any interest in classical music before becoming a judge. She could recognize just about any traditional Irish air and recite its title in Gaelic and English. But with classical music she was at sea once she got beyond *Ode to Joy* or *Claire de Lune* or *Rhapsody on a Theme of Paganini*. Still she listened, thinking that classical was as good for her head as traditional Irish was for her spirit.

She flipped through a *New Yorker*, reached the end, and plucked another off the pile. For the last week, every day had been worse than the one before. Learning that her marriage was over was one thing; seeing a man shot dead not five feet from her was something else. She wished she could have a glass of wine, but the tightness of her waistband across her belly argued against it.

She put aside her second *New Yorker* and closed her eyes, but the horrible images behind her eyelids forced her eyes to snap open. She reached for another magazine.

Her cell phone rang. She knew it wouldn't be Hugh; even if he had heard of the shooting he wouldn't call. This wasn't like the last time. She lifted the phone, stared at the strange number for one more ring, then answered.

"Is this Judge Conover?"

"Who's calling?"

"Gary Martin."

"Oh, Gary. Hi. It's Linda."

"I heard what happened," said Gary. "Horrible."

"Horrible doesn't do it justice."

"I'm glad you're all right. You sound all right, anyway."

"Not really, but thanks," said Linda. "Where are you? You sound like you're outside somewhere."

"I'm right in front of your house."

Linda went into the front den and saw Gary sitting in his wheelchair on the sidewalk, bundled in a parka with a blanket across his lap.

"How did you . . . ?" she said. "Did I ever tell you where I lived?"

"No," he said.

"Then how did you find me?"

"Uh, the Green Book," he said, his voice inflecting like an incredulous teenager.

"Oh," she said. "Right."

A judge's home address was not public knowledge, nor was it a state secret. Home addresses and contact information for all high-ranking public officials were published in something called the Green Book. Gary likely had no access to a copy, but just as likely knew someone who did.

"Can you come out?" he said.

She eyed him through the window, saw him brush back a curly

lock from his forehead, saw him smile his earnest smile. The same old Gary, just crippled beyond repair.

"Sure," she said. "Give me a sec."

She went into the hallway and took a coat from the closet. She was about to open the front door, then reversed direction to the elevator and descended to the basement. After all, this was Gary outside in the cold night air, not some stranger. Something had happened today that Gary understood all too well. And the truth was, now that she had a taste of solitude, she didn't really want to be alone.

She went out through the door beneath the stoop and walked up the concrete incline to the wrought-iron gate.

"Hey, over here," she called.

Gary did an exaggerated double take, then rolled in her direction.

"It's good to see you, Gary," she said, lifting the heavy latch.

"It's good to see you, too," he said.

The gate creaked as she pulled it back, and they hugged as comfortably as two people could hug with the arm of a wheelchair between them.

"What's this?" she said, feeling a hard edge beneath the parka.

"Something I brought to brighten your night."

"God knows my night needs brightening," she said. "Do you want to come in?"

"How do I do that?"

"You'll see."

Gary followed her into the basement. Halfway down a dimly lit corridor, Linda opened a door.

"An elevator?" said Gary. "How coincidental."

"More like fortuitous in both the correct and the misused senses of the word," said Linda.

She stepped aside while Gary backed into the tiny car, then squeezed in after him. As the car rumbled upward, she explained why the house came to have an elevator and how she and Hugh came to own it.

"Nice story," said Gary. "But a slow elevator."

"Luckily it isn't a skyscraper." She was about to add that she probably wouldn't be living here much longer, but decided she didn't need to say it and Gary didn't need to hear it.

The elevator leveled at the first floor, and the door opened.

"Want anything to drink? Eat?"

"Seltzer?" said Gary.

"Have you ever come to the right place," said Linda.

"That's what I was hoping," said Gary.

They went down the hallway and into the kitchen. Gary nudged the wheelchair sideways against the long granite counter while Linda went behind and poured two glasses of seltzer. She settled onto a stool opposite Gary and pushed her coat off her shoulders.

"Cheers," she said.

They clinked glasses.

"So, what will brighten my night?" she said.

Gary reached into his parka, pulled out the silver urn, and, with a magician's flourish, set it on the counter.

Linda caught herself between a cry and a swallow, then started coughing because the seltzer went down the wrong way.

"Is that what I think it is?" she finally managed. She put down her glass.

"Depends on what you think it is," said Gary.

"The stolen urn?"

"The missing piece," said Gary. "Yep. This is it."

"But why? How? Were you . . . ?"

"Involved in the heist? That would be some story, right? Hero court officer implicated in daring courtroom invasion. But it's nothing so interesting. I just figured it out."

"Figured what out?"

"That the piece never left the courthouse," said Gary.

"But how did . . . ?" Linda stopped.

"How did I figure it out? Me? A court officer? How did I find it when everyone else in the world was looking for it? I spent a lot of time on the Internet, reading and looking for clues. I sued the court system. Did you know I sued the court system?"

Linda shook her head.

"Well, I did," said Gary. "Only I wasn't interested in money. I was interested in what I could find out about that day, what no one else knew, what no one else was supposed to know. I got security feeds that proved to me those two bastards left the courthouse and the piece wasn't with them."

"Impressive," said Linda. "Brilliant."

"Thanks," said Gary. "But it wasn't because of brains. It was because no one thinks about this piece the way I do."

"You actually went to the courthouse and found it yourself?"

"Nah. Mike actually found it. He was my man on the scene, my boots on the ground. I'd tell him where to look, and he would go look, and when he didn't find it in one place, I'd send him someplace else."

"And where did he—did you, I mean—find it?"

"A place called the plenum. Know it?" Gary waited till she shook her head. "Few people do. It's a storage area on the mezzanine level between the third and fourth floors."

Linda slid the urn close and ran a finger over the low-relief Roman soldiers, deer, boar, and mountains.

"You need to give it back," she said.

"To who?" said Gary. "There's no rightful owner. You know that."

"The auction house actually has legal possession."

"Screw the auction house. I don't give a damn about the auction house. Mike had some cockamamie idea of waiting for the trial to be over and selling it to whoever won."

"This isn't a windfall, Gary."

"Hey, nobody knows that better than me." He slipped his hand into his parka and adjusted something. "I don't care if the piece is worth five million dollars, ten million dollars, a billion dollars. It's not for sale. I needed to find this piece. It was essential that I find this piece."

"Why, Gary?" She pulled her hands off the counter and folded them across her belly. "Why was it essential to find the piece?"

"Don't you remember?"

"Remember what?"

"That day," said Gary.

"Of course I remember that day. No one who was there ever can forget that day."

"I don't mean the heist. The heist is where everything went sideways. I'm talking about before the heist. Just before. The last time you and I and this piece were together. That's as close as we got."

"We?" said Linda.

"I. We. What's the difference. It's as close as I got."

"To what?"

"To giving you this."

Gary slipped his hand into his pocket again and, with the same flourish as when he produced the urn, pulled out a book. He let it sit on the counter between them, then pushed it toward Linda.

"*The Missing Piece*?" she said.

"Open it," said Gary.

With one hand, Linda fanned the pages.

"Not like that," said Gary. "Here."

He opened the front cover, bent it back, and creased it so that the book lay open-faced on the counter. Linda read only a few words of the inscription before her mind disengaged and her thoughts turned elsewhere.

"Well?" said Gary.

Linda forced a grin, gave a tiny shrug. Gary started talking, but she didn't hear the actual words. She was measuring, assessing. She was essentially in a cul-de-sac formed by walls, appliances, and the counter. She could reach the back door, but it was locked and bolted and chained. Not an easy exit. She could vault over the counter, get behind Gary, and make a break for the front door. It had fewer locks to handle, and if she ran fast enough she could put significant space between herself and Gary. But she couldn't be sure she would hit the floor cleanly or run without tripping. She could just fly around the counter and run past him. Catch him by surprise.

She drained the last of her seltzer, silently toed her slippers off her feet, gently pushed back her stool. Gary was parked facing the back door. Once she got past him—if she got past him—he would need to turn a complete one-eighty in a tight space before he could chase after her. That would be her move.

She waited until he lifted the book again, took his eyes off her so he could turn another page and crease it flat. Then she bolted.

The surprise worked. She ran around the counter and right past Gary.

"No!" he yelled.

She crossed from the tiles of the kitchen to the hardwood parquet of the hallway. She heard the screech of the wheelchair's tires, the whirr of the wheelchair's motor. But she was flying down the hallway, past the living room on one side, the elevator door on the other. She reached the doorway into the den. Up ahead was the foyer with its closet, its coat tree, its umbrella stand, its small desk where she dropped the mail. She focused on the front door, playing out the order in which she would turn the locks. Deadbolt first, latch second. Luckily, the chain wasn't set.

She had drawn even with the coat tree when Gary caught up. Something—the wheelchair's footrest, she instantly realized—clipped her heel and tripped her. She tried to get her feet under her, but her tumbling momentum drove her to the floor.

Gary stopped beside her. With one huge hand, he grabbed her ankles together and lifted her feet. She tried to kick herself free, but his hand held fast. She heard the clank of metal as he locked the handcuffs around one ankle and then the other.

The husband of the couple who lived in 4D returned home from his late shift just after midnight. With his wife already asleep inside, he carefully separated the keys on his key chain. He quietly turned back the dead bolt, then slipped the second key into the other lock. From down the hall came the rattle and click of a door unlocking. He glanced quickly down the hall and saw it was the door to the apartment where the man in the wheelchair lived. The man was quiet and rarely left his apartment. His girlfriend was a nurse, coming and going at all hours. They were both big people.

He opened his own door, intending to avoid any chatter that would disturb his wife. But he thought it would be polite to wave, so he turned and instead of his neighbor saw a naked man crumpled against the doorjamb. The man stumbled forward and fell to his knees. Then he pushed himself up and began to crawl. His skin was pale and splotchy. Yellow saliva dripped from his mouth. He rose up on his knees and stretched his arms in supplication.

The husband from 4D closed himself in his apartment. He threw the lock and the dead bolt, then he called 911.

They were in the living room. Linda sat in the corner of the sectional, her legs drawn up, her feet cuffed at the ankles, her arms hugging her belly. Gary buzzed around the room in his battle chair. He already had taken her cell phone and the two cordless landline handsets, and now he was pushing a chair and the coffee table to block the doorway that led into the hall. Despite her fear and confusion, Linda couldn't help but notice how easily and deftly Gary worked the chair. It was fast and it was precise, more appendage than machine.

Gary's last move was to push away parts of the sectional to

create a space next to the corner piece where Linda sat. He backed into that space, then reached a hand toward Linda's knee.

"Don't touch me," she said.

"Okay. No problem." Gary withdrew his hand. "We'll get there."

"Get where? We're not getting anywhere."

"Back where we were. Before."

"We weren't anywhere before."

"Yes, we were." Gary reached into the pocket of his parka and dropped a fistful of objects onto the sofa. "We did a lot together. Museums, restaurants, the park, the zoo. We were building something hour by hour, souvenir by souvenir, memory by memory. Look. This is evidence. You can't deny evidence."

"Gary, I don't deny that we had a good time. I don't deny that I liked you and appreciated you, because I did. Truly. But things were different then. We were both in a different place."

"No, you need to see things the way I see things. We weren't in a different place then. We've been in different places since, but lives are like big gears, always turning. Moving away and then coming back together. I know. I spent lots of time thinking about these things. And now we are all back together: you, me, the missing piece, and *The Missing Piece*."

"Gary, I never even heard about that book until tonight."

"That's because the gears already were turning that day," said Gary. "I suspected it, but I really didn't understand it. I was going to give you the book that day. Ursula moved out over that weekend, so the decks were clear. But then Kearney switched me and Foxx and then you had that fight with the judge. So even when Kearney put me back in on that security detail, there was no time for it. The closest I got was when you and I were standing there and looking at the piece. But the time wasn't right, and I thought, Hey, there's always later. I didn't know later would be so long."

He opened the book.

"Gary."

"No. We are here, and it is now. I am going to show you the book, and you will understand." He turned the page. "Here is the main character. He looks like a cheese wheel with a large hunk cut out. He's on a quest to find a piece the exact size and shape to fill what he's missing. Some pieces are too big, others too small, a few come with missing parts of their own, or extra parts that he can't accommodate. All he wants is to roll along smoothly through life, but none of the pieces he tries fit perfectly and he thumps along like a flat tire. And then he finds the perfect piece, and the two roll along merrily into the future."

"I don't know where you're going with this," said Linda.

"You don't? Linda, you're my missing piece."

"But I'm married, remember? And you're with Ursula."

"Not anymore. She's with Mike now."

"McQueen?" said Linda. "I know he's your friend, so don't take this wrong. But I don't see him with anyone."

"He's with her. Right now. Trust me. And your marriage is a temporary problem with a simple solution. You don't love Hugh. You never loved Hugh. He was your hook for becoming a judge. Okay, so you became one. But you're still Linda, and we fit together. You can't deny that."

"But not perfectly," said Linda. "And you want perfect. You deserve perfect. I have my own missing pieces. I have my own baggage."

"No!" Gary shouted. "You're perfect!"

"I'm not," Linda said softly. "There are no perfectly shaped pieces out there. Everyone has a dent or a bump or an odd angle. People choose the ones who best fill what they lack. But nothing's perfect."

"No. It happens. I know it happens. And I have proof. Finding that piece was proof. See, when I got out of rehab, Mike and some of the guys chipped in and bought me a computer. They figured if I was stuck in my apartment, the computer would be my connection to the outside world. I was hurting, Linda. I was hurting pretty bad. The computer wasn't the answer. And then I began to use it to learn about the treasure, you know, demystify the thing that put me in a wheelchair and took me away from you. I trolled the Internet, looking for word that the piece had been found, or sold, or turned up in some Middle Eastern bazaar. I never found anything, and so I got to thinking that the piece never left the courthouse. Those bastards got away, but they left it behind, hidden somewhere. And then an idea popped into my head. It was like a revelation. I knew that if I found the piece I could have you back."

"But there is no connection between me and the piece," said Linda.

"Of course there is," said Gary. "When you spend time alone like I did, all those weeks and months in rehab, you start to think in supernatural ways. This piece is what binds us. Not just then, not just now, but forever. It brought us together, it got me shot."

"You got shot because someone wanted to steal it," said Linda.

"No, no, no, that's the wrong way to look at it. Events tried to pull us apart, but it brought us back together. Think about it. Standing in the courtroom just before the trial began. You and me. Together. It was my last happy moment, the moment I held on to all these years. Now I have everything. The piece that was missing and the missing piece."

"Gary, we had something special," said Linda. "We truly did. And I remember standing there with you. I've thought about it over the years, too. Fondly. Sadly. Ruefully. But as much as I want to go back to that day and have it end differently, things are just too complicated now."

"You and Hugh, right? I told you. Simple solution to that. You get a divorce. Hugh won't give a damn. He's not your destiny. He never was. I'm your destiny. And Ursula's not a problem anymore, either. Last time she moved out. This time . . . well, the decks are clear once again."

"What happened to her, Gary? What did you do?"

"It doesn't matter, not anymore."

He pushed the joystick forward and shot away from the sectional. She watched as he worked the wheelchair like a bulldozer, quickly shoving aside the chair and the coffee table that had blocked the doorway. She felt sick to her stomach, not the morning sickness of these last few days, but something deeper and more primal. Something that wouldn't go away with a sleeve of saltines or a glass of seltzer. Ursula was dead; she knew that. And Mike? Well, if he wanted to sell the piece that was right now on her kitchen counter, he probably was dead, too.

Gary rolled back beside the sectional. He snaked an arm across her belly and yanked her onto his lap. She flailed and she punched, but it was like pummeling a walrus. He twisted her until she was sitting on his lap, then squeezed her till she stopped fighting.

"That's better," he whispered into her ear.

He rolled to the elevator, opened the outer door, and backed into the car.

"Where are you taking me?" she said.

He punched number two.

"Where do you think?" he said.

CHAPTER 40

Foxx tracked the cell phone to the pocket of the shirt he'd tossed into the laundry basket only an hour ago. He considered letting it ring through, then decided after a day like today that wasn't such a wise idea. At least he could thank her for saving the phone from a watery grave.

"Get down to Gary Martin's apartment," said Bev.

"Now? What happened?"

"That's what I want to know."

It took Foxx almost an hour to get from City Island to the Upper West Side, but he didn't miss much of anything. Bev and one of her investigators waited in the hallway outside Gary's apartment. The apartment door was open, and a police officer stood guard at the threshold. Beyond, in the once ornate foyer, a man wearing a medical examiner windbreaker talked with a detective. They moved sideways, and a tech entered stage right, guiding a gurney with a body bag. Something clenched in Foxx's gut.

"Gary?" he muttered.

"No," said Bev. "Someone named Ursula."

"Gary's girlfriend," said Foxx. "Shit. Where's Gary?"

"Nowhere," said Bev. "Neighbor saw Mike McQueen stumble

out of the apartment. Naked, disoriented, drunk or drugged. EMTs took him away."

"Any ideas?"

"None," said Bev. "I don't know if McQueen's a suspect or a victim. No one's telling us anything."

Except for a small sitting room at the front of the brownstone, the master bedroom suite took up the entire second floor. There was the bedroom itself, his and her walk-in closets, and, in the rear, a large bathroom.

Linda's eyes were open, but she took in little as Gary rolled them off the elevator. If she felt sick to her stomach before, she felt like she was having a total physical breakdown now. Her legs felt like jelly while her chest heaved and her arms shook uncontrollably.

Gary spun them into the bedroom.

"Are you cold?" he said.

She didn't answer.

Gary pulled up beside the bed, which had a flouncy comforter and a frilly bed skirt, cubbies built into a teak headboard, spindles for a footboard. It was a high bed, so he raised the seat of the wheelchair and pushed Linda off his lap and onto the mattress. She immediately rolled away, but he grabbed her by the waistband of her sweats and pulled her back. She bucked wildly and pounded his forearm with her fists.

"Stop!" he yelled.

She only bucked harder.

He pinched her face in one hand and forced her to look at him.

"Stop, goddammit!" he yelled. "We're here for the night. Get used to it."

She settled down. He let go of her face, patted one cheek gently, then trailed his hand along her shoulder and down her arm before locking onto her wrist. He backed away enough to turn the chair and inspect the bed.

"Okay," he muttered. "Okay."

He let go of her wrist, scooted the wheelchair to the foot of the bed, and hooked his fingers on the metal links between the two rings of the handcuffs. He pulled, and she slid down the mattress until her feet touched the spindles. Quickly, he opened one ring, looped it around a spindle, and locked it around her ankle again.

"There," he said, shaking the cuffs. "Comfortable?"

"No."

"You will be."

He scooted back to the top of the bed, lifted her head and shoulders, and shoved two pillows underneath.

"Better?"

Linda only grunted.

She watched as he cleared everything off the night stand on "her" side of the bed, anything she could reach in the cubbies over her head—a crystal bud vase, a decorative ceramic tile, a china teacup embossed with a gilt *Herself.* He took the cordless landline handset from its cradle, dropped it onto the floor, and rolled over it with his wheelchair. She could hear the plastic breaking. Then he dropped the phone cradle and rolled over that, too.

Linda closed her eyes until the sound of cracking plastic stopped. She didn't expect that Gary would leave the bedroom phone intact, not after he took care of the phones downstairs, not after he dropped her cell phone somewhere deep into the cavernous pockets of his parka. She saw him now spinning slowly in the wheelchair as if making one last inspection.

"Where are the light switches?" he said. "Oh, never mind."

There were two banks, one just inside the door and the other beside the headboard. They were complicated, controlling the ceiling fixtures, spotlights, accent lights, the reading lamps. With one swipe of his hand, he killed them all.

The bedroom had no windows. Ambient light came in through the sitting room, but dimmed to a fuzzy gray as it reflected down the hallway and into the bedroom. Linda stared up at the dark ceiling. She heard the wheelchair roll around the foot of the bed and along the other side. Hugh's side. For a moment, that simple thought gave her some comfort; then it didn't.

She heard Gary fumbling and grunting in the dark, then two solid thunks as something, probably his sneakers, hit the floor. He was quiet for a while, and then she heard a hissing sound and realized he was peeing into a plastic urinal. A moment later, the smell reached her nostrils. She nearly gagged.

Gary capped the urinal and shoved it into its sleeve on the side of the battle chair. He never really noticed the smell of his own urine, but tonight it seemed particularly pungent. Maybe he hadn't drank enough during the long hours of waiting for Mike to bring the missing piece. Maybe he was just plain nervous. It certainly had been one hell of a night so far.

He shrugged out of his parka and hung it over the back of the battle chair, balancing it because Mike's service piece weighed heavily in the left inside pocket. He set his elbows on the armrests, leveraged himself off the seat, and pushed his pants down so he could sit without pinning them with his ass. It took some effort to push and pull them over his dead legs, but eventually he got them off.

Then he began his maneuvers. He raised the seat and spilled himself onto the bed. He landed awkwardly, then pushed and pulled and finally twisted his torso for his legs to follow. They didn't, and so he lay gasping, his hips turned almost ninety degrees, and his legs crossed. He rested a while and then worked himself till he lay completely flat on his back.

Linda felt Gary's every move through the mattress, but now he was quiet and still. At another time and in another place, she might have felt sorry for the enormous effort it took him simply to climb into bed. But this wasn't the time or the place. Still, she sensed a definite expectation in the air. He wanted her to say something or, God forbid, do something. She did not intend to do either.

She stared at the ceiling, not wanting to cast even the slightest glance in his direction. She had no idea of the time. She thought he had come at about ten, but ever since he ran her down as she tried to escape time seemed to have stopped. He'd taken away the bedroom clock.

And so she lay as still as she could, her shallow breaths and his deep drafts in counterpoint. And then:

"Linda," he whispered.

She stayed silent, kept her breathing steady.

"Linda," he said, more sharply.

Again, she stayed silent.

"Linda," he shouted.

"Yes," she said. She tried to sound calm because if she sounded calm maybe she would stay calm. But her heart pounded and the shakes returned to her arms.

"I have to explain something," he said.

"You have a lot to explain," she said.

"Well, this is important," he said.

A smart remark crossed her tongue, but she swallowed it back.

"I can't come to you," he said. "I just don't work that way anymore. I can't lie beside you and get a hard-on just thinking about you. Not like I could before."

He paused. In the silence, her body gave one last shake, then calmed.

"I can still have sex, though," he said. "Just like any other guy, except it's not in my head anymore. Not even a little bit. I need you to come to me. I need you to manipulate me. That's how it works now. I just want you to know that you don't need to be afraid of me."

"Okay," she said.

"And I wanted you to know what you need to do for me."

"Gary, that isn't happening."

Gary sighed.

"I know," he said. "Not yet."

They lay in silence for a long time before Linda rolled away from him as much as the cuffs allowed. She tucked one hand between her thighs and pressed the other to her womb and thought about the baby she needed to protect.

Foxx didn't know much about medicine, but he knew about vital signs. The monitors over McQueen's bed told a dismal story. Blood pressure low, heart rate low, oxygen absorption low. McQueen himself looked terrible. His skin, always raging with acne, was splotchy. His cheeks were sunken. His eyes, without his aviator glasses, were small in his head. He coughed suddenly—the only sound he made since Foxx sat down—and shook his head hard enough to dislodge the oxygen clips under his nose. Foxx realigned the two jets beneath his nostrils. The oxygen monitor showed a brief spike, then settled back into the dismal range.

"Hey, Mike," Foxx whispered in his ear. It was his third attempt at communicating. "Mike. It's Foxx."

"Foxx, where am I?"

Foxx tweaked the oxygen clip.

"That better?"

"Better," said McQueen.

"You're in the hospital. We need to know what happened. Where's Gary?"

"Piece," said McQueen.

"Peace?" said Foxx. "Gary's at peace?"

"Piece," said McQueen. "Treasure piece."

"The piece from the treasure? The stolen piece?"

"Found it."

"Gary found it?" said Foxx.

"I did."

"Where?"

"Courthouse. Gary knew."

"Gary knew what? About the piece."

"Uh-huh." McQueen coughed, then took a deep slurping breath. "Urse."

"What about her?"

"How is she?"

"She's in another room," said Foxx.

An alarm sounded. The cardiac monitor flashed. The heart rate that had been so slow skyrocketed over 140. The cardiogram running along the bottom of the screen twitched like a seismograph.

Foxx ran outside for help, but a team with a crash cart already raced in his direction.

"Coding!" someone yelled.

Foxx jumped aside, and the team piled into McQueen's room.

"You'll need to leave, sir," said a nurse.

They slammed the door and closed the blinds.

Linda had no sensation of falling asleep. Only after replaying the dream in her head—a quickly evaporating discussion with Hugh— did she realize that she had drifted off. She had no idea of the time. It could have been twenty minutes, or maybe only twenty seconds, since her last waking thought.

The bedroom was still dark, the mattress perceptibly tilted because of Gary's bulk. She rolled onto her back, then pushed herself to keep her distance from Gary, who smelled like a mix of sweaty body odor and funky sleep. Suddenly, he snorted, and just as suddenly the energy of the room changed.

Linda held her breath.

"Hey," he whispered. "Hey, you awake?"

"Uh," she moaned. She did not want to admit she was awake,

but at the same time did not want to pretend that she was asleep. So far, his claim that he could not approach her appeared to be true. Still, he could hurt her in other ways.

"I need to tell you something," said Gary.

What now, thought Linda, though she stayed silent.

"I need to tell you exactly how I got shot," he said. "I saw the whole thing happen in slow motion, like a train wreck or a car crash. They told us to turn around and face the bench. Remember? I didn't think they were going to shoot. They were going to run, and I wanted to get one last look at them to see if I could spot some quirk or mannerism that might help me identify them later. One of them slipped through the doors. The other one stood over Mike. He started to turn toward the door, and Mike grabbed his ankle. I said to myself, Mike, you stupid ass. And then I saw the gunman turn and the gun swing around with him and I moved to get in front of you because I knew that gun was going to go off.

"I didn't feel any pain. There was a sudden loss of balance, and a slow topple to the floor. Somebody yelled, '*He's bleeding.*' And I wondered who was bleeding." He paused. "I took a bullet for you."

CHAPTER 41

"McQueen is dead," said Foxx.

"Did you talk to him first?" said Bev.

"Yes, and I'm sorry, too. Thank you for your condolences."

"Foxx."

"Yeah, I talked to him. He said Gary had the missing treasure piece, which he, McQueen, found in the courthouse."

"That's it?"

"He also asked about Ursula. I didn't tell him she was dead. Then he coded."

"Atabrine," said Bev.

"What?"

"He had Atabrine in his system. Quinine."

"But that's not lethal."

"It can be in high-enough concentrations. And McQueen was not a well man. He had serious kidney and liver problems."

For Foxx, this was the type of revelation that immediately made sense because it was all of a piece with McQueen's bad complexion, contentious personality, and terrible work ethic. Chronic illness was a logical underpinning.

"He have any idea where Gary went?"

"Never got that far," said Foxx.

"Well, he shouldn't be too tough to find," said Bev. "He's in a wheelchair. We've got calls into all the major ambulette services in case he dials one up."

Foxx grunted.

"I spoke to Belcher. After Conover formally declares a mistrial this morning, she'll have the option of working in chambers or taking a leave for the rest of the month."

"Whatever," said Foxx.

"My sentiments exactly," said Bev.

Linda woke to light. Not a lot of light, but definitely enough for her to see that she had gotten through the night. Somehow. Without a clock or a phone, she tried to reason what time it might be. Mid-October, three weeks past the equinox. Equinox meant twelve-hour days and twelve-hour nights. In general terms, 6:00 a.m. to 6:00 p.m. So what could it be? Seven o'clock? Later? She was due back at the courthouse at nine thirty to declare a mistrial and disband the jury. Other than her own sense of duty, she had no obligation to handle these technicalities. Sharon had been gracious in yesterday's aftermath and would understand if she didn't show up.

And then she remembered Bernadette.

She pushed herself up and then squirmed forward to ease the cuff pressure on her ankles. Gary lay on his back, with his hips turned away from her and his legs crossed like the legs of a marionette.

"Gary," she said.

He groaned, then sank back into sleep.

"Gary." She poked his shoulder. "I need to use the bathroom."

He shook his head and then opened his eyes.

"What was that?" he said.

"I need to use the bathroom."

"Now?"

"Yes. Now."

He dragged himself to the edge of the bed, slowly rotating his torso until his back faced the wheelchair. He gripped the two armrests like a gymnast on a pommel horse and, with a grunt, lifted his butt off the bed and dropped himself heavily onto the seat. His legs, still crossed at the ankles, stayed on the bed. He reversed the chair, and his legs fell off, his heels hitting the floor with two solid thuds. He stopped the chair, then used his hands to lift one leg and then the other to set his feet on the footrest.

He rolled alongside the spindle and used a key to unlock one of the cuffs.

"There," he said.

"Can you take the other off, too?"

Gary made no move.

"It hurts," she said. "And I'm not going to run."

He hesitated, then unlocked the other cuff. Linda drew up her legs and rubbed her ankles with her hands.

"Thank you," she said, and dropped herself to the floor. "I'm just going to make it."

She hurried down the corridor between the two walk-in closets and closed herself into the bathroom. The door and the lock were weak, more suggestions of privacy than barriers against intrusion. But she clicked the lock anyway, then turned on the lights and the ventilator fan. The bathroom had a single frosted glass window over the toilet. She climbed onto the toilet lid and quietly lifted the sash as far as it would go. The screen popped out easily with a push. It sailed downward, bounced off the awning, and landed on the deck with a crack.

Dammit, she thought. But several seconds passed, and Gary did not react.

She poked her head out the window. No lights were on in the brownstones across the back gardens, no one sat on a deck drinking coffee. She could start screaming, but she didn't know her neighbors and doubted anyone would take her screams seriously. Besides, Gary would hear. He'd break through the flimsy door in a second, and who knew what he would do . . . which made the awning more inviting.

She ran her hand along the inside edge of the window, considering whether it was big enough. She'd need to go out feet first and wriggle her body through, all the while gripping the window frame. The awning was ten feet down. With her arms extended she'd be about six feet tall, which meant her drop to the awning would be only about four feet. The patio furniture was still on the deck. If the awning held—*if* the awning held—she could slide down to the edge and jump onto the love seat.

A slim chance, she thought, but her only one right now.

She lifted one leg through the window, then contorted herself enough to fit her second leg through. She sat on the sill, her legs dangling outside and the rest of her still in the bathroom. The opening was just large enough for her to roll herself onto her belly. As she began to roll, she heard the doorbell. Then the pain hit her.

Gary had his pants on and one arm in a shirtsleeve when the doorbell rang. He froze. The bathroom door was still closed. Linda did not call out to him, which meant she might not have heard it.

The doorbell rang again, twice quickly now, as if the person was impatient. He punched his other arm into the sleeve. Again, Linda did not call, so he rolled out of the bedroom and into the sitting room. Turning the battle chair sideways and leaning close to the window, he could see down to the stoop. Bernadette.

"Shit," he muttered.

Bernadette pressed the doorbell one more time, then backed away from the door and looked up. Gary jerked away from the window. The doorbell did not ring again, and after a few seconds he returned to the window. Bernadette was on the sidewalk now, drifting slowly toward Broadway with her cell phone to her ear. Linda's cell phone buzzed in Gary's parka, which still hung over the back of the battle chair. It buzzed until Bernadette went out of sight.

Storm's over, thought Gary.

With Judge Conover's courtroom still an active crime scene, Foxx received instructions to set up in a different courtroom with a different clerk and six other court officers. Public proceedings be damned, no one except the lawyers and the jurors would be allowed inside. It would take Linda barely more than a few minutes to declare a mistrial and disband the jury.

Foxx removed the cardboard covers from the two small door windows, then unlocked the doors. Pinter and Braman were waiting in the corridor, along with three people with press credentials Foxx happily suggested should take a hike. The court reporter set up her steno machine. Billy Cokeley rushed in, saw that nothing was happening yet, and immediately relaxed.

Foxx tried to analyze the bad feeling in his gut. Mike and Ursula were dead. Gary was missing. And then there was this thing about the treasure piece. He was under orders not to disclose any of this to anyone. He was to observe and report, just like always. But that bad feeling still gnawed at him, and he suspected that it might be related to none of the above.

The clerk gave Foxx a sign, and Foxx went to the jury room to count heads. Seven of the eight jurors were there, the men still wearing their jackets and the women sitting with their purses clutched on their laps. Foxx put together some words of reassurance. The judge would be here soon, the proceedings wouldn't take more than a few minutes, their jury service would be over, they wouldn't be called back for at least four years.

As Foxx descended the stairs to the robing room, his cell phone buzzed.

"Is she there?" said Bernadette.

"Not in the courtroom," said Foxx. "Don't know about chambers."

"I was at her place," said Bernadette. "She didn't answer her door."

"She could be on her way."

"Yeah, except she would have told me," said Bernadette. "She's not answering her cell phone, either."

"Are you still at her place?"

"No. Heading toward Broadway to pick up the two train."

"Let me make some calls. I'll get back to you."

Gary rolled back into the bedroom and began to work a sneaker onto his foot. The bathroom door was still closed and there was no sign Linda had heard the doorbell. He wondered if Linda had planned for Bernadette to drop by on her way to the courthouse. If so, somebody somewhere would figure out something was wrong. Soon.

"Gary."

Did Linda just call his name? He wasn't sure.

"Gary."

He definitely heard her that time. Her voice sounded weak, but tense.

"Linda." He drove toward the bathroom.

"Gary, help me." There was a cry in her voice.

He stopped at the door.

"It's locked," he said.

"I can't open it. Break it. Hurry."

He used the battle chair like a battering ram. Pulled back, shot forward. Pulled back, shot forward.

"Hurry," she cried.

On the third try, the doorjamb splintered.

Linda sat on the toilet, her sweatpants pooled at her ankles, her head in her hands. She looked up. Her face was wet, her eyes red from crying.

"Something bad happened," she said.

She sat back, and Gary saw the blood glistening on her thighs. She tried to stand up, but dropped back onto the seat.

"Help me," she said.

Gary nudged the battle chair toward her.

"Give me your hands," he said.

Linda reached toward him, and he gathered both of her hands in one of his.

"I'm going to back up slowly and pull you forward. The rug is soft. I want you to lie down."

"Okay," she said.

He eased back the joystick, pulling her off the toilet. There were bloody streaks on the porcelain, bloody water in the bowl. He kept easing back, and she went from standing to kneeling to lying face-down on the rug. She rolled onto her side, clutched her stomach, and groaned.

"What is it, Linda? What's wrong?"

"I need a doctor."

"But what's going on? Why are you bleeding. Is it your period? Is it . . . ?"

"Gary, I need a doctor. Call 911. Please."

He reached back into the parka. Pulled out Linda's phone. Fumbled it. Caught it. Saw that Bernadette left a voicemail.

There was lots of blood, and Linda was in terrible pain.

"Hurry," she whispered, as she drew her knees up to her chest.

He pressed the nine, and then the doorbell rang.

He backed out of the bathroom, zipped through the bedroom.

"Gary," Linda called weakly.

But Gary had a hopeful idea, a better idea, an idea that didn't involve the police or EMTs. He drove to the sitting room window, and sure enough, Bernadette was on the stoop, punching the door-bell as if this time she would not go away. Gary went to the elevator, made it down to the first floor, drew Mike's service piece from inside the parka.

Then he answered the door.

"Gary?!" said Bernadette.

She spotted the gun and tried to back away, but Gary grabbed her wrist and pulled her inside.

"What are you doing? Where's Linda?"

"Upstairs bathroom. She's in trouble. Come."

He pushed her into the elevator.

"What kind of trouble?" said Bernadette.

"She's bleeding."

"Bleeding from what? Gary, what are you doing here?"

He didn't answer. The elevator stopped on the second floor, and Bernadette ran off. Gary rolled after her. Bernadette already was kneeling over Linda when he reached the bathroom.

"Holy shit," said Bernadette. She patted Linda's cheek. Linda groaned, then opened her eyes.

"Hey," she said.

"Hey," said Bernadette. "You okay?"

"Do I look it?"

"Is it like a heavy period?" said Gary.

"Period?" said Bernadette. "Are you an imbecile? She needs a doctor."

"No doctor. You need to fix it."

"Gary, that's crazy. I can't fix this."

"You'll fix it," said Gary. He waved the gun. "Give me your cell phone."

Bernadette took it from her jacket pocket, looked at it as if weighing exactly how stupid it would be to punch in 911, then handed it over.

"Now fix it," said Gary.

Bernadette opened the door to the vanity.

"Dammit, Linda. Don't you have maxi pads?"

"Ran out. Didn't think to buy any."

"Towels. I need towels," said Bernadette.

"Linen closet in the hallway," said Linda.

Bernadette turned to Gary. "Get 'em. As many as you can." She snorted. "Fix it. What an asshole."

Gary backed quickly down the corridor. The linens were behind a door in the hallway that looked just like the door to the elevator. Gary pulled towels off the shelves, piling them on his lap.

Staccato thoughts zipped through his head. Was he too rough with her last night? Cuffing her, dragging her, bowling her over with the battle chair. She had whaled at him, and he had bearhugged her until she calmed down. Could he have caused her to hemorrhage?

Something didn't seem right, but he wasn't sure what it could be. He had no time, either. He needed to get back to Linda. He added one more towel to the pile on his lap, then turned toward the bedroom.

And then he had it.

There was one thing he hadn't told Linda last night, a small detail from the day he was shot that didn't seem important at the time. He hadn't realized he was shot, but as he lay on the courtroom floor and the blood seeped into his shirt, he noticed a funny smell that evoked a boyhood memory—the smell of his palm after holding a handful of old pennies. It was later that he learned it was the smell of his own blood.

If anything, all that blood in the bathroom should have a distinctive smell. He didn't know what that smell might be—salty, funky, maybe even fishy. But he knew one thing with certainty: there was no smell in that bathroom.

He rolled back into the bedroom, slowly now because the emergency was over. He stopped at the bathroom door. Linda was sitting up now, her back against the vanity. Bernadette knelt beside her. She seemed to be working between Linda's legs, but her back was to Gary and she blocked his view.

"Towel," she said, raising a hand over her shoulder.

Gary dropped the whole pile of towels on the floor beside the battle chair.

"Towel," Bernadette said again. When Gary didn't respond, she began to turn around.

Gary lifted the gun off his lap.

"Get up," he said.

"I need those towels," said Bernadette. "She's lost a lot of blood."

"Get up," said Gary. "And step away from her."

Bernadette stood up, allowing Gary to see Linda. Linda's sweatpants were pushed down to her knees, but her panties were in place. As if Gary needed any further proof.

He tossed Linda a towel.

"Clean yourself up," he said.

She started to protest, but he cut her off.

"Clean yourself up. I don't know whether that's paint or some kind of makeup, but it isn't blood."

Linda wiped her thighs, pulled up her sweatpants, and stood up.

"You stay in here." Gary pointed the gun at Bernadette. "You come with me."

Linda slowly walked to Gary. Once she was in reach, he yanked her onto his lap and pressed the gun against her chin.

"I don't like being played for a fool," he said.

In the bedroom, he raised the seat of the battle chair and spilled Linda onto the bed. Neither said a word as he cuffed her by the ankles to a spindle. He gave the cuffs a shake, then drove back to the bathroom.

"Your turn," he told Bernadette, patting his lap.

CHAPTER 42

Foxx used the robing room phone to call Linda's chambers and then Judge Belcher's chambers. No one in either chambers had seen or heard from Linda, and that bad feeling in Foxx's gut worsened. He replayed last night's taxi ride and his short time in Linda's house. The bittersweet feel of his departure had lingered into the night before fading. Now he wondered if it was a clue to something he might have missed.

He used his cell phone to call Bernadette. Her phone rang and rang, then kicked into voicemail. He started to leave a message, then cut the call because at that moment, Judge Belcher burst through the stage entrance, already wearing her robe.

"I've decided I can't keep these lawyers and jurors waiting around," she said. "Obviously something's come up with Judge Conover. Everyone here?"

"The lawyers are," said Foxx. "Missing one juror at last count."

"Count again. I need to get this done and move on to the other seventy-five problems on my desk."

Foxx climbed to the jury room and counted the same seven jurors. Then he descended all the way to the basement and out the back door.

* * *

Linda sat up as soon as the elevator door opened.

"What did you do with Bernadette?" she said. She had tried to listen as Gary took her friend away, but after the elevator landed and the whirr of the wheelchair faded, she heard nothing.

"She called me an imbecile," said Gary. He stopped at the foot of the bed, his hand quivering on the joystick, which caused the whole wheelchair to tremble. He did not look at her.

"That's just Bernadette, Gary. She always talks like that. She doesn't mean anything by it."

"She called me an imbecile," he repeated. "An asshole, too. I'm not an imbecile. I'm not an asshole. I found the missing piece."

"And that was amazing," said Linda. "But I still need to know. What did you do with Bernadette?"

"I don't want to talk about it."

"Look, Gary, it's not too late. You can leave. I won't press charges. Bernadette won't press charges. You can take the piece. I never saw it. I'll deny to the death that I ever saw it. We'll give you an hour, two hours, whatever head start you need. You can go wherever you want, sell the piece to whoever you want."

"No, no," Gary wailed. "That piece means nothing to me. When I go, you're coming with me."

"Well," said Linda. She reminded herself to stay calm, to measure her words. "Here is where things get complicated. Bernadette panicked when she saw me because she knows something that you don't know. Gary, I'm pregnant. I was pregnant once before, and it ended in a miscarriage. She knows that, too."

Gary pressed his hands to his temples.

"I don't want to hear it," he said.

"It's the truth. Sorry. I know how much it hurts you. But it's the truth."

"Enough!" Gary shouted. "I don't want to hear any more."

He spun out of the bedroom.

Gary bumped the battle chair up to the sitting room window. The early morning sunshine had dimmed behind a line of clouds. The sky was a flat gray, the leaves still hanging on the sidewalk trees were a dull brown.

His problem was not so much Linda's resistance than his own failure to think things through. He'd started this without a firm grip on all the consequences. It all seemed so simple: show her the missing piece, read her *The Missing Piece*, return her to that day, and let the gears of their lives reengage. After that, forward motion, smooth rolling, the cheese wheel with its missing piece firmly and perfectly in place. But it didn't work out, not the way he envisioned it, so he went to plan B. Hold her, lie beside her, wait for her to come to him and fit herself into the big missing piece of himself.

Well, that didn't happen.

She'd warned him, he realized now, when she said she wasn't perfect. It wasn't modesty, it wasn't even denial. She had an appendage. A baby. Some goddam appendage. And then she tricked him. And then Bernadette showed up to make it two against one. He had a mess on his hands now, with no plan C.

Mike had an old saying about girlfriends and girlfriends' friends. "It's not your girlfriend who fucks you up," he'd say. "It's your girlfriend's friends you need to worry about." Nobody ever gave Mike much credence, probably because he never seemed to have a girlfriend. But damn, thought Gary, Mike might have had more wisdom than he got credit for. Too bad Mike and the missing piece were mutually exclusive. He would have been a good guy to have around right now. An extra set of eyes, an extra pair of hands, a different set of ideas. Someone who could think up a plan C.

And then Gary had his plan C. And this plan C had everything to do with Mike.

Gary played pocket pool with the cell phones in his parka, mulling this new idea over because he wanted to be sure he considered all the consequences. He would leave, like Linda said. Only he wouldn't go just anywhere, and he wouldn't go alone. He and Linda would go to Mike's cabin in the Catskills. He had been there once, late that first summer after the heist. It was a shambles, but it was built at ground level, and he could get the battle chair through the front door. They could rough it till he thought of something better.

He grabbed his phone. The private ambulette service he used would charge him dearly for a trip upstate. But the driver would ask no questions. And, after all, money was no object. He didn't just have all the money from the fund-raiser; he also had the missing piece.

Speak of the devil and he appears, thought Linda. Pretend to miscarry and a miscarriage might visit you.

She lay on her side, having pushed herself down toward the footboard so that she could draw up her knees. The wave of cramping slowly ebbed. She could hear Gary talking. The words were unclear, but carried the cadence and rhythm of a phone call. Silence followed, and Linda slowly stretched out and eased onto her back.

The wheelchair whirred, and Gary rolled into the bedroom.

"You said I should leave," said Gary.

Linda sat up. "That's right," she said warily.

"Then here's the deal. I'm leaving, and you're coming with me."

"Gary, I can't do that."

"You're going to do that. This isn't a negotiation."

"I won't do that."

"You will do that. A car is on the way. We are leaving."

Linda slid herself so she could hug her legs to her chest and press her forehead against her knees. Then she lifted her head and stared at Gary.

"I'll go with you on two conditions. First, you let me see that Bernadette's all right. Second, you let her go."

"I'm not doing that," said Gary.

"Then I'm not going with you," said Linda. She lay back down and rolled onto her side.

"I give you my word that Bernadette is all right," he said. "But I'm not going to let you see her. We will leave and when we get where we are going, we will call someone and let them know she is here."

"Who?"

"Captain Kearney."

"What about Foxx?"

"Kearney. That's the deal. And stop playing me."

Linda sat up. "Okay, I'll go with you. Let me pack some things."

"Linda."

"I'm going with you to some unspecified place for some unspecified length of time, and I'm supposed to go with only the clothes on my back?"

"Fine," said Gary.

He drove to Linda's walk-in closet. There were rows of dresses and skirts, racks of sweaters and slacks, pairs and pairs of shoes. Up above, on a shelf, were suitcases. He moved under the shelf and raised the battle chair's seat as high as it would go. His hand just caught the handle of the lowest suitcase. He pulled, and three tumbled down on him. He dragged the largest back into the bedroom and opened it on the bed.

"I didn't see anything but fancy stuff in there," he said.

"That's because all the unfancy stuff is out here," said Linda. "Uncuff me and I'll pack."

"No, you tell me where."

But before Linda could answer, Gary's cell phone rang.

"Are you fuckin' kidding me?" he said. "Okay, okay."

He ended the call.

"They're on their way. Dammit."

"Who's on their way?"

"The car," said Gary. He unlocked the cuffs. "Okay. You pack. Fast."

After Gary opened the cuffs, he backed the battle chair into the doorway in case Linda tried to run. There was no other way out, unless she wanted to try the bathroom window. Linda moved quickly, opening dresser drawers, lifting out piles of underwear, jeans, and sweaters. It was a promising start to plan C. Still, he locked one ring of the cuffs to the arm of the battle chair.

Ten minutes later, his cell rang.

"You're kidding. You're not kidding," he said, and hung up. "Jeesh, all these years they make me wait. Now they're early and up my ass about it."

Linda laughed, really laughed, and for a moment it seemed to him that they weren't at odds. She stuffed one last sweatshirt into the suitcase, pressed down the lid, and snapped the locks.

"Ready," she said.

There was something almost sprightly in the way she said that one word, and he thought maybe something had happened in these last few minutes. Maybe he had scratched through the shell of the last few years to the feelings he believed she had for him underneath.

He backed the battle chair into the hallway, angling it to block the path to the stairs on the off-chance she might run. But she rolled the big, heavy suitcase out of the bedroom and swung open the door to the elevator.

They both looked at the tiny space.

"You'll need to back in first," said Linda.

Gary shook the open ring of the handcuff.

"Oh please, Gary. You think I'm going to run and leave you here with Bernadette? Let's go if we're going to go. Get in there."

Gary backed in, briefly tensing at the thought that Linda might run. But she rolled the suitcase right in after him and began to wedge it in beside the battle chair.

"Don't do that," said Gary.

"Okay," said Linda. She set it crossways in front of Gary. "Now there's no room for me. How about this?"

She lifted the suitcase and stood it on the arms of the battle chair, blocking Gary's view as the door closed and the elevator started down.

Then it stopped and went dark.

"What happened?" said Gary.

There was no answer.

The elevator had a control panel on each floor, and on the second floor it was in the linen closet. Linda, after jumping out of the car before the doors slid shut, hit every switch with the idea that one of them had to kill the power. She heard the motor cut and, one second later, Gary start to shout. She backed out of the closet and listened at the elevator door. Gary was stuck between floors, cursing like a madman.

"Have fun," she said.

She sprinted to the stairs.

She searched the first floor from front to back. Foyer, foyer closet, front den, living room, another closet. No Bernadette anywhere. She reached the kitchen. The silver urn still stood on the counter. The back door chain was still in place. It was here or the basement.

Gary couldn't believe it. He couldn't fuckin' believe it. She had tricked him, played him, screwed him.

He threw the suitcase off his lap. It hit the wall and bounced back, so he threw it off again. Goddam shitty little elevator didn't even have an emergency light. It was fuckin' pitch black.

"Linda!" he yelled again. "Goddam you!"

Ridiculous, he realized, stupid. A waste of energy. He needed to get out of here somehow. He ran his hands across the elevator car door. It was a two-piece slider, which meant it had an edge where one piece slid over the other. He turned the battle chair sideways, jammed the footrests against the side wall, and twisted himself so he could hook all his fingers along that edge.

He began to pull.

"Bern, hey, Bern."

Linda leaned over the kitchen counter, but Bernadette wasn't back there. Behind her, Gary had stopped cursing. Instead, she heard grunts and thuds coming from the elevator shaft.

She reached the back door and, though she doubted Bernadette was out there, looked through the window. The deck furniture was still in place, the screen from the bathroom window lay beside the love seat.

Beside the back door was the door to the pantry.

"Bern?" said Linda.

Then she opened the door.

Gary eased off to give his arm a rest. The sliders had moved a couple of inches, but he needed better leverage to open them all the way.

He knew he was close to the first floor. He could hear Linda at a distance, calling for Bernadette. Once Linda found her, his time would be up.

He spun the battle chair so that it faced in the opposite direction. He braced his arm along the first slider and locked his palm against the edge of the second. With his free hand, he pushed the joystick forward. The wheels bit, the motor groaned, and slowly the sliders began to give way.

Bernadette lay among cases of bottled water and piles of canned vegetables. Her ankles and wrists were bound with plastic garbage bag ties. A cloth napkin was stuffed in her mouth.

Linda pulled out the napkin. Bernadette gagged and then sucked air.

"Bastard," she said. "Where is he?"

"In the elevator," said Linda. "Stuck between floors."

"How'd you manage that?"

"Never mind."

"Well, what the hell's this all about?"

"Never mind that, either. We need to get the hell out of here."

The ties were too thick to tear off. Linda went into the kitchen. She needed a scissors, but with the constant thumping coming from the elevator she was too jittery to remember where she kept them. She opened the silverware drawer and grabbed a steak knife instead.

Back in the pantry, she knelt in front of Bernadette. Louder banging sounded in the hallway.

"What's that?" Bernadette whispered sharply.

"Don't move," said Linda, sawing the knife into the ties that bound Bernadette's ankles.

There was a second bang.

"Stand up and turn around."

Bernadette got to her feet, and Linda started working on the ties that bound her wrists behind her back.

After opening the sliders another couple of inches, Gary was getting nowhere. The battle chair's motor strained, its tires spun on the floor of the car, the heel of his hand hurt like hell. He eased off the joystick, if only to dampen the pain, then began to goose it rhythmically. Back and forth, back and forth, like rocking a car out of a snowbank. The tires held their traction, and the sliders, ever so slightly, began to move.

Grunting, he kept up the pressure. He was going to break this door. He didn't mind the pain. In fact, he welcomed it, he reveled in it. It was much better than the three years of radio silence between his legs and his head.

It happened suddenly. The sliders gave way, and the battle chair lurched forward, crashing into the wall of the car. More light seeped in now. He could see Linda's suitcase upended against the back of the car, the open gashes where the battle chair's footrests cracked the faux wood paneling. The light was coming in from around the door to the first-floor hallway.

Almost there, he thought.

Leaning over the armrest, he pushed the door. It rattled on its hinges, but wouldn't open. Still, after wrestling with the sliders, forcing this door would be easy.

He spun the battle chair to face the door. He jammed the joystick forward, then immediately pulled it back. Two hits and the door cracked lengthwise. One more and it flew open. The front wheels of the battle chair fell off the floor of the car, but the rear wheels had enough torque to drag them back up.

Four feet below, Gary saw the parquet hardwood of the first-floor hallway. He heard whispers, anxious whispers. And then the whispers stopped.

Linda found Bernadette, which meant he had only a few seconds to stop them. Four feet. He couldn't just drive out of the elevator. The battle chair would tumble forward. Land on him. Probably kill him.

He quickly shrugged into his parka and detached the cushion from the backrest. He secured the gun inside the parka, held the cushion in front of his face and chest like a surfer on a boogie board. Then he leaned forward until gravity took over.

* * *

The doorbell rang as Linda sawed into the ties behind Bernadette's back.

"Who's that?" said Bernadette.

"Gary's driver."

"What?"

"He was taking me away," said Linda.

"Where?"

A tremendously loud thud resounded in the hallway.

"What was that?" said Bernadette.

"Don't know," said Linda. She cut through the tie. "Let's go."

They ran out of the pantry and crossed behind the end of the granite counter to where they could see down the hallway to the front door.

"Damn," muttered Linda.

"Shit," breathed Bernadette.

Gary lay facedown on the floor, literally filling the width of the hallway. He shook his head, pressed his hands against the floor, and lifted his head and shoulders.

"Back door," Linda whispered.

They did a quick about-face and attacked the locks with all four hands until they heard a loud bang and the wood above their heads splintered.

Foxx gave up on the phone calls. Last he tried, both cells kicked immediately into voicemail. That didn't bode well. He got off the subway train at the Broadway and Seventy-second Street station, ran up Broadway to Linda's street, then turned east. The street had solid lines of parked cars on both sides. Up ahead, way up ahead, at what looked to be approximately in front of Linda's house, a van was double-parked. Foxx ran right down the middle of the street. As he got closer, he saw that the van wasn't approximately in front of Linda's house; it was directly in front. The rear door on the passenger's side was open, and a wheelchair ramp angled down to the street.

Foxx shuffled between two parked cars and onto the sidewalk. A small man stood on Linda's stoop, pressing the doorbell.

Foxx took the steps in three long strides.

"What are you doing here?" he said.

"Picking up a client," said the man. He spoke with a South Asian accent.

"Gary Martin?"

The man stuttered. Foxx opened his jacket and pressed his court officer's shield to the man's face.

"Gary Martin?" he repeated.

"Yes, yes. The client is he."

Foxx tried the door. Locked.

A crack sounded inside. Foxx knew that crack well. It was the report of a gun, not just any gun, but a gun of a certain caliber. He knew that report from the shooting range where regulations required him to requalify every year. It came from a Glock 9mm, a court officer's service piece.

"You got tools?" he said. "Crowbar? Tire iron?"

"Tire iron in the back," said the man.

Foxx shoved his phone at him.

"Call 911. Give this address and say 'shots fired.'"

He ran down the steps, lifted the rear gate of the van, found a tire iron on a heap of oily rags. As he wedged the iron between the door and the jamb, the man said, "Shots fired," into the phone.

And then another shot crackled inside.

Linda and Bernadette cowered on the floor behind the counter. They could hear Gary grunting, panting, his belt buckle scraping the floor as he dragged himself toward the kitchen.

"We gotta do something," said Linda.

"Someone's at the door," said Bernadette.

"Yeah, lotta good that does us."

"They musta heard the shots. They must be calling the cops."

"We can't assume that," said Linda. "They could be running away, too."

Gary fired again. This time a hole opened in the ceiling near the back door. Shattered plaster rained down.

"Dammit," said Linda.

They were safe here, but only for the moment. Gary was crawling into the kitchen now. His grunting was louder and his belt buckle made a different scraping sound on the tiles. He couldn't lift himself up and over the counter. But he knew where they were, and they knew that once he reached the end of the counter he'd have them trapped.

"How many shots do you think he has?" whispered Bernadette.

"I don't know. You were the gun expert."

"Long time ago. Court officer guns used to have clips of nine. That's all I remember."

"We don't know if it's a court officer's gun," said Linda.

Someone started banging on the front door.

"They're back," said Bernadette.

The banging sounded like metal on wood. But unless it was a firefighter with an ax, Linda knew that the door would hold much too long.

"He's going to crawl around and corner us," said Bernadette. "We should wait till he gets close, then jump over the counter and run."

"We'll have no cover," said Linda.

"We'll be behind him. He'll need to turn himself to get a shot at us. We can run upstairs."

Bernadette rose on her knees as if to peek over the counter. Gary fired at the same time. A spotlight exploded, bits of broken glass and plastic fell on them.

Scratch that plan, thought Linda. She took a deep breath. Gary's belt buckle scraped again on the tiles. He was directly on the other side of the counter, about six feet from the end. If he could put a slug in the ceiling above them, he could turn himself enough to squeeze off a couple of good ones as they ran down the hallway.

The front door would hold. Gary would reach the end of the counter. They needed to end this themselves. There was no other way.

Linda slid across the kitchen, reached up to the counter, and fell back to the floor. One hand pressed against a sudden pain in her belly, the other held a carving knife. She slid back to Bernadette, expecting another shot but hearing only another scrape of belt buckle on tile.

"Are you okay?" said Bernadette.

"I'm fine."

"You're not fine. You were holding your belly."

"I'm fine. It's just a twinge. I've had enough of this shit. I'm ending this. I'm going over the top and onto his back."

"No, you're not."

"Why not?"

"Because I'm doing it."

"But this is all about me. Something I did or said to him without knowing."

"That doesn't matter right now," said Bernadette. "I'm doing it. You're not well and you have a baby to carry."

She lifted her pinkie. Linda stared for a moment, then locked her pinkie around it.

They pulled apart. Bernadette kicked off her pumps, shed her jacket. She took the carving knife from Linda, held it first as a sword and then as a dagger before going back to holding it as a sword.

Behind them, Gary's belt buckle scraped again. At least he's on his stomach right now, thought Linda.

Bernadette went into a crouch.

Good luck, mouthed Linda.

See you in a minute, Bernadette mouthed back.

She pushed herself up and over the top.

Gary was tiring fast. Even with many months of constant exercise devoted to keeping his arms and upper body strong, he still hadn't exerted himself like he had this morning. But he was near the end. The end of the counter. The end of everything.

The old firing range mantra came to mind as he pulled himself another few inches forward. Two in the head and two in the body. He didn't need so many shots. He needed only three. One for his girlfriend, one for his girlfriend's friend, and then one for himself.

In between pulls, he could hear them on the other side. Talking about him. Plotting. He rolled onto his left side so he could look up at the counter. They could jump over and run down the hallway. He needed to be ready for that.

He rolled onto his stomach, measured the distance to the end of the counter. One pull, maybe two, and he'd be within reach of the end. He'd stay on his left side from that point on, hook his left hand on the corner of the counter, keep his right hand on the gun.

He needed only one more pull to reach the end. But as he rolled onto his left side, something dark fluttered above him. Something large, falling.

The girlfriend's friend.

He saw a glint, felt his cheek rip. The girlfriend's friend had a knife in her hand. Her first swipe had cut his cheek, and now she straddled his hips, her shoulders twisting as she coiled for a second swipe. He pushed himself up, rocking her backward enough that the knife flashed passed, missing his face. She regained her balance and pushed forward while swiping at him again with a backhand. He caught her wrist and slammed it against the counter. Once, twice, and the knife fell from her hand. Blood ran from a slit below his eye, gathered in his mustache, and seeped into his mouth. He pressed the gun to her forehead.

Linda heard things go wrong: Gary's triumphant grunt, Bernadette's terrified cry. She jumped up, grabbed the closest thing to a weapon, and vaulted over the counter.

She landed on Gary's chest, knocking him back to the floor and pinning his arm beneath her. She struck him on the head. The gun went off, and she struck him a second time.

"Linda!" cried Bernadette.

"No," she said.

"Linda!"

"No, no, no," she said, pounding Gary each time, feeling his skull soften with each blow until Foxx pried the missing piece from her hand.

Foxx pulled her to her feet, and she collapsed against him. She sobbed into his chest until a pain stabbed her belly and her breath caught in her throat.

"Sit me down," she said. "Gently."

Foxx guided her around the counter and eased her onto the floor. Bernadette, her slacks soaked with the blood from Gary's gut wound, knelt beside Linda and stroked her hair. Linda closed her eyes and hugged her belly, then flinched at another stab of pain.

"No way," she said. "Not this time."

CHAPTER 43

The August term of court is the quiet time of year at 60 Centre Street. Trial lawyers take vacation. Judges take vacation. The courtrooms stay locked and dark. Those who do work try to accomplish what cannot be accomplished during the rest of the year. This year, the librarian started a top-to-bottom cleaning of the dusty, overburdened library stacks. Jessima helped.

The work was arduous, unstacking and dusting every book on every shelf, dusting the shelf, and then restacking the books. During the week before Labor Day, the most quiet week of the quiet term, Jessima reached the mezzanine level. As she unstacked a set of digests, she heard something slip down behind the small wooden bookcase. She looked into the thin space and spotted a motion folder.

Jessima knew the folder was important and wondered why it was hidden behind the bookcase. It was the kind of find she would have reported to Damien. But she hadn't seen Damien in almost a year. For all she knew, he was dead.

Jessima needed to do something with the folder. The librarian didn't want it, so she walked half the hexagon until she reached the fifth-floor security desk. She handed it to the officer.

"Thanks," said Foxx.

*   *   *

"I won't deny I was angry with her," said Mark Garber. He and Foxx were walking along the outside of City Hall Park. Tour buses idled, their fumes thickening the unseasonably hot air. Sweat darkened patches of Mark's new uniform, the red smock issued by the office supply store where he now worked.

"But I'm not angry with her," he continued. "Yeah, she let me go. But she was the only person during my whole time at Sixty who I can honestly say was up front with me."

Mark admitted everything, not that Foxx needed the admission. He just wanted to confirm the timing.

"That's it down to the minute," said Mark. "I don't think I'll ever forget."

They got as far as the corner of Chambers Street before it was time to part ways. Farther up Centre Street, the facade of the courthouse angled into Foley Square.

"This is as close as I've gotten since I left," said Mark.

The basement of the mission was not a flophouse. It had cots, but only for the half dozen souls who worked there regularly. Ronan Hannigan was gone. After he lost his case and then the appeal, he went off looking for other windmills to tilt and other unfortunates to shepherd.

Damien Wheatley lay on one of the cots. His chest was sunken, and his ribs looked like church pews beneath his T-shirt. Foxx nudged the cot with his knee, and Damien sat up. With his dreadlocks gone, his face looked gaunt, his cheek scar more prominent.

Foxx sat on the adjoining cot.

"You met Judge Johnstone in the coffee shop that morning, right?"

Damien nodded, and Foxx moved on to more important matters.

* * *

Linda dangled a tiny plush pony in front of Emily. The baby, who everyone agreed had her mother's bright eyes and her father's black hair, swiped a dimpled hand at the pony and smiled.

Foxx knocked on the open door. Chambers had a much different decor now, with a bassinet and a changing table replacing one of the sofas in Linda's private office. A template for the modern judge, she had announced the day the furniture arrived, studiously not modifying *judge* with *female* or *divorced*.

"Order to show cause," said Foxx. He handed the folder across the desk.

"Braman again?" said Linda.

"Read it this time," said Foxx.

"Bossy, huh? Bernadette's rubbing off on you."

Foxx said nothing.

Linda sat down to read the order and Braman's supporting affirmation. Foxx dangled the pony. Emily cooed.

"I suppose if Braman can't find his client I'll allow him to withdraw from the case. Gives me the rest of the day off and another month before the trial." Linda stroked her initials on the signature line. "Do you think Leinster is hiding?"

"I think he's dead," said Foxx.

He made photocopies of the order, then went down to the robing room. He peeked into the lavatory, then called the court clerk on the intercom and asked to see the lawyers. A moment later, Braman, Pinter, and Cokeley filed in.

"The judge signed the order to show cause and stayed the trial," said Foxx. He handed a copy to each of the lawyers.

"I don't plan to oppose," said Pinter.

"Neither do I," said Cokeley.

Professional courtesy at its finest, thought Foxx, as the three lawyers headed toward the courtroom door.

"Mr. Braman," said Foxx. "I need a word."

Braman waited until the courtroom door closed behind his adversaries.

"What can I do for you?" he said.

"For me, nothing," said Foxx. "But there are a couple of people who need to speak to you."

He whistled. Bev stepped out of the lavatory as a man came in the stage entrance. Bev looked neat and precise as ever in a business suit. The man wore a raincoat. Braman looked back and forth between the two, confused.

"Mr. Braman," said Bev. "We have evidence to prove that last October you made an implied promise to Mark Garber that you would hire him if he gave an affidavit to support your motion to disqualify Judge Conover from the Roman silver trial."

"Implied promise," said Braman, laughing. "That's a good one."

"It gets better," said Bev. "You read the affidavit and thought it was too weak to convince Judge Conover to disqualify herself. But then, someone offered you personal information about the judge. She was pregnant, which presented you with the chance to scare her off the case. So you hired two goons to assault her. When that didn't work, you submitted the order to show cause. But Mark, who had second thoughts about selling out his judge, intercepted it."

"This is absurd," said Braman. "Who the hell are you?"

"The inspector general," said Bev.

"You don't have any jurisdiction over me."

"Maybe not," said Bev. "But he does."

The man in the raincoat opened his hand to show an NYPD detective's shield in his palm.

Braman bolted. He pushed through the door and into the courtroom, where a court officer blocked the narrow passage between the clerk's box and the rail. Braman bounced right off him.

Foxx and Bev followed at a distance as the detective escorted a handcuffed Braman to the elevator and then across the rotunda and out the front door. They stopped at the top of the steps.

KEVIN EGAN

"Third time and the trial still doesn't go forward," said Bev.

Foxx said nothing. He rapped a pack of cigarettes against the heel of his hand as he watched Bev walk down the steps, her skirt swinging against the backs of her legs. At the curb, the detective bent Arthur Braman into the back of a squad car. Then he and Bev got into a black sedan.

Foxx lit a cigarette. He would smoke his entire ration of six today. Smoking helped him think, and he wanted to think about Gary and Mike and how the Salvus Treasure either corrupted or killed everyone who came near it. There shouldn't be a trial. Not now, not thirty days from now, not ever. The Salvus Treasure, missing piece and all, should stay crated in the basement of the auction house until the ground opened up beneath it and it disappeared forever.

He took a last drag and flicked the butt. It spun out over the steps and landed in a flurry of sparks. A moment later, Ivan swept it up with his broom.